"About last night—"

"I do not believe that there is anything to discuss," Lillian interrupted quickly, looking away.

Nick suddenly realized that he had no idea how to broach the subject. Taking a deep breath, the words tumbled from his mouth. "I, well, I need to know . . . well, if you might be expecting an offer of marriage."

She gasped, shock shimmering in her gaze. "Is this some sort of hoax?"

"I don't jest about matrimony," he grumbled. "You were innocent a few hours ago and no matter how it happened, I was the one who . . . well, ended that condition."

"It's not an illness."

"Of course not." Bloody hell, if this wasn't turning out to be nearly as bad as being drugged and trussed. "But under the circumstances . . ."

"There are no circumstances that would induce me to marry, Mr. Redford. To you or any other man."

Other AVON ROMANCES

In My Heart *by Melody Thomas*
In Your Arms Again *by Kathryn Smith*
Kissing the Bride *by Sara Bennett*
Once a Gentleman *by Candice Hern*
The Princess Masquerade *by Lois Greiman*
The Princess and the Wolf *by Karen Kay*
The Sweetest Sin *by Mary Reed McCall*

Coming Soon

The Return of the Earl *by Edith Layton*
Taming Tessa *by Brenda Hiatt*

And Don't Miss These
ROMANTIC TREASURES
from Avon Books

A Dark Champion *by Kinley MacGregor*
An Invitation to Seduction *by Lorraine Heath*
So In Love: Book Five of
The Highland Lords *by Karen Ranney*

SARI ROBINS

ONE WICKED NIGHT

AVON BOOKS
An Imprint of HarperCollinsPublishers

This is a work of fiction. Names, characters, places, and incidents are products of the author's imagination or are used fictitiously and are not to be construed as real. Any resemblance to actual events, locales, organizations, or persons, living or dead, is entirely coincidental.

AVON BOOKS
An Imprint of HarperCollins*Publishers*
10 East 53rd Street
New York, New York 10022-5299

Copyright © 2004 by Sari Earl
ISBN: 0-06-057534-4
www.avonromance.com

First Avon Books paperback printing: July 2004

Avon Trademark Reg. U.S. Pat. Off. and in Other Countries, Marca Registrada, Hecho en U.S.A.
HarperCollins® is a registered trademark of HarperCollins Publishers Inc.

Printed in the U.S.A.

10 9 8 7 6 5 4 3 2 1

For Nanci,
the bestest sister in the whole wide world

Acknowledgments

I will be eternally grateful to my family and friends, especially my mother and father, who continue to enthusiastically champion my efforts. I want to specially acknowledge the following people for their faithful support:

Dorothy Rece

Joahnna Barron of Athena's Salon and Spa

Griffin for introducing me to the remarkable mother-daughter team of Carol Nagel and Liz Hayes

Mr. James Paradies

Janine Katins

Lowenstein Yost and Associates

Lyssa Keusch and May Chen

Frances Drouin (and to Eloisa James for the introduction)

Jerla Gross, of Charlotte, North Carolina, and Mairi Hamilton, of the National Gallery, London, for graciously providing information about Queen Charlotte Sophia

The incomparable Julia Quinn

The superlative Avon Books team, including (but not limited to): the Art, Sales, Marketing (Adrienne!), Editorial, Managing Editorial, Foreign/Subsidiary Rights and Publicity departments. Thank you!

Finally, my husband and children who gave me the opportunity to follow my passions and meet my deadlines

Prologue

May 1810
London, England

"**H**uzza for Randolph!" a shout filtered through the trees of the moonlit grounds.

"After him!"

"The first to the fountain wins the purse!"

"It's a wager!"

The sounds of many feet striking pebbles invaded the pine-scented air, and a sense of panic overwhelmed Miss Lillian Kane. She had fled the ballroom in a desperate bid for relief from the jarring bodies, discordant music and the overwhelming effort of maintaining her façade as grand mistress to the Marquis of Beaumont. She did not admit to anyone that the disapproving stares and critical whispers stung at her dignity, making her feel like an overused pincushion.

Like a swarm of irate bees protecting its hive, the

established elements of polite Society were defending the pecking order, the very stability that she threatened to upset with her charade. But her choices were limited, as was her ability to break free of her past, so she would withstand the onslaught with her self-respect intact (if a bit battered). Still, a woman could only endure so much.

"I'm winning!" came a man's shout from nearby.

It seemed the respite that she desperately needed to refurbish her social armor was under siege. Her garden sanctuary was being overrun by chirping, merry revelers, and she was not up for carousing.

Turning, she abandoned her refuge by a bubbling fountain and raced down the path in the broken shafts of moonlight, then spun left and dashed down another lane. Slipping behind a large pine tree, she prayed that the shadows would hide her until the merry party passed.

Suddenly a large, gloveless hand grasped her arm and pulled her back up against a broad chest.

"Don't move," a deep voice commanded from behind. "There's a snake by your feet."

She started, then froze, frightened enough to obey. Holding her breath, she searched the ground until she caught the outline of a coiled form at the base of the pine tree where she had taken her refuge. Beady golden slits watched her unblinkingly, and she wondered if it was poisonous. Either way, she would not welcome the encounter.

In the stillness, her rescuer's warm breath caressed the bare skin of her shoulders, making the fine hairs of her neck stand on end. She realized that the staccato beating of her heart was not simply from fear of the snake. The man's proximity made her skin tingle with awareness. He was tall and smelled pleasantly of almonds, of all things. As his firm hand grasped her arm and his broad chest pressed against her shoulder blades, she was surprised by how titillating the simple contact was. She had not even seen his face, and yet inexplicably, she was stirred.

Lillian wondered who he was and what he was doing hiding out in the darkened woods. Her heart skipped a beat. He could be a thief or a madman, or worst yet, one of those actors hired for the theatrical production tonight. Steeling her spine, she pushed aside her irrational fears. The man had averted her from an unfortunate encounter with a snake and had done so without making a fuss or alerting the revelers of her presence. All in all, she could reasonably ascertain that he did not mean her harm. Nonetheless, his nearness was disconcerting and entirely improper (not that she was inclined to be prudish, but still . . .). She wondered if there was a way to somehow chase off the snake.

As if heeding her silent wishes, the serpent twisted, then slithered away under the brush.

Lillian let out the breath that she had been holding, and she turned just as the stranger released her arm. "Thank you. I did not see it."

The man was brawny, and at least a head taller than she. Lillian was forced to step back to look up at him, but even then, his face was cast in shadow.

"It was not poisonous, but it would have given a nasty bite." His deep voice held the cadence of the London streets. He wore a wooden tipstaff hanging from the band by his hip.

"You are one of the Bow Street Runners retained to save the guests from pickpockets," she surmised.

"Police officers assist with any trouble they might find, ma'am."

"What are you doing out here?"

"I came out to take a breather." His rumbling tone held a hint of defensiveness.

"It seems I'm not the only one escaping the horde," she replied lightly, trying to unruffle his feathers. She was the last person in the world to begrudge him a few moments of peace. "And I am most grateful that you were here."

"Here is the fountain!" a male voice shouted from nearby. "You see, I was not lying. They *are* naked."

"Shall we swim with the nymphs?" another man cried in a voice steeped in champagne and revelry.

Lillian grimaced. Cavorting in fountains was Mr. Hurt's only means of gaining a view of exposed ladies' flesh.

"I shall be your sea nymph, Lord Danby," Mrs. Parsimmon cooed. Lillian just barely contained an unladylike snort. She disliked the sinuous widow, who seemed to thrive on scandal-mongering and bedding other ladies' husbands. Lillian might not be an advocate of the marital state, but she felt that it ought to be respected, once assumed.

"I thought I saw Lillian enter the gardens," Russell Mayburn commented. "She came this way, I was sure."

Without thought, Lillian stepped deeper into the shadows. If she had had no desire to make her presence known before, Russell's obsessive company made it even less appealing. His infatuation was becoming an outright embarrassment. It was appalling for him to be so determined to "free" her from his brother's protection. Not only did Lillian not wish to be "saved" but she also disliked being a public barb between the already fractious brothers.

"If you are looking for solitude," the police officer whispered, "I can show you the way."

She was obviously doing a terrible job at being inscrutable and mysterious tonight. These were some of her supporters—well, at least not her detractors. Despite the disapproval of many pillars of Society, some of the younger, "smart" set thankfully chose to welcome her. It seemed that she was a rebel behind whom many rallied as a minor means of thumbing their noses at the powers that be. That the Bow Street Runner could read her distaste so plainly shamed her. Still, he did not seem to be judging her, as so many others did. Despite herself, she was intrigued.

Tall and brawny, he seemed one with the trees around him. A slash of moonlight fell across his features. His eyes were like beacons in the darkness, golden and compelling. Her breath grew heavy and her body warm. It felt good, and she was curious enough to ignore the warning clamoring in her brain. Nodding, she turned, and he led her past an overhang of roses heady with bloom.

"Perhaps your Lillian, Lady Janus, had a rendezvous?" Mrs. Parsimmon offered with a thick drawl.

"Lillian does not have your taste for debauchery," Russell defended. "She is the finest . . ."

As they wove through the trees, the voices faded away, replaced by whispering leaves.

In the silvery moonlight, Lillian studied her rescuer's broad back. He had ebony hair, long past the collar, and he sported a black woolen cloak. His worn leather boots made little sound on the carpet of pine needles.

Lillian knew she should be on her guard, alone in the wood with an attractive stranger and not a soul to hear if she cried out. Yet, he was a police officer, one behaving perfectly well, and she felt *safe* around him. As if no harm could touch her when he was near. Silly, really, since she knew nothing of the man, yet she sensed it just the same.

They came out of the wood and happened upon a stone edifice with archways, which continued through the grounds. He stopped, waiting for her to join him. In the moonlight she could finally discern his features, causing her heart to beat even faster than when the snake had been near. A strong forehead fringed with thick black brows. Sharp cheekbones, shadowed with a shade of scruff that ended in a cleft chin. His nose was jagged, with evidence of a break or two, and topped wide, smooth lips that seemed to lure her gaze like a child to candy. His shapely mouth eased the severity from his features, making him brutishly handsome. His was a mouth to make a woman long for a lingering kiss.

Lillian mentally checked herself. She was not one to have her head so easily turned. Dillon was the only man she could even consider being involved with and that suited her just fine. It must be the surroundings, she decided. And, she had to admit, the man's natural appeal. She wondered how aware he was of his own magnetism.

"Would you like to see something?" he asked, breaking her unbridled thoughts.

Her cheeks heated and she prayed that she had not been standing there staring at him like a ninny. She lifted a shoulder, tentative. "All right."

He motioned for her to go deeper into the alcove. After hesitating a moment, she followed. He pointed to a corner near the ceiling. Two small eyes stared out, and she could just barely discern the outline of a broad head and a ruff of feathers. Unbidden, her lips lifted at the corners.

"Barn owl," he explained.

"Wise soul, hiding out in the darkness."

"On a beautiful night like tonight she should be flying free."

"If staying secreted is her choice, then she *is* free."

He studied her face in the darkness. He did not move, yet inexplicably her skin warmed. Then he stepped out of the alcove into the moonlight, and she followed.

"Have you ever heard the story of why the owl is a creature of the night?"

She shook her head, diverted. "No."

"Some say that the owl had stolen the rose, a coveted prize bestowed for beauty. Angry, the other birds punished the animal by only allowing it to come out at night."

"I thought that it was good luck to see an owl."

"Perhaps tonight it is." White teeth flashed in a smile so compelling that she returned it before she realized that she had.

"What is your name?" she asked, slightly breathless.

He bowed. "Mr. Nicholas Redford, at your service, Lady Janus."

She straightened. "I do not recall being introduced."

"Most of London knows the lady who refused Lord Beaumont's hand, instead to become his mistress."

She grimaced and turned away, as her fanciful sense of security fled. He would believe her the worst sort of lightskirt, easy pickings for an attractive man such as him. Was he even now considering how simple it was going to be to seduce her?

"I must get back to the house now, my lady," he said, surprising her. "I have already been away from my duties for too long." The man *was* trustworthy, and conscientious to his responsibilities, it seemed. "And although solitude is its own reward," he continued, "it might not be such a good idea for you to remain out here alone." There was no trace of an offer in his tone, and she was relieved. She did not need further complexity in her life, and here was a man who seemed ripe with prospects for complications.

Unfortunately, she knew that she must return to the ball as well. Dillon would be looking for her, and he relied on her as a barrier in these social contexts nearly as much as she counted on him. Nonetheless, she felt almost weighted down by the prospect. She was exhausted from the constant push-and-pull between Dillon, his father, Russell, Society, and her dreadful stepfather Kane. She felt as if she were dancing on the edge of a knife blade, ever in peril of blunder and blood.

Where was the harm in stealing a few moments more of freedom?

"Do you believe that there is danger to me here?" she stalled.

"Not on my watch. But I cannot be everywhere, my lady."

She exhaled softly. "I suppose returning to the ball is not such a terrible fate when you consider the alternative. Owls, snakes and drunken fools."

He smiled, and she felt it down to her toes. "Perhaps not. May I escort you, my lady?" He offered her his elbow.

"I am relying on you, Mr. Redford. I have no earthly idea where I am."

A slight thrill shuddered through her as she took his proffered arm. He would have made a superbly noble knight in a fairy tale, she mused. For a moment she enjoyed the picture: Redford, resplendent in shining armor, charging on a stallion, lifting her up and rescuing her from the torment of drunken fools and hateful gossipmongers. She smiled to herself. In truth, there could be no happily-ever-after with Mr. Redford. Not only was the man below her in class and of a profession that would threaten her status in Society but she could never leave Dillon for him. It would destroy the marquis.

Still, she could not keep herself from covertly studying the handsome police officer. He had to be almost thirty, or so. She wondered what made him tick.

"It must be fulfilling to be a police officer," she mused aloud. "Catching criminals, helping others, claiming rewards." She bit her lip, hoping that she was not treading on unwelcome waters. Members of her station usually did not discuss employment satisfaction with the other classes.

He hesitated a moment before answering, "It puts bread on the table, my lady." His voice held a tinge of discontent.

"You wish to be something other than you are?" she asked, relieved that they could speak so easily. There was something liberating about the garden's cloak of darkness.

"Hovering behind ferns watching polite Society frolic is not the best use of my skills."

"So what would you do instead?"

"I intend to open my own firm."

"Enterprising," she replied, impressed. "Using your policing skills?"

"And others I have yet to have the opportunity to utilize."

"From where will you get your clients?"

"There is always someone in need of help, my lady."

"Including damsels silly enough to jump before looking?"

"*Especially* damsels who jump before looking."

They shared a smile, walking side by side in silence. Lillian appreciated how he shortened his long stride to accommodate her shorter gait.

Too soon the house drew near. Lillian found her feet slowing of their own accord; she was not quite ready to lose his engaging company and not nearly ready to return to her gilded cage. Still, this was the life she had chosen, and, considering the alternative, she could not complain.

She cleared her throat. "It would probably be best if we part here, before entering the house." She felt him stiffen beside her. Her hand slipped from his arm self-consciously, and she took a small step, putting space between them. "Thank you."

He paused, as if only then realizing that he was being dismissed. "Of course." He bowed formally.

Her cheeks heated. "It's just, well, people might talk—"

"A lady's reputation is not to be trifled with," he intoned the accepted wisdom.

"Yes, but I—"

"Ah, there you are, darling." Dillon, the Marquis of Beaumont, stepped onto the terrace in his perfectly elegant attire. Notwithstanding the slightly mussed flaxen hair under his bicorne hat, he did not appear the worse for wear from being left alone. Title and a hefty birthright overcame any social inelegance, it seemed. Likewise, they gave Dillon the quality of being a first-rate catch for any young lady.

She noticed that Mr. Redford's shoulders squared, and he closed his cloak. Was he discomfited to have been found in her company? They had done *nothing* wrong.

Dillon's cool gaze roved over Redford dismissively and then fixed on her. "I have been wondering where you had taken off to. Everything all right, darling?"

"Fine," she answered. "I lost my way and—"

"Who is this?" Dillon motioned to the police officer.

Lillian spied Redford's lips quirk, and she wondered what he found so amusing. Then she realized that Dillon had an oddly affected way of leaning his head back so that he could look down at "the help."

"This is Mr. Redford, the courageous police officer who—"

"Simply guided a lady back to the house, my lord," Redford interjected, smoothly, facing away.

She looked from one man to the other. Dillon with his nose up, Redford with his chest out. They were like tomcats stalking each other, each with its fur on end. Ridiculous.

"Dillon, Mr. Redford is being modest. He—"

"—was glad to be of service, my lady," Redford interrupted mulishly.

"Well, then, my thanks to you, my good man." Dillon reached for his purse.

"That is not necessary, my lord," Redford stated, turning away.

"Of course it is," Dillon replied, tossing a coin into

the air. It clattered onto the stone steps, rolling down to the pebbled path below and flattening with a clank.

Redford stared at the coin a long moment, as if he would rather starve than pick it up.

Lillian looked away, embarrassed by the awkward situation and unable to remedy it. Dillon was oblivious to his boorishness, and nothing she could say would make him fix it. And how could she assuage the police officer's pride without pricking it further?

Redford straightened. Then, without a word, he nodded to Lillian, strode up the stone steps, and swept into the house, not once looking back.

"Inexcusable manners on that one," Dillon huffed. "Probably gets away with it most of the time because of his looks."

"I had not noticed."

Dillon popped open his snuffbox, took a pinch and sneezed. Wiping a handkerchief across his nose, he drawled, "The man's manner is indefensible, and I shall have to have a word with our hostess."

"It is not worth your time, darling," Lillian stated quickly. "I have forgotten the man already." She climbed the stairs and locked arms with him. "I would love a glass of champagne. . . ."

He looked down at her, his brow furrowed and his blue eyes filled with concern. "But you don't like how you feel out of control when you drink. . . ."

She was feeling unsettled and in need of *something* to soothe her nerves. "I am in the mood to be reckless. Will you protect me from myself, darling?"

"I always will, but if I know you, you will take two sips and then beg off."

"You are probably right. How about a game of casino, then?"

"I would love to play casino!" Russell exclaimed, stepping through the French doors.

Dillon scowled. "You love anything that Lillian loves."

"She has good taste, what can I say?"

Lillian put on a game face, trying not to appear as worn out as she felt. "The more the merrier, I suppose."

Russell sent Dillon a look of triumph.

"Lillian is on my team," Dillon declared. "Find yourself another partner. Come, darling."

As they stepped inside the French doors, Lillian stole one last look at the gardens. Out there somewhere an owl hid cloistered in darkness, and for a moment Lillian wished so could she.

Chapter 1

Thirteen months later

Lillian sat alone at the dining room table in her dishabille, enjoying a cup of cocoa and the *Morning Post*.

"Bravo, Mr. Redford," she whispered to the empty room. There it was, the notice that she had been searching for during the past few months.

Mister Nicholas Redford
Enquiry Agency
15 Girard Square, London
Established 1811

She had followed his illustrious career in the papers with the apt attention of a woman in thrall. Although slightly mortified by her fascination, no one knew of it except her dear friend Fanny, who would

15

never tell a soul, so she saw little harm. In fact, the man was fodder for her most sensational flights of fancy, and Lillian was not about to give up her favorite escape. There were nights when she excused herself from festivities simply to enjoy the company of his deliciously imagined kisses.

Often the dashing police officer was a crusader saving her from a marauding infidel, or from a ruffian come to steal her away. She schooled herself to recognize that these were girlish fantasies and not in any way related to the lead performer himself. She wondered if she would ever encounter the handsome Mr. Redford again.

The only excuse she could have for seeing him was to retain his services, something she could not quite imagine doing. What excuse could she have to retain an enquiry agent? The possibility of hunting down her natural father flitted through her mind, but she instantly dismissed it. Beyond having caused her mother infinite heartbreak, the dastard had deserted the poor lady when she had been with child. Such an unfeeling blackguard did not deserve to be found.

So Redford would remain a deliciously decadent player in her imaginary fantasies; her own private champion. Looking around to ensure that no one was near, she folded the newspaper along the lines of the advertisement and gently tore along the edge.

"Happy birthday, darling," Dillon yawned, ambling into the room.

The paper ripped across the wording with a loud tear. "Blast," she muttered, flipping over the broadsheet and pushing it aside before he could see.

"You woke early for me?" she asked. He was the

picture of a young boy roused from sleep, with his tousled blond hair and air of lethargy. She smiled up at him affectionately. "Now I know that I rank."

"Of course you do, darling," he intoned, rubbing his red-rimmed eyes. "I wanted to be the first to thank you for being born." He bussed her on the lips, and his clove-scented breath reminded her of an escapade long ago.

"Do you recall our first kiss?"

"How could I forget?" He grinned. "The butler found us in the pantry."

"How is crotchety Mr. Jenkins?"

"Still scaring the cook and chasing the maids, I'm afraid. But father will not let him go. Says he keeps everyone out of his hair, and he will not give that up." He sat down beside her. "Speaking of which . . ." Reaching into his gown pocket, he pulled out a velvet-covered box and set it on the table. "For you."

"I do not need gifts, Dillon. You have given me so much already."

"Father insisted."

She bit her lip, knowing that this gift came with unstated terms. Opening the lid, she gasped. Diamonds glittered like a circle of stars on black velvet. "It is far too indulgent," she avowed quietly.

Lifting the bracelet, he draped it across her wrist. "Nonsense, you are worth every gem."

It felt like a manacle, heavy with its demands made with luminous insistence. She yanked her sleeve down, extinguishing the glare. "It is a beautiful gesture, Dillon. But it will not make me change my mind."

"Do not be so cynical. It is a gift for your birthday."

"Dillon . . ."

He shrugged. "So what if we want you to stay when the year is out? It is encouragement only, nothing more."

"I will not be a puppet dancing on your father's strings—"

"But you will destroy me, instead." He crossed his arms, anger infusing his handsome features.

"Stop being dramatic." Carefully, she placed the dazzling bracelet back in the case and closed it with a snap. "My plans are not subject to debate, by either you or your father."

"I can give you all the money that you need—"

"The waters might flow between you and your father, but there are expectations involved and you know it."

"He has been more than reasonable—"

"Which is why I endeavor to deal plainly with you both. I told you from the onset of this arrangement that it is only until my four-and-twentieth birthday."

"How can you deny him his happiness when he has done so much for you?"

She stood, frustrated. They had been over this ground before. Granted, they only seemed to discuss it on or around her birthday, almost as if Dillon discarded the thought until then, but they *had agreed*. "His efforts were not completely selfless, but more importantly, it is about my happiness, not his. I will stand on my own two feet when I am able and not rely on the generosity of others."

"It was never a handout between us." Dillon frowned with injury. "We have been friends since birth, and I would never turn my back on you."

His accusation hung in the air, but she was not

about to let him make her feel guilty. She moved to the window, staring out at the enclosed rear garden. "Will you be joining us today at Mr. Wigley's Great Room?"

"I have already seen the Panoramic View of St. Petersburg."

"Fanny has not. Besides, I, at least, was unable to absorb the entire scene in one viewing. I have examined it twice already and continue to be pleasantly surprised." She glanced at him, hoping for a truce. "Please join us for my birthday outing."

"Aren't you afraid of Kane jumping from behind a tree and stealing you off to marry his dupe?" he scoffed.

"I do not make light of your fears, Dillon," she stated quietly. "Why must you belittle mine?"

He would not meet her eye; instead he toyed with the velvet package.

She walked toward the door. "I am going to get dressed."

"Lilly?"

She turned.

Standing, he held the box out to her. "It is a gift freely given."

Tilting her head, she accepted it. "Thank you."

"I apologize." He opened his arms.

She came to him then, encircling his lean waist and resting her cheek on his chest. She welcomed his familiar musk cologne and the support he gave.

He kissed the top of her head. "It was ill done of me to ridicule your situation. Kane is a dastard and you are wise to take care."

"You know better than any other how he treated me. You were witness to the bruises and the grief."

"I know. It's just, well, I have been so happy these

last two years and I never want it to end." He shrugged, struggling to voice his feelings. "Never in my lifetime have my father and I been so at peace. Never have I felt so . . . *connected*, to Society, to my peers. With you, I fit, perfectly. We are made to be together. If only you would see that."

She looked up at his dear face and tried making light. "I simply see things differently from down here."

"But you are happy with me."

"I cannot imagine being with any other, but—"

"If only you were not so irrationally set against marriage."

"Irrationally?" She pushed out of his arms. "Irrationally?"

"Perhaps I used the wrong word. Excessively, maybe."

"Excessive? My fears are excessive?" She set her hands on her hips. "Tell me, Dillon, how was it that my stepfather Kane had free reign to mistreat my mother? *Because he could*. As her husband, he held every shred of power over her person, her money . . . her home. She was *nothing* to him, and he treated her as such. *We* were nothing."

"You cannot think that I would ever—"

"I will never give anyone that power over me. I had to suffer his authority for eleven years, and that was more than enough for a lifetime. And my mother . . ." Thinking of the frail, despondent lady with lovely golden hair and sad sapphire eyes, her resolve hardened. "It may have been a fever in the end, but she was broken in spirit long before then."

"Had your grandparents understood earlier—"

"Granted, they only realized after Mother was gone. But realistically, what could they have done before then? He was the patriarch." Crossing her arms as if to ward off the memories, she hugged herself. "Had Kane fought them for me, he likely would have won. He is named on my birth records. To the world he is my father, and do not think that he did not hold that over my head from the day I was born."

"Your grandparents regretted arranging that marriage."

"Perhaps. But deep down they were still relieved to have given me a name."

"Would you have preferred it otherwise?"

She shrugged a shoulder. "I will never know, will I?"

Quiet befell the room. She sighed. "I do not wish to quarrel with you, Dillon. I just need you to understand that my feelings signify."

"So we do not marry, and remain as we are."

"Until my inheritance comes to me."

"For one more year."

"Please understand, Dillon. I have dreams, and in them I am other than a man's mistress. I want to travel the world, see phenomena beyond my imaginings . . ." In all of her dreams, she did not know exactly where she would end up or what she might be doing, but in all of them she ruled her destiny with a free spirit, unencumbered by any man.

His blue gaze shimmered with vulnerability. "Are you unhappy with your decision to be with me?"

"Never. I might not have liked my choices, but you have been wonderful, Dillon. And I am grateful."

He reached for her hand and clutched it in a firm grasp. "I would never let anything happen to you, darling."

"I know." She squeezed his hand. "Pray Kane knows that as well."

"He does not touch you now—"

"Not for want of trying. I fear that it is only yours and your father's influence that truly keeps him at bay. And even then, he is like a hooded serpent lazing in the sun yet ready to strike if the opportunity presents itself."

Lord Cornelius Kane sank into the tall leather armchair at his club, nursing his brandy and his rotten mood. He had escaped to Brooks's in the hopes of avoiding his man-of-affairs, who was becoming a dratted nuisance. The bungling idiot did not seem to understand the basic concept of credit. Perhaps it was time to retain a new man-of-affairs. If only he had the blunt to pay for it.

Platter-faced Mr. Pitts ambled across the parlor, wearing breeches that fairly screamed last year's fashion. Kane turned his shoulder to the man, sending the message that he was not welcome near the square of armchairs by the fire. "They'll let in anyone these days," he muttered.

"What's that you say?" Lord Felton leaned forward, causing the leather to creak noisily.

"Nice day," Kane pasted on a false smile. The old man was as deaf as a doornail.

"My Sophie always loved the spring," he sighed.

"Don't turn maudlin on me, old man. It'll send me into a panic."

"Lady Janus?" the ripened gent's rheumy eyes brightened. "She is yours, isn't she?"

As always when Lillian was the topic, Kane's lip curled in distaste. He hated the month of June. It was a reminder of the birth of the she-devil spawn that had thwarted his best efforts for a reasonable existence. And he deserved a tolerable life as much as the next nobleman, perhaps even more so. He hardly ever skipped on a bill, always paid on a wager and almost never cheated at cards. He was a good man, yet he felt like the angels were sitting upon high, pelting stones at his head every time he was about to land on his feet.

His clever funding scheme was unraveling; Cecilia was making noises about telling her husband about the whole thing (and their affair, but he did not care overmuch about that; Lord Langham should be thanking him for keeping hog-buttocked Cecilia occupied), creditors were knocking at his door, and his favorite valet had off and died on him (at least it saved him from having to pay a month's wages).

What he could not understand was why everything had to come unstitched at the same time. Sighing, he sipped the brandy slowly, mindful that he could not order another; his bill was outstanding and he could never let anyone suspect that he could not meet his obligations at Brooks's. It was one thing to let a tailor go unpaid (one could always pretend that the workmanship was shoddy), but a man's club was his sacred domain. And here he sat in a bastion of recreation, unable to imbibe. His father would be rolling in his grave at seeing his dear son suffering this indignity. Lord Cornelius Kane *economizing:* What was the world coming to?

Emptying his glass, he eyed the room, looking for a lackey to buy him a drink. A young man standing by the far mantel caught his eye. Or perhaps the man seemed to be studying him? The blond buck's morning coat was beautifully tailored (it had the look of a Weston cut), his chapeau bras was perfectly seamed, and his Hessian boots were not even scuffed on the heel, they were so new. The man was probably related to someone deep in the pockets.

The man's eyes locked on Kane's with intent. Some unknown fire burned in that light blue gaze. The man pushed himself away from the mantel and sauntered over. Kane leaned back, wondering how many drinks he would be able to milk from his quarry.

"Lord Kane?"

"Yes."

"Lord Russell Mayburn."

The name rang jarringly in Kane's ears. Anyone related to the Marquis of Beaumont earned his instant enmity. That Mayburn was Beaumont's brother made his company insupportable.

"May I?" The man motioned to the chair.

He'd rather have an appointment with his dreaded man-of-affairs. Kane turned sideways in his seat, adding vinegar to his tone. "I would *prefer* that you did not."

The impudent dandiprat sat anyway.

Kane grunted. Today's youth were devoid of respect for their elders.

Mayburn motioned to a footman. "Brandy for two and cigars. Your best, mind you."

Kane frowned to himself. Perhaps one drink with the gent would not kill him. He shifted in his seat, pique rising with the idea that, in fact, bilking this particular dupe of a few drinks would be more satisfying than usual.

After settling in with their brandies, Mayburn started, "I will get straight to the point, my lord. It is about Lillian."

So the man used her Christian name. Slut.

He was probably another one of her admirers come to extol her virtues. Brandy or not, Kane was hardly about to sit through this. Gripping the leather, he stood.

"I want to get her away from my brother," Mayburn continued.

Kane blinked, then lowered himself back into the chair. He examined the young man with new regard. That light in his eyes was fervor, and it seemed that Lillian was its focus. He could be a prodigious tool, this one, if wielded well.

"Why would you wish to end their affair?"

"Because she can do better."

"Meaning you, for instance?"

"I would never allow her to remain a kept woman. She deserves to be married with full rights to such stature."

Kane sighed for effect. "Your brother uses her."

"Abominably. But she does not see it."

"You two are close?" Kane asked, already knowing the answer. Only a select few knew of the acrimony in the Kane family. Lillian was always one to keep her skeletons in the cupboard. To her disadvantage in this instance.

"She is exceedingly dear to me. But my brother unjustifiably resents our relationship."

"She loves him, I hear. Perhaps it is for the best that they remain together?"

"How can you say that?" Mayburn cried, slamming his fist onto his thigh. "She has no prospects with Dillon. She can bear no recognizable heirs. Deuced if I can understand why my father allows him to treat her so disrespectfully. But he has always indulged Dillon beyond what is defensible. If no one else will save Lillian, then I will."

"And how do you propose to do this?" Kane inquired, his mind racing to make the best use of this man.

"I don't know." The gent sulked. "She has refused any opportunity to run away."

"So you came to the conclusion that . . ."

The man blinked, his gaze as blank as parchment. "What?"

Nodding encouragingly, Kane led, "That it is your brother who must be removed. . . ."

"To where?"

Not the sharpest tack in the pile. "Away from Lillian."

"So instead of her running away, *he* leaves?"

"Excellent notion."

Mayburn shook his head. "Dillon will never leave her. He has it too good. He gets everything he wishes from her." His cheeks reddened. "Pardon."

Kane waved him off. "I know of these things and they do make my blood boil, but there is naught that I can do."

"But if he were gone—"

"With your brother out of the picture, Lillian will no longer be under his manipulative sway." Kane leaned closer, and Mayburn leaned in as well. "She would then be, say, *open* to other, more constructive, influences."

Mayburn exhaled softly, excitement shimmering in his gaze. "That would be most excellent. For Lillian, of course." He frowned, scratching his head. "But how to accomplish this? He does not visit the country, nor take the waters at Bath. In fact, he hardly ever leaves Lillian's side."

Although he would not admit it to the young man, Kane had tried tricking Beaumont into leaving

London. Or at least leaving Lillian for an extended time, to naught. Urgent messages calling the marquis to the country. Fake funeral announcements of relatives. Even illicit invitations from some of the most tantalizing specimens the demimonde had to offer. The bloody man was like a cork stuck in a bottle, unwilling to be removed.

"It is her birthday today," Mayburn pronounced, pulling Kane from his frustrated musings. "I was wondering what to give her."

"Arsenic, perhaps?" Kane muttered under his breath.

"Wh-what?" Those dull eyes blinked. "Do not even jest about such matters! Lillian is the light of London. A fair creature of—"

Clearing his throat, Kane interrupted, "A book, perhaps."

"Will you call on her today?"

"No, Beaumont does not allow it." Not since Lillian had told the meddlesome marquis about the encounter in the solicitor's office. Kane really could not have been blamed for his outburst over the fact that his father-in-law, Lord Janus, would leave his entire estate in trust for a worthless chit. Well, it would bring any man to violence.

"Interfering wench," Kane muttered, recalling how Lillian had tried to stop him from throttling the solicitor who had imparted the wretched intelligence. Who could blame him for striking her? It was self-defense and only what she deserved, not a fortune to call her own.

"Pardon?" Mayburn eyed him oddly.

"I meant wretched interfering of him. Beaumont influences Lillian, turning her against me." It was Lillian who had turned Lord and Lady Janus against him, convincing them to change their wills. She was the source of his current ill state. Because of her, he was denied his rightful legacy. Barred from the funds that were his due. It was her fault that he had been forced to enter into that funding scheme that was now falling to shreds. It was only because of the scheme that he had formed his liaison with the troublesome Cecilia Langham. Lillian was the linchpin to all of his problems, and his only solution, to marry Lillian off and siphon the funds, was denied him by the protective Marquis of Beaumont.

Like lightning, an idea flashed in his mind. His heart began to pound and his face broke out in a sweat. It would solve all of his problems, tying them up in one neat little bow. Anticipation rushed through him, making him almost shake with excitement. He had not been this elated since his cousin Louis had died of the pox, making him a baron. The plan was inspired in its simplicity. He was even more brilliant than he had ever supposed.

Trying to keep the enthusiasm from his tone, he declared, "I am grateful that you had the fortitude to approach me, Mayburn. Your concern for my daughter does you great credit."

"Thank you, Lord Kane," the man stated warily, as if unused to such flattery. No wonder, the numskull could not have much opportunity to attract it.

"It has planted a seed in my mind. One that, I believe, with a bit of careful tending, can grow into the remedy that will be Lillian's just due."

Mayburn straightened, looking quite manly, thanks to that Weston cut. "Really? You think it is possible?"

"Yes. But there are some things that I need you to do for me."

"Anything, my lord, anything at all."

"You can start by telling me everything you know about your brother and his relationship with my daughter. . . ."

Chapter 2

"**G**ood day, Lillian."

Lillian started. "Russell! You surprised me." She tried not to show her irritation at the interruption. The servants were usually quite good about not allowing visitors into her private garden.

"I thought that Dillon could not stand cats," he stated, dubiously eyeing the kitten in her lap and the many felines roaming the grounds. "They make him sneeze."

"He indulges me. Besides, they do not enter the house."

She felt crowded with him standing over her, and she certainly did not expect her visitor to sit on the pallet alongside her. So she gave Blackie one last scratch behind the ears, placed the feline down onto the ground, and stood.

Brushing off her gown, she asked, "What brings you here this afternoon?"

His smile was pleased. "I have the perfect gift for your birthday."

"Oh, you needn't have bothered, Russell—"

"But of course I did. And it is only a week late because I was having it made." He turned, reaching for something on the ground behind him.

Smiling faintly, she tried to rally herself for the appropriate gratitude. She found it hard where Russell was concerned. With Dillon, at least, she could express her feelings plainly. The regard between them was so secure that she felt free to speak her mind and know that their relationship would only be better for the honesty between them.

With Russell, she felt as if she were walking on eggshells. He was a sweet boy—young man, she corrected herself—and Lillian felt certain that he would grow out of his infatuation with her soon enough. Until then she did not wish to crush his spirit.

He spun, grinning, with a hatbox in his gloved hands. With a dramatic flair, he lifted off the cover and lowered it so that she could see.

"A bonnet," she cried, not exactly sure why he would choose such a personal gift. But it was a nice gesture. "How lovely. Thank you, Russell; it was quite thoughtful of you."

"Ah, but it is not simply any bonnet, Lillian. It has the Mayburn crest stitched onto the front. With our family motto, An enemy to one is an enemy to all."

And there it was: a snarling lion surrounded by spiky swords—the Mayburn crest—on the crown of the bonnet, with silly yellow ribbons splayed generously around it. Who in the world would wear such a thing?

He practically preened. "I selected the additional blue feathers for your beautiful eyes."

"Why, it is just . . . lovely . . . of you to have gone to such trouble."

"My lady, if you will pardon me?"

She turned, relieved at the butler's interruption. "Of course, Hicks. By the by, the new uniform looks well." Cream and black had been her choice, and it suited his tea-skinned coloring.

A slight smile just barely flitted across the butler's impenetrable veneer. "Thank you, my lady. Visitors here to see Lord Beaumout."

"Inform them that he is at his club."

Hicks pursed his lips, saying tentatively, "The leader of the party is Solicitor General Dagwood, my lady."

"The Solicitor General? Here?" Foreboding overwhelmed her; Kane had been too quiet of late. What was he up to now? It was around the time of her birthday, and the sands of time until she could claim her inheritance were thinning. Recalling Dillon's recent charges, she hoped that she was simply being highly strung. That Kane had given up on taking her funds. But she doubted it. He viewed them as his, stolen by her even though she'd had nothing whatsoever to do with her grandfather's decision to change his will.

"What could the Solicitor General want with Dillon?" she murmured under her breath.

Russell grasped her hand. "Do you wish to sit, my dear? You seem upset."

"No, thank you." She gently shook off his hand. "I am fine." She bit her lip. "Do you know, Russell, what exactly the Solicitor General does?"

Russell smiled, obviously pleased to have been

consulted. "The man is a commoner, chosen from the ranks of the prominent barristers to serve the Attorney General. It is all very convoluted and political."

"But what is his function?"

"Well, he is a Law Officer of the Crown."

"But what does he do?"

"It is a bit complicated. You should not concern yourself—"

"I will endeavor to keep up with your explanation, Russell. Pray tell me everything that you know about his role."

He sighed. "If it pleases you."

"It does."

"Very well." He straightened, as if giving a homily. "The man is assigned the task of representing the Crown on legal matters. This can entail serving a function in the courts, providing legal advice, questions involving public welfare."

"When the rights of the Crown are involved."

"Yes," he replied, as if surprised that she understood. "And more. Law Officers are consulted in the most important instances. For intricate legal matters involving debts to the Crown, thefts from the Crown, exceptional prosecutions . . ."

"Are you feeling unwell?" she asked, alarmed. His cheeks had reddened, making him suddenly appear fevered.

He swallowed. "I just recalled something . . . that I . . . neglected to do."

"Something serious?"

"Yes. No! I mean, it can wait."

"If you are so concerned, you may leave through the back gate, if you wish."

"No, no. I will come with you," he replied, wiping his brow with a handkerchief. "I have never met the Solicitor General and wish to ensure that all is proper."

"Very well. Where is he, Hicks?"

"I asked them to wait in the front drawing room."

Russell took her hand and rested it on his arm. "Don't worry, Lillian, I will take care of you."

Butterflies were swarming in her middle, and she was glad for his company. Whatever scheme Kane had afoot, she was thankful for the support of Dillon and his family. Her situation depended on their esteemed place in Society, and Russell's presence could be beneficial.

The Solicitor General was much younger than she would have imagined for a Law Officer of the Crown. Despite the streaks of silver at his temples, much of his hair remained jet black, and his pallid face bore few of the telling lines of age. He had firm, if regular, features, but what was most distressing were his eyes. They were like black coals of burning ambition.

The man bowed. "Solicitor General Dagwood, at your service."

"Lord Russell Mayburn." Russell nodded. "And may I present Lady Janus."

Lillian's nod was cool. The man smelled of cigar, a cloying odor that she always associated with overgrown boys patting themselves on the back.

The man waved to his companions. "May I introduce Police Officer Kim and Police Officer Kelly of the Bow Street office." Each man wore street clothes with the requisite tipstaff hanging from his hip.

One of the police officers stepped forward and unscrewed that very brass-topped tipstaff, revealing a parchment inside. He handed it to the Solicitor General, who held it up. "This is a warrant for the arrest of the Marquis of Beaumont."

"On what charge?" Lillian cried.

"Murder."

Russell's face blanched.

Lillian felt her knees wobble, as if a violent wind had swept into the room. *Kane.* This had to be Kane's doing.

Anger infused her spine with iron, and she stepped forward. "Who is Lord Beaumont supposed to have murdered?" she inquired derisively. "Or is the victim a fabrication as well?"

"Lady Langham."

"He hardly even knows her!"

The impetuous man smirked. "He *knew* her better than you obviously know him. They had been having an affair, I am sorry to say." He did not appear apologetic in the least, with his pointy chin jutting out and his know-all nose high in the air. "Lady Langham threatened to tell her husband of the affair, and Beaumont killed her."

"I have never heard so much twaddle in all my life!"

"Calm down, Lillian." Russell laid a hand on her arm. "We do not know the facts. Does my father know of this charge?"

"*Meritless* charge," she interjected, crossing her arms.

"The Duke of Greayston will be informed once his son is in custody."

"He will not allow this to stand," she declared. "And rightly so. Dillon is incapable—"

Dagwood turned to Russell, as if she were unworthy of his attention. "Is Beaumont here?"

For a moment she was a young girl back at Helmsridge, as valued as a piece of the furniture, perhaps even less so because she had to be fed.

"We have a warrant for his arrest," the Solicitor General continued, bringing her back to reality. "We can search the residence if you insist upon it."

"He is not here," Russell replied.

"Pray tell where he is."

"I would not know."

Russell was right; she needed more information to be able to untangle Kane's web. Trying to recall everything she knew about the heavyset brunette with small eyes and a calculating manner, she stepped forward. "How did Lady Langham die?"

Dagwood raised his chin. "She was battered to death with a fire poker."

Russell pressed her arm. "This is not for—"

"Lord Beaumont is incapable of such violence."

"Tell that to Lord Langham, who mourns his wife."

"When did this happen?"

"Last night."

"That matters have proceeded to arrest so quickly may indicate that all of the facts are not in order," she suggested, noting the look of irritation flashing across the police officers' features.

"Has Lord Langham offered a reward for a quick arrest?" Russell asked, blessedly aiding her line of reasoning.

"Of course. But it is inconsequential—"

"Not to the runners," Lillian supplied.

The Bow Street Runners' faces darkened.

"The *police officers'* integrity is impeccable," Dagwood intoned.

"But are their facts?"

Dagwood raised a supercilious brow. "Tell me, Lady Janus, where was Lord Beaumont last night? With you, perhaps?"

Her mouth opened, then closed. He seemed so blasted sure of himself, as if he knew the answer before having asked the question. What would be the best response to help Dillon and not land him in even deeper waters?

"I take your silence as a no," Dagwood declared smugly. "We will find Beaumont and arrest him. A title and money will not help him to escape justice."

Lillian wiped her suddenly moist brow. "May I ask one final question, Solicitor General Dagwood?"

Shooting the police officers a look of exasperation, he pinched his face in a patronizing smile. "Of course."

"Why are you involved in this matter?"

"Law Officers often conduct prosecutions."

"Why handle it personally?"

"I am trying to avoid a miscarriage of justice," he declared, puffing up his chest.

"Are you sure that you are not trying to use Lady Langham's death as a stepping stone for your own ambitions?"

He stiffened, and alarm flashed in his black gaze, quickly clouded by an affronted mien. So it was true. Dillon was only a pawn, being hounded by a man heady with the whiff of ambition.

Not even bothering with courtesies, Dagwood swept from the room. The two men followed at his heels.

Lillian paced, anger fueling her limbs.

"How could you have accused him of that, Lillian?" Russell cried. "The man is a Law Officer of the Crown!"

"I can't quite believe that I said it either," she admitted, chewing on her thumbnail. "But it's true. The man can't see his nose for the ambition that blinds him."

"Now you have only earned his ire."

"It makes no difference as to how he will proceed." She fell into a chair, trying to brake her racing thoughts and untangle them for purpose.

"Do you wish to lie down?"

"What?"

"You must be distraught. . . ." Russell seemed the one overcome; his face was white, and his eyes were round with alarm.

Reaching out, she squeezed his hand. "Do not fear for your brother. Things will be all right."

"But how?"

"All I know is that we are going to need help." Mr. Nicholas Redford came to mind. She grimaced, thinking of how just a week before she had dismissed the notion of ever needing to retain the investigator. Ironic.

"The Solicitor General would not dare arrest Dillon unless his evidence was secure," Russell mumbled.

She looked up sharply. "What are you saying?"

"Where was Dillon last night?"

"Don't even consider the possibility!"

"Dagwood obviously knows something that we do not. Something damning."

She certainly knew something damning. Damning, but it might just save Dillon's skin. But how to use that knowledge?

"But what if it is true?" he cried. "What if we don't know Dillon at all, but we're blinded by the regard we hold for him?"

Dragging her attention back to the poor boy, she squeezed his hand. "Listen to me, Russell. Your brother did not kill anyone. He is the kindest, gentlest of men. He is incapable of the deed Dagwood described. I do not care if ten righteous vicars swore on dog-eared Bibles that he had done it. I will never believe it so."

He looked away, his brow troubled, his lips pinched.

She lifted his chin, forcing him to meet her gaze. "So when you read the nasty headlines, or hear the gossipmongers wagging their tongues, remember that Dillon did not kill anyone."

"Your loyalty is admirable." He jerked away his chin, standing.

"It is not loyalty, Russell. It's common sense."

He turned, facing the window. "Pray that we can all remain so steadfast." After a moment, he asked, "Shall I go to Dillon's club and warn him?"

She realized that she was chewing on her cuticle, a habit she had considered conquered long ago. Lowering her hand, she shook her head. "No. We cannot stop it. Go to your father. Tell him everything. He will know what to do."

"What about you?"

She did not believe in coincidences, only the failure to act on them. "I am going to see a man about an enquiry."

Chapter 3

Lillian's palms were sweating inside her kid gloves as she climbed up the stairs of the town house at 15 Girard Square. She was about to encounter the flesh-and-blood man she had been fantasizing about for almost a year. She was terrified that he would take one look at her and just *know*.

She pushed aside the irrational fear. She was here on a mission of the greatest importance and did not have time for girlish stupidity. Besides, the man might not even remember her.

Her footman, Gillman, opened the door, and the hinges cried out in protest. Swallowing, she entered the hallway at the top of the stairs and looked around. There were four sets of doors, and she had no idea which way to turn. There was little light, the hallway bore no sign, and it smelled uninvitingly of mold and inexpensive tallow candles. Now which way to go?

"Perhaps this one, my lady?" Gillman inquired, pointing to the first door.

She nodded, and he swung it open.

"No. This is simply a storage room of some kind." It was filled with trunks and boxes.

A buxom woman of about thirty wearing a faded blue dress appeared at the threshold of the next door and fairly preened with excitement at seeing visitors. "Welcome, my lady. Will you be needin' the services of the finest investigator in the King's land?"

Gillman closed the storage room door.

"Mr. Redford's enquiry agency?" Lillian stepped forward.

"Yes, my lady. Please come in."

Lillian followed the woman into an airless office with a single secretary, a lone wooden stool and a threadbare armchair. Mr. Redford's agency did not exactly match her fantastic dreams. Still, it was not a nightmare.

"I am Miss Mabel Brink, Mr. Redford's assistant. I don't do investigations, mind you, just help out around the office." She had a kind face, with deep lines fanning russet eyes, as if from a good measure of smiling. Still, her smile appeared shaky, just the same.

She waved to the tattered armchair. "Please be seated."

Lillian sat, setting her parasol across her lap. Her trusty footman positioned himself by the door.

"May I offer you some tea, my lady?"

"No, thank you. I am here on a matter of importance. Is Mr. Redford available?"

"He'll be back shortly." Her brow puckered, and

she bit her lip as if to contain her emotion. "He's over at Andersen Hall."

"Andersen Hall?"

"The foundling home, from where we hail."

Lillian recalled reading something in the papers about Redford being an orphan. Suddenly the woman's face became splotchy and her lower lip's quiver heightened to a quake. Looking around to see if there was anyone else to tend to the woman, Lillian realized that except for her footman, they were alone.

"Here." Lillian held out her handkerchief. "Are you unwell?"

"Thank you," she muttered, taking it and pressing it to her moist eyes. "Excuse me, my lady. I am not usually such a puddle of woe, but it's been a bit of a tough time." The woman sniffed into the linen, obviously trying hard to keep her distress in check.

"I understand."

"I'm just so very thankful that I have Nick." Miss Brink held out the sodden cloth. "Sorry, I made a mess of your pretty hankie."

"You keep it." Lillian did not see a ring on her finger. Still, she wondered if it was more than just helping out around the office between Mr. Redford and his helper. The woman did have pretty russet eyes, and men often preferred buxom women. But it was none of her affair.

"Will, ah, Mr. Redford be away much longer?"

"He is over at the orphanage, dealing with only Lord knows what, with the headmaster's death." She let out a noisy sigh, seemingly collected once again.

Lillian tried to keep down her panic. "Is Mr. Redford handling another matter?"

"Don't you fret, my lady. He is available for hire. In fact, the work'll do him good. He's beside himself with Dunn's death, same as all of us, perhaps more."

Her shoulders sagged with relief. "Dunn?" The name rang a bell. "Mr. Uriah Dunn, the head of the orphanage?"

"Yes, God rest his beloved soul. He was murdered."

"Murdered!" Lillian straightened. Was it an epidemic now?

"Frightful day, isn't it, my lady? When a man is killed for trying to help a poor sod."

"What happened?"

Her fists curled. "Conrad Furks. The bloody thieving bugger." Her cheeks reddened. "Ah, pardon my foul tongue, my lady. It's just, well, our Dunn never could turn a soul away. Even if they was a bastard in the truest sense. And now he's dead for his trouble."

"They are sure it was this man who did it?"

"Conrad was caught bloody as a butcher, stealing Dunn's watch."

"How horrible." Lillian shuddered. "At least they have the fiend in custody."

"But what's to become of the children? And Andersen Hall? Everyone there and even us still, we depended on Dunn like fish do water. And poor Nick. . . ." She sighed forcefully. "Those two were closer than any father an' son I ever saw. Caused a right bit o' resentment from Dunn's son Marcus—"

"That's enough, Mabel," a deep baritone rippled through Lillian's middle.

She stood, her heart suddenly in her throat.

He loomed in the doorway, not the Apollo of

moonlight but a man of hard angles and dark strength. Even the eyes that had blazed with golden fire in her dreams were dimmed with brown frost. She could not believe the transformation in him. Perhaps the moonlight and memory had softened his face to haze, or perhaps it had all been a dream.

She felt his gaze burn across her, and her cheeks tingled in response. He might look different in the daylight, but his effect on her was still the same. She felt breathless, and suddenly overwarm.

"Lady Janus." He nodded curtly.

Her vocabulary was suddenly bereft of words.

"This is Lady Janus?" Mabel shrieked, standing. "The very lady who set Society on its ear?"

"Enough, Mabel," Redford chided. He motioned for her to precede him into the adjoining office. "If you would, please, my lady?"

Mutely, she obliged, feeling his wolfish presence behind her with every tingle that raced down her back.

The chamber was immaculate, with a large wooden desk and chair, and two brown leather sofas facing each other. Its very ordinariness gave her tattered confidence a lift.

Instead of sitting behind the desk, he motioned her to one sofa and dropped into the other. "Welcome to my humble agency."

"Congratulations on opening your firm." She began the speech she had practiced on the carriage ride over, "I am here to—"

"You look different in the daylight," he mused aloud, that deep cadence rippling through her.

A traitorous blush warmed her cheeks. So he *did* remember their first encounter. "Ah, how so?"

"Your hair is not so much golden as strawberry."

Uncomfortable with the intimate perusal of his gaze, she coughed into her hand. "I am sorry for your loss, Mr. Redford. Mr. Dunn was well regarded in all circles."

He locked his hands, glancing down. "They did not come any better than he."

The moment stretched between them. Suddenly he stood as if he could no longer endure her company. "I cannot help Lord Beaumont."

"How?—"

"Word travels quickly when a peer of the realm is indicted."

She tasted leather and realized that she was chewing her gloved thumb. Grasping her hands in her lap, she asked, "Why will you not help me?"

"I will not take a case where the person is clearly on the wrong side of the law."

She rose. "But Dillon is innocent."

"Because he told you so?" His brows lifted in disbelief.

"Because he is incapable of doing what they said he did." She stepped forward. "I have known Dillon my entire life. He could not hurt a fly."

His face darkened. "Rage makes animals of men."

She felt for his loss but could not allow him to dismiss Dillon because of it. Especially when Dillon's situation was her fault. "I know that Dillon did not murder Lady Langham as well as I know that the sun rises in the morning. I fear that it is because of me that he is in this mess."

"You?"

"Lord Kane has been looking for a means to separate Dillon and myself—"

"Lady Langham was the target," he interrupted.

"But Dillon is being blamed. Kane is behind it, I tell you."

"This was a crime of passion. Not the work of a disapproving father."

"Kane is more than a disapproving father. He is a man without conscience. He must have known Lady Langham well enough to have created this deception—"

"Although you may not wish to believe it, the police officers have compelling proof of Beaumont's guilt." He rubbed his hand over his eyes, as if tired. "You may wish to reconsider your loyalties."

"I would sooner cut off my arm."

"Laudable, but it will not help the defense."

The clench on her parasol was so tight that it caused her hands to shake. She loosened them, trying for calm. She had not realized how much she had been counting on Redford's help. The man emanated confidence like a fashionable impure exudes perfume. Knowing of his achievements, of the many felons he had seen swing for their crimes, of the ostensibly vanished valuables he had found, of the estate contests proven to be false claims, she knew that with his assistance, Dillon would have a real chance at freedom.

"What . . . what is so convincing about the evidence they claim to have?" she asked.

"You really wish to hear the unpleasant particulars?"

"Please."

He hesitated, studying her, perhaps wondering just how forthright he should be. "The police officers have love letters between the pair. Beaumont's handwriting has been identified."

"Lies." Not wishing to be the personification of

the affronted mistress, she leveled her tone. "What else?"

"A note on Lady Langham's stationery threatening to tell her husband of the affair."

"Is it addressed to Dillon?"

He tilted his head. "No, but with the other evidence . . ." At the dubious look on her face, he added, "Beaumont's bloodied handkerchief was left near the body."

"How do you know that it belongs to him?"

"It is stitched with his initials, and the merchant confirmed that it was Beaumont's special design."

That was damning indeed, but it still did not change the fact that Dillon was innocent. "That is hardly enough foundation upon which to hang a man."

"Men have swung based upon less."

"What do you know of the police officers involved, Misters Kim and Kelly?"

He tilted his head, seemingly impressed that she knew them by name. "They are good men who are thorough in their work."

"They are being well rewarded to see Beaumont arrested. Do they receive a bonus if he hangs?"

Nick crossed his arms, knowing where the lady was headed and not wishing to go down that road. Her frustration shimmered off her in waves. Ivory-gloved hands fisted around her silly parasol as if it were a sword, and her peaches-and-cream cheeks were tinged with red spots of color. Her questions were good, he had to admit, giving her the aura of an avenging goddess, yet it was all based upon myth. Beaumont was guilty.

He waved to the door. "I am sorry, my lady. But I

cannot help you. I suggest that you contact my competitors, Sir Patrick or Mr. Martin."

"And if he is innocent?"

"Then a trial will prove him so." Nick wouldn't bet a farthing on it.

"That is not always the case."

"True, but in this instance we are not dealing with someone without the means to defend himself."

"A barrister argues facts, Mr. Redford. But he must have them at his command in order to sway the judges. That's what we need you for."

"I cannot be swayed, my lady."

Her lush lips pursed. "Is this because of Headmaster Dunn?"

It was like a black veil lowered over his eyes, and for a moment all he could see was blood. A chill rippled through him, as if a ghost had walked across his grave. He felt every ounce of sympathy he had had for her shriveled to dust. He was never one to suffer manipulation easily, and he was not about to let anyone use his grief over Dunn's murder for their own ends. "My answer will not change. You can bat your pretty eyes and sashay your hips until dusk, but I will not take Beaumont's case. Good day."

"I have never—" She pressed her lips together, her gaze flashing azure fire. Those gloved hands clenched and unclenched on the meager parasol. "This is not about me," she whispered. "This is about justice."

"Ask Lady Langham's family about justice," he retorted. "I have seen too many injustices to worry overmuch about a murdering marquis."

She turned away, facing the window. In the glass,

he saw the reflection of her glistening tears. He contained his grimace. That old trick never worked on him.

She certainly had the package to please, though. Petite, so that he could encircle that tiny waist with his hands. She had a derriere that begged to be clasped; its rounded curves enticed a man to imagine treating her as anything but a lady. He could lift her up, carry her downstairs and deposit her in her carriage to get rid of her. The very thought heated his blood to a slow simmer. But if he laid his hands on her, he doubted that he would want to stop with simply removing her person.

But she was a nobleman's woman, kept content by gifts, gold and ornament, things he did not possess as of yet. She would never be satisfied with a man who earned his own way. Likewise, he could never be with a woman who had tossed away her virtue like yesterday's wash.

"How can I prove to you that Beaumont is not guilty?" she asked, turning.

"A woman of the world such as you cannot be so naïve." His tone was gruffer than he intended.

Her back stiffened. Lifting her chin, she stated coolly, "And if there is some proof of his innocence that no one knows about?"

He shrugged. "Between the police officers' evidence and Solicitor General Dagwood's involvement, I would be hard-pressed to trust any exculpatory proof. In fact, I would do my best to ensure that he swung. *Nothing* burns my blood more than watching a guilty man walk free."

She pursed her lush lips and tilted her head, finally acknowledging that he would not bend to her will. She nodded and swept from his office, the scent of lilies floating in her wake.

Slowly he spun on his heel and stepped over to the window.

After a few moments, Mabel moved beside him and followed his gaze. "She certainly left in a huff."

Nick shrugged, focusing on the street below. Lady Janus was crossing the thoroughfare as if she owned it, her harried footman a few steps behind.

"You refused the case." It was a statement.

"Of course."

She let out a noisy breath. "Damnable shame." After a moment, she sniffed. "Did she show any interest . . . in a non-business capacity?"

"Are you daft?" he scoffed. "I have no title, and my bank account is meager."

"That never seemed to stop you before." She raised her brow knowingly.

"Working for me does not give you leave to discuss my personal affairs, Mabel—"

She snorted. "No, knowing you since the day you dawned, does. Besides, your affairs have not been particularly interesting of late. It's all business with you these days."

"Launching one's own enterprise can do that to a man."

"All work and no play makes for some very lonely nights."

"It beats suffering the snores of forty other boys," he jested, trying to make light.

Staring out the glass, her gaze grew troubled. "How are things at Andersen Hall?"

The weight of a thousand responsibilities pressed on his shoulders. "Not good."

"A job would have been helpful to you, and to us. We could certainly use the blunt."

"I will never go back on my oath, no matter how attractive the one asking." He looked down at his hands, large and bony. Not a gentleman's hands, nor a laborer's, but a craftsman's of a different sort. "Dunn taught me that my skills are tools to ensure that justice is done. I will not allow them to be corrupted in pursuit of the mighty coin."

"I know, I know. But to work for Lady Janus . . . well, she is really quite beautiful." She sighed. "Like a fairy with that lovely goldish hair—"

"I had not noticed anything beyond her calculating manner."

"She seemed nice to me. And I always liked the idea that she chose her own path and would not marry. . . ." Dropping into the couch, she shrugged. "Never did quite understand why not, but all the same, it took gumption."

"She is cheeky, if that's what you mean. But I suppose that comes with the territory." He watched through the window as Lady Janus accepted her footman's hand and stepped into her luxurious carriage. The driver flashed the whip and the horses pranced.

"Well, I think that it's deuced nobby how she landed a title without having to take a man along with it. How do you suppose she did that?"

"I expect that for her title, descent must have been through the female line." At the confused look on Mabel's face, he added, "If there was no male heir, then the lady takes."

"Fancy that." Pulling a linen from her pocket, she fingered it with a wistful look on her face. "What will happen to her now, I wonder."

"She will be fine," he replied, turning his back on the window. "She is a survivor. The lady will probably have another titled protector before her handkerchief lands on a ballroom floor."

Somehow, the thought did not soothe.

Chapter 4

"Vingt-et-un" Dillon called the game over, flipping his cards and exposing an ace and a king.

"You've been very lucky today, Dillon," Lillian remarked, trying to hide her disappointment that the game was proceeding so rapidly. She could care less about her lost coins, instead fearing for how to fill the remainder of the afternoon.

For three days Lillian had visited him at Newgate Prison, bringing fresh baked goods, books, and tidings of the outside. They waited in a purgatory of sorts, for the first volley in the courtroom. Torturously slow, the clock ticked onward.

Lillian had managed to maintain a stiff upper lip by keeping life a whirlwind of activity focused on Dillon. He was doing better at Newgate Prison than she might have imagined. Thanks in large part to the fact that his father, the Duke of Greayston, was greasing Warden John Newman's greedy palms. Not every prisoner got to inhabit a room in the Warden's residence.

Her eyes shifted about the small space. It was decent enough, with a bed, a chair and secretary set, a couch, table, chairs and a hearth. Certainly better than the unspeakably overcrowded, pest-ridden part of the prison where any other man awaiting trial would be housed.

"I really would like to see a newspaper," Dillon remarked, pulling her attention back to him.

"What is the point of reading the papers?" She handed him the deck. "They will only upset you."

"I just feel so disconnected. If it weren't for your visits, and the barrister's, I would feel completely isolated. I thought it might help." He dealt the cards. "Do you think that they might print a retraction when all is said and done?"

Lillian would not bet a pickle on it. "What they should do is headline an outright apology. You deserve it."

"That bad?"

"I never appreciated how inaccurate the news accounts were until now. Facts that I know as true they depict as wholly false. It's really quite astonishing."

"Then I suppose you are right in keeping them from me." He peeked at his cards. "I certainly don't need any more bad news."

It was as if a scythe hung over Dillon's head. But she would paste on a happy face if it killed her. "The proceeding tomorrow will go well, Dillon. You will see."

"Dagwood is running the show."

Her fists curled. "I know that the Solicitor General believes that he is just doing his job, but I swear he pushes too far."

"The barrister, Mr. Kent, says that if things go well tomorrow, then the matter will never even go to trial. I will be free."

Reaching over, she squeezed his hand. "Let us keep our thoughts positive then."

"I cannot wait to see what the investigator has scratched up."

Lillian tried not to be pessimistic about Sir Patrick and his findings. She had attempted to meet the man, but he'd claimed to be too busy to see her. She had buoyed her spirits by rationalizing that he was occupied with freeing Dillon. Moreover, the Duke of Greayston had promised to pass on her suspicions about Kane. There was little more she could do.

"Has Sir Patrick not reported to you?" she asked, as if it did not signify.

"Father is handling everything. And trying to take care of Mother as well."

"Any better?"

"No. She will not remove from her bed." He studied his cards, asking with feigned nonchalance, "Has Russell come to see you again?"

"I am disappointed that he has not yet visited you. But he has promised to come to court tomorrow."

"Well, at least he checks in on you. I never would have guessed that his infatuation would actually turn out to be for the good." He motioned to her cards. "You know, Lillian, the game cannot proceed unless you look at your hand."

Her cheeks heated. "Sorry." A two and a three. Could her luck get any worse? "Russell seems to have matured in the last few days. I'm hoping that it is a permanent change."

"It is about time, is all I can say. The man is nearing two-and-twenty."

"Perhaps you will see a difference in him tomorrow."

"*If* he shows up for the proceeding."

"He has committed to come and give his support. He will be there."

"What about Fanny?"

"Fanny is not good with these things, as you know. But she has made me pledge twenty different ways to Sunday that I report to her as soon as the proceeding is done."

"Well, let us hope that you have good news to convey."

The next afternoon Fanny strode into her drawing room, anxiety worrying her brow. "Well, how did it go? Is Dillon in the clear? What did Sir Patrick have to show? Did the Solicitor General retract his evidence?"

"Oh, Fanny. It was dreadful." Lillian's stiff upper lip crumbled to ash as she practically fell into her dear friend's arms. "The matter proceeds to trial in less than two weeks."

"There, there. Tell me what happened," Fanny coaxed, pushing her into the chaise and sitting beside her.

Lillian yanked out the handkerchief that she had been clutching during the ordeal. It was in tatters. Bunching it up, she pressed it to her watering eyes and took a deep breath. "That horrid Solicitor General said the most dreadful things about Dillon. That he was a blood-soaked fiend, and . . . oh, Fanny, if you could have seen Dillon's face. . . ." Tears pricked her eyes, blurring Fanny into a featureless haze of red hair and milky white skin. "He winced with every charge, as if it was a knife thrust. I have never seen him so pale. . . ."

"I think we both could use a drink." Fanny stood. "Scotch'll do."

"The judge hung on Dagwood's every wretched word, clearly biased. And that oaf Sir Patrick. Oooh." She brandished her fist. "I just wanted to shake some vigor into him. He just sat there like a useless shrub as each piece of evidence was presented. I swear, Fanny, the man must sit home counting his coin, for he has done nothing since Dillon's arrest."

Fanny poured scotch into the snifters at the sideboard. "It has only been a few days. Not so much time to be able to clear a man of murder charges."

"Time is a luxury we do not have! In less than two weeks a trial will decide whether or not Dillon hangs! And no one seems to be doing a blessed thing about it!" Pressing her face into her hands, she sobbed, allowing the tears that she had been suppressing ever since Dillon's arrest to break free. The waters poured unreservedly, like a dam that could contain itself no more, and, at this moment, she could not see them ever running dry.

"Drink this."

A tepid glass was pressed into Lillian's hand. She lifted it to her lips, and the smoky liquid seared her throat. She shuddered. "The barrister Greayston hired appeared dazed. And the poor duke sat there looking as if he were carved from stone. Russell actually had to support his father when they left the courtroom; the poor man was so grieved. I cannot imagine his anguish."

"Did you tell the duke the idea you had to save Dillon?"

"He told me that he 'would rather have his entrails consumed by maggots.' "

"Oh, dear. Greayston was never one for subtlety." Fanny dropped onto the chaise. "I do not like to say I said so, but I did." She sipped her drink. "At least he did not threaten you."

"I am just glad that we were alone in the barrister's office after the courtroom debacle, and no one had to hear his bellowing." The memory of another meeting two years ago in a solicitor's office flashed through her mind. The poor solicitor, a wraith of a man, really, had been no match for Kane's fury. Lillian could not say that she had been surprised at Kane's aggression, but never before had it been so public. Her stomach churned recalling the will reading and how Kane's brutal fist had smashed into her face, busting open her lip. The flow of blood had seemed endless. A shudder quaked through her at the memory.

In one sense, she realized, Kane's overt violence had been a good thing. It had been the breaking point for her, giving her the impetus to take a chance on a fool's scheme and try to change her life forever. The inheritance had become the light at the end of a tunnel, glimmering faintly with promise through the darkness.

"Are you all right, Lillian?" Fanny inquired, her arched brows bowed in concern.

"Yes." She shook off the memories; she had more pressing matters to deal with now. "I'm fine."

"Greayston always was a terrific bully, especially when you told him something he did not wish to hear." Fanny scowled. She had been Greayston's mistress long ago and apparently had left him instead of the other way around, which was what usually happened. The woman had fallen in love with someone else and followed her heart.

Lillian blew her nose. "Well, it was awful."

"What, exactly, did Greayston say?"

"That he would destroy me if I even breathed a word of 'such falsehood' to the public. That a 'fetid lie' would not serve his son." Lillian hugged herself. "It was like there had never been any history between our families, he was so hostile."

"Even your good relationship could not hold a candle in the face of his fears. In this instance, one cannot really blame him. It was a terrible idea."

" 'Truth will come to light; murder cannot be hid long,' " Lillian quoted. " 'A man's son may, but at the length truth will out.' "

Fanny smiled wistfully. "I've always loved Shakespeare's *Merchant of Venice*. But no matter how compelling, it is fiction, dear."

"But it bears truth. And my specific . . . knowledge of certain things is the only means I have that might save Dillon."

"You must leave matters to the barristers and the investigator. Greayston will not allow his son to swing."

"You don't understand, Fanny. There is little they can do to exculpate him; the deck is stacked so high. If you could have heard the supposed evidence of the affair, you would realize. They presented Lady Langham's letters to her lover that conveniently have 'Beaumont' scratched across the outside, and a foul innkeeper who went on and on in wretched detail about secret assignations between Dillon and Lady Langham and fighting between the lovers. It was all so"—she shuddered—"neat. And foul. And the judge seemed to swallow it whole."

"But you did try to help. . . ."

"With naught to show for it!"

Fanny rubbed Lillian's arm, worrying over her like a mother hen. "Do you really believe that it would have made a difference if it had been Redford sitting in the courtroom today instead of Patrick?"

Lillian thought about it a long moment. "I do. There is something about Redford. The man is so blasted confident you want to knock him in the chest and, at the same moment, trust him implicitly to get things done. I do not believe that he would rest until an innocent man was let free."

"I have heard that Redford is known for never breaching a confidence. Why not tell *him* the truth about Dillon?"

"He would not believe me." Lillian huffed, trying simply to imagine it. "In fact, he would probably laugh and hoist me out the door on my sassy bottom."

"Sassy bottom?"

Lillian's cheeks heated. "He told me not to bother using my feminine wiles on him."

"What, *exactly*, did he say?"

Lillian shifted uncomfortably. "I cannot precisely recall. . . ."

Fanny's painted red lips pursed, and she raised a perfectly arched brow. "You remember every word that was ever said to you. Now spill."

"Something like," she cleared her throat and deepened her voice condescendingly, " 'You can bat your pretty eyes and sashay your hips until dusk, but I will not take Beaumont's case.' "

"He wants you."

"Yes, to go away."

Fanny smiled indulgently. "The man noticed you.

He wants you. And who can blame him? You are a masterpiece."

"Your masterpiece."

"No longer." Fanny shook her head. "I may have shown you how to walk, how to talk, how to dress, how to thread those bushy eyebrows, but it is all Lillian now."

"Well, that transformation might have saved me once, but a well-arched brow will hardly keep Dillon from the hangman's noose." Lillian's eyes burned warningly, and she blinked. "Kane. That man will be the death of me. I had hoped to be finished with him that day in the solicitor's office when we learned my grandfather had willed all his money to me instead of Kane. When he attacked the poor solicitor, busted open my lip and I ran away to Dillon . . ." Tears spilled down her cheeks. "I do not know what I would have done without him, and you. . . . And now," she sobbed, "I am causing Dillon's end. . . ."

"Now, now," Fanny cooed, wrapping a solid arm around Lillian's shoulders. "It is not your fault that Kane is such a fiend."

"But I brought his wrath upon Dillon."

"But you cannot control Kane's machinations. What you *can* do is expose him for the devil that he is."

"How?" Lillian sobbed.

"Get Redford on your side. The man is known to be more dogged than a drunk with a tankard in his sights. If Kane is behind this, then Redford will see justice done."

"If?"

"Have you any proof?"

"Well, no."

"That's what you need an investigator for."

Lillian sniffed. "I don't know, Fanny. The man seemed so dead set against even considering Dillon's matter."

"And you have never overcome crushing odds? Three years ago, you were a timid wallflower, hiding out on the margins of polite Society, hoping not to be noticed. You were a graceless waif—"

"I was not *that* pitiful. . . ."

"Well, you did have steel in your spine, only it was hidden under the most horrific posture."

Lillian grimaced, recalling the painstaking exercises that Fanny had taught her. She would never look at a broomstick in the same manner again.

"Do you know why I agreed to help you?" Fanny asked.

"For the money?"

"Well, that too." Removing her arm, she continued, "But also because you never saw yourself as a victim. All of Kane's ill treatment, and you never assumed that it was your fault."

"Why would I?"

"Sadly, some people do, giving the tyrant power over them. I have seen it many times. Luckily for you, you never had to deal with self-recrimination as well."

"Well, I certainly had my share of self-doubt. I was deuced terrified every time I had to be seen in public; sick as a cat on a regular basis."

Fanny waved dismissively. "Stage nerves, nothing more."

"Tell that to my maid. I must have gone through fifteen gowns a day."

Besides Fanny, servants had been the only ones to witness the backbreaking hours of posture exercises, modiste fittings, elocution lessons, dancing and movement instruction. How many hours had she spent before a mirror, flirting with her reflection, making polite conversation with the terrified chit staring back at her, ready to mock her efforts?

"But you overcame your nerves just as you overcame Kane. Why? Because you *refused to let him win*." Placing her glass on the side table, Fanny wagged a delicate finger. "I cannot take credit for your life today, but I can say that I taught you that once a woman sets her mind to something, she is capable of anything."

"What I learned from you and Dillon is that I cannot do everything on my own. I need help sometimes, the more steadfast the better." Sighing, she nodded slowly. "Perhaps I am not quite ready to fold my cards."

"Good girl." Fanny squeezed her hand. "Show Kane what he can do with his schemes."

"But how in heaven's name am I supposed to get Redford on our side? How can I impress on him that Dillon did not do what they say he did? Redford said that he would disbelieve anything set before him."

"He needs to feel it where it counts, darling."

"Where is that?"

"You have been a high-stepping mistress for over two years, Lillian. Think about it."

Lillian's mouth actually dropped open. She did not bother to force it closed. "Have you gone round the bend?"

Fanny lifted those expressive shoulders, famous from her years of acting on Drury Lane. "You are the one who has been dreaming of the man for months. . . ."

"The Redford I met four days ago was hardly the Apollo of my fantasies."

"How so?"

"He was so dark, closed, hardly even attractive. . . ."

"Now, that I find hard to believe. I have seen the man, and he might not be an Apollo, but Ares, the god of war, certainly comes to mind."

Stroking the rim of her glass with her finger, Lillian would not meet her friend's eye. "He did not seem particularly violent to me—"

"Not violent, hot-blooded. Couldn't you sense it?"

Lillian shifted uncomfortably. "I do not know what you are talking about, Fanny. All I know is that I don't think that I can do it."

"Then Kane wins."

Lillian sagged against the back of the chaise. "Therein lies the rub."

"Listen, Lillian. Your transformation two years ago. It was about creating a fantasy. You needed to go from drab wallflower to luminous lily. We knew that the pillars of Society would never accept you, but we wanted to make you so very fascinating that you would be an asset to any social gathering. You became the woman every man wanted and the charmer every woman wanted to be. Charisma. It's what gives Napoleon his power."

"I thought it was his army that did that," Lillian quipped.

"Where he leads, they follow. His magnetism charms his subjects into doing his bidding. Charisma is the key."

"Some might argue that it cannot be taught."

"Perhaps not. But it can be feigned. Create a fantasy and then live it." Fanny waved a languid hand.

"It is the same with Redford. You have months of imaginative gold to work with. Take your fantasies and spin them into treasure. In the bedchamber it is all about the imagination. Give him a fantasy, and he cannot say no."

"What if *I* wish to say no?"

"The way that you have been going on about him?" She snorted. "You will probably be in seventh heaven."

Lillian's cheek heated. "Assuming even that this is our best option, the man will believe that he is being manipulated, so he will refuse to be seduced."

"Then you must give him no choice, darling."

Lillian bit her lip. "We do not have much time. The trial is less than two weeks away." She sipped at her scotch, wondering if this was all a pipe dream.

"I have something in mind that can be arranged tonight."

"Tonight?" Lillian sputtered, choking on the harsh liquid.

"You have allowed Kane to command this skirmish. Now is the time for you to be the general."

"What are you talking about?"

"You seduce Redford and he'll take the case. Once Redford understands that Dillon could not have killed Lady Langham, he will not stop there. He will be your greatest soldier, fighting on *your* side."

"He *is* honorable—"

"No, he's smart. There is lots of money to be made off capturing the true culprit. Apart from Lord Langham's sizable reward, Redford has just opened up a new firm. The exposure will be a reward in itself."

"Justice sounded a lot less calculating."

"Here, he can have both. A win for all."

"But must it be tonight? It seems so . . . soon."

"You have already waited three and twenty years to overcome Kane, Lillian. What will it take, the next solar eclipse?"

"If I am to do this, I suppose it will be better in the dark. . . ."

"That's the spirit, darling. Think moonlit grasses and a potent young buck."

"Ugh, you are making me think of hunting. Not exactly the metaphor I need at the moment."

"What would work better for you?"

"Sacrificial lamb?"

"Whatever you say, dear." Fanny's face lit up. "That's it!"

"What are you talking about?"

"When all else fails, go with the Scriptures. I am thinking Abraham sacrificing Isaac."

"I am not following you, Fanny."

Fanny rose and paced, excitement making her bottle green gown swoosh with every sashay. "Don't you mind, Lillian. I am going to take care of everything."

"Everything?" Lillian grinned hopefully.

"Except for the most important thing, Miss Sassy. Not that I wouldn't mind. Redford's just the kind of man to cause a girl to give up on sleeping and eating."

Lillian adjusted her skirts, uncomfortable with the frank conversation. She was used to Fanny talking about such things, but not when they related to her. "So what is the plan?"

"Well, I need you to draft a note to Redford. I was never very good with my letters. Then go home and take a scented bath. Then come back here around dusk. And bring some of those pretty night rails that we bought last month. *Not* the one that *you* picked out, mind you." Fanny beamed wickedly. "Tonight is *not* the night for you to look like a nun."

Chapter 5

~~⁕~~

Nick walked into Tipton's Tavern, his emotions more knotted than a briar patch. Ever since Dunn's death, Nick felt like he wore a mantle of grief as part of his everyday wardrobe. It was with him when he rose, when he moved about town, and when he returned to his single bed at night. It was a barrier separating him from the rest of the blithe world that was not experiencing his heartache.

Dunn had come to Andersen Hall and transformed it from a foundling home of despair to one where children budded with hope. He'd given his charges the one thing that everyone else seemed intent on denying them: *dignity*. It had taken time for Dunn to win the trust of the children at Andersen Hall, most especially that of Nick Redford. But that fragile thread had grown into the fabric of caring, a safety net in a cold, cruel world. Nick would be for-

71

ever grateful for that support. It had given him the
confidence to venture out, to make something of
himself. And he knew that that net had been inter-
woven with Dunn's greatest gift of all, the belief
that his children were *worthy* of success.

Nick loved Dunn more than he could ever love
the father that he had never known. Grieved for that
caring educator with every fiber of his being. It was
like a weight on his soul, sinking him down.

But on a day like today, when the clouds split and
sunlight speared through, the mantle of sorrow
slipped off. And he felt irrationally guilty about it,
like he was being unfaithful to Dunn's memory by
his lack of grief. Yet Nick knew that Dunn would
have chided him for feeling this way, if he were yet
living.

To find a missing bauble, to compile evidence securing a case against a thieving man-of-affairs, to
prove a claim in a contested will; these were the
easy tasks in life. Unraveling his own feelings was a
labyrinth that seemed without egress. So Nick
pushed it all aside for examination at a later time
when he would feel up to it; a time he knew would
never come.

"Good day, Joe." He nodded to the barkeep.
"Have you received any messages for me?"

Joe, a bald, wizened chap with a lame leg and a
sharp eye, shook his head. "Nothing for ya today,
Nick. Heard Dunn's son Marcus was in town. Is it
true?"

The mantle weighed down as if creeling stones
had been set on his back. "Yes. But I haven't spoken
with him."

"I heard that he's become an officer and a hero."

"That's the story they're telling." Shifting his

shoulders, Nick slipped onto a stool and rested his arms on the scratched wooden bar. "I'll have a beer."

"Nick." Dr. Winner patted his arm.

Nick was not in the mood for conversation, but he liked the good doctor. Moreover, Winner was an old crony of Dunn's. "Hello, sir. Sorry, I did not see you."

Winner dropped onto the adjacent stool. "No matter."

"Gin for my friend, Joe," Nick requested.

The barkeep spit into a glass, rubbed it with a cloth, then poured the drink.

"Suddenly you're a man a plenty, Nick?" Winner inquired with a raised brow.

Nick shrugged, sipping his beer. No one needed to know about the bank draft in his pocket. Besides, it would not be his for very long. Between Mabel's wages, the bills piling up on his desk and tithe for the orphanage, it would all be ancient history soon.

After a moment, Dr. Winner cleared his throat. "I heard that you turned down the Beaumont case."

"Blast Mabel and her loose tongue!"

"She knows that I would never tell a soul."

"Still—"

"It takes a man of integrity to think with his conscience instead of his bank account," Winner remarked. "Dunn would be proud of you."

Grief was like a blade slicing through him. Those were the very words that he had striven for his entire life, it seemed. It was a standard rarely to be met, because Dunn was a noble man above others. The headmaster had been kind to all of his charges, but Nick felt especially blessed that Dunn had chosen to cultivate their relationship. Dunn had gone from instructor, to guide, to confidant in their time together. Perhaps how it might be between a father and son. Nick had always been an orphan, but when Dunn had been around, he had not felt like one.

Something must have shown on his face, for Winner laid a hand on Nick's arm and gave it a squeeze. "I know that you are broken up about Dunn. We all are. I wish that I had a cure to ease your pain. But there is no better medicine than time."

Nick inclined his head, indicating his appreciation. "You're right, it's everyone's loss."

"You and he were especially close, Nick. He thought of you as a son. Especially after that mess with Marcus."

"Worthless sod." Marcus had had the one thing that every child in Andersen Hall had wanted—Dunn as a flesh-and-blood father. Yet he had thrown it away, breaking Dunn's heart. No one knew why.

"You and he never did get along." Winner sighed. "Although he seems to have made something of himself. Worked quite closely with Sir Arthur Wellesley, I heard. Helping give Napoleon a well-deserved thumping." He sipped from his glass. "I'm hoping he will assist me with the board of trustees."

Nick snorted, disgusted. "Marcus only knows how to help one person—himself."

"It's been seven years since he left; he's bound to have changed."

"I'll believe it when I see it. But I would not stake the orphanage on the likes of Marcus Dunn."

"It might just come down to that."

Shock rippled through Nick. "You can't be serious."

"We are going to have a deuced time keeping the doors open unless some considerable funding comes up soon. And then there's the matter of securing a new headmaster."

"No one can replace Dunn."

"Someone will have to, or Andersen Hall will be no more."

The children's faces sifted through Nick's mind. The thought of their future without Andersen Hall made him want to kick up a riot. "We cannot allow that to happen."

"The key is finding a headmaster who is vested in the place. Who loves the institution and its charge as more than simply a job. . . ."

"Banish the thought, sir." Nick shook his head. "No matter how committed I am to the children, I'm not the man for the job."

"You never know until you try. . . ."

"I know what I am good at. Administration does not even make the roll. And raising finances?" Nick snorted. "Can you picture me sniffing the ton's skirts to try to drum up funds?"

"Well . . ."

"You know that I am not built for that sort of thing, and I would only bring ruin on the institution."

Winner grimaced. "You do have a tendency to be impolitic."

"You mean frank."

"In polite Society that is one and the same."

"So you agree. I would make a terrible headmaster."

"Perhaps." Winner nodded. "But I am sure that there are other ways for you to contribute to the institution."

"I always will."

They drank in silence.

Nick thought about Marcus's war record. Marcus had never been one to deal well with authority, as was inordinately apparent from his inexplicable clashes with his father. Yet to be noticed by the likes of Sir Arthur Wellesley? Despite himself, Nick was impressed. Marcus might have been a selfish bastard, but he was quick on his feet and sharp with a blade. Apparently he had made good use of his skills on the Peninsula.

Winner waved a nonchalant hand. "What we need is to find someone to publicly express support for the institution. Someone with great influence in Society. . . ."

Nick studied his beer, trying to keep the astonishment from his face. Could Winner possibly know about his new client? No one knew besides . . . *Dunn.*

Winner shifted on his stool, seemingly agitated. "So how is the enquiry business doing, anyway?"

"Fine." Nick drank, reluctant to share the news. It was still too fresh, too startling . . . and it was all the more bittersweet because Dunn had set it up, still trying to help Nick succeed even from the great beyond.

The doctor started tapping his boot heel into the leg of his stool.

Nick refrained from shaking his head at Winner's nosiness. Typical Winner. Dunn had always said that he was as curious as a cat.

"No happenings you would like to share with an old friend?" Winner lured.

Nick allowed himself an inner smile, knowing that Winner was right. What was the use of good tidings if you did not share them? Still, he had to make the fine doctor suffer a bit. Dunn would have insisted. "Ask Mabel. She seems to know everything."

The tapping increased. "I am asking you."

"Oh yes, there is something."

Winner's boot stilled.

"I had new business cards printed. Want to see one?"

The man scowled. "Tarnation, Nick. Stop being coy. Did it come through or not?"

Nick let the good doctor wait another moment, before nodding. "Dunn came through."

"Damn," Winner breathed, slapping the bar. "The queen of England herself." He grinned. "If Dunn were here, he'd be buying us all a round!"

"Yes, he would. He would also be begging me for details. It's not every day that a misbegotten orphan gets to meet the queen of England."

"You met the queen of England?" Winner shrieked. "Queen Charlotte?"

"Is there another?"

The man actually hooted.

Nick smiled. "I am glad that I have finally impressed you, sir."

"No, laddie." Winner slapped him on the back. "You impressed me the first day that I met you, drippy-nosed stripling that you were. I just never mentioned it. So, what's she like?"

"Who?" Nick teased.

"Devil take you! Queen Charlotte!"

"Well," Nick began slowly. "She was nothing like what I had expected. I mean, she was regal, like any queen, I suppose. But she was not like the renderings that I have seen."

"More inspiring?"

"Smaller."

"Undersized?" Winner asked, his gaze horror-struck.

"No, just not as tall as in her portraits. I suppose they must put her on a pedestal when they paint those things."

"Is she as plain as they say?"

"She has too much intensity to be plain. Her eyes seemed all-knowing. As if she could see through to your birth and know every skeleton in your cupboard."

"Upon my honor," Winner breathed, his eyes wide with wonder. "Glad it was you and not me standing before her. I would have been in shark's waters for sure. So what are you required to do for her?"

"Investigate anything that might crop up."

"You mean, you might not actually have to do anything?"

"Actually, no."

"But you did get paid?"

"A sizable retainer fee." Nick patted his coat pocket. "After Mabel's wages, there will be a nice donation for the orphanage."

Winner's cheeks reddened and his eyes flashed with excitement. "This is a grand opportunity, Nick. Fortuitous. Just when we need a person of influence—"

"I believe in Andersen Hall as much as you do, Doctor," Nick interrupted. "The children need it to remain a safe haven where they can learn a trade and succeed. But I can hardly ask the queen of England for favors."

"Well," Winner wagged a finger, "one never knows what opportunity might spring from another."

"Please don't say a word, sir."

"You should be crowing about this one."

Nick shrugged. "I am happy, of course. But crowing is a bit too much effort for me these days."

"Dunn would want you to be happy, Nick. It's all he ever wanted for you."

Nick almost smiled, remembering the burly headmaster. "No, he wanted me to be happy, hardworking, honorable, righteous, provide for a family . . . the list goes on."

"He was a bit of a tyrant."

"A beloved one at that."

Winner scratched his shadowed chin. "So when will you settle down, Nick? You're almost thirty. Almost as old as me."

Nick swirled the beer in his mug, watching the foam spin. "I do not think that I am cut out for having a family, sir."

"Why the hell not?"

Nick shifted his shoulders, feeling that unseen mantle drag on him. "Well, I've never had one, for one."

"Perhaps not in the traditional sense. But being at Andersen Hall was like having a big family. Well, maybe not. But look at you now; you're the queen's man, for heaven's sake."

"Please don't tell anyone, sir."

"Your secret is safe with me."

"Thank you." Finishing his tankard, Nick stood.

"Where are you off to in such a hurry? We have some celebrating to do."

"You enjoy yourself, Doctor." Nick tossed some coins on the bar. "I have to go see a prospective client."

"Anyone I know?"

"Miss Fanny Figbottom."

"The stage actress?"

"Can't imagine many women having that name."

"I saw her once in a production of . . . what was it now? Oh, I can't recall. Something about someone dying and a great love affair. All I know is that she had these milky white shoulders that seemed to have a life of their own. And those hips, well, she certainly is aptly named." He coughed into his fist. "Not that I notice those things, mind you. I went for the culture." He looked up. "Did you ever have the chance to see her?"

"She was *ages* before my time, sir," Nick ribbed.

"So were many other great things, you gutter-snipe," he retorted, joking. He sipped from his drink. Then, licking his lips, Winner sighed dramatically. "Miss Figbottom. I would love to meet her in person."

"I cannot introduce you until I meet her myself."

"Very well, but I want a full accounting."

"You are assuming that there will be something worth sharing."

"With a woman like Miss Figbottom, there always is."

Chapter 6

Nick was led to a wood-paneled drawing room with mint-colored walls, bottle green chintz furnishings and pea green drapes. Splayed before him was a plush carpet depicting a view of the ocean's multilayered emerald waters. The former actress must be inordinately fond of green, he mused.

A hearty fire flamed in the hearth, and the drapes were drawn, giving the chamber an intimate feel. The two wide-backed olive chairs faced each other before the grate, with a mahogany table resting between them. On the table sat two glasses filled with a burgundy liquid. A crystal decanter filled with the same was positioned beside them.

The carrot-headed butler waved for him to have a seat. "My employer will be a few moments." The man had the stout build of a laborer and a less formal mien than most butlers.

"Miss Figbottom, she's the famous actress, isn't she?"

"Yes, sir. Retired now."

"You need not 'sir' me. What is your name?"

"Stanley."

"How long have you been with Miss Figbottom, Stanley?"

"I have known Miss Figbottom for almost thirty years."

Nick did the sums in his head of when the actress must have been on Drury Lane. "But you have not always been her butler?"

"No, sir. Not always." A twinkle flickered in his pale blue gaze.

Nick nodded, sensing that there was a story underlying this relationship. Curious about his potential client, he inquired, "May I ask how you two met?"

"When I was a stagehand, sir. With Mr. Lowell's Traveling Troupe of Players. Miss Figbottom was the lead in almost every production. The best thing that ever happened to the troupe."

"And now you are her butler."

"I consider myself a jack-of-all-trades, Mr. Redford. I do *whatever* is required, regardless of designation."

Nick did not like the satisfied smile on his face. Like a cat who'd cornered the mouse. He pushed aside the feeling; the man was probably serving his employer in the boudoir in addition to his other duties and wanting to crow about it. Well, it was none of his affair.

"Now, my task is to make you comfortable, Mr. Redford." He motioned to the chairs by the flaming hearth. "I have taken the liberty of pouring you Cognac."

Cognac. He had not had the opportunity for such an indulgence in a very, very long time. If he had to name a favorite libation, Cognac headed his list. Either Miss Figbottom had done her research, or he was having an exceedingly lucky day.

"Aged twenty-five years," Stanley added, with a pleased smile. "Miss Figbottom will be a few moments. So please make yourself comfortable."

He left the room and closed the door with a loud click.

Miss Figbottom must have been in sore need of investigative assistance, for she was going to great trouble to put him at ease. Nick eyed the snifter longingly. Twenty-five-year-old Cognac and somehow smuggled into England despite the war with France. Still, he hesitated. He had a personal rule about no spirits while working. Unless, of course, he was gathering information at a tavern and needed to grease the wheels. Since Miss Figbottom obviously wished for him to imbibe, their interview likely would proceed more smoothly if he did . . . and surely, seeing as it was already poured, he could not let such a fine tipple go to waste. . . .

Slipping into the cavernous chair, he raised the snifter to his nose. The burned, oaky scent teased his senses. He sipped. Velvety fire.

A sigh escaped and Nick leaned back, allowing himself a brief moment of repose. The fire popped and hissed. This was *fine*.

A part of him wished Miss Figbottom would take her time. But he knew that the sooner he was done here, the sooner he could be back in the office. This was not his favorite part of the job. The sale. The negotiation. And when a woman was involved, the possibility of tears. The fire crackled, and heat wrapped itself around him like a thick blanket. The urge to stretch his legs was unbearable, and he soon felt the soles of his boots warmed by the flame. His muscles unwound themselves as his shoulders relaxed. It seemed the tension of these last few weeks was no match for a good drink, a soft chair and a roaring fire.

Before he knew it, the glass was empty. He wished he could have more, but he wanted to keep his head about him, so instead, he waited, letting the fire warm him. Time stretched, and he eyed the decanter. If she was going to keep him waiting like this, surely she could not expect him to simply sit there. And if she wasn't going to show at all, it would be a terrible waste of some of the best Cognac he'd tasted in a long time. He lifted the crystal decanter and poured himself a hearty measure more.

"To Miss Figbottom," he murmured as he raised the glass in toast. "And the . . . water of life."

"Legend has it a knight in the sixteenth century created Cognac," a husky female voice stated from near the door.

Blast him for not hearing her enter. Quickly, he set the glass on the table with a graceless thud and stood. His knees turned to jelly, and he had to lean against the chair back for support. *What the hell was wrong with him?*

"Miss . . . Figbottom." His voice echoed oddly in his ears. Shock rippled through him: He couldn't be this foxed from only one glass . . .

She sashayed deeper into the room, the swoosh of

her emerald gown grating on his ears. "Story has it, the knight thought he would burn in hell once for murdering his unfaithful wife, and a second time for killing her lover. Hence he 'burned his wine' twice and put it in the far corner of the cellar. Whereupon he promptly forgot about it."

He seemed to be looking at her from down a long tunnel, and she was a blur of green gown, pale skin and flaming hair. "What . . . is . . ." His mouth was not working properly. "Wrong . . . with . . . me?"

"Finding it years later," she continued as if he had not spoken, "he must have felt a bit better, or worse, about his destiny because he decided to imbibe. And acidic, poor wine was reborn as Cognac."

The room spiraled around him in sickening green waves, and he fell back into the chair with a thump.

"The story is completely false," she stated in devilish tones, leaning forward and bracing herself on the arms of his chair. The scent of roses enveloped him, making his stomach lurch.

"The drink . . ." he slurred.

Her face swam before his eyes; the skin ghost white, cat green eyes, devil-red curls and scarlet lips formed in a smirk. "We know that Cognac was born by accident. An offshoot of economies of trade. But the myth is much more affecting."

"I'll see . . . you . . . in hell . . . for this," he whispered, barely able to keep his eyes open.

"The road to hell is paved with good intentions," she murmured, pressing a kiss to his forehead.

All went black.

"Fanny, what have you done?" Lillian cried from the doorway.

Her friend stood over the canopied bed where Redford lay stretched out on his back, his sleek, bare skin glistening in the candlelight.

"What?" Fanny turned. "Oh, get that horror-struck look off your face. He will be fine. The alchemist said that he might have a bit of a headache, but he will be fit as a fiddle all the same."

"And you trust this?" Lillian shrieked.

"Look at him, he's breathing soundly and shows no ill effects from the tonic."

"You could have killed him!"

"Piffle."

Her friend's confidence reassured her, and Lillian's feet edged forward. She was afraid but too fascinated not to look. Her breath caught; the man was a masterpiece of smooth, pale skin rippling over fluid brawn. His head rested to one side, spreading his collar-length glossy black mane over his shoulder. His arms bulged in repose over his head, held there with colorful silken cords tied from wrists to bedposts. This position opened his chest like a fan of undulating muscle.

"Oh, my," she breathed, spellbound by the dipping hollow of his navel. Heady warmth washed over her, and more than anything she longed to graze her hand across the sprinkling of black fuzz that ended abruptly at the silken white sheet at his waist.

"He is a beauty among men, isn't he?" Fanny marveled.

Lillian swallowed. "You would know better than me."

Setting hand to hip, Fanny grinned. "That's true. And I must say, he's as well favored as any man I've had the good fortune to bed in the last few years."

"Look at those scars." Lillian pointed to the slashes of white on the moon-pale skin of his chest and arms. "I wonder what happened to him."

"The man was an orphan; it could not have been easy."

Something inside Lillian tightened at seeing Nick Redford so vulnerable. He was not a fantasy but a flesh-and-blood man with history, feelings and hurts. "Fanny, this is not right—"

"Now for the prize," Fanny declared. Reaching forward, she lifted the sheet.

Lillian grabbed her hand. "Fanny!"

"This is a golden opportunity. You might as well enjoy the view."

"It just doesn't seem right."

"And drugging him was? Besides, where's the harm, the man is out cold."

Guilt clashed with fascination inside Lillian. Where *was* the harm at this point? She was going to hell anyway, she might as well glance a peek. Slowly, she released her friend's hand.

Lowering the sheet, Fanny beamed. "Oh, *my*."

Lillian straightened.

"Pretty astounding that those parts cause so much trouble in this world," Fanny opined.

Lillian tilted her head. "When he is resting and all, well, it does not look so daunting."

"Daunting? Dear Lord, Lillian. I'm coming to believe this is an act of charity, me exposing you to a man other than Dillon. I love him dearly, mind you, but the man clearly is not a good influence on you. That, right there, is heaven's perfect tool of pleasure, and a mighty well formed one at that."

"Look at those thighs," Lillian murmured, raising her hand to her lips. The thighs were brushed with a delicate cover of dark fuzz on sea-foam white skin. "Each one around is as big as my waist."

"Go ahead," Fanny encouraged, stepping aside. "Touch him. He will not wake."

That navel just begged to be stroked. She felt the yearning deep in her middle, like a ticklish hunger that could never be satisfied with food.

"He will not wake?"

"Go ahead, Lillian."

Swallowing, she tentatively stretched out her hand. Her fingertips swept across the gentle slope of his rib cage. "Like a baby's bottom . . ." she marveled, her heart charging with excitement. She explored that delicious dip in his navel, then raked her fingers through the crisp black hair. A ticklish heat swamped her, and she felt the unholy desire to press her mouth to that very abdomen and taste him. She licked her parted lips. "He is beautiful. . . ."

"His face is not bad either."

His angular features had softened; the hard lines coalesced into a smooth, handsome visage. The worry had eased from his broad brow, his lids were closed, and his mouth was slightly open in repose.

Leaning over, she traced a fingertip along that sumptuous bottom lip. It was velvety soft. His warm breath enveloped her finger.

He groaned.

She jumped, clutching her friend.

Fanny grasped her hand. "Do not fret. He is tightly bound."

They watched him with baited breath. He did not move or make another sound.

Lillian struggled free of Fanny's hold. "This is depraved, Fanny. We are fondling an unconscious man."

"Yes, it is a bit wicked, isn't it?" She grinned unabashedly. "I have not had this much fun in years."

"Fanny!"

"Must you sour all my grapes?" Fanny moaned. "It feels like ages since I've had a good tumble, and this is amazing inspiration."

"Even if he is not awake, we must respect his dignity. It's only proper."

"There's nothing proper about what we're doing tonight, Lillian. So get that idea right out of your head."

Despite her better intentions, Lillian spared another look at that poetic convergence of man and muscle. "Don't you think he's cold?"

"Stanley stoked the fire. Besides, when Mr. Redford gets you in his sights, he'll be hotter than burned bisque."

"Dear Lord, the servants must know! What must Mr. Stanley think?"

"Don't you mind about Stanley or anyone else. You just worry about Redford here." Fanny sashayed to the door.

"You can't just leave me here!" Lillian cried, suddenly panicking.

"I have done everything in my power to get you to this point, dear. Now it's time for you to do your part."

"But Fanny! I can't do it if he's unconscious. It defeats the whole purpose."

"He should wake in an hour or two."

"But . . . but . . . what do I do until then?"

"Whatever you wish," Fanny cooed, slamming the door closed behind her.

The key turned in the lock with a deafening *click*.

Chapter 7

The scent of hearth spices beckoned Nick to consciousness, and he became aware of soft down beneath him. A fire was nearby; he could feel its wafting warmth. He exhaled a shuddering sigh of relief. He had had a nightmare, of that much he was sure, but the specifics eluded him. He could only recall trying to struggle with some unknown fiend, but his arms would not function.

A sense of impotence stained his consciousness. He swallowed, and, surprisingly, that tang of fear seemed to still lace his tongue, intermingled with something sour. Like aged goat cheese.

He felt ragged, as if he had overslept but not quite gotten the rest that he needed. A late night at Tipton's Tavern perhaps? His memory was fuzzy, his senses dull.

He peeled his gummy eyes open and saw that he

was lying on a canopied bed with fluted, ivory columns supporting a mint green embroidered tester. He tried to rise, only to realize he was hindered. His arms were fastened.

"What? . . ." His cry came out as barely a croak. His throat felt burned to ash. He yanked his arms again. They were tied with silken cords. *What the hell was going on?*

Panic pulsed through him, bringing with it sharp awareness. For the first time, he took a good look at his situation. He was as bare as the day he was born, with a thin sheet covering him to his waist. He was in a fancy bedroom with one white paneled closed door. Probably locked. A dresser, a divan and two armchairs by the fire. Wait. One of those chairs was occupied. Pulling on the bindings, he stretched as high up as he could to see. He could not have been more stunned if it had been Father Christmas.

A lush young woman lay curled up asleep in a corner of the chair, her back to him. She wore a rail of the flimsiest silk in a color that reminded him of a lush peach. Golden red curls cascaded loosely over her shoulders and down her back like a wealth of silk. The swell of her derriere pressed against the skin-thin chemise, giving him a view that, on any other occasion, he would have appreciated.

What the hell was happening here? He felt too awake for this to be a dream, and too cross for it to be a fantasy. Though he had had a few offers, he had not once felt the inclination for erotic sport. His brain scrambled for memory. Green furnishing. Cognac. Miss Figbottom.

His inability to function.

Poison.

"Bloody hell!" Though his throat burned raw, it felt good to scream.

She jerked awake.

He heaved his arms, struggling to pull free. "You'd better keep me tied! I'm going to kill you when I get my hands free!"

Uncurling, she sat up and turned.

Shock stole his breath. "Lady Janus?"

She blinked, her gaze clouded, her hair mussed from sleep. Seeing him, her eyes widened.

"Untie me," he urged.

She just sat there, as if afraid to move. Was she likewise a hostage in this nasty game?

Her chest rose and fell as if she were out of breath, drawing his gaze to the swell of her creamy white breasts.

He ripped his mind back to his predicament. "Were you drugged? Are you unwell? Untie me. I can help you. We'll get out of here. . . ."

"I can't." She swallowed, slowly rising. She was half-naked, but he couldn't think about that right now.

"Why not?"

Her eyes slid away.

He felt the knowledge slam into him like a blow. "You did this to me."

She shook her head no, then slowly yes. "It was not my idea, but . . . yes, I am the reason. For Dillon, Lord Beaumont . . ."

He had never felt the inclination to hurt a woman before, but the powerful urge pulsed through his blood like vengeful fire. His hands clenched and unclenched, eager for violence. He was panting, his heart clapping against his rib cage. How dare she?

Poison, shackle and whatever she had in store . . .
His anger ripped through him like a mighty cy-
clone, ready to wreak havoc in its wake.

"You bloody bitch!"

"This seemed the only way to—"

"You think this will convince me to work for
Beaumont?" he cried derisively as his mind raced
through alternatives. This was her home territory;
no hint of rescue if he called out. It was unlikely he
could change her mind. So it was up to him to break
free.

Her chest, neck and cheeks were flushed red with
discomfiture. "I need to prove to you that Dillon did
not kill Lady Langham."

Eyeing the bindings, he saw that they did not
look particularly complex. If he could keep her talking, she would be distracted while he freed his
hands.

"Prove it, then," he sneered. "I am a captive audience."

"First I will have to, um . . ." She stepped forward.

Alarm surged through him; he needed time to
worry the knot. Seeing the pitcher on the bureau, he
stalled, "What the hell did you poison me with?"

"I don't know what it was."

"At least give me a drink. My throat burns like
fire."

A small spark of guilt flashed across her features.
Good. She should feel culpable. Guilty as hell, in fact.

Taking a deep breath, perhaps even a relieved
one, she turned toward the dresser. The flimsy rail
clung to the alluring curve of her derriere. This was
no time to be distracted. He tore his eyes away from
her bottom and hastily worked on the binding at his

right wrist. Damned his fumbling fingers. The binding budged a smidgen but did not come undone.

She faced him, holding the mug before her in both hands like a shield. She took one step closer, and then another. At least she was frightened of him, what little satisfaction that brought.

She reached the mug toward him, touching the cool ceramic to his lips. Oddly, she seemed most careful not to touch him.

Even though he had only asked for it as a ruse, the water was a welcome balm on his sore throat. Rivulets dripped down the sides of his mouth and onto his chest. She seemed diverted by their progression. As the water made its way down to the sheet, she averted her eyes. Not exactly the playful seductress, was she?

"Enough?" she asked.

He couldn't free himself with her watching, so he nodded.

She turned, resting the mug on the nightstand. He made quick work with his hands. The bond was loosening beneath his fingers. But he was not quick enough.

She faced him again, her eyes sweeping the length of him as if trying to work out something. He was not used to such open examination and felt his skin prickle despite himself.

"It's a little late to inspect the merchandise," he derided, the sense of impotence fueling his anger.

Her face reddened further, the blush crawling across that lush swell of bosom. "I wish it were not so," she murmured, as if resigned. "But this is how it must be."

"You're just trying to make excuses, and there are no excuses for your despicable deeds."

"An innocent man's life is at stake. Hopefully soon you will understand." Stepping back, she slowly lifted the edge of her rail to the knee, exposing shapely, white calves.

He swallowed, his heart hammering to a new sort of danger. Moving closer, she rested one knee on the mattress. The smell of lilies permeated the air.

"Perhaps I could get a real drink? Scotch? Brandy?" he stalled, hoping for more time to work the bindings.

"Perhaps later." Pulling herself onto the bed, she climbed atop him, straddling him between supple white thighs.

He felt seared where her skin touched his about the waist. Despite himself, his shaft swelled, grazing her buttocks. He withheld a groan. Blast his traitorous body. She settled herself on top of him, the heat between her thighs making his cock burn to be inside her. His breath shortened to a pant.

Azure eyes met his. Tense and wary.

"Don't think you're so original," he scoffed, trying to keep the lust from his voice. "I've had plenty of wenches try to seduce me into taking a case." But never so intricately planned and never by someone who looked good enough to eat. It was usually a desperate widow who, as a last-ditch effort, shoved her bosom in his face and made suggestive remarks. "It's never worked before, and it won't work this time either." Heaven help him, he was starting to wonder if he actually wanted to get out of this black widow's web.

Laying her hands on his bare chest, she leaned forward, providing him with an incredible view of lush cleavage. She shifted above him, lowering herself to his hips. The buttery caress of her thighs caused his cock to harden to iron.

"It's only a stiff staff. Doesn't make a bit of difference to anything," he told himself as much as to her. He would be damned if he was going to let her manipulate him into anything beyond sex. He had made no promises, certainly didn't owe her a thing.

Her lips parted, and she inhaled a quivering breath that he felt all the way in his shaft. Her eyes fastened on his nipples, and beneath that piercing blue gaze, the nubs peaked.

"This is a mistake," he bit out, knowing that if things went one step further, he would be gone.

She licked her lips, shifting above him with a maddening rub of silken flesh. She removed her hands and stared at him, not doing much of anything.

His body fairly throbbed with the need for release. Yet she did not touch him anywhere except for her inner thighs. Uncertainly, she eyed the door. Her brow knotted with unease. Something didn't make sense.

"What the hell is going on?" he demanded, wanting her to either get on with it and end his torment, or stop this madness completely. At the moment, he was actually wishing for the former.

Again, her gaze shifted to the door. Was she waiting for someone to come crashing through to save her? The absurdity of it made him want to scream.

"I can't do this," she muttered under her breath. The look of distaste was clear on her face now. She was no longer even pretending to be enjoying this little seduction. As if he was unworthy of even that small pretense.

Then it hit him like a cannonball; she dreaded

bedding him. Hell, she seemed barely able to endure touching him. She was lowering herself and couldn't stand it. The wench would sell herself to a noble, openly living in sin, but couldn't bear the thought of lying with a man of his class.

Her eyes met his, and for the first time since this madness began, they looked certain. "I can't do this," she confirmed his assessment. "No matter how important, I just can't see it through."

Climbing off, she sat on the edge of the bed, her legs stretched before her. Her face was turned away, as if she couldn't stand to look at him. "I just cannot bring myself to do it. Not for Dillon. Not even for me. . . ."

His teeth clenched, and he felt unsated lust and fury surge through him.

"This was a mistake. I'm sorry. . . ." The mattress dipped as she moved to push off it.

Furious, he tore at the bindings. His right hand ripped free.

Grabbing her about the waist, he flipped her over onto her back. His body covered hers, capturing those supple curves beneath him. Quickly, he freed his bound hand. Hunger and rage surged through him. He would have his satisfaction. She knew it, too. Her eyes were wide with shock, her mouth rounded in an astonished O.

He would teach her a thing or two about dipping with the lower classes. He was going to leave her begging for more.

"You want to play games?" he whispered huskily in her ear. "You should have asked about my rules."

Chapter 8

Lillian's breath caught as she stared, stunned, into tempestuous cocoa brown eyes. Her captive was now the conqueror, eager to exact revenge for her offenses. Shocked, she tried to push herself up, but he was a block of iron, pressing her deep into the feather mattress.

Snatching her wrists in his hand, he stretched them high above her head. She felt the wooden bedpost graze her knuckles, but it was too broad for her hands to grab. Her heart raced and her mouth dried to dust. His head slowly lowered, and a black lock of hair fell across his eyes. She winced, steeling herself for the punishment she knew she deserved.

His lips hovered over hers, and his warm breath wafted over her. The scent of almonds and Cognac teased. Suddenly his mouth was gone, and a surprising shaft of disappointment slashed through her.

Heat encased her nipple, burning through the thin fabric of her shift. She gasped, realizing that he had taken her breast full in his mouth. Her body shuddered with an unholy hunger she couldn't place.

He looked up, passion burning in his dark gaze. "You're the one who brought me here. Now it's time to finish what you started."

Icy shivers raced down her spine. This was not the way it was supposed to have happened. Not the way Fanny had promised it would go. She should have anticipated that Redford would not be played so easily. She should have known that she was toying with fire.

He pressed an open kiss to her throat, searing her skin with his tongue.

Her mouth went dry. Alarm swirled in her belly.

"Mr. Redford . . ." she started huskily, hating how her voice betrayed her.

"So formal," he breathed. "The women who tie me up usually have the decency to use my Christian name."

"You've done this before?" she cried, aghast.

"Haven't you?" His husky voice rippled through her.

Heaven's no. "Listen, Mr. Redford . . ."

"Yes, *my captor?*"

His words caused a hot ticklish sensation in her middle. Oh, dear.

"You have a request for me?" he purred, lifting her earlobe with his tongue. She felt his teeth nibble down on the soft flesh. She gasped. A shock rippled through her, straight to the heated joint between her legs.

"I am at your command, *my lady,*" he murmured,

the salutation coming off as anything but deferential. "Perhaps you wish for me to take your breast in my mouth again?"

As if heeding his words, her nipples lifted and hardened.

His eyes fixed on her nipples as they pushed up against the flimsy silk. "I'll take that as a yes."

She felt his mouth on her nub, as if the thin rail did not exist. She bit her lip to contain a groan. Her body was betraying her, exposing the deep longings that had filled her lonely nights. She had never expected to know a man's touch, to experience the feel of a man's hard body pressing into her with desire. Her senses were unprepared for the limb-melting assault. And for the responding fire within her that yearned to be stoked.

Redford's tongue circled her nipple with hot, languid strokes, smoldered her already overheated skin and causing the most unholy dampness between her thighs. Part of her mind cried to unleash her hunger. To stop being so restrained . . . so afraid of losing control.

From a young age she had learned to be careful, mindful of her every move for fear of raising Kane's ire. That pattern followed her still. After breaking away from her stepfather, she'd guarded her every step in Society. It felt like every action in her life was measured, every move studied. *Chaos beckoned*. She longed simply to *let go*.

A small groan hummed through his mouth, sending ripples of pleasure reverberating through her breast straight to her feminine core. Heat surged and her brain muddled to mush.

Her lips parted and she closed her eyes, surrendering to sensation. His hot, wet tongue. The arousing rub of his skin against hers. Wetness pooling between her thighs.

Her hips rocked. She moved beneath him as if riding to some unknown rhythm that he played on her breast.

Suddenly his mouth broke free and cold air stiffened her nipple even more.

"Or perhaps," he breathed, hovering over her belly, "there's some other place you'd like my mouth."

Excitement whipped in her belly at his frank suggestion.

He pulled her arms down toward her head, and the tresses teased her fingers. With his knee he pushed her leg up to the side, her other imprisoned against his unmoving thigh. He pushed the night rail up around her waist. She felt suddenly exposed.

Cool air teased her open flesh and she trembled. Slowly, he lowered. His hot tongue flicked across her inner thigh and her hips bucked.

"Oh, God," she cried out before she realized it.

"Not yet, my lady. There's more."

More? Lord help her.

His tongue slipped between the secret folds of her flesh, sending tremors shooting through her core. He slid up and down in her wetness, driving her to madness. Sensation soared. His mouth fixed on her hard nub and sucked. She cried out.

His head lifted. "You liked that?"

She was panting, her heart pounding. She felt like she was in a race, trying to catch up but not quite making it.

His tongue flicked across her womanhood and she gasped.

He looked up, watching her. Sweat glistened on

his forehead. His breath was shallow. His gaze smoldered to near black with fiery passion. His mussed raven hair lay across his forehead, making him look wild, brutish with masculine strength. He was a warrior god, *a stranger*. Yet her body seemed to know him. Welcome him, even.

"Tell me you want me," he urged.

It was true. She desired him. Hungrily. Desperately. She always had. For all of the convoluted reasons for this seduction, none of this would ever have happened if not for the simple fact that she desired him, like a starved woman beguiled by forbidden fruit. And now this. This unbridled passion. This beckoning desire to abandon control, to lose all restraint. *To capitulate to his passionate onslaught.* It was all too much to deny.

"Yes?" he asked.

"Yes," she breathed, amazed by how easy it was.

"I want you too," he murmured, pressing an open kiss to her inner thigh. The rough yearning in his voice sent her final trepidations flying off.

Bracing his hands alongside her, he moved up her body in a long, slithering stroke. He lay on top of her. His member, hard like granite, but searing like fire, pressed into her innermost thigh. He shifted. The head of his manhood pressed into her core, causing liquid fire to surge inside her. She heard herself moan.

"What is your command, my lady?" He pressed himself against her nub, rocking gently. Her hips rose to meet him. "You only get what you ask for."

"Please," she moaned.

"Please what?" His shaft slid in her wetness, slick with desire for him.

She shook her head. She couldn't say it. She didn't even know the words.

"Tell me where you want me to put it."

Her heart slammed against her chest. She felt like she could cry from wanting him so badly.

"In . . . inside," she whispered, her face burning with shame. But she did want him there. Needed him to fill her.

His manhood slid lower, edging near the entrance to her core.

She held her breath.

His hips bucked forward, ramming his shaft deep inside her, infiltrating her most delicate muscles. She screamed as her maidenhead tore. Shock rippled through her and she shuddered, closing her eyes to the truth of it. He was inside of her. Deep, full, stretching.

She was panting, fear and wonder surging through her. She had done it. She was an innocent no more.

"You conniving bitch!" His face was a mask of contained fury. "What schemes do you play?"

She caught her breath. "No schemes. You . . . wanted . . . proof . . . for Dillon—"

"This doesn't prove a bloody thing!" He reared up on his elbows, glaring down at her.

His manhood shifted. A thrill shot through her, and she gasped. That's when she realized that the pain was gone, just as Fanny had described.

She swallowed. "We need to talk about this . . . about Dillon . . ."

"Damned Beaumont. He's not the one *swiving* you right now."

She froze and blinked, an unseen pain slashing through her heart. She turned her head away, unable to endure the fury in his gaze. This was the most intimate connection she had ever had with anyone in her life, yet she felt his anger like a battering ram, hammering at the invisible walls of her self-worth. The man looked like he reviled her. Mortification swept over her like a torrent. She felt none of the heat she had felt before, only coldness from deep in her heart. What they were doing was not *right*.

"I only did this to prove . . . that Dillon . . . did not murder Lady Langham."

"Bullocks!" He pulled out, slick and wet, leaving her cold.

He showed no discomfiture at his nakedness, standing bold and magnificent in the candlelight. He raked his hand through his dark hair, obviously troubled. He turned and leaned both arms on the back of the armchair, giving her his back. His shoulder muscles bunched with tension as his hands clenched and unclenched.

Apprehensive, she pulled the sheet over her, wondering what to do now.

He turned and she felt his wrath like a bonfire; she was paces away yet imagined that even her eyelashes singed.

"Tell me," he demanded darkly. "Does Beaumont appreciate you whoring yourself out and giving it away for free?"

She swallowed, wanting the feather mattress to cleave open and engulf her whole. But that would not save her or Dillon. Ignoring the terrible shame shuddering through her, she focused on her purpose. "I was an innocent," she whispered.

"A parlor trick, perchance?"

Anger overcame her humiliation. "Have you ever bedded an innocent before?"

His cheeks tinged, and a shadow passed through his eyes.

"So you know that I'm not lying," she affirmed, wondering who he was thinking of.

"It proves nothing," he growled.

"It proves that Dillon, the marquis, and I have never . . ."

"Which, some might argue, confirms why he sought entertainments elsewhere."

"Devil take you, Redford!" Her anger built and she fed it, preferring to be outraged instead of humiliated. "He's not capable—"

"What makes you so sure?"

"Dillon does not . . . Dillon is not . . ." How could she put the secret into words? Taking a deep breath, she muttered, "Dillon is uninterested in females."

Understanding flashed in his eyes. "Black spy take me! He's a backgammon player?"

"A what?"

"A sodomite."

Her cheeks flamed and her jaw worked. "I-I suppose. I don't ask many questions. It is none of my affair." She swallowed. "Dillon never would have had this great love affair that the Solicitor General claims. He hardly even knew Lady Langham; he most certainly did not care enough about her to kill her. He is innocent. But no one knows the truth of it. *Except for you.*"

"Devil take it! You deceived me. Drugged and trussed me. And now you expect me to work for you?"

"This is not about me. It's about saving an innocent man."

His eyes blazed black with anger. He strode across the room to the wardrobe, all golden pale skin over rippling muscles. Yanking open the door, he snatched out clothing, tossing items to the floor.

"Now you understand—"

"All I understand is that you are a fraud. You lie, deceive. And Lord only knows why, but I don't give a plumb's uncle."

She rolled onto her knees, hugging the sheet to her breast. "I would not lie about this! It would destroy Dillon's family—"

"So instead you stoop to kidnapping? To unwanted sexual advances?"

Her cheeks flamed. "It seemed the only way to show you that you were wrong, to get you to assume Dillon's defense—"

"A cobweb pretense," he sneered.

"I would not have done these things otherwise!"

"The only thing more pathetic than a charlatan is one who deludes herself into believing her own lies." He snatched a coat and turned to the door. It rattled, still locked. Dropping the garment, he grabbed the knob with two hands and yanked. Wood splintered, and the door flew into a far wall with a loud bang that made the furniture rattle.

Bare as a Greek god, he strode out the threshold, not once looking back.

Chapter 9

"**T**he cad," Fanny intoned, giving Lillian's shoulders a little squeeze. They sat side by side at the scene of the crime, draped in silken sheets and gloom. "He is a scurrilous dog, a lout of the worst order."

"Calling him names does not make it better, Fanny," Lillian countered, hugging the pillow on her lap. "Especially since he is not in the wrong. We deceived him, drugged him, tethered him and tricked him. How could we have expected him to act otherwise?"

"But you did not do it to him. I did."

"I might not have tied the bindings, but I certainly abetted your offenses. Moreover I—"

"They were not offenses. Hell, most men would have paid mightily for the pleasure of such sport, and with a virgin no less."

"Nicholas Redford is not most men."

"I gather." She scowled. "I still don't understand what was so terrible—"

"We tried to take away his choices, Fanny. His choice about bedding me. About helping Dillon. I attempted to exploit his principles. As if I could force him to do my bidding by playing fast and loose with his code of honor. It's despicable."

"Don't be so hard on yourself, Lillian. You were only trying to do what's right."

Guilt, sorrow and shame swept over Lillian like a torrent. And she had brought it all upon herself. "Was I?"

Leaning back, Fanny eyed her skeptically. "You can never convince me that you acted with evil purpose. It's not in you."

"It was deuced convenient that the man I needed to bed for Dillon's sake was the one I happened to have been dreaming about for almost a year." She shook her head, overwhelmed by her folly. "I'm beginning to think that he was right. I forsook my morality under the pretense of good intentions."

"What the blazes are you talking about?"

Lillian struggled to put her disgrace into words. "My innocence was like this invisible shield that helped protect me whenever I came across the likes of Lady Furgesen or Mrs. Bute—"

"They're just uppity matrons who haven't—"

"They are pillars of Society, Fanny, and they may be right about me. I might have been playing the part of a hedonistic lightskirt who had thrown away her respectability on a whim, but now I am her. I am ruined. A debauchee in truth, no longer just in rumor."

"Nonsense! You are no seductress. Hell, you were more scared than a rabbit in bowshot."

"Not so frightened that I could not go through with it."

"He had you pinned. He is much larger—"

"Stop it, Fanny. The man had me begging for more."

Her grin was wicked. "It was that good, eh? Wish to God I could've traded places with you tonight. I was downstairs playing piquet with Mr. Stanley and lost a crown sterling."

"At least you can win it back," Lillian grumbled, but she felt a smidgen better. Fanny always did have a way of making light of a wretched fix.

Fanny patted her hand. "Don't you fret about your maidenhead. You didn't need it anyway. You've sworn never to wed."

Lillian plucked at the silken sheet. "Still . . ."

"Have you changed your mind about that now?"

"Most decidedly not. We have worked too hard to keep me out from under Kane's thumb. I am not about to suffer under another man's dominion."

"Not all men are like Kane."

"We have been over this ground before, Fanny. Even if I married as well as, say, Dillon, a cage will not suit me, no matter how gilded."

"So where is the harm in losing your maidenhood? Now, at least, you sampled something you never expected—a taste of passion."

"But at what cost? Even if some part of coupling wasn't terrible—"

Fanny snorted.

"All right. It felt good."

"Good?"

"Fine. It was fantastic."

"Earth-shattering?"

Lillian blinked. "Why, that's a very good description."

"Blast, if I do not get a man in my bed soon I might as well close shop and become a nun."

Their eyes locked, and they burst out laughing. Lillian laughed so hard that tears burned her eyes. Suddenly it did not seem so funny any longer, and a sob escaped from her throat.

"There, there, dear." Fanny hugged her. "What's done cannot be undone."

"Why do I feel so awful?" Lillian sniveled. "I mean, I never expected him to hold any affection for me, but to feel so wretchedly—"

"Ill-used?"

"Yes. But that's not right. That must have been how he felt. Right? I'm confused."

"For women sex is a strange brew, Lillian. One can never quite know how it will make you feel, especially when it's over."

"If it feels like this, then I never want to do that dastardly deed again."

"Rubbish. It's usually wonderful. Besides, the first time is typically the worst."

"Really? Was it for you?"

"Well . . ." She winced. "My situation was not exactly like yours. . . ."

"Whose is?" Lillian scoffed, wiping her eyes. "So what happened when you did it for the first time?"

"After my first time I wanted to shout to the rooftops with joy, thinking that I had passed a major milestone on my way to living happily ever after. As if the sex was the highway I needed to cross to get there! Harrumph! I pictured myself in a nice house, a lovely husband, babes around me . . ." Waving her hand, her lip curled. "What a cock-a-hoop pipe dream! Dickey Atwater had no intention of marrying me or any other woman unless he was being held down with a boot at his back and a noose over his head."

"Did you love him?"

"I was fifteen at the time and hardly knew what I liked for breakfast."

"How dreadful."

"It was not so terrible." Fanny shrugged. "My father sent me packing, ashamed of my wanton behavior. My mother slipped seven farthings in my pocket, all she could spare, and I started walking. After about a day and a half and only a farthing left, I came across an old barn with people drifting in and out. It was late, dark already, and I was beginning to get cold. I used my last coin to get inside, and had to beg at that. It was a theatrical production. Christopher Marlowe's *Tamburlaine*."

"Providence?"

"Divine intervention." Fanny sighed, staring off. "Looking back, I can say judiciously that it was a mediocre performance, not the best that Mr. Lowell's Traveling Troupe of Players had to offer. But back then, I thought it was heaven on earth. I hung about until the troupe was finished and then introduced myself to Mr. Lowell. By midmorning, Fanny Figbottom was born."

"So it all turned out for the good."

"Some good, some bad. But life's like yesterday's soup. You just have to make sure that there's enough spice to keep it entertaining."

Lillian nodded, feeling somewhat improved. "My only consolation is that with Redford not helping with Dillon's defense, now at least I do not have to see him. Lord, I pray that I never have to lay eyes on the blasted man again."

"How do you think that Dillon will take it?"

"After the last round in court, retaining Redford was the only thing keeping his spirits afloat."

"Are you going to tell him what you did?"

"Heavens no! He would be appalled. I will just explain that I failed to secure Redford's aid." Lillian rubbed her eyes. "He will be crushed."

"Well, Lillian, no one can say that you didn't give up your golden treasure trying."

"Very funny." She looked up. "I don't suppose that I can convince you to come with me to Newgate Prison?"

"I must draw the line at hostage taking, Lillian. A woman can only do so much."

Lillian sighed, having expected this answer. "It is not so terrible. Dillon is quartered in the warden's house. Thankfully Mr. Newman will stop at nothing to further his efforts to make money."

"It's a very old practice of letting out a portion of the warden's residence, and by a fiction treating it as an element of the other side of the prison where most prisoners are housed. All above board." Fanny nodded sagely. "And you couldn't pay enough money to drag me there."

"Then I suppose I'm on my own." Lillian squared her shoulders. "It is time to stop crying over spilled milk and move on." Now, if only her spirits would rise to match that idea.

"Good show." Fanny waved her fist. "A bath, some new clothes, some warm cocoa, and you will be fit as a fiddle."

"Thanks, Fanny."

"What are friends for?"

Despite her intentions, Lillian could not seem to gather up enough energy to actually move off the bed.

After a moment, Fanny bit her lip. "Speaking of moving on . . . I know that you do not wish to address this, Lillian. But it might not be such a bad idea to have a plan. In case something happens to Dillon."

"What would you have me do? I cannot bear to think about a future in two short weeks where Dillon is dead. It's too awful."

"Well, let us work this through together. Shall we?"

Lillian shrugged.

"You have one year until the money comes in. You need to be in London to claim it. That does not mean that you cannot travel abroad in the interim."

"Yes, traveling about on the war-torn continent sounds lovely, Fanny. Can't you just see it? Me running madly as Napoleon's cavalry nips at my heels."

"It was your original plan once you claimed your fortune."

"Well, matters have taken a turn around the bend, now, haven't they?"

"It has always been your dream to go to Italy."

Images of the Leaning Tower of Pisa, the Roman ruins, the canals of Venice flashed through her mind. "The books probably overstate it."

"Don't be so glum. I am sure that it's divine. Imagine, being swept off your feet by a gorgeous Italian blade. Love in Venice . . ."

"Love is a disease I intend never to catch."

Fanny's eyes widened. "You cannot mean that!"

"It wasted away my mother as effectively as any

ailment could. She pined for the bastard who spawned me until the day she died. And did he care? Did he even once contact her? Did he ever want to know about me? Obviously he was not so stricken."

"Stricken? Love is the fruit of life's feast. The cream in every pudding."

"And your great love turned out so well?"

"It never died, I tell you. Even though my beloved Ned is gone, I cherish him still."

"But if he was alive and you, *heaven forbid*, deceased, would he feel the same?"

"Of course. He loved me well."

"I do not doubt your feelings, but do men succumb as strongly? Are their feelings steadfast? Or do they simply lose interest like a stallion that moves on to the next mare?"

"I will admit that many men stray, but there are plenty who remain faithful."

"Out of happiness or laziness or simply having no choice?"

Raising her hand to her heart, Fanny shook her head. "I cannot believe what a cynic you are about the greatest emotion a person can experience."

"Is that how men view it, do you think?"

"I suppose . . ."

"Or are men more interested in the next young stunner with a big bosom or curvy bottom to pass by?"

"My father adored my mother even though her hips widened with every child. My grandfather was the same with my grandmother, who was by no stretch a beauty. And my many uncles with their wives, at that." Her gaze grew wistful. "The men in my family knew how to love well."

"Did your father love you well when he set you out on the street?" Lillian wished the words back in her mouth the moment she had said them.

But Fanny did not seem injured, instead answering seriously, "He regretted it all of his days, Lillian. My mother told me that he had expected to find me in the quarry where I used to hide when I was a young child. But in the morning, I was not there. He searched the roads for two weeks before giving up."

Lillian pressed her hand to her mouth, aghast. "He thought you were dead?"

"That I had succumbed to a highwayman or some such. He was wracked by guilt over it."

"Did he ever know what happened to you?"

Fanny shook her head, her face dropping with sadness. "I used to dream of returning to my village, dressed in a gown more expensive than ten pigs, wearing fine jewels, riding in a fancy carriage . . . I wanted to see the look on my father's face, make him eat crow. . . ."

"But?" Lillian asked, fascinated. This was a window into a side of Fanny that Lillian had never seen.

"By the time I finally got around to contacting my mother, he was gone."

"Is she still alive?"

"No. I suppose birthing and caring for all of those children was a bit too much for her." Exhaling loudly, Fanny straightened. "What about you, Lillian? Don't you wish to have children of your own?"

Lillian swallowed hard, thinking of the babies she would never bear. "In denying marriage, I forfeit any right I have to bring a child into my life."

"But do you wish for children?"

Lillian sat, mute, unable to lie or endure stating the truth.

"I, personally, do not," Fanny declared, laying her hand to her generous bosom. "I suppose I am too self-centered to be responsible for another living being."

"I challenge that. You mother me like a hen does chicks. You help me when I need it, let me bend your ear—"

"Drug and truss your bedmates . . ."

Lillian's lips lifted. "You are the only friend that I would trust for such a delicate task." She frowned. "Seriously, Fanny, any child would be blessed to have you as their mother."

"I suppose that I might not be so bad at it." Fanny sniffed noisily. "But I'm too old. I would rather come visit you and your brood."

"How old are you, anyway?" It was a perpetual question, yet to be answered. Between her dyed hair and face paints, Fanny almost seemed ageless.

"None of your bloody nosey business. And don't change the subject. We are talking about you and babies. Haven't you ever even considered it?"

Lillian toyed with a feather from the pillow. "Growing up, as a game, I would try to envision how my children might look. Would they have Grandmother's aristocratic nose? Grandfather's bushy brows?"

"Only if it's a boy. Otherwise, we must call someone to thread that nasty brow. What else?"

Lillian shrugged. "It does not signify. They were the imaginings of a head-in-the-clouds young girl Fanny. I am no longer that silly child."

"No, now you are just a silly woman. You have your whole life ahead of you."

"These are my choices, Fanny. Let them be."

"And if I believe that you are making a terrible mistake?"

"Then I will be the one to suffer the consequences."

Fanny sighed. "You always do."

They sat in silence, a cloud overhanging the room. Looking up, Fanny brightened. "I just realized one good turn from this mess."

"Pray tell?"

"You will never have to go through losing your innocence again."

"And that's a good thing?"

"No, Lillian. It means from now on, no more pain, only pleasure."

"And who do you suppose I am going to bed, Fanny? Mr. Stanley?"

"He's not half bad, once you get the uniform off."

"Oh," Lillian groaned, yanking the pillow atop her eyes. "I did not need to know that, Fanny. Now I will never be able to get the image out of my head."

Chapter 10

The guard led Lillian and her footman to the warden's small quarters on the prison grounds where Dillon was housed. She was going to use Fanny's old trick of keeping her chin up, hoping that it would come off as cheerfulness. She needed to put an optimistic shine on her bad news. But how to do that when the idea of Dillon's life depending on Sir Patrick did not imbue confidence? When she had this terrible sinking feeling roiling in her middle?

At the guard's knock, the door opened, and they were led through the musty-smelling hallways to Dillon's room.

"Lillian!" Dillon jumped up from the secretary, where he had been drafting a missive. A wide smile brightened his features, but he was looking thinner, more haggard. Older than his five-and-twenty years.

He clutched her hand and bussed her cheek. "I'm so thrilled that you've come." His voice quivered slightly, and she realized that he was trying to present a brave front, for her sake. Dear Dillon.

The footman set the basket upon the table by the hearth.

"You may wait in the usual place, Gillman."

"I will be just outside the front door, my lady." The young man bowed. "Please call if you require anything."

"Thank you, Gillman."

The guard sent Dillon a knowing look and then closed the door with a wink. Lillian blushed deeply, grasping what the guards thought she and Dillon did on these visits.

"What's wrong?" Dillon asked, apprehension lacing his tone.

"What makes you think something's wrong?" She looked away.

"You're wearing too much face paint, for one. You're as white as a ghost." He skimmed his bare finger down the bridge of her nose. "Your nose is shiny and your eyes are red. You've been crying."

She swallowed. "Oh, Dillon, I could never hide a thing from you."

He gently gripped her arm. "Tell me what's troubling you. It can't be worse than the promise of a Newgate frisk or hornpipe."

Reminded of the dreaded hangman's noose, her failure loomed large.

"I brought scones and some of Cook's strawberry jam . . ." she offered. "Let us sit—"

"If there is bad news, I would have it now, Lillian." He frowned. "It's not Kane again, is it? I asked

Father to look after you and even sent Russell a letter instructing him to have a care for your person."

"They have been wonderful, thank you. I appreciate your concern. But I am worried for you, here in this dreadful place."

"Well, in less than two weeks I will no longer require John Newman's lodgings." His blue gaze perked up. "Have you heard from Redford yet? I assume that he will wish to question me. I have an empty calendar these days, so finding time will certainly not be an issue."

"Well, Dillon." She swallowed. "Mr. Redford's schedule is another matter entirely. He is quite occupied—"

"But you are quite right," a deep voice rumbled from behind her, sending a familiar ripple through her middle. "He does need to question you."

Dillon looked up, his eyes bright.

Lillian blinked, shocked beyond speech.

Nicholas Redford stood in the doorway to Dillon's room, fully clothed and yet just as overwhelming as when he was as bare as a Greek god just hours before. Her pulse quickened, and awareness of him made her skin swim with warmth. He showed no ill effects from the wild night—still handsome, brawny and dripping with galling confidence. He carried a cane in one hand and a bottle of brandy in the other. Warden John Newman stood beside him, a similar bottle in the crook of his arm.

"Excellent show!" Dillon grinned. "And you even brought the tipple!"

"I imagined that you might be a bit thirsty."

"I'm parched as hell, if you please."

"Mr. Nicholas Redford at your service, my lord."

He bowed. "I'm the new investigator Lady Janus retained to see you freed."

Redford stepped near, and part of her could not believe that he was actually standing before Dillon, saying that he was going to take the case. Was she dreaming? Had her mind finally cracked? Had she had a taste of Fanny's tainted Cognac? Why did she have to look like such a carriage-wreck this morning?

"Thank the heavens. Now we don't have to rely on the cabbage-headed Sir Patrick. I was beginning to think that my goose was going to be cooked."

Redford waved a hand. "I will not interfere with Sir Patrick, milord. My role is simply to ensure that in the short time frame of the proceedings, no rock has been left unturned."

Lillian was thrilled, but stricken. Just a few hours ago this man had been lying between her legs, and his insults rang fresh in her ears. She had been hoping never to see him again and yet here he was, jumping into the fray to make things right. She did not know whether to leap for joy or run out of the room crying.

Warden Newman scratched his craggy cheek. "You might actually have a shot at avoiding the Lord of the Manor of Tyburn, milord. This one's worse than a kissing jack at a ball. He'll never give up until he gets what he wants."

Redford set the bottle on the table. "And foremost in my plans is seeing an innocent man freed."

Dillon stared at him a long moment. His gaze glistened, and he blinked rapidly. Whipping a linen from his pocket, he wiped his eyes. "So sorry. I just . . ." Sniffing, he folded the cloth into squares, not meeting anyone's eyes. "It's just, well, besides

Lillian . . ." His gaze met hers and his lopsided grin quivered. "Well, most people try to pretend, but besides Lillian, no one has truly believed me. Until now."

Lillian's heart swelled. At that moment it was all worth it. Every despicable act that she had done was redeemed just to see the hope rising in Dillon's gaze. She had proven that Dillon was not the man Dagwood presented him to be, and Redford knew it. Soon, hopefully, so would the rest of London.

She squeezed his hand. "Everything is going to be all right now, Dillon. If anyone can maintain your innocence, Mr. Redford can."

"Well," Redford shrugged, "I cannot perform miracles. But if the evidence is out there, and I do believe it is, then we will find it."

Tears burned the back of Lillian's eyes, but there was nothing left to shed. "I told you justice was not blind, Dillon. You just needed a little faith."

"You've always been the one of our twosome with faith in your pockets, Lillian. Me, I usually just relied on you," Dillon remarked, stuffing the linen into his coat. "And as usual, it is to my benefit."

"Lady Janus?" Redford studied her.

Her heart lurched.

"Do you like puzzles?" he asked in that deep voice that made her inside tremble.

She dared not meet his gaze. "As much as the next person, I suppose."

"I assure you, not nearly as much as the person standing next to you. And you are a puzzle, indeed."

Peering at him through her lashes, she could not decipher his meaning or the strange look in his eyes. Suddenly, she could not wait to depart. "I'm sure that you two have much to discuss, so if you will excuse me."

Dillon squeezed her arm. "Thank you, Lillian. You are the most capital girl on the face of the earth."

Her smile was wooden. "I will try to come see you on the morrow." Her cheeks warmed, and she lowered her voice. "Oh, by the by, Fanny sends her regards."

"How is darling Fanny?" Dillon asked loudly.

"Miss Figbottom?" the dratted Redford asked in a falsely innocent tone. "The famous actress, perchance?"

Dillon looked up. "One and the same. She's bang up to the mark, our Fanny. She and Lillian are like two peas in a pod. Sisters could not be closer."

"Oh, really?" Redford's gaze was infuriatingly interested. "And how is it that you know each other, Lady Janus?"

"I introduced them," Dillon explained. "About two years ago—"

"No use boring Mr. Redford and the good warden with stale tales, Dillon." Lillian glared meaningfully at Dillon. "I am sure that they have much more interesting matters—"

"Oh, no, I *really* wish to hear this," interjected the blasted investigator.

"Perhaps I will share it another time," Dillon replied. Apparently the euphoria of feeling like the world was not ending had loosened Dillon's lips, but thankfully, now he was recovered. "Say, in about two or three weeks."

"Yes, when we are finished celebrating your release." Lillian kissed Dillon on the cheek and nodded to the men. "You have much to discuss. I bid you my leave."

Keeping her eyes trained on the scraped floorboards, she stepped to the door, making certain to stay as far as possible from Redford. "Good-day, gentlemen." To her shame, she almost fled.

She was down the hallway and almost to the main entry when she heard Redford's booming call. "Lady Janus!"

She did not stop but motioned to the guard to open the door.

"Lady Janus!"

Redford arrived to stop the door midswing. He held the edge in his gloved hand, blocking her exit.

He loomed over her, and she realized that it would be easier to ignore a rampant carriage than it would be to ignore him. She stood stiffly, not about to let him see how much he unsettled her. Yet her faithless cheeks flamed. "Yes?"

"I was wondering. How do you fare this day, my lady?" His voice rippled through her middle, bringing fresh memory of his touch, his heat and him inside of her.

Her mouth went dry.

"I, myself, am a bit fagged. Not enough sleep, I suppose."

She stood frozen, trying very hard to concentrate on the sliver of courtyard outside, which she could see through the partially open door. His nearness caused her heart to dance. Dash her weakness!

"Did *you* sleep well this night?"

His infuriating needling made her want to kick up a row. She hated that he felt at liberty to toy with her. Loathed how he must see her. Despised that she gave a fig about his regard.

"Why do you ask?" She raised a brow. "Do I look weary?"

"Actually," he drawled, and the hairs on the back of her neck rose, "I was just thinking how tantalizing you look this morning."

Liar.

"I am well rested, if that is what you mean, Mr. Redford. I had a most uneventful night. So much so, in fact, that I can hardly recall it. If you will excuse me, I am a very important person with many vital things to do."

Catching her jibe, his lip quirked slightly, and he considered her a moment longer. Then he slowly opened the door, allowing her passage. "I look forward to calling upon you this afternoon, my lady."

She started. "What? Why?"

"For your help, of course. With Beaumont's defense."

Alarm shot through her.

"With the trial less than two weeks away," he continued, "I will need to know everything about Beaumont and those around him, including you."

Was this a ruse? A cruel trick of some sort to get her on her back once again? Did he consider bedding her a bonus to his fee? She burned with mortification, then realized she had to tell him about Kane. There was validity to his request. But that did not mean that she trusted him. Not by a hair.

"Will you be in residence?" he inquired.

Finally, she faced him, fluttering her eyelashes. "Oh, but Mr. Redford. Will you be able to suffer my feminine wiles? All of that eyelash batting and hip sashaying might be a bit overwhelming."

"I think I can handle it."

Ooh, how she wished to wipe the smirk from his face.

"Perhaps, but you *cannot handle me*." She strode out the door, confident that she had gotten her message across. She refused to be the brunt of his jest, the foil for his barbs. . . . Oh, dear. Her belly flipped at the inadvertent innuendo. She was going to have to be very careful around Nicholas Redford. Very careful, indeed.

Nick watched her from the doorway, wondering how the blazes he was going to deal with the exasperating Lady Janus. Something about her pricked his senses, and usually not in a gentlemanly fashion. Toying with her had not exactly been a kind turn. But tying and trussing him the night before had not been precisely hospitable.

After leaving Miss Figbottom's house, he had been furious, raging, in fact, over the women's chicanery. But in the darkest hours of the night, when his anger had cooled, he could not escape the evidence. No man could live with a fiery woman like Lady Janus and keep his hands off of her. Which meant that Beaumont was uninterested in females and would likely not have been drawn into an affair with Lady Langham. The facts raised too many questions leading to only one answer: Beaumont might be guiltless. A pawn, perhaps, in a greater game. This deduction had left him deeply troubled.

He had fought the possibility that Lady Janus might somehow have been justified in her transgressions. But in the end, he'd had to accept the fact that she had taken the absolutely perfect course for opening his eyes about Beaumont's innocence. She had completed her charge with results. He, however, had not, and he was sore as hell for it this morning.

She had turned him from enraged martyr to willing lieutenant in a few short hours. She had played him flawlessly; he could not in good conscience let a guiltless man swing if he had the means to stop it. Lady Janus and her tricks, his wounded dignity, his aching body: None of it signified if a man's life hung in the balance.

Lady Janus had done what she'd needed to do to save a wronged friend. Nick could scarcely believe that she had handed him her innocence to prove her point. One had to admire her loyalty, and her gumption. Moreover, he was not too much of a bastard to admit that it had been a hell of a wild night. One he would never forget as long as he lived.

Watching her shapely rump gently sashaying down the pathway, he recognized that he hungered for her still. He itched to have her and finish the job she'd started. And soon. Problem was, she was an innocent. Hell, he might have busted her maidenhead, but she was no lightskirt waiting to be flipped. Her reticence, her blushes, they all made sense now. And he had considered himself a first-rate investigator!

John Newman stepped beside him, sneering, "I'd love to split the beard of that lassie."

Fury hotter than fired iron flashed through Nick. His hand was around the man's throat in an instant, smashing the warden up against the wall. "Shut yer foul trap!"

"Drop him!" a guard cried from down the corridor. Racing forward, he hoisted his bludgeon.

The warden raised his palms upward and the guard froze, waiting. "You'd best be letting me down, Nick. Don't let that temper of yours overtake good sense."

Nick's body had reacted before his mind could catch up, and he realized that his vehemence was in part anger with himself for making those very same erroneous presumptions. Still, the message had to be clear. "Don't let your foul mouth even breathe near the lady."

"I didn't know it was like that, Nick. No harm done. No harm done. Stand down, Jackson. All is well. All is well."

The guard lowered his club to his thigh, but no further.

Nick eased his fingers and dropped the warden back onto his boot heels. Straightening Newman's coat, he murmured softly, "If I get wind that anyone, and I mean anyone, touched the lady, then it won't just be the Lord of Tyburn Manor doing the hanging around here."

"You know me, Nick. Now that I know the lay of the land . . ." At the murderous look in Nick's eye, he added, "So to speak. Then I won't be making that same mistake again." Adjusting his coat, he sniffed. "You should have told me, by the way."

Nick glared.

"Oh, you don't tell tales, I know. But if I'm going to help you, then I'll need to know what's going on."

"Nothing's 'going on.' "

"And I'm a beggar's brother."

Nick tried to lighten the darkness ringing his composure. He forced himself to recall that he had always liked John Newman. One usually knew where you stood with the man—at the other end of your purse. He was plain about his lack of morals and greedy demands. But he was no lecher.

Forcing a jovial tone, Nick jibed in reply, "Oh, and your sister sends her regards."

Newman grinned. "There's the old Nick. No worries. No worries."

Nick stared out into the courtyard after the woman who had turned his assumptions upside down and made his blood stew to boil. "You know me, Newman. No worries at all."

Chapter 11

Nick was led through the corridors of Lady Janus's house, fascinated by the austere decor. He had expected lavishness, he supposed, but instead he'd found mostly dark paneled woods, intricately carved ceilings and pale, unadorned walls. Lady Janus was proving to be very different from what he had supposed.

"My lady is in the garden, sir," the butler explained as they proceeded to the rear of the dwelling.

They neared an alcove housing the back entry, and Nick paused. "If I may ask you a few questions, ah? . . ."

"Hicks, sir." The man halted and turned. He was in his forties, stout with graying ginger hair, clear brown eyes and a long, hawkish nose.

"May I ask how long you have been in Lady Janus's service, Hicks?"

The butler coughed into his hand. "Just over one year, sir."

"Being in your position allows for a certain awareness of the goings-on in the household. . . ."

The man nodded, guardedness clouding his gaze.

"That knowledge stretches to Lord Beaumont as well?"

Hick's eyes darted about. "I suppose that's true."

"Are you uncomfortable answering these questions, Hicks?"

"Yes, sir. A good butler must be discreet. But seeing as my lady has requested that all of the staff do your bidding to the fullest, I will answer you as best as I can."

Nick hid his surprise. Lady Janus apparently understood the importance of his labors and was making an effort to ease them. "Any enemies of Lord Beaumont come to mind? Injured party seeking revenge, that sort of thing?"

"No, sir. To be quite honest with you, sir, Lord Beaumont is well liked."

"Below stairs as well?"

Hicks stiffened, eyeing the empty hallway. "The staff likes him well enough. He's not as good as some, and a whole lot better than others."

"A bit of a prig."

Hicks's cheeks reddened. "I never said that."

"No, I did. But ruffling someone's feathers does not warrant a hanging." Rubbing his chin, Nick asked, "Anyone to benefit from his absence? Anyone particularly fond of Lady Janus?"

"Lady Janus does not entertain other men, if that's what you're aiming at."

"Not on her part but on someone else's. Say, any flowers arrive from an admirer? Gifts?"

"No, sir. She is a fine lady, and a good employer as well. Wages are always paid on time without any of the haggling that oft goes on."

"Who owns this house?"

"Duke of Greayston, sir. And it's a good thing."

"Why do you say that?"

"His Grace and Lord Beaumont's younger brother, Lord Russell Mayburn, regard Lady Janus well. They'll watch out for her."

"You believe that Beaumont will not be back?"

Hicks shrugged. "If you're to trust the papers, he's already hung."

"You don't think that Greayston will turn her out?"

Hicks's eyelids flickered. "I did not suppose so. . . ."

"When was the last time someone gave you a house in Mayfair out of the goodness of their heart?"

The butler stiffened.

"If I do my job, Hicks, then hopefully no one will need to find out how well the Duke of Greayston regards Lady Janus," Nick remarked, scratching his chin. "Any changes in the comings and goings since Beaumont's arrest?"

"Well, Lady Janus spends most days at the prison now. Lord Russell usually comes to check on her in the evenings." He shrugged. "He tends to leave about nine. The maids say that she's exhausted these days and can hardly keep awake past ten." He scowled. "She's so quiet, one could hardly believe that it's actually the Season. Last year at this time it was balls until dawn, rounds of social calls, picnics, riding in the park—"

"Is there anything more you believe would be helpful for me to know?" Nick interrupted. He knew all about High Society's diversions and did not need a recitation. "Or anyone else I might wish to speak with?"

Licking his lips, Hicks shook his head in the negative. "It's a good position here, sir. Better than most I've ever held. I'm hoping not to have to leave it."

"I'm not sure what will happen, Hicks. All I know is that I am going to do my duty to see Lord Beaumont freed. The rest is none of my affair."

"Very well then." Hicks nodded. "Shall I take you to Lady Janus?"

"Yes, please."

Nick followed the butler down the steps into the garden. The narrow path was lined with rosebushes, the pink buds peeking out from emerald leaves. From his years helping tend Headmaster Dunn's garden, Nick knew the roses were soon to bloom. But the heady scent was not yet evident in the garden; only pine and damp marked the air. The moss sank deeply with his every step, masking the sound of his footfalls as they trod toward the rear of the garden.

Hicks's steps slowed as they neared a large oak tree. He stopped and motioned for Nick to proceed.

Lady Janus's voice filtered through the greenery, "I love you dearly, Jack, but I cannot countenance this behavior any longer."

Jack? The lady had a paramour?

Nick shot Hicks a questioning look.

The man grimaced as if he were embarrassed.

Devil take Lady Janus and her household of liars! Was everything about her a falsehood and everyone around her embroiled in chicanery? Disgust rose in Nick's gut. Had he been a cat's paw of the first order? A dupe for her dastardly tricks? He pushed past the butler and stepped quickly around the oak, fairly stomping over the gnarled roots.

He stopped short. Lady Janus was alone amid the foliage.

Spying him, she frowned. And was that a flash of guilt coloring her creamy cheeks?

"Where is he?"

She blinked with an artificial innocence an actress could study. "Who?"

"Show yourself, you bastard!"

Lady Janus turned to her butler. "Who is he talking to?"

Hicks lifted his shoulders.

Scanning the garden, Nick saw that the walls were a head taller than him and the spiked iron gate was closed. So the spineless scum was probably hiding behind a tree. Nick hardly cared any longer. The focus of his ire stood before him, the black widow of this web.

"You can stop acting now," Nick charged. "I've had enough of your bloody schemes. Someone else can be your chump."

"What in heaven's name are you talking about?" Lily white hands set on rounded hips; she played the affronted dame to perfection.

"Pretend all you like, but it doesn't change the fact that I'm not going to help you or your lovers."

Artful azure eyes widened. "But you've accepted Dillon's case. You cannot desert him now."

"I was duped into taking the matter under falsehoods. I will not help your reprehensible marquis."

"You cannot quit!" she cried, stepping forward.

"Watch me." He turned and marched toward the rear entry. "You and your lover Jack can try to save Beaumont yourselves or do whatever the hell else you do. I don't care."

"Jack?" Lady Janus gasped.

He opened the spiked iron gate, eager to get away from the witch. *This is the last time I'm going to be taken in by a pretty face and a curvaceous bottom,* he swore. *From now on, all facts, no figures.*

She rushed forward, her hands raised in mock surrender. "I confess, Mr. Redford! You found me out."

He stopped. "So you admit it?"

"Jack is here in the garden. Pray, let me call him, and you will understand."

"I have no patience left for your trickery—"

"I swear to you on my mother's grave, sir, that I have no tricks left. I exhausted my allowance of them last night." Turning quickly, she cupped her hands around her mouth, calling, "Jack! Jack sweetling!"

He huffed at the endearment. Jack had to be a dandified pup to respond to that summons.

"Jack, darling!"

A cat with shiny black-and-white fur meowed and stepped out from under a shrub. Lady Janus crouched down and opened her arms. The cat jumped into her lap. The lady stood, cradling the large feline.

"Mr. Redford, may I introduce Jack."

"That's Jack?" he scoffed. "The one you cannot countenance any longer?"

She nodded toward the green pallet on the ground nearby. "This naughty boy has been misbehaving again."

Hicks stepped over to the pallet and lifted it up with two gloved fingers, making a face of disgust. "I'll have Miss Lonnie wash it yet again, my lady."

"Thank you, Hicks."

"And I will ask Cook to prepare a repast," the butler offered quickly. Hicks nodded to Nick. "Mr. Redford, at least, will be needing refreshment."

"Perhaps, perhaps not." Her sky blue eyes locked with Nick's, and he saw the challenge within. "Will you be staying?"

Nick scowled, starting to feel idiotic, but not quite believing it. "That's Jack?"

"Yes, the king of the jungle in these parts."

His eyes slowly scanned the yard. Many more shapes moved about, stalking, sleeping and cleaning themselves. It was a veritable garden of felines.

"All of these cats belong to you?"

"Actually, none of them are mine. They just visit me now and again."

Noting the plates set about in the grass, he realized, "Of course they do. You feed them." He unfurled his hands and rubbed his eyes, feeling the veritable fool. "So there's no lover hiding in the bushes."

"Only if she's yours."

Bloody hell. He was not usually one to misjudge on scant evidence. He must be more exhausted than he thought. And, he had to admit, there was something about Lady Janus that touched a nerve.

Peering at her, he wondered how to undo the damage he had done. To his chagrin, her lips were bowing up, but she was trying to conceal her smile in the cat's fur.

"It's not funny," he insisted, realizing that it was. His own lips lifted, but he forced them down. "It's not amusing in the least."

Hicks rolled his eyes and spun on his heel, carrying the offensive pallet far away from him. "I'll tell Cook that two will be dining."

Lady Janus grinned at Nick. "It's hilarious. You thought that Jack was my lover!"

"I heard you speaking to a Jack, and, well, I jumped to conclusions," he replied halfheartedly, amazed at his folly.

Her sparkling eyes wrinkled at the corners. "I've been accused of many things in my lifetime, but cavorting with a feline . . . well, that is a first."

Suddenly the absurdity of the situation burst full bloom upon him, and a guffaw erupted from his throat.

Lady Janus chuckled, holding her hand to her belly. "Oh, my, it feels good to laugh."

He realized that he had to agree. Something inside him had loosened, and he felt better. Had it been so long? He could not recall the last time that he had had a good laugh, and at himself, no less. He grimaced. "I owe you an apology, my lady. I must be more tired than I thought."

Her smile vanished, and he was unexpectedly sad to see it go.

Looking down, her strawberry curls fell in front of her face as she dropped the cat. Jack sauntered off, his nose and tail raised high in the air.

"I do not know what ill effects you might be suffering from that tonic . . . ," she murmured, biting her lower lip.

"Miss Figbottom's doing, I presume?"

"Fanny bought it from an alchemist." She kicked at a rock, not meeting his eye. "He said that you might have a headache but should be fine."

"No headache. I'm just suffering from a case of acute embarrassment."

Looking up, she grasped her hands before her in supplication. "I am the one who is shamed, Mr. Redford. It was ill done of me and Fanny, no matter our intentions."

Intentions. He was reminded of his formidable task here today. Now he felt even more compelled to see it through. He cleared his throat. "Yes. Well, that is something we need to address before we can proceed with the investigation."

"I suppose it was too much to hope that we could forget the whole incident?" Her blue eyes pleaded.

He was tempted to forget it himself. But he knew that it would not do. "It would just leave us at sixes and sevens."

"I assure you, I am not confused."

"Look, we must work together to see Beaumont free. So we had best clear the air as soon as possible."

Lillian nodded and straightened her back, as if bracing herself for an onslaught. "As you will."

Nick suddenly realized that he had no idea how to broach the subject. Taking a deep breath, the words tumbled from his mouth, "I, well, I need to know . . . well, if you might be expecting an offer of marriage."

She gasped, shock shimmering in her gaze.

"From your expression, am I to understand that you do not anticipate such an offer?"

She blinked. "This is the last thing in the world I ever expected from you," she stated breathlessly.

"Why?" he asked irritably. Did she think him such a boorish cur?

"What compels you to ask?" she asked, her eyes narrowing suspiciously.

He shifted his shoulders; this was probably one of the most difficult conversations of his life. "In my book, when a man lies with an innocent lady, then he has to live with the consequences."

"Is this some sort of prank? Are you trying to get back at me?"

"I don't jest about matrimony," he grumbled.

"But what happened . . . was not exactly a typical debauching."

"You were innocent a few hours ago, and no matter how it happened, I was the one who . . . well, ended that condition."

"It's not an illness."

"Of course not." Bloody hell, if this wasn't turning out to be nearly as bad as being drugged and trussed.

Crossing her arms, she raised a perfectly arched brow. "And what makes you believe that I might be interested in a proposal of marriage from you?"

"Under the circumstances . . ."

"There are no circumstances that would induce me to marry, Mr. Redford. To you or any other man."

He was a bit surprised by the vehemence in her voice. And even though he was relieved, he was also just a little irritated to be dismissed so lightly. "I was just trying to do the right thing."

Exhaling loudly, she shook her head. "I appreciate your consideration, Mr. Redford. But please understand that I have no intention of ever marrying. Am I clear?"

"Abundantly."

Awkward silence stretched long between them. The leaves rustled in the trees, and a cat shrieked somewhere in the garden.

Lady Janus bit her lip. "Given that we are speaking plainly, Mr. Redford, there is another point I wish to settle." She swallowed. "Since we are going to be working together . . . I must make it perfectly clear . . . that well, there will be nothing untoward between us."

What? Did she think that he was going to jump her bones at the first opportunity? That he was a beast in heat, slobbering for a taste of her wiles? He was not nearly that desperate.

"I do not mix business with pleasure, my lady," he bit out. "*I* have no problem containing myself."

Her peaches-and-cream cheeks flamed red as she obviously recalled her passionate cries of the night before. It was answer enough.

He laid his hand over his heart. "Rest assured I would not touch you if King George himself ordered me to. If Napoleon's army—"

"Your assurance is most reassuring," she interrupted, pique making her eyes flash.

"Excellent. Now that that's settled, perhaps we can eat? I really am quite famished."

Her mouth worked as if she wanted to say something more but could not find the words. Finally, she spun on her heel and marched toward the house.

Nick smiled. No doubt about it; something about Lady Janus definitely pricked at his senses. And he got a kick out of watching her struggle with her fiery nature. He usually had a rule about mixing business with pleasure, but in this case the two seemed in each other's pocket. Oh, yes, he had the feeling that this investigation was going to be *really* interesting.

Chapter 12

Lillian could hardly eat a bite for the butterflies swarming in her middle. She was mystified by Nicholas Redford's unenthusiastic offer of marriage and appalled by the fact that she had to actually sit across the table from the man who had had her begging for him just a few hours before. Gallingly, the source of her discomfiture did not seem affected in the least by her presence. He sat at the table—broad, dark and stunning—wolfing down his food as if this were his last meal.

"Slow down, Mr. Redford. Cook usually prepares more than enough to feed a horse."

"Headmaster Dunn always said that I ate like one," he remarked, stopping his fork in mid-thrust. Slowly setting the utensil onto the table, he lifted his goblet and gulped his wine.

"It was ill-mannered of me to comment so," she

spoke quietly. "In fact, my servants would be well satisfied if I followed your example. Quite inappropriately, they say that I eat like a bird." She knew that it was only because they cared, and she was glad for it, to be sure.

"You've been a bit preoccupied, I suppose." Lifting his fork, he dug into his ham once more.

"Frazzled, more like it. Ever since Dillon's arrest my life has been . . ." Her cheeks heated. "Chaotic."

"Growing up in an orphanage, we learned to eat when we had the chance. Nothing—not nerves, disasters or bloodshed—could keep us from a hot meal."

As she was reminded of his origins, another twinge of guilt nagged at her for her comment. Not even bothering to pretend any longer, she pushed away her plate. "You seem so self-reliant. It's hard to imagine you as a needy child."

"Every child is needy in one way or another. That's why I'll never have any."

She leaned forward. "Really?"

"Well, I certainly don't need to produce the heirs."

"But don't you want to perpetuate your name?"

"My given name represents nothing beyond the place where I was abandoned as a babe." At the questioning look on her face, he added, "Redford is a distortion of 'reed ford.' A river crossing."

"And you do not wish to have children because they are helpless?" It seemed the antithesis to his code of honor.

"Children need a good father, and I don't know how to be one." It sounded like a frail excuse, but then again, she had never been an orphan in a foundling home. She had no idea what he had been through.

Redford tossed down his napkin and pushed away his plate, obviously wanting to end the topic. Nodding to the footman, he sipped his wine. "I think that it is time for us to discuss the Beaumont matter, my lady. If you are finished with your repast, that is?"

"Of course." She wondered how he could be so cool about something so awful. Perhaps that was how he dealt with it.

She nodded dismissal to the footmen. "Thank you, Gillman, Jones. Some privacy, please."

The footmen nodded and left, Gillman closing the door softly behind him.

"In my office you mentioned that you believed you were the cause of Beaumont's predicament," he stated, shifting sideways in his seat to face her fully. "Tell me who you believe murdered Baroness Langham and why."

She took a deep breath and dove in. "Lord Cornelius Kane is my father by name—"

"Not naturally?"

She shook her head. "My mother was forced to marry him when the man who seduced her took off." The words came out more easily than she would have supposed for such a well-kept secret.

He motioned for her to go on.

"Kane was deep in dunn territory, and the creditors were knocking. My mother was in a fix. My well-heeled grandparents arranged the marriage, thinking it would solve all of their problems. Kane was a baron, for heaven's sake, they thought. They did not suspect that he was such a cancer to those around him."

"How so?"

Lifting a shoulder, the familiar numbness that came when she talked about her childhood swept over her. "With Kane one is usually either worthy or unworthy. My mother and I were special cases—worthless. My mother suffered the yoke of marriage like a personal cage, with Kane as its jailer. She was too delicate to suffer his fits of anger, so she crawled into a shell. One that eventually cracked."

"And how did he treat you?"

"Let us just say that if it were not for my grandparents taking me to live with them, I don't know how long I would have outlasted my mother."

Nick crossed his arms, and she could not help but notice the muscular bulges in his brown wool coat.

"So we have established that Kane is a fiend and can be violent. True?"

"Yes," she replied, tearing her mind back to more important matters. "But it is not an animalistic aggression."

"Because he is an aristocrat?" His tone was cynical.

"No," she replied, wondering why he even bothered making a distinction. "Because his violence is not for violence's sake but when he feels that it is justified."

"He thought it was justified to raise a hand to you as a child?"

"Yes. In his mind, it was perfectly reasonable."

"Why do you believe that he killed Lady Langham?"

"I have wracked my brain for an answer, but I have no idea. Her husband is an acquaintance of Kane's and apparently doted on his wife. Still, I hardly knew the lady; we traveled in different circles."

"But Kane did."

"Yes."

He scratched his chin. "So what does he gain from targeting Beaumont? The satisfaction of hurting you?"

"My grandparents came to regret joining their only daughter with Kane. They changed their wills, placing everything in trust for me. Kane views the fortune as his, stolen from him, by me."

"It could not have been his if your grandparents could pass it on to you."

"That small fact escapes him."

"But how does he profit by targeting Beaumont? He still does not gain access to the funds."

"I lose my protector and dear friend, something that Kane has wanted for a long time. Thus, I am susceptible to his devices."

"Which are?"

"He has threatened to lock me in a mental institution. . . . As a woman I have little recourse under the law. As my father, he maintains all rights if I am unmarried." She shrugged. "He has intimated that he would marry me off to a patsy who would sign over my funds in exchange for arranging the match. . . . It's all about power over me and my inheritance."

"I apologize for asking such personal questions."

She waved a hand. "How else are you to understand this devil's labyrinth?"

"Many of my clients are not as cognizant of that fact, making my job all the more difficult."

"We have less than two weeks. I cannot afford to be reticent."

"Still, I thank you for being so forthcoming." He shifted his long legs beneath the table. "The scandal-broth was that Beaumont had offered for your hand. It would seem a simple solution to your quandary."

"As I told you outside, I have no intention of ever marrying."

"I thought that you were simply trying to soften the blow. You actually meant it?"

Crossing her arms, she scowled. "Leg-*shackle*, marriage *bond*, parson's mouse*trap*, wed*lock* . . . after enduring Kane's domination as a helpless child, am I to sign up for the same treatment my mother suffered?"

"I am not following your reasoning. At least in marriage, the man has a legal responsibility toward the woman. Being a kept woman—"

"I agreed to this arrangement to keep me protected until my four-and-twentieth birthday, when the trust will distribute the funds to me outright." She scowled. "Thankfully, my grandparents had the forethought to make it so that if anything happens to me before my four-and-twentieth birthday, then everything goes to charitable causes."

"So Kane gets nothing if you predecease your claim."

"Exactly. And I have already drafted an ironclad will that if I should die after collecting my inheritance, then it all goes to charity as well."

"But you still might be susceptible to Kane's machinations even once you get your inheritance."

"I intend to be out of the country, with my funds secured out of his reach."

Scratching his head, Nick recapped, "So Beaumont agrees to help you because . . . ?"

"He is my dear friend."

"Why did he not simply set you up outside the country at a hidden location?"

"Because he has no funds. His father holds the purse strings."

"Ahh. So the duke knows of his son's predilections?"

"Greayston does not wish to face it. He simply hoped that by financing this arrangement, it would calm some whispers and likewise might influence Dillon to become interested in the fairer sex. At a minimum, Dillon gets a great reputation as a lady-killer without actually having to do anything he does not wish to."

Nodding slowly, Redford clearly understood the logic.

She crossed her arms. "I have a question for you, Mr. Redford."

"Certainly."

"If you never intended to have children, how does that correlate to your asking for my hand in marriage?"

Setting his large palms on the tablecloth, he shrugged. "I did not actually ask for your hand, my lady. I simply inquired if you anticipated an offer of marriage."

"And if I had said yes?"

"The chances were slim."

"Because of how I lost my innocence?"

"Because you are a highborn lady accustomed to a certain lifestyle that I cannot, at the moment, provide. I did not expect you to give up that life for a man you considered so beneath you as to drug and truss him to get your way."

Shame washed over her, but she ignored it, instead asking, "So you did not actually mean it?"

"Oh, I did. I took your innocence, quite willingly at that point."

Her cheeks heated and she looked away.

"And," he continued, "I was honor bound to at least inquire about expectations of marriage. But I had the feeling what your answer would be."

"An easy way to fulfill your code of honor," she muttered, surprised by the disappointment filtering through her.

Leaning forward, he lifted her chin with his finger. "Do you wish to change your mind?"

She met his cocoa brown eyes. Amusement filled them, and they creased at the corners—understandable, given her protestations moments before about never marrying.

"I suppose my questions smack of injured pride," she confessed sheepishly. "Oh, and for the record, I would have drugged and trussed an earl or duke just as easily. I do not discriminate when it comes to convoluted schemes to prove a point to help my friends in need."

His lips widened into a white smile that she felt down to her toes. A man really had no right to be that attractive. She returned his smile, feeling like a truce of sorts had settled between them.

Releasing her chin, he stood. "I am off to the Bow Street office. I need to unruffle a few feathers before they get tied in a knot."

She was saddened that the interview was over. The man was surprisingly easy to talk to.

She rose, and he quickly pulled back her chair. He was over a head taller than she, so she tilted her head up and remarked, "That is very politic of you."

"Not politics, my lady, survival. An enquiry agency will not last long in London if it doesn't get along with the Bow Street office."

Her guilt haunted her. "I-I had not realized that

taking this case might put your business in a bad spot."

"Nothing I haven't been in before, I assure you. Just this time I'm going to do a better job of getting out of it before I'm stuck. There's nothing worse than having your supposed friends be the ones gunning for you."

She bit her lip. "That brings me to something that has been bothering me, Mr. Redford."

"Yes?"

"The evidence against Dillon. The bloodied handkerchief . . . his love letters . . ."

"Those were truly his letters?"

"Foolishness, he told me. A prank from when he was away at school." She grimaced. "He seemed reticent to discuss it and I did not press him. The question is: Who took them from Dillon's possession and left them with Lady Langham's corpse?"

"For the first query, to be frank, if I did not know better, I would say that they came from you."

"Me?"

"You have every access to Beaumont's personal items. But, seeing as you went beyond the pale to have me retained, I would be hard-pressed to believe it so." He scratched his chin.

"My guess," he went on, "is that someone close to Beaumont, possibly in his home or in his service, planted the articles."

"I had feared that answer." Clutching her hands before her, she shuddered. "It is awful to think that an enemy swims about like a shark pretending to be a guppy. With Kane, at least I always know where I stand."

Reaching forward, he clasped her bare hand. "For all of your legal protections, you might very well be in danger, my lady. You need to be vigilant. Have the servants be on their guard. Take an extra footman with you when you go out."

His warm grasp reassured her. "Thank you, Mr. Redford, for taking my concerns seriously. Many of the gentlemen that I know would not necessarily have accepted my beliefs as valid." Grimacing, she added ruefully, "Too frequently women, especially ones who have taken my route, are discounted as less than bright."

"Only a fool would dismiss such grave concerns."

Tilting her head up, she smiled warmly at him. "Then it is very well that you are not a fool."

"Lillian!"

Russell stood in the doorway, a look of horror on his youthful features.

Lillian self-consciously released Redford's hand and stepped back. She did not need Russell getting the wrong idea about them. "Russell. Your timing is good. Mr. Redford here probably has some questions for you."

"Who the hell is he to question me?" he shrieked.

"Calm down, Russell, it is not what you suppose. Mr. Redford is an investigator hired to exculpate Dillon."

"What was he doing taking liberties with you?"

"He was not taking liberties, Russell. You know as well as any what a difficult time this is. He was simply—"

Russell advanced into the room, his lips bowed downward and his blond brow wedded in a disapproving scowl. He pushed himself between them and glared up into Redford's face. "Lillian is too kindhearted to see you as you are. But I will not allow you to take advantage of this situation to your own despicable ends."

Redford coolly raised a brow. "And what ends might those be?"

"You know exactly what I mean!"

Redford opened his hands wide as if to show his lack of deceit. "I can see, Lord Russell, that Lady Janus has a champion in you."

"Young Russell is quite reliable in his regard," Lillian supplied, wishing that Russell were not so fervent but appreciating his consideration nonetheless. "He and his father have been more than kind during this ordeal."

"Then I leave you in good hands." He bowed. "I will try to report back to you within the next few days, Lady Janus. If you need to speak with me sooner, please send word to my office, or to Tipton's Tavern on Kenbridge Lane. Someone is always at the tavern to hold messages for me, and I frequently check by." He nodded in farewell. "Lord Russell."

Swiftly Nick strode from the room.

Lillian turned to Russell. "How dare you jump on him like that? That's the man who is going to set your brother free!"

"He was clutching your hand!"

"Which you do on many occasions, but I have yet to brand you as a libertine." She crossed her arms. "Don't be a Holy Willy, it does not become you."

Russell's pallid cheeks tinged, and a look of guilt flashed across his face. "Still," he insisted, pointing to the table. "You actually ate with the man."

"So what?" she cried. "Is breaking bread suddenly a crime?"

"He is in service. It is unseemly."

"Stop being such a snob. He is retained by me, but he is far from in service." Suddenly the stupidity of this argument hit home. "If I want Hicks or Gillman or anyone else to sit at my table, that is my prerogative. I need not explain myself to you."

His mouth worked. "But, but, it's not right. . . ."

Rubbing her temples, she scowled. "I have a headache now, Russell. If you will excuse me, I am going to lie down."

Hicks hovered in the open doorway. "Please see Lord Russell out, Hicks. And I am not accepting visitors."

"My lady?"

"Yes, Hicks?"

"Mr. Redford asked that I post additional footmen at the front and rear entries. Shall I do so?"

"As I said, all of the staff is to do his bidding to the fullest. We are in his hands for the moment." She left the room and headed up the stairs.

Despite her headache, Lillian felt suddenly better than she had since the onslaught of this dastardly affair. Redford was taking command of the situation. She could not help but feel reassured.

Chapter 13

"**H**e is a dastard of the first order, I tell you!" Russell Mayburn insisted later that afternoon at his club.

"Lower your voice, Mayburn," Kane chided, irritated by the intrusion. Reading the afternoon paper was a sacred pastime, something the young clod seemed unable to appreciate. Kane wished that he could simply send Mayburn off with a slight and be done with him. But he needed the gent, so snapping the newspaper wider to give a hint would just have to do.

"He grabbed her hand and was exceptionally familiar." Mayburn pushed aside the broadsheet and peered far too closely for tolerability's sake into Kane's face. "On my honor, his intentions are foul."

Disgusted, Kane shoved the idiot back into his chair. "Stop making a fool of yourself over the slut."

Mayburn rebounded. "She is not a slut!"

"Lower your voice." He noted the heads turning toward them and realized that he would actually have to deal with the whelp. He folded the paper and tucked it under his leg. No one was going to read it before he did. "You just said that she was allowing him to molest her."

"He was doing no such thing!"

"Then what are you getting in such a snit about?"

"The man is toying with her affections." The buck's lips curled into a frown, reminding Kane of a petulant adolescent.

"I hate children, so stop acting like one, Mayburn."

"But she said that he was an investigator come to free Dillon."

Kane did not give a fig about Lillian's affections. But he did care about this new turn. "What was his name again?"

"Redford."

Bullocks. He rubbed his chin. "This will not suit."

"Well, what can we do about it? He is working on the matter and supposedly has some questions for me. I don't know why." Mayburn's eyes widened. "Do you think that he suspects something?"

"Don't be a nincompoop." As if the man could stop himself. "They know nothing."

Mayburn's shoulders sagged. "Of course. So what shall we do? We cannot have him hanging about. The man is trouble."

"Lillian hired him. She will just have to fire him."

"She's given Redford leave to order the servants about. She seems quite set on him. And you know Lillian, when she makes up her mind about something, it sticks."

Kane knew no such thing. "Well, we just have to change her mind for her then."

"How?"

"If she is threatened, she retreats. Always has."

"You threatened her?"

Kane showed a placating smile. "When *others* threatened her, she usually ran. I saw it when I watched her play as a child. Patterns from youth often repeat in later age."

"I do not countenance frightening her. It seems so . . . bullyish." The greenhorn quivered like a girl.

"Ah, but my dear boy, who do you think that she will run to if she is upset?" Kane allowed a grin to lift his lips.

"Who?"

"Her stalwart friend. The man who has been faithfully visiting her every day. . . ."

Awareness lighted the idiot's gaze. "Me?"

"Yes. It is a double objective. Scaring Lillian is only a simple means to an end. Redford will be out of the picture and you more firmly set in it."

Mayburn frowned. "But it seems so . . . aggressive."

"We will not truly harm her. We *must* not harm my dear child." If Lillian died, then the trust funds passed on to charitable causes, and unfortunately Kane was not listed among them. That was the only fact keeping her alive these past two years.

Mayburn inched forward in his seat. "So what should we do?"

"She needs to be frightened enough to toss Redford out on his ear."

"Should we send her a letter?"

"Child's play. You must be serious if you wish to see the matter properly done."

Mayburn stiffened. Then his eyes slid about the room. "Everything that you have said has come true, sir," he whispered. "But there is something important that we have not yet discussed."

Kane had been waiting for the cabbage-head to figure it out. "Lady Langham's demise?"

Relief flashed across his features. "Yes."

"Terrible tragedy that one, and poor Langham is wrapped up in grief over it. The poor sod had no idea what would happen when his fury finally overtook him."

"What?"

Kane could just see the clouds forming in the lad's dull gaze. "He had confessed his anger to me, you see. His wife was having an affair, and he was distraught about the whole thing. But he loved her truly, and his distress was more than any man could possibly bear. You know about deeply committed love, don't you?"

Mayburn blinked, as if surprised he had been asked. Then his brow puckered. "I do," he whispered, nodding sagely.

"Hence, poor Langham's anger overcame him. But he is so repentant that the archbishop of Canterbury, if he knew, would be the first to forgive him. The man's practically beside himself with remorse. The only good thing to come from the wretched situation is helping Lillian."

Mayburn's mouth opened and then closed as he scratched his head.

Kane rushed on before the stupid sod's mind might actually recognize the fabrication for what it was. "Thank heavens you had the foresight to deliver your brother's personal items to me. Now we can save poor Langham and see about freeing Lillian from Beaumont's damaging influence."

The clod blinked, bewildered.

"So at the end of the day, you will have your Lillian, she will be free of your brother's evil clutches, and I will finally have the funds that were mistakenly granted to her. Lillian will have no need for the money, as she will have yours. So you can sign those papers I gave you. Then the real Marquis of Beaumont takes his rightful place."

"Me," he breathed, grasping the only point he was meant to.

"And soon you will be the Duke of Greayston."

"Russell Mayburn, the Duke of Greayston..." He puffed out his chest like a rooster.

"God willing. And all of that property, all of that money goes to you. Lillian will *hardly* need the funds that are my due."

Mayburn's mouth opened, then closed, and then opened. "Yes, I suppose it is only right for good to come from evil."

"Exactly. Now we just need to ensure that Redford does not discover poor Langham's part. The man is devastated, no use torturing him further. So here is what you will do...."

Spotting Dr. Winner sitting at a table in the corner of Tipton's Tavern, Nick wove through the crowd. The scent of beer, sweaty bodies and mutton filled the air. It was the dinner hour, and the crowd was thick, as was usual for this time of evening.

The barkeeper, Joe, regularly had his wife cook

the dinner, and Winifred scratched up the best mutton stew in town.

It had been three days since Nick had last seen the good doctor. Three days since he had had his dramatic turnaround and assumed Beaumont's case. It felt like a mere few hours, though, and time was running short. But Nick knew that he worked better when his eyes weren't burning with tiredness and his belly wasn't crying out for sustenance. His usual Thursday evening visit with Winner was the perfect excuse for a lift.

He sat down with a grunt, setting his walking stick against his chair. One never knew when a cane might come in handy in a raucous bar. "Sorry I'm late. I am dog tired."

"You're too young for griping, Nick," Winner reproved. "You need at least another ten years on you before you're entitled to grouse like an old man."

Nick rubbed his weary eyes. "Long nights turning into long days."

Winner sat up. "Miss Figbottom turned out to be more than just a retainer? It's been three days and you have not bothered to come by and tell me. How dare you, Nick? But I can forgive if you make me forget. I want details, man. Down to the last sway of those wicked hips!" He waved to the serving girl. "Ursula, bring the beer!"

Nick almost groaned from his loose tongue. "Miss Figbottom changed her mind about hiring me. I'm working for Beaumont now."

"Beaumont!" Winner cried, aghast. "The man's positively drenched in blood."

"Things are not always as they appear." Nick had certainly learned that lesson well.

"But the papers—"

"Do you trust me to do the right thing, sir?"

Eyeing him, Winner leaned back. Slowly, a smile broke out on his face. "Oh, but this is going to be good. I can't wait to see Dagwood fall flat on his overambitious arse."

"Don't go betting against the odds yet, sir. Knowing something and proving it are worlds apart."

Flashing a saucy grin, Ursula ambled over. The young barmaid slapped a tankard down before each man, and froth dripped in rivulets down the sides, splashing onto the table. She was a plump maid with buxom breasts and what Mabel would have called "first-rate birthing hips."

Ursula sent Nick a wink and nodded to Winner. "How ya farin', Redford?"

"Fine, thanks." Shifting his eyes away, he sipped his beer. Ursula did not need any encouragement. To Joe's disappointment, his daughter was one to fish in the closest pond.

"Hey, Doc, can I ask you a question?"

"Certainly, Ursula."

"I've had this rash, see? For like a month." She shoved a fistful of snarled brown hair behind her ear, exposing a bright red spot on her cheek. "And it itches."

From the wooden bar, Joe yelled, "Stop chatting, Ursula, and get back in the kitchen!"

Adjusting the platter on her hip, she turned, shouting, "As if you never chat up the customers!"

"Ursula!" the barman warned, laying his palms on the bar.

Looking back at the men, she rolled her eyes.

"The man's more of a pain in the arse than 'e's worth. If 'e weren't my pap, I might just quit. Still, I get to meet some mighty fine fellas here." She leaned her elbow on the table so that her loose blouse gaped open, giving Nick a generous view. "I can slip free around midnight, Redford. If yer interested."

Nick veered his gaze from the sight of her lush white breasts as suddenly a slighter figure with peaches-and-cream complexion came to mind. He cleared his throat. "I have a previous appointment."

"Give Basilicum a try, Ursula," Dr. Winner suggested quickly. "That rash should clear up before you know it."

"Thanks, Doc."

Joe approached, anger exacerbating his limp. "Next time I ask ya to come over, Ursula, ya come. Yer mother's working like a horse and the food is getting cold." Grabbing Ursula's arm, he pushed her toward the kitchen. "Now go!"

Rubbing a hand across his bald head, Joe snorted. "Young 'uns these days make you just want to tear your hair out. Winifred thinks she's going to marry off the lass. The sooner the better, as far as I'm concerned." He tossed a folded note onto the scratched table. "This came for you a couple of hours ago, Nick. T'was a footman named Gillman. In Lady Janus's service."

"Thanks, Joe. And thanks for getting his name."

Nick reached for his purse, but Joe waved him away. "It's on yer bill, don't worry."

"Thanks."

Nick slowly unfolded the foolscap. The script

flowed with elegant curves, reminding him of its author.

> *Mr. Redford,*
>
> *I appreciate that you must be engaged with the weighty demands of your investigation. Nonetheless, Dillon has asked me to solicit a report from you. Time grows short, and he is most anxious for intelligence of your progress. I must confess, I am eager for news as well.*
>
> *We can meet at Newgate, but if you prefer not to take the time to journey there, you may call upon me at my residence. If you intend to call today, please do so before five o'clock or after seven. If that does not suit, you may find me then at Litchfield Park in the gazebo by the eastern entrance. There, I will be visiting with my dear friend Lady Rece, as we are wont to do.*
>
> *Thank you for your efforts on Dillon's behalf.*
>
> *Lady Janus*

"What's wrong?" Winner asked. "You look as if you've already eaten Winifred's mutton, and I know you haven't even ordered yet."

"I love Winifred's mutton," Nick replied distractedly. He felt a twinge of guilt in his gut. He usually did a better job keeping in contact with his clients, but Lady Janus did not need him, not really, and his efforts were better targeted elsewhere. The lovely lady was smart enough to take precautions for her safety, and she had done well enough without him before now. Moreover, even with Beaumont out of the picture, Russell Mayburn was hanging about. Nick was busy with a time-sensitive murder investigation, for heaven's sake.

But the flimsy excuses rang hollow in his mind. He considered the last few days and recognized that despite her frequently invading his thoughts, Nick had been avoiding Lady Janus.

Slowly, he realized that he was afraid of becoming diverted by her. The lady was too exquisite by far, and her character seemed to grow in his estimation with each moment that he spent in her presence. A dangerous combination for the man who had sworn never to touch her.

Still, he should have checked in on her just the same. He was one of the few people aware of the menace against her. The idea of a threat to her tickled at his conscience. He reread the note.

" 'I will be visiting with my dear friend Lady Rece, as we are wont to do,' " he murmured under his breath. Why did that bother him? *Because if she did it on a regular basis, then others might expect her to be there.*

He stood. "I think I'd better go check on this."

"Where are you off to, if I may ask?"

Classic Winner, curious as a cat. But where was the harm? "Litchfield Park."

"Don't take a hackney. You're better off on foot this time of day. Take Northland. And do you have an umbrella? It looked like rain."

Nick brandished his cane. "This will have to do." Nick threaded his way through the customers, heading out the door.

Through her thin muslin skirts, the stone bench in the gazebo was cold under Lillian's bottom. She pulled her silk spencer more tightly around her neck, hoping to ward off the evening's chill. The outer garment was probably filthy by now. What had she been thinking, putting on a thin white silk spencer for her meeting with Lady Rece in the park? *Was I trying to appear chaste?* she wondered, annoyed with herself. Hard to do when the eggshell muslin gown she wore underneath hugged her every curve. She did not fool herself; she had dressed on the slim possibility that Redford might show.

Despite her insistence that nothing occur between them, gallingly, she still wanted to look her best when he was around. The problem was, most of her wardrobe was for a worldly high stepper. Even though she was no longer an innocent, she was hardly a Cyprian, either. It was like she was in a sort of sexual limbo, from which she doubted she would ever emerge. Fanny had explained that she had not really experienced the full act of sex, and she wondered if she ever would.

Where was Redford, anyway? It had been three days, and she had not heard from him. She had spent most of the interim at the prison, and she had made it her business to be in residence in the evenings. Maddeningly, no one had called. Not even Russell.

Dillon was growing anxious for word, and Lillian was almost ready to chew off her thumb from worry. Granted, Redford was probably very busy, with such a short time until the trial. Nonetheless . . .

She wondered if he was avoiding her. Could she have been wrong about the truce between them? Still, he should have reported to Dillon at least. Lillian had been inordinately relieved when Dillon had asked her to contact Redford. She had not had the nerve to go to Redford's office or Tipton's Tavern herself, but she had sent notes. Calling on him would have felt almost like begging for attention, the last thing she wanted to do.

Still, she seemed destined to have the man in her thoughts.

Hence, her completely unseasonable garments.

She peered out into the darkening evening. It seemed later than half-past five. There was no sound of a carriage approaching or even footfalls on the gravel nearby. Where was everyone these days?

Was Redford at Tipton's Tavern having a beer? Sitting with his cronies, laughing about how he had tasted Miss Lillian Kane's bungling charms?

Her belly flipped with mortification. Even though she knew that it was pure fantasy, the fear lingered. No. Redford was too honorable for that. Wasn't he?

Thank heavens Lady Rece had asked to meet for a visit tonight. The woman could talk sense into a looby with a loose screw. Not that she could really tell the lady anything about Redford. Lady Rece did not know her secrets. She was more like a supporter in the wings. But a cherished one. Lady Rece maintained their friendship despite her husband's staunch disapproval of Lillian, which made Lillian fully aware of how much the lovely lady really cared.

She and Lady Rece had met at the milliner's one fortuitous afternoon. Over tea they had realized that they had not a blessed thing in common, yet they had seemed so similar it was astounding. They had become fast friends. Lillian and Lady Rece tried to get together about every week or two, but they'd missed their last visit because of the whirlwind events surrounding Dillon's arrest. So they were due for a chat.

Lillian realized that two of her dear friends in Town were significantly older than she was. Fanny had to be at least thirty (probably older, but who knew?), and Lady Rece was well into her forties.

"I wonder if I should go fetch an umbrella, my lady?" Lillian's footman Gillman stepped forward, his shoe heels clomping loudly on the wood-planked porch. "It looks as if it might rain."

Roused from her musings, Lillian finally took note of the impending storm. The air was thick with moisture, and leaves flashed agitated on a restless wind.

"Yes, it smells like rain," she observed, recognizing that it was not as late as she had assumed; the sky was simply darkening in anticipation of the storm.

As if confirming her words, lightning flashed. Seconds later, thunder clapped overhead, fairly shaking the rooftop with a shuddering boom. Deadly quiet shrouded the gazebo, only to be broken by the pitter-patter of a shower.

"Oh, dear," she muttered as realization dawned. Paper-fine white silk and water did not mix. If her ensemble got wet, it would be like plaster. She wanted to groan from the ignominy of it. Thank the heavens Redford had not chosen to meet her here. Now she just prayed that he did not decide to await her at home.

"It's just a little rain," she muttered to herself. "You'll not melt." No, but she wanted to. She had been a fool to try to impress an uninterested man. She was acting like a girlish ninny. A mistake she would not make again.

She nodded to her footman. "That is a good idea, Gillman. Thank you. Also, ask Jon Driver and the other footmen to bring the carriage closer. I fear that Lady Rece has been delayed."

"Yes, my lady." Nodding, Gillman stepped off the porch and into the darkening woods.

The winds whipped the tree branches into frenzy. Darkness oozed up the stairs of the gazebo like spilled ink on a desktop. The rain intensified, hammering the rooftop like tiny pellets.

Unease filtered through her. Lady Rece had not shown. Now Lillian was alone, unguarded in an open gazebo in the woods. She stood, feeling the sudden urge to get out of there.

Hearing a sound behind her, she turned. A man in black stepped out from the shadows and up the rear steps of the porch. She ran screaming for the stairs.

Chapter 14

In the gloom, Nick cursed under his breath as the rain lashed at his face and glazed his woolen cloak wet. This was ridiculous. Lady Janus had probably come, taken one look at the rain clouds, and left in her nice dry carriage before the storm. Why the hell was he out here risking a chill when the rest of the world was home safe and dry?

His boot heel slipped on a rut in the path and he tripped, just barely catching himself. Still, he pressed on, knowing that he could sooner disregard that sinking feeling in his gut as ignore a ravenous stomach. They were both signals to him that something needed doing, and without delay.

He shifted his heavy cape more fully around his shoulders, glad that he had thought to wear it tonight. He cursed the gods for mocking him so. "Couldn't have the rendezvous on a cloudless spring morning, eh? That would be too convenient. Blasted fool's errand." He prayed it was so.

A scream shattered the night, jolting his heart and raising the hairs on the back of his neck.

He spun and tore down the path, heading toward the sound. Fear lent his boot heels wings. Coming out from the cover of trees, he spied a structure in the distance. The faint outline drew his racing steps, and he charged up the wooden stairs two at a time. The sight before him froze him in his tracks.

A man swathed in black clutched Lady Janus tightly before him. His ebony arm snaked about her shoulders, and he held a glittering dagger perilously near her throat.

Her face was as white as her coat, and her eyes were wide with terror. Fear gripped Nick so hard that he felt as if the knife were at his own throat. That would have been far preferable.

"Let her go or I'll see you bloodied before a moment's gone," Nick growled, stalking forward.

"You're not supposed to be here!" he shrieked, his voice muffled by the thick scarf at his face.

Nick froze, not wanting to panic the man into doing harm. "Calm down."

"No one wants you!" he screamed, yanking Lady Janus closer to him. "Go away!"

Nick would sooner cut off his own arm, but he did not say so; instead, he studied his quarry. The bastard's face was covered in black paint. He obviously did not wish to be recognized by voice or features. He had not killed Lady Janus when he'd had the chance, which indicated that he had some other goal. First and foremost Nick wanted to see Lady Janus safe, then get acquainted with the scurrilous dog.

Never taking his eyes from the blade, Nick shifted closer. "If you let her go, then I will go as well. It's that simple."

The blade quivered. "No! You leave now!"

"Perhaps we can discuss a trade of some sort . . . ," Nick stalled, slowly advancing. "I didn't catch your name—"

"Stay away!" The bugger stepped backward, dragging Lady Janus with him. If he moved just a couple more steps, his back would be against the latticed wall. No way out except through Nick.

"I suppose it is getting late. With the rain and all, leaving might not be a bad idea." Nick slowly turned as if he were leaving.

The fiend's arm lowered just a pinch.

Nick swung his cane in a high arc and downward onto the man's knife arm.

The knife clattered onto the floorboards as the man shoved Lady Janus forward and raced out the back of the gazebo.

Nick caught her as she spun and dropped heavily into his arms. "Get him!" she shouted as the villain dashed past them and down the steps.

"I'm not leaving you alone," he growled, watching the bastard dart into the trees. He fought the urgent impulse to give chase. There was likely no way he could get the bastard now. And Lady Janus's safety was his primary concern. But given half a chance, he'd skin the man alive.

"Where the hell are your servants?" he demanded. Thank the good Lord for his intuition. Thank Lady Janus for sending the note. Still, he wanted to shake her for putting herself in such danger in the first instance.

"I-I don't know. Gillman left for an umbrella. I

brought extra footmen like you suggested, but they waited by the carriage. It is not far, and I thought that it was safe. . . ." She raised an unsteady hand to her head.

Nick decided that he had more important things to do than chastise her. "Are you hurt?" he asked with concern.

"He hit me when I tried to get away."

Lightning flashed, illuminating the trees. Thunder boomed. Nick hugged her close, as if to ward off the violence.

Looking down, he scanned her face. "Blast, I can't hardly see you."

Lightning flashed again. In the brightness, he saw the line of blood trailing down her forehead. Something constricted inside him, making him thirst for blood of a different owner. He had been pushed to kill before and had never enjoyed it, but he might just make an exception for that black assailant.

"What's wrong?" she asked with alarm.

He realized that he was clutching her too firmly. He loosened his grip and forced his temper to settle. No use coiling himself up; he needed to think about more than just doing violence.

"I must check that wound." Ripping his glove off with his teeth, he explored her skull with his fingertips. An egg-sized lump was already forming on the side of her head. A small cut lined her scalp where the handle must have struck her. For her sake, he tried to temper the rage pulsing through him as he considered what he would like to do to the owner of that blade. Nick had always had a problem with men who preyed on vulnerable women. Something about it just made him want to bang heads.

Cautiously raising her hand to her scalp, she winced.

"Bad?" he asked, suspecting that it ached like the dickens.

"Feels like I had a night of merry mayhem without the merry."

Some of the tightness in his chest eased. She was jesting; she could not be so terribly harmed. He nodded. "I want to get you out of here."

"My thoughts exactly."

Helping her stand, he was glad to see that she was not too unsteady on her feet. Still, he hoisted her into his arms, just in case. He should not have been surprised, but she was amazingly light considering her forceful personality.

"I'm not an invalid. Put me down."

"Your balance may be affected—"

"And your life may be if you don't put me down this instant!"

He gently set her on her feet but kept his arm wrapped about her waist. He was not about to let her fall.

"Thank you. I really am . . . fine." She was putting on a good face, he had to admit, but she was shaken. "What . . . what do you think happened to the servants?"

"I don't know. I did not see anyone." And no one had come. Which was not a good sign.

"They would never leave their post unless . . ." Her voice quivered slightly. "We must find them."

Instinctively, his grasp on her tightened. "No. We will get you safe first. I can come back and look for them later."

"We cannot abandon them. What if that man . . ."

His instincts were telling him to leave, and he was not about to ignore them now. "He wanted you. And the last thing in the world I am going to do is give him the opportunity to return with reinforcements."

"I had not thought of that." She shuddered in his arms. "But to leave seems so wrong—"

"Do you trust my judgment to do what's right?"

The question hovered between them.

Slowly, she nodded. "I do."

"Then we need to get going. I'll not give that bastard a second chance."

Eyeing the pouring rain and the darkness, he eased her closer to prop her weight onto him. "I hope you don't mind a little rain. I don't think that Noah's going to show up on his ark to save us."

She did not seem to appreciate his jest; she only hesitated at the top stair.

"What's wrong?"

"It is of no consequence. Let us go." She leaned into him. Her body was stiff with tension.

He slowly led her down the stairs, and sheets of water poured down, soaking them in an instant. The soft grass sank slightly under his feet, and once on the path, he was careful to mind the ruts and puddles.

"The carriage was here," she declared, eyeing the empty grasses.

"Come," he urged, keeping his arm locked around her and continuing down the path. "I will find out what happened and do what I can, but your safety must take precedence."

Lightning cracked and the sky rumbled. Nick kept their pace slow and steady, ready for anything and more than ready to do a bit of damage if the blackguard returned.

"God is trying to tell me something," she muttered, shuddering with cold.

He pulled her closer, concerned. "God's been trying to tell me something since the day I was born. I just try not to listen."

Doused by the rain, they gradually trudged through the park, side by side. The trail was slick and muddy, and he gripped her firmly to keep her from falling. He tried to ignore how good she felt in his arms; this was neither the time nor place for his randy thoughts.

As they progressed through the trees, she seemed to relax in his embrace, leaning more into him. She was probably drained from her ordeal. Still, she did not complain once, although he knew that she had to be in more than a bit of discomfort from her injury. Lady Janus wasn't turning out to be the fancy powder puff she appeared to be.

Exiting at the west gate, Nick allowed himself a momentary sigh of relief that they had made it to safety. He led Lady Janus toward a busy intersection, where he hoped to find a ride. The streets were deserted, the smart folk staying where it was warm and dry.

He leaned closer to speak in her ear, and rain streamed off the rim of his hat and down her collar. "Sorry about that."

"Don't be. I cannot get any wetter." Her features were grim. "Thank heavens—at least the rain seems to be easing."

The rain had lightened up to a drizzle. The darkness had lessened as well, the clouds seeming to have drifted east. Nick looked down at Lillian, noting the tightness of her lips and the unnatural pallor of her skin. The once fluffy feathers of her bonnet were limp hunks clinging to her cheek. He brushed a flaccid plume from her face.

"We should be able to get a hackney around the next—" The words froze on his tongue as he took in the state of her attire. Dear Lord, she looked like a sea nymph ready to seduce him senseless! Her white spencer clung to her rounded curves, showing off every nook and cranny of her glorious form. Her generous breasts curved enticingly, emphasizing her hard nipples in magnificent detail. Her every sweeping curve was clearly discernible through the thin, wet fabric. Unable to help himself, he peered behind her and was so stunned that he almost tripped. The gentle sweep of her derriere was deliciously outlined for his intimate perusal.

He swallowed, noting that his chill had suddenly waned and heat swamped his body, especially at his groin. He pushed away all licentious thoughts. This woman was in his care. Injured, cold, beautiful, hot-blooded . . .

He would pretend to be indifferent. A knight in service to his lady. Focus on his charge: safeguarding the lady.

He cleared his throat. "May I ask you a question, Lady Janus?"

"Yes."

"Was that attacker Kane?"

"No. Kane is taller, more aggressive, actually."

"What do you mean?"

Her shoulder lifted slightly. "Kane would have knocked me first, for good measure. This man only struck me when I struggled."

The distinction was not lost on him. But that she should be so nonchalant about the violence made something constrict in his chest. Kane was going to have to be met, and soon.

Her smile was stiff. "I am just grateful that you came along when you did. Thank you."

"Me, too. But I have to ask, with all that is going on, why did you choose to meet Lady Rece in the park?"

She wiped some rain from her eyes. "It is not unusual for us to visit in the park, and so I thought nothing of it when I received her note . . . dear Lord!" She raised a hand to her mouth, her eyes wide with fear. "Do you think that Lady Rece is in trouble? That something untoward happened to her?"

He gave her what he hoped was a reassuring squeeze. "Do not jump to conclusions. There could be a number of reasons why she did not show. This weather, for one."

Lillian let out a long breath. "You believe so?"

"Yes."

She grimaced. "I suppose anyone with sense would have noticed the incoming storm. Anyone with intelligence would have realized that nothing unusual is just that these days."

"Do you typically meet in the gazebo at the park?"

"Yes."

"And who knows of this?"

"Well, I suppose all of my staff. Some of hers. Fanny, Dillon . . . it is no secret."

"Why there?"

"Lord Rece knows that Lady Rece and I are friends, but he does not approve of me. Hence, we

choose to meet in not too public a place so as not to
ruffle his feathers. It is better for Lady Rece all
around, since I am socially on the margins."

She said it dispassionately, as if this was par for
the course. He had not fully appreciated what Lady
Janus had given up in assuming her persona. It
made her choices and Kane's menace all the more
compelling.

"Why did you come?" she asked.

"I received your note, and, well, it gave me
pause."

"You thought that I might be in danger?"

"There was no indication of it," he assured her,
finding it difficult to explain the sense of foreboding
he'd had. "I just was unwilling to take the chance."

"It was foolish to think that I could continue with
my customary practices."

"Your assumption was not so wide of the mark.
You have done well for two years—"

"But you suspected that there might be a danger
to me. Why did I not see it?"

"I am an outsider to your daily life. It is easier for
me to see things that fit and things that seem off."

"Shouldn't it be the opposite way?"

"No, actually. Which is why I can make a living
doing what I do. If people could see their own
foibles, notice the contradictions in others, well,
then I would be out of a job."

They walked along in silence.

"I would feel much better if we could stop by
Lady Rece's residence to ensure that she is well,"
Lillian stated. "Even Lord Rece could not fault my
presence under the circumstances."

"I'm not taking you anywhere but to a warm

bed." His cheeks heated as he realized his inadvertent innuendo. "I mean your bed . . . alone," he added, ready to bite his own tongue.

Lillian blinked, taken aback by his slip. Mortification overwhelmed her. Had he noticed her indecent attire? Well, there was naught she could do for it now, and he *had* seen it all before. And touched her and tasted her . . .

"You're quaking," he declared. "Here, I don't know why I didn't think of this sooner." Shrugging off his cloak, he hung it on her shoulders. She felt overwhelmed by weighted wool and yet relieved to be covered.

"Thank you," she murmured. Looking down, she observed how the mantle scrunched on the ground at her feet, it was so long. "This will not do. I cannot walk like this, and you have no cloak. No, please take it back. I insist."

"And I insist that you wear it." His face had taken on an obstinate glower.

Well, she had to agree that despite being wet, it was toasty inside from his body heat. And she was no longer indecent. Still, this was ridiculous. "Mr. Redford, if I may offer an alternative?"

He nodded.

"At this point, where is the harm if you wear your cloak but simply wrap it around us both?"

"Very well."

Lifting the mantle off her shoulders, she felt relieved of the weight, and a bit chilly. After setting the cloak on his shoulders, he enveloped her in a warm cocoon. His arm snaked around her waist and pulled her closer, and she could not help the ticklish thrill inside her as she embraced his torso. Her temperature rose—and not just from the wool. She looked down to hide the blush that must be tainting her cheeks.

"Much better, thank you," she supplied, trying to pretend like she wasn't half-naked, hanging on him like a clinging vine. She wondered at the faint scent of almonds he wore.

They resumed walking down the thoroughfare.

"How is your head?" he asked. "Any better?"

"It's fine," she lied. It hurt like the dickens, but she could hardly think of her aching head with his muscular thigh brushing hers with each step. His burly arm held her close, and he tended to lift her slightly onto her toes when there was a furrow in the road. Help like this could almost make a girl want to be rescued more often.

As they stepped around the corner, they came upon a small party of rough-looking men hovering in an entryway out of the rain. Redford turned to one side, blocking her from view. She was both relieved and horrified in one stroke. That settled it; he had definitely noticed her indecent state. But he was too much the gentleman to speak of it and was kind enough to ensure that no other saw her mortifying condition. She shot him a grateful glance and his gaze was kindly apologetic, as if he was sorry to point out her condition.

A warm, reassuring sensation flitted in her middle at his gallant behavior. Nicholas Redford knew how to be a gentleman. He might not have been born one, but he certainly exercised the qualities.

Her heart fluttered deliciously as she thought of him dashing up those gazebo steps with knightly purpose. Every word out of his mouth, every step he had made had been calculated to protect her from harm. Then when they had neared those rough-looking men in the alcove and he had hidden her from view, it had been so . . . stirring. Like he had tapped into some heretofore unknown feeling that made her feel safe, protected and yet womanly with power. He wanted her to trust that he would take care of her.

For the first time since her grandfather's death, Lillian felt the urge to let someone else drive the unsteady chariot that was her life. To release the reins to another, if only for a few moments. She never felt comfortable giving Dillon the lead. He was wonderful but had a dim worldview that irritated her. She could not do it with Fanny either; Lord only knew where they would end up. But for a few precious moments, she would allow Redford to lead.

Lillian might have been wet, cold and aching, but deep inside something warm and pleasurable kindled.

Chapter 15

~~~~~~~~◦◦◦~~~~~~~~

Lillian barely looked up as Redford hailed a hackney and helped her inside. He gave directions to the driver, sat down beside her and slammed the door closed. Without even asking, he pulled her into his burly arms and enveloped her, wrapping the cloak tightly around them both. Now that she was finally off her feet, exhaustion hit her like a cannonball. She felt each aching muscle like it was a hawker screeching for attention.

Her cheek brushed against the wool of his cape, and the scent of almonds once again teased her senses. "Why do you always smell of almonds?"

He rubbed his hand up and down her arm to warm her. "Most people don't notice."

"I have an affinity for scents," she replied, wiggling her toes in her sodden shoes and grimacing with disgust; they felt like icy prunes.

"Well, please don't tell the gents at Bow Street," he joked. "It will soil my roguish reputation."

"Your secret is safe with me. But I must confess I never saw you as a man who indulges himself with perfumes."

"How do you see me?"

She shifted uncomfortably. "I don't know. Self-reliant. No-nonsense."

"No frills, you mean?"

"Yes, I suppose so."

He shrugged, his deep voice rumbling low near her ear. "The scent is not of my choosing. It was a gift."

"Oh." Images of scarlet-haired coquettes flashed in her mind, causing a startling sinking feeling in her middle.

"Not by a woman," he added quickly.

She raised her brow.

"It was a gift from Mr. Evans."

"The old soapmaker?"

"Yes."

"Why, may I ask?" she inquired, sensing a story behind the present.

He sighed. "I suppose we do have some time on our hands." He settled deeper into the seat, pulling her close. "When I was growing up, a few of us were sent to help out at Mr. Evans's shop during Christmastide each year. It was his busy season, and it allowed us to earn a few pence for the holidays. In my second season there—"

"Pardon, but how old were you then?" she interrupted, trying to imagine him as a boy. Dark, mischievous but likely quiet. Not one for tall tales or putting worms in girl's bonnets, she would venture.

"Ten. Most of the boys were older, but Dunn allowed me to go along."

"He seemed like a very special man," she stated slowly, reminded of their last unhappy exchange on the subject and wishing to make amends.

His body stiffened, and he was silent.

"I'm just, well, very sorry. I did not mean to pry." But she was probing and she knew it. She was insatiably curious about the man. She had thought that she had known so much about Redford from the accounts in the newspapers. But she seemed to know naught about him, really. Exploits in the broadsheets did not translate into understanding a human being, his motivations, his dreams. . . . It was no surprise that she was at sixes and sevens about Redford and hardly knew which way was north as far as he was concerned.

"It is no great secret," he remarked, shrugging. "Dunn was like a father to me. I had no one, and his own son was . . . let us say, very different from what Dunn would have hoped."

"It sounds like a beneficial arrangement for you both." So why did he sound so disturbed about it?

"It was good for me, no doubt. And Dunn appreciated our friendship. He loved me well, but no matter how dear I was to him, I was never his son. There were times when I did almost wish to be of his blood, I'll admit, but it was not the right of it."

"And this saddened you?"

"Mostly, I was upset for Dunn. The rift with Marcus brought tremendous heartache to him."

"What happened between them?"

"Marcus was smart, quick on his feet, a bit of a rake. Somehow, if there was trouble about, Marcus would be found in the middle of it. Dunn's approach was to try to discipline the rowdiness out of him, mostly with chores and lost privileges. Not that Marcus didn't deserve a thrashing now and again . . . but it seemed that with every punishment, there was retaliation. Marcus was a wild stallion, you see, and Dunn tried to break him. It was only a matter of time before something had to give."

"What was it?"

"I don't know. Dunn would not speak of it. Marcus left for the Peninsula. Dunn was never the same after Marcus took off. He tried to hide it, but we all knew. He never fully recovered . . ." His voice trailed off with sorrow. After a moment, he straightened. "But I digress. I was telling you the story about Mr. Evans's soap shop. Do you wish to hear it, or am I boring you to tears?"

"No, please go on." She was anxious for every crumb he might offer about his childhood, so very different from hers.

"Well, the shop was pandemonium during Christmastide, but Mr. Evans was a sharp gent, and he realized that someone was filching from the till."

"Did he accuse you?"

"No, he blamed my friend John William. John was a braggart. All talk but no deeds. He might have mentioned the easy money within reach, but he did not have the brass neck or the stupidity to actually steal a farthing."

"So what happened?"

"I begged Mr. Evans to give me a chance to prove John William innocent."

"So you knew even then that you wanted to be an enquiry agent?"

"I did not realize until years later exactly what I

wanted to be. But I suppose, looking back, I already had the proclivity for untangling facts."

"Were there that many mysteries to solve at the orphanage?"

He shifted. "Many of the children were curious about their parents. . . ." He shook his head, stating slowly, "I confess I was hoping to distract you, but still, I can't recall the last time I went on so extensively about myself . . . this is really not very interesting."

"Please, I am anxious to know more."

"Why?"

She lifted a shoulder. "We have had such very different lives. I suppose I wish to understand what you have seen."

"What purpose could it serve?"

"Well, you did save my life tonight. Perhaps I need to fashion the appropriate reward?" She wanted to swallow her foot and never speak a word again in her lifetime! Glue her lips sealed and then add a sewing patch for good measure. Her face flamed. "I mean, I don't mean . . . heavens, I don't know what I meant . . ."

"I know what you meant." Nick nodded slowly.

"You do?"

"Yes, you've figured out that the soap was a reward from Mr. Evans and you are wondering if it pleased me."

She sagged against him, relieved. "Exactly." She knew that he was trying to help her save face, and she appreciated his gallantry. Many gentlemen would not have been able to resist that easy setup. Especially after the way Lillian had treated Redford over the course of their acquaintance.

"Please tell me more about the pilfering in the

soap shop," she asked, ready to take his lead and leave her tongue-slip far behind.

After a moment, he sighed, continuing, "So if John William was not the villain, then Mr. Evans still had a thief in his shop."

"Who was the crook?"

"Mr. Evans had an assistant, Ezekial Jones. He was taking a portion of the money and ensuring that it never made it to the till."

"How did you discover this?"

"If you watched him long enough, it became clear. He probably knew that I suspected him. But I was a miserable, ten-year-old orphan. Who would take my word over his?"

"So you set out to prove his chicanery."

"Jones slept in a back room in the shop. I asked Mr. Evans to send him on an errand, and then we searched his room."

"And?"

"And he had stuffed his pillows with blunt. Money he never could have made on the up-and-up as a shopkeeper's assistant."

"Not exactly the way to endear Jones to his employer. Mr. Evans must have been very appreciative of your efforts."

"That was when he rewarded me with almond soap."

"And what else?"

"That is all."

"You stopped a thief from pilfering under his nose, exposed a lying turncoat who had betrayed his trust, and he gave you a miserable bar of soap?" she cried, aghast, pulling back to look at his face.

"Calm down," he soothed, grinning down at her,

amused. "He gave me almond soap for as long as I wish it."

"What does that mean?"

"For as long as I live, if I wish it. A box is sent to my residence the first Tuesday of the month."

"Every month?"

"Since I was ten."

She leaned back into his embrace, mollified. "Perhaps he is not so tightfisted after all. Still, Mr. Evans no longer owns the establishment."

"He had specific provision for my 'account' written into the terms of sale."

"I have never heard of such a thing."

"Neither had Mr. Shafer. But he does not mind having me as a customer, as I make certain to keep an eye out for his shop."

"And no one causes trouble when Nicholas Redford is about."

"That's stretching things a bit far, my lady." He shifted slightly.

"I heard about the thief of Robinson Square. How he never robbed a house on your watch."

"Happenstance."

"Not according to the *Times*, Mr. Redford."

"You can't believe everything you read in the papers."

"Very true, but—"

The carriage swayed as it took a turn around a bend, pressing Lillian deeper into his embrace.

"Sorry," she muttered, her skin flaming, and not just with embarrassment.

"Think nothing of it," he assured her coolly, ostensibly unaffected by the close proximity.

She tried to follow his lead, to pretend that there

was nothing out of the ordinary about their situation and that she wasn't enjoying it as much as she was. The coach righted and she relaxed, but he did not loosen his hold. She did not mind.

After a moment, he scratched his chin. "I have a request, my lady."

"Yes?"

"I mean no disrespect or untoward familiarity, but, well, I would really prefer it if you called me Nick."

"Nick" felt so intimate, and she was uncomfortable taking what felt like such a dramatic step. Especially since she was half-naked, hugged close in the man's arms. Particularly since she felt his nearness like a fever that she wanted to catch. She seemed to need reminders that there was nothing going on between them. That she had to maintain her distance.

"I would not want to take liberties . . .", he ventured.

"Of course you're not taking liberties," she replied. The man *had* just saved her life.

"It just feels like we've been through so much, yet to still be so formal. . . ."

He was right. After the things that they had done . . . and yet not done. Despite the mistaken assumptions between them, a fragile trust was growing. He was an outsider, yet he knew all of her secrets. He had saved her life tonight. Had been more gallant than most men of her acquaintance would have been.

"Nick," she mouthed. The name suited him; masculine, sturdy and make-no-bones-about-it succinct. So did the almond scent. . . . She straightened, insight piercing her like a lightning bolt. "The man in the park! He wore Dillon's fragrance!"

She felt his body tense.

"What cologne?" he asked.

"Canterbury violet."

"Many men wear it," he commented. "Nevertheless, we can assume that we are dealing with a gentleman who can afford the finer things and probably travels in Beaumont's circles."

"Which is why he disguised his face and voice tonight." She shuddered, but this time not just from the cold.

The coach rolled to a halt.

"Oaks Square," the hackney driver called.

The door opened and Hicks stood outside, the drizzling rain shimmering on his cream-and-black butler's uniform. "My lady! Thank the heavens! We feared the worst when Jon Driver and the men could not find you."

"The servants are here?" Lillian cried, relief flooding through her. "Is everyone all right?"

"They were held up by a highwayman!"

"No!" Her heart constricted for her loyal servants. "Was anyone hurt?"

"They are all well and whole, my lady. But frightened out of their minds. And when they could not find you, they lost the last wits they did have."

The hackney driver leaned over from his perch. "A highwayman, did you say?"

"Have you reported it?" Nick asked.

"Gillman is on his way to the Bow Street office. But we must send word that you are safe and well." Hicks stepped forward. "Pray tell that you *are* well, my lady!"

"I am fine, Hicks." Highwaymen in the heart of Mayfair. Was this Kane's doing? she wondered. He had never gone to such lengths. But that did not mean that he was incapable.

"Lady Janus is not fine," Nick insisted, interrupting her thoughts. "But she will be in a few moments. Please pay the driver, Hicks, and get out of the way."

Nick maneuvered out the door and eased her from the carriage. Clamping his arm around her waist, he drew her up against his hard form. She was a bit embarrassed by his embrace, but she *was* feeling a bit drained from all of the excitement.

"Has Lady Rece sent any word?" Lillian asked Hicks, worried for her friend.

"I dispatched Jones to Lady Rece's residence when you did not return. She claimed that you had called off your meeting until tomorrow."

Lillian was relieved, but troubled. She had sent no such postponement.

Just then, Fanny cried from the threshold, "Oh, thank the dear Lord in heaven!" She advanced down the steps. "I called just when your servants returned. I've been half mad with worry! Were you robbed? What happened? Are you hurt?"

"Give the lady a chance to get inside before peppering her with questions," Nick suggested brusquely. "She may be whole, but she's had a difficult night."

Lillian was thankful for Nick's interference, feeling suddenly unequal to inquiries. Fanny's good intentions aside, as long as everyone was well, all Lillian wanted was to get dry, warm and decently dressed. Now that she was out of the hackney, she felt the wind knife through her like winter's frost. She shivered, keen to get inside.

Fanny eyed Nick warily but turned to the servants hovering in the doorway. "Stand aside. Don't badger Lady Janus."

The footman rushed down the steps with an umbrella and held it over their heads as Lillian and Nick managed the stairs.

Candles flooded the windows with welcoming light, and Lillian was so glad to be home. If not for Nick's intervention . . . well, she did not want to think of how this night might otherwise have turned out.

Chapter 16

"Prepare a hot bath for my lady," Nick instructed once they had breached the vestibule of her home. "Tea and biscuits, too. Then I want a full accounting from Jon Driver."

Hicks rushed back toward the kitchens and the maids scurried away.

"This time I'll not take no for an answer, my lady." Hoisting her into his arms with amazing ease, Nick headed toward the staircase.

Lillian did not have the energy or inclination to fight him. Even his warm, brawny chest failed to diminish the dreadful chills that were making her feel as if icicles lived beneath her skin.

"It's the third door on the right, Mr. Redford." Fanny hounded their every step up the stairs. "Are you ill, Lillian? Injured?" Alarm made her usual throaty voice shriek.

"Just cold, Fanny." Lillian shivered. "Cold, wet and miserable."

Nick headed down the hall and kicked open the chamber door.

He studied the room, and after quickly scrutinizing every stick of furniture in the chamber, from the mauve canopied bed to the rose-colored silk Grecian settee, he decided on her favorite chair, the threadbare floral wingback by the hearth. He eased her down into the seat, turned and whipped the rose-embroidered coverlet off the bed to wrap it around her shoulders.

"Thank you," she mumbled, nuzzling her freezing nose under the blanket.

He leaned over her and carefully removed her hat, wilted plumes and all. "Let me have a look." His fingers skillfully but gently examined her skull. "You still have a bump, but the cut has almost closed."

"The burning has stopped," she replied, realizing that it had. In fact, all she was feeling was rather cold and sodden, from her flooded feet to her tender head.

Just then the butler and maids clamored up the back staircase and charged into the room, hauling all sorts of implements for the bath. The housekeeper, Mrs. Marx, bustled behind them, carrying a tray with tea, the keys at her waist clanking with her every shuffling step.

Mrs. Marx handed Lillian a cup, and she gratefully sipped the burning Hyson. Heat slithered down her throat and into her hollow belly. "Thank you, Mrs. Marx. Hicks, please prepare a bath for Mr. Redford in the guestroom next door. And do your best to find him something to wear, would you?"

"Yes, my lady." Hicks turned and left.

Nick shook his head. "Thanks for the hospitality, but I'm going to speak with Jon Driver."

Lillian did not like the pallor of his skin or the color of his lips. "You will not be of any use to me if you catch a chill . . . Nick."

Pressing his fist to his chest, he bowed. "Your concern moves me, my lady." But she caught the glint of amusement in his gaze.

"Please do me the courtesy of humoring me . . . Nick. I would hate for you to be so disobliging as to die on me."

"I promise not to expire," he stated mockingly, bowing, "until I have spoken with your coachman." Then he spun on his heel and headed out the door.

Stubborn oaf, Lillian thought affably.

Fanny's eyes were weighing the circumstances. "What in the blazes is going on, Lillian?"

Not meeting her friend's gaze, she explained, "I was supposed to meet Lady Rece, like we usually do. But it seems someone had sent her a note—"

"I'm speaking of you and that dark Adonis, not the blasted correspondence with Lady Rece!"

"Can we discuss this later?" Lillian murmured as she nodded toward the servants. Although they were trying very hard to feign nonchalance, their motions had slowed down to a crawl as soon as Fanny had asked about Nick. "I'm a bit frigid at the moment."

Fanny nodded, her face softening. "Warm up in your bath, my dear. Then we will chat. My curiosity is piqued. Piqued indeed."

Once deep in a scalding, lily-scented bath, Lillian finally felt like a person again. In the sudsy water, her skin no longer felt frozen, her chills had waned and she felt wonderfully relaxed. It felt so good.

"So how in heaven's name did Redford go from furious injured party to knightly savior in the span of three days?" Fanny asked, stretched out on the divan.

Had it really only been just three days? It felt like a lifetime. "Apparently, Fanny," she stated, thankful that the maids were gone and the door closed, "our outlandish plan actually succeeded."

"I knew it!" Fanny slapped her hand on her thigh. "I just knew it would work. Never underestimate a sleeping draught, a see-through night rail and a plan."

"I'll try to remember that," Lillian ribbed.

"Give me details, please."

"Well, Nick met me at the prison the afternoon of our little escapade and told Dillon that he was going to do his best to set an *innocent* man free."

"So it's Nick now?" Fanny raised a brow.

Ignoring the lure, Lillian continued, "You should have seen Dillon's face, Fanny. He actually teared up when Nick gave him the news. It was well worth everything."

"Hmmm. So Redford is on our side. But how does that bring him to Litchfield Park this night?"

Lillian pushed a cloud of bubbles around her knee. "Dillon asked for a report. So I let him know where I might be found."

"Might be found? Ha! *You've* got yourself a bit of a crush. Not that I blame you, my dear. He has that dark, brooding air that women can't resist."

"I do not have a crush." Lillian glared. "It was a smart thing to do under the circumstances."

"Under the circumstances the smart thing to do was to stay home, safe and dry."

Lillian's face fell. "I know. I feel like a fool."

"Well, no harm done. So your servants lost a few coins. Better than their lives."

"A highwayman in the heart of Mayfair. I never would have guessed that Kane would go so far."

"You believe it was him?"

"Or his lackeys. One attacked me, a wretched fellow who Nick believes is a gentleman behaving as anything but."

"Did you recognize him?"

"He was disguised. Thankfully, Nick came along just in time. He, at least, realized the possibility of danger."

Fanny scrunched her face. "Hmmm. The man came running to your rescue, very interesting."

"It was brave, is what it was. You should have seen the way he handled the dastard. Cool as ice, and the man was dispatched, one, two, three." Lillian snapped her fingers as the stirring image flashed in her mind. "It was really quite . . . remarkable."

"Cool in a fix and handsome as that?" Fanny brushed her hand along her hip, stating throatily, "What a package. No wonder you're infatuated."

"Oh, stop it, Fanny. There is nothing between us."

"Then you are out of your wits. Redford is a sharp blade. One of the most stunning men I've ever had the good fortune to lay eyes on. And that body! Well, the man's fine even with his clothes on."

"I try not to think of him with his clothes off," Lillian confessed. "It's a bit too distracting."

"That's the point," Fanny declared, popping open

her fan and waving it rapidly. "I'm just . . . well, I just hope Dillon doesn't find out. Although he should not blame you. No matter the truth of your relationship, men are selfish bastards and don't like to share."

"Well, the possibility of an affair is moot, so drop it. Nick cares naught for me. It is a simple business relationship, nothing more."

"I can tell by the way he carries you about and ministers to your delicate body," Fanny chided in a disbelieving tone.

"The man swore that he would not touch me if King George himself ordered him to," she grumbled. "Not exactly a Romeo with his fair Juliet."

"Why would he say such a thing?"

Suddenly finding it vitally important to clean her cuticles, Lillian grabbed the soap and attended to them. "Well, I told him that we could not have anything untoward between us."

Fanny flipped her fan closed with a snap. "Have you cracked?"

Lillian straightened in the tub, defensive. "It's for the best. Where can a relationship with Redford ever lead? There are a hundred reasons it will never do. I'm a kept woman. The man's got more principles than ten vicars combined. Besides, I will not marry. And he despises the wedded state as much as me."

"You sound perfect for each other."

"Perfectly wretched." She sank back in the tub.

Fanny's eyes narrowed. "You're afraid that you are going to fall in love with him."

"I will never suffer that malady." Lillian examined a pile of suds in her hand. "It's not an option."

"So he's a free man? You don't care if he samples other wares?"

"Beyond the investigation for Dillon, it's none of my affair what he does."

Fanny stood. "Then you won't mind if I stop by the guestroom and help warm his bath—"

"Don't you dare!" Lillian sat up so quickly that the water splashed over the side of the tub and onto the thick Turkish carpet.

Her old friend eyed her knowingly. "None of your affair, eh?"

Shock blazed through Lillian at her own violent reaction. She slowly sank back into the bath, realization dawning. Heaven help her, she *was* growing fond of Nicholas Redford!

"Oh, Fanny," she cried. "I cannot . . . I will not . . ." Lillian leaned forward, imploring, "Please help me stop it, Fanny."

"You really wish to end your feelings?" Fanny inquired, adjusting her emerald skirts and lounging on the divan.

"Absolutely!"

Fanny sighed. "Then there is only one thing you can do," she replied, tapping the closed fan against her painted red lips. "Sleep with Redford."

"What?" Lillian shrieked.

Tossing the fan aside, Fanny wagged a delicate finger. "Fighting the attraction between you will only make it more intense and significantly more difficult for you two to interact. You do wish to work together for Dillon's sake?"

"Of course, but I think bedding Nick would be the worst thing for me to do."

"If you bed him, then the tension will disappear.

You can cease focusing on each other because the pressure has been *released*, the temptation has been satisfied."

Her argument had merit, but it made Lillian uneasy. "I still don't think that it's a good idea, Fanny."

"You consider love akin to a malady. Yes?"

Lillian nodded.

"How do you treat a cold? I will tell you." She waved her hand in dramatic affect. "You give in to your body's need. You focus on it, take to bed, rest, and tend to your body's travails."

"Wouldn't the act of coupling intensify the feelings instead of quelling them?"

"In the beginning, perhaps. Sometimes it can dampen feelings completely. Like when the sex is bad. When it's awful, then the feelings can be quashed in an instant."

Bad? Nicholas Redford? Lillian crossed her arms, sighing, "If only. Somehow I cannot fathom it being awful after what happened the other night."

"Don't rub it in!" Fanny exclaimed. "I'm having enough difficulty talking about sex as it is."

Lillian shook her head. "It just doesn't seem right, Fanny. Me cavorting with Dillon's investigator while he withers away in prison."

"What on earth does Dillon have to do with it?"

"What if I distracted Nick?"

"And you aren't now?"

The clock chimed the hour of nine, and Lillian could hear shuffling feet and deep voices in the guest-room next door.

Fanny slipped off her half boots and wiggled her toes, sighing. "If I were in your shoes, I'd be living every moment as if it were my last."

"What do you mean?"

"With a scoundrel like Kane hovering over my shoulder, the possibility of imminent doom, well, I'd be making every moment last. Passion, hell, just having *fun* would rise in importance."

"As if it's low on your list of priorities now?" Lillian scoffed, but she heard the logic in her friend's words.

"Don't you agree?"

"Even if I did wish to follow your advice, Fanny, Nick has sworn not to touch me. So your suggestion is impossible."

Fanny smiled mischievously. "Is Redford sleeping here tonight, perchance?"

"I have invited him to."

"Visit him tonight, Lillian. See what happens. Perhaps you can be even more persuasive than King George."

"Nick?" Lillian tapped lightly on the guestroom door about an hour later. "May I come in?"

It was still early yet, just after ten, but the servants had retired for the night, as was usual these days. Lillian had not kept them about either, knowing that she might be making a nocturnal call.

"If I could have a word with you, please?" Silence greeted her. She wrenched nervously on the tie to her dressing gown, wondering if she should tiptoe back to her room. But Fanny's words had convinced her; if she had the chance for a taste of passion, she should jump on it. And how frequently would the man of her fantasies be sleeping in the next room? "Live every moment as if it's going to be my last," she murmured, reaching for the door.

Her hand was damp with nervous sweat as she slowly turned the brass knob.

"Nick?" she whispered, edging into the room. "May I come in?"

It was a foolish question, because she was already crossing the threshold. Still, if he sent her on her way, she would respect his wishes. No matter Fanny's confidence, Lillian still had considerable doubt that Nick would even wish for an affair with her. And in the end, it might be disappointing, but it really might be for the best. Then she would know for certain that her feelings would not be reciprocated, ending them forever. At least she hoped that would be how it worked.

The fire had burned low to embers; the scent of lavender soap filled the air. The plush carpet sank under her slippers, and she was surprised that there was no sound of movement in the room. Perhaps he was already asleep?

The bed was empty, its sheets turned down. A tray of food loaded with empty dishes rested on the far table by the high-backed chairs near the hearth.

That's when she saw his bare feet, stretched out before him, as if warming by the fire. Just the sight of that moon-pale skin made her breath catch.

"Nick?"

She stepped around the chair.

A low snore emanated from his slightly open mouth. He had fallen asleep sitting up, a goblet of wine still in his hand. His raven hair was loose, just grazing his shoulders, his face relaxed in repose and his eyelids smooth with sleep.

Her heart softened at seeing him so. The poor man was exhausted. It was likely her fault, and here she was thinking about passionate trysts. Her selfishness mortified her. Raising her hand to her mouth, she realized that she needed to stop thinking of herself and simply be a better friend to this outstanding man. For a start, she would do what she could to see him comfortable this night. She owed him at least that much.

Carefully she removed the goblet from his grasp and set it on the table. Treading softly over to the bed, she lifted off the coverlet and gently wrapped it around his legs. She felt odd stuffing the bedspread about his waist, but he seemed exhausted beyond being disturbed.

Hoisting up his feet, she realized that she had not noticed before how long and slender his toes were, with crisp dark hairs dusting them. Slowly, she curled the coverlet under his heels. Still he did not rouse.

As quietly as she could, she added another log to the fire. Turning, she watched the rise and fall of his chest for a few moments, softly mouthing a prayer that the angels of repose guard him safely until dawn. It was the prayer that her grandmother used to say over her bed every night.

A feeling of wholeness overcame her. This was how it should be. Nick had helped and comforted her this evening; she would do him the same good turn. He deserved it, after all.

Turning, she went back to her room.

Chapter 17

"I see this investigation as having three fronts," Nick explained to Lillian the next morning over kippers and eggs. "First, Lady Langham. I believe I am beginning to understand why she might have been the target."

"Really?" Lillian set down her fork, too excited to eat.

"Yes. I questioned her servants, and she *had* been having an affair."

"With whom?"

"Neither her maids nor footmen seem to know. Whoever the man was, he was very secretive, meeting Lady Langham mostly at a house off of Manchester Street. It's vacant now, and the agent has conveniently taken off on holiday."

Lillian's hopes slipped downward. "Oh."

"But I came across an interesting gent the other day, leaving Lord Kane's residence."

"You went by his house?" Somehow the thought of Nick near Kane brought Lillian a sense of unease. Not that she worried for Nick, but he was going up against the monster of her childhood.

"It seemed prudent to assess his movements. I have ascertained that he hides out at his club most days. Probably to avoid his creditors. The man is deep in dun territory."

"Kane likes to live well." Her fists clenched as she recalled her mother wearing faded garments with multiple mends while Kane was always dressed in the height of fashion. "Living well is not cheap."

"He has failed to pay his man-of-affairs the last three months' wages."

"The gent you met leaving Kane's residence was Mr. Danneman?"

"Danneman was fired and apparently took off to Cornwall. This fellow's name is Stein, and he had just left his notice on Kane's desk."

"What intelligence did Mr. Stein have to offer?"

"The man was only Kane's man-of-affairs for a few months, so he was not as helpful as I would have liked. But questioning him revealed that Kane and Lady Langham were involved in a shady investment scheme."

Lillian leaned forward. "What kind of scheme?"

"One that's been around for years because it is effective at playing on people's greed."

"That would do well in London," she remarked, nodding. "How does it work?"

"Some scoundrels set up a false venture opportunity. The first investors reap handsome rewards. They usually reinvest and attract other shareholders. They even work to solicit many of the new backers with tidings of their great gains. The original scoundrels take what they want, covering their thefts with the new deposits. But eventually the money dries up."

"Then what happens?" she entreated, fascinated.

"Everyone is left with empty pockets except for the thieves, who are usually long gone."

"Lady Langham was one of the thieves?"

"Yes, she and Kane were in on it together. Apparently the investors were starting to wake up and suspect the scandal."

If this could be proven, then Kane would be locked up for his crimes. She tempered her hopes. It sounded too good to be true. "Is there proof of Kane's involvement? Would Stein be willing to testify?"

"Kane has covered his tracks well. At this point it would be Stein's word against his. But I'll unearth the evidence. Nothing can remain hidden for long."

Her spirits rose at the conviction she heard in his voice. She had no doubt that Nick would do as he said. The man was probably one of the most capable she had come across in her lifetime. "But if Lady Langham was in partnership with Kane, then why kill her?"

"Remember the note that Dagwood has on Lady Langham's stationery where she threatens to tell her husband all?"

"It did not have an address or salutation!"

"Exactly." He tilted his head approvingly.

"And it may have been referring to the scheme!"

"You might make an enquiry agent yourself, Lady Janus."

She felt her blush down to her toes. "Lillian, please."

Cocoa brown eyes met hers, and she felt drawn into dark, heady pools. Her lips parted, as she felt suddenly breathless, lost in his smoldering gaze. The world fell away, leaving only the delicious heat simmering between her and this dark Adonis. She had to fight the compelling desire to reach across the table and touch him.

He coughed into his hand and looked away, breaking the spell. "I'm curious, do you wear lily perfume because of your name?"

Stealing a small sigh, she reminded herself that this was the man who had sworn never to touch her. It was time to stop acting like an infatuated lass, since Nick, at least, was keeping this relationship on a businesslike plane.

"It was Fanny's idea," she offered. "I prefer other scents—lavender, vanilla—but I've grown accustomed to it now."

"Hmmm." He shook his head as if to dispel a thought. "So, onto the second front: Beaumont. About his secret—"

Alarm shot through her. "You cannot tell anyone what you know!"

Holding up his hand, Nick shook his head. Despite the closed doorway, he lowered his voice. "I assure you, it is not my intention to save a man by ruining him."

Her shoulders sagged, relieved.

"Besides, it would do little good," he added. "What I need to know is where and what he was doing on the night of Lady Langham's murder. He lied to me. Sent me on a wild-goose chase, wasting some of the precious little time we have. I need to confront him. To tell him that I know his secret so he need not hide anything."

Lillian swallowed, miserable. "If you do that, then he will know that I broke my promise to him."

Nick extended his hand as if trying to soften the blow. "If you came with me, then it might help assure him that I would not breach his confidences."

She did not answer, knowing what she needed to do but not looking forward to the conversation.

"It's important, Lillian." He looked grim. "Or I would not ask."

"I suppose we can go this morning, if that suits you," she sighed.

"The sooner, the better. I will have to find witnesses to confirm his whereabouts. No one necessarily needs to know *what* he was doing with others, so long as there are people who can say where he was at the time of the murder."

"What is the third front?"

His face hardened. "Kane."

A surprising thrill shot up her middle at the force she heard in his voice. Kane had always been her own personal monster, and she had never had someone willing to challenge him. Nick's eagerness could make a girl swoon.

Trying to stop the unfamiliar flutter of her heart, she cleared her throat. "How will you deal with him?"

"Exculpating Beaumont will hopefully lead to Kane. But since I doubt the bastard will lay on his laurels and not stir up trouble like last night, I intend to keep you close to me at all times."

Her face flamed, and Lillian could not keep the pleased smile from her lips. She had a champion, it seemed. Nick might not have been retained to help her, but he seemed to have assumed her cause. With

Nick Redford around, she might actually see Kane get his due.

She bit her lip to keep her smile from splitting her face. "I must confess, I will feel safer with you around. Thank you, Nick."

He looked away as if uncomfortable. "It's the smartest thing to do under the circumstances." He stood and walked over to the sideboard. Serving himself, he added, "Besides, you're a sharp lady, you travel in Beaumont's circles. You can help me speed the investigation along."

A loud knock boomed on the door.

"Come," Lillian called.

Hicks stepped inside. "Lady Rece is insisting on seeing you, my—"

"Lillian?" Lady Rece swept into the room behind Hicks, her burgundy organza gown swooshing with her every stride. "There you are! What on earth is going on? First we make plans, then you postpone them, then your servants do not know where you are to be found."

Nick turned, setting his dish down on the sideboard.

Lillian rose and greeted her friend with extended arms. "Oh, Lady Rece. I am so sorry to have worried you."

The matron squeezed Lillian's hands affectionately, then she noticed Nick and frowned.

Lillian did not want her to get the wrong idea about having a handsome man joining her for breakfast. "Lady Rece, may I present Mr. Redford." She motioned to Nick. "Mr. Redford is investigating Lady Langham's murder. He also, thankfully, came to my aid last night when I was attacked at Litchfield Park."

"Attacked?" Lady Rece flicked open her fan, waving it wildly. "I believe that I need to sit down."

Nick leaped forward and yanked out a chair. Lady Rece fairly fell into it, her feathered turban sliding over her eyes.

"Oh, give me my vinaigrette," she begged. "In my purse."

Lillian grabbed her bag and yanked opened the drawstrings. Lady Rece might be a stalwart friend, but she was fainthearted when it came to violence of any kind. Moreover, she tended to succumb to the vapors quite easily, hence keeping a revitalizing vinaigrette always on hand.

Snatching out the tiny silver box, Lillian opened the hinged container and set it under Lady Rece's nose. The scent of vinegar filled the air.

"What the devil is going on in here?" a loud voice boomed from the doorway.

The owl-haired, wiry Viscount Rece stood in the threshold. A look of aversion lined his features, and he held his walking stick before him like a weapon. "Dorothea!" Dropping his cane, he rushed to her side, and Lillian quickly backed away.

"I'm fine, Donald," Lady Rece huffed. "A foul wind overcame me."

"Unsurprising in this place." His lips pinched.

Lillian was surprised at the strength of his animosity. But this was her home, and she did not have to suffer his antagonism. She opened her mouth to protest, but Lady Rece shot her a quelling look.

"Behave yourself, Donald." Lady Rece adjusted her turban and straightened. "You are a guest here."

"Not for long, I trust." Nick stepped forward warningly.

Rece rose. Even at his full height he was a hand

span shorter than Nick. He glared at him. "I will be out of here as soon as I collect my wife." He turned to her. "I told you not to come here, Dorothea—"

"I needed to see that Lillian was all right. She was attacked in the park last night."

Rece turned to her, his bushy gray brows raised mockingly. "In Mayfair? Unlikely."

"It's true," Nick supplied. "By my own hand I saw the attack undone. Lady Janus was only there in anticipation of seeing your wife. Which begs the question why Lady Rece did not show."

"I received a note postponing our appointment until today."

"Do you still have it?" Nick asked.

"I suppose I must."

"Will you bring it here, so that we may see it?"

Lady Rece turned to Lillian. "You did not send it?"

Lillian shook her head.

"This makes positively no sense whatsoever," Rece declared. His azure eyes filled with contempt. "Who would go to such great lengths to attack Lady Janus?"

"It is not your concern, Lord Rece," Nick stated coolly. "Suffice it to say that there will be no more meetings in the park."

"You can bet money on it!"

"I've had about enough of your unwarranted hostility toward Lillian," the matron scowled at her husband. "She is my friend."

"Lady Rece." Lillian stepped forward. "Your friendship means a lot to me. And I would not wish anything untoward to happen to you. So perhaps it is not such a terrible idea for you to stay away from me for a time."

"But—" Lady Rece pushed her slipping turban out of her eyes.

"Last night," Lillian continued, "when I thought that something had happened to you. . . . well, it made it so much worse." Guilt overwhelmed her. "I would not ever wish to see ill befall you, but for me to be the cause . . ."

Silence enveloped the room.

Even Rece had the decency to look away.

Lady Rece's lower lip quivered. "I don't like this. Not one bit. Do something, Donald."

"What do you wish for me to do, darling?" His tone was clipped. "The lady is obviously entangled in a dilemma, and I have to agree with her. You should not be involved."

"Friends do not desert each other at the first sign of trouble."

Lillian took her hand. "You are not deserting me. I have Mr. Redford to help me, the greatest investigator in London."

Nick coughed into his fist, embarrassed.

"This shall not do." The matron rose on unsteady feet with Lillian providing support in the front, her husband from behind. Nick pulled back her chair.

Lady Rece sniffed. "I will call upon you in three days' time, Lillian. And to ensure that all is well, my husband will accompany me."

Rece looked as if he had swallowed a sour grape.

"Friends rally at trouble; they do not shy from it. I will see you in three days, my dear." With that and a final squeeze of her hand, Lady Rece swept out the door.

Lord Rece watched her go but did not leave. "I will not have anything adverse happen to my Dorothea."

"Neither would I," Lillian concurred. "If she changes her mind, I will understand."

"Dorothea does not change her mind, once settled."

"Sounds like someone else I know," Nick muttered.

Lillian set her hands on her hips. "If she calls, Lord Rece, I will not turn her away."

Rece frowned. "Of course not. She would be devastated." Lifting his cane from the floor where he had dropped it, he added, "I suppose she feels a sense of responsibility toward you."

Lillian's brow furrowed.

"We have . . . never been able to have children," he explained haltingly. "Dorothea has always wanted a daughter."

Lillian was touched but disagreed. She did not see their relationship in this light. Perhaps it made the man feel better about his wife's choice in friends if there was some reason. For why else would Lady Rece associate with such a disreputable light skirt? If it weren't for her regard for Lady Rece, Lillian would have demanded that the man leave.

They stood awkwardly in the dining room and still Rece did not depart. Lillian wondered what he wanted from her. A promise that she would not pursue the friendship with his wife? Well, she was not about to give it. Especially after Lady Rece's staunch support this morning.

"I knew your family," Rece finally broke the quiet. "Years ago. We had a . . . falling out."

"Kane tends to have that effect on people," Lillian replied, crossing her arms.

He looked at her oddly.

She shrugged. "Kane is not a kind man, by any stretch."

He tapped the cane against his leg. "I suppose I may have allowed that anger to color me against you."

That was probably the closest thing to an apology the man was able to muster. "Well, since I adore Lady Rece, I suppose I will have to let that color me toward you."

His brows lifted, and she could almost discern a twinkle in his blue eyes. "I can see why Dorothea likes you."

Lillian raised a brow but did not reply.

After a moment, the man nodded curtly. "Have a care, Lady Janus. My Dorothea will be most upset if anything happened to you." Swinging his cane, he strode from the room.

Lillian dropped into a vacant chair. "I do not like drama with my breakfast," she muttered.

Nick recovered his plate from the sideboard and sat. "Do you usually face such animosity in higher circles?"

"The younger set tends to favor my company. I am deemed somewhat of a novelty. Yet I am not received in most of the homes where I was welcomed when I was with my grandparents. The majority of the matrons in polite Society will not speak to me." Her shoulder rose in a nonchalant shrug. "But I do not care. Rece was always particularly hostile toward me. Now I know why. Kane is like a poison to everything he touches."

"He did not say that his quarrel was with Kane," he replied, lifting his goblet.

"Who else could it have been with? My grandparents were some of the most admirable people to ever live. And my mother could not clash with a flea." Toying with a fork, she remarked, "If only she'd had more of a backbone, then perhaps she would have refused to marry Kane. I know she did not want to. Then I wouldn't be in this fine kettle of fish."

"No, you'd likely be in a kettle of a different variety."

"You are probably right. Being an unmarried woman with a child would have been inordinately hard for her. And she was not the strongest of women to begin with."

"Lord Rece has the reputation for being reasonable, not quick to anger. So it must have been a serious quarrel for him to have carried the grudge for so long." Nick slipped a piece of bacon into his mouth.

"I do not care to know anything about it. I have a bellyful of strife; I need not hear more."

She had been feeling so good, and now she felt as if she had been ripped through briars. Why? She should be feeling glad for Lady Rece's support. Her husband did not account.

"I expect that I don't wish to be the reason that a husband and wife are at odds," she stated slowly. "A friendship should not have unwarranted costs."

"Every relationship carries a price—not financially, of course."

"Even marriage?"

"Especially marriage. It's like pouring everything into one unstable connection."

"Why unstable?"

"Because it has to end."

"Not all marriages fail."

"Of course they do; someone dies. In the end, one spouse is left behind. Alone. Until death do us *part*."

She felt a pain tear at her heart for the scars he carried. No wonder he did not want to marry, did not wish for children. He could not bear loss; he had had his fill of it.

"Fanny says that love is the fruit of life's feast, the cream in the pudding."

He shrugged. "Then that's one meal I'll just have to miss."

"Perhaps that's not a terrible approach," she murmured, not quite believing it. "If there is no love, there can be no love lost." Yet, her grandparents had embraced her in a loving family. They had taught her that life was a struggle to be enjoyed for its sweet and bittersweet moments. She knew that if they could voice it, they would say that any heartache was worth it, to have experienced the joy. She had her own reasons for not bringing a child into her life, but fear of heartache was not one of them. In fact, her reasoning was the opposite. No matter her own selfish desires for a child, since she would not marry, she would not burden an innocent babe with the life of a scandal-ridden unwed mother.

He watched her a long moment. "You seem sad."

"I was just thinking about my grandparents. They'd always hoped that I would marry. Preferably to Dillon." She shook off her melancholy and tried for a smile, but it was slight. "Perhaps I should have the carriage brought around? We can go visit Dillon this morning." She sighed. "It seems that Newgate Prison has become my new haunt these days."

"That reminds me. Can we get any more of that

Cognac from the other night?" He grimaced. "Untainted, of course."

Abashed, she felt her cheeks heat.

"I need it for bribes," he explained. "At Newgate things move more smoothly if the wheels are greased."

"You mean the palms."

"Those too. Besides the usual state of affairs, John Newman is a font of information if you dig enough. Digging at Newgate can only mean two things, bones or bribes."

"Believe it or not, Fanny sent a few bottles over to your residence. An apology of sorts, for drugging you, and all."

"Is she sorry?"

"Actually, she's quite pleased with herself."

He snorted and then ate his eggs. After a moment, he wiped his napkin on his lips. "Was it her plan or yours?"

"Her idea, my execution."

His face darkened.

She had not meant it the way it sounded. Mortified, Lillian rose. He moved to stand, but she motioned for him to remain seated.

"I will go call the carriage." Turning, she left him to his meal.

Chapter 18

"You are very quiet," Nick opined as the carriage rocked on its way from Newgate Prison.

"Dillon was not very happy with me," Lillian replied softly. "And who could blame him?"

Nick's gaze softened. "He did not take it too badly, once you had explained your reasons."

"Thank you for not letting on about how I imparted the intelligence to you."

"Of course not." He waved a dismissive hand. "The important thing is that he seemed to understand that I would not breach his confidence. You are obviously very dear to him, and he trusts you well." Tilting his head, he inquired, "But that is not the only thing bothering you?"

Lillian bit her lip. "I just . . . well, I had no idea that such places existed."

"Where there is a demand for such services, there will always be someone willing to meet it."

"I suppose I am just naïve, but a brothel just of men . . . for men . . ." Looking out the window, she tried to thrust the disquieting images from her mind.

"It answers the question of why no one stepped forward to claim that Beaumont was with them on the night of Lady Langham's murder."

"So it was not helpful in the least?"

"No. I'm sorry."

She sighed, adjusting her skirts. "You had to try."

They rode along, the sounds of carriage wheels, horses' hooves clattering on stone, and street vendors hawking their wares filtering through the cabin.

"Halt!" a loud voice boomed from outside the carriage. "Halt, by order of the queen!"

Nick stuck his head out the window just as the coach rolled to a stop.

"What is happening?" Lillian asked, peering over his shoulder.

A rider wearing a scarlet coat trimmed with gold braid sat atop a gray charger, trying to keep the mount under control in the congested street.

"What does a royal servant want with me?" she asked.

"I suspect he's more interested in me," Nick remarked, swinging the door open and stepping down to greet the man.

Lillian tried not to ogle as she watched the men converse, the servant on his steed and Nick on the ground. If only the street noise would tone down, then she might be able to hear the discussion. She did not dare attempt to get out and join them, but she listened carefully for any stray bits of conversation.

The man in the ornate royal livery was scowling and seemed upset, and Nick was arguing with him. Dear heavens! She marveled at Nick's gall. Nick raised his voice, and even from her perch, Lillian could see the liveried servant's cheeks blanch. After a moment, the man nodded curtly. Nick spun on his heel and marched back to the carriage.

Yanking open the door, he looked up at her. "There is an emergency regarding the queen. Would you do me the favor of taking me to Windsor Castle?"

"An emergency? The queen?" she sputtered, aghast. "Of course."

"Follow that servant to Windsor Castle posthaste!" he ordered the coachman. Then he stepped inside and slammed the door shut.

Through the window Lillian saw the servant wheel his horse around and charge through the crowded streets, making way.

Jon Driver shouted, "H'yah!" and the wheels of the carriage rolled into motion.

Lillian blinked and turned to Nick. "Windsor?"

"I am on retainer to the queen."

Lillian was flabbergasted, impressed and alarmed. "Is Her Majesty unwell?"

"I have no idea, but I doubt it," he remarked, staring out the window, his face etched with tension. "I'm no doctor, just an investigator."

"But how did he find us?"

"Warden John Newman sent the royal servant after us. Apparently the man had been dashing about Town looking for me."

"You." She shifted in her seat. "So I was not requested at Windsor?"

His nod was terse.

"Nick?"

"Yes?"

"I don't think that it's such a good idea for me to come with you."

He shifted his shoulders. "No matter."

"You were called upon, Nick. I was not. One does not simply 'drop in' on Queen Charlotte."

"They need me, I'm with you. They will be appreciative of your help."

"Appreciative? I am not welcome in most homes of the *ton*, I am certainly not received by royalty. My very presence will cause you a devilishly awkward situation."

"Don't you wish to be of service to Her Majesty?"

Lillian closed her mouth, scowling. He obviously had no idea what he was dragging her into. And he was trying to manipulate her at that. She bit her lip, realizing that he had played her well. It was a chance in a lifetime to help the queen. Her Majesty had been a beloved friend to her grandfather, and she was Lillian's favorite member of the royal family. Although Lillian would not proclaim it too loudly where the Prince Regent could hear.

But Lillian was no longer just Lord Janus's granddaughter; she was the Marquis of Beaumont's paramour. She licked her lips. "My very presence might get you sacked, Nick. Please let me off and take my carriage. Gillman can escort me home."

He crossed his arms. "I am not going haring off to Windsor and leaving you behind to fall victim to Kane's clutches."

"I'm not that helpless, Nick. I can take precautions—"

He swung sideways, facing the window. "No."

Having a champion was nice, but having a dictator was unacceptable. "I have done just fine the last two years—"

"Like you did last night?"

She stiffened. "That is not a mistake I will make twice."

"Neither will Kane or whomever he is working with. They have less than two weeks to see Beaumont hang, Lillian. They are growing desperate."

"They're not the only ones," she muttered.

"Do you or do you not want my help?" His cocoa brown eyes had taken on a dangerous glint.

"Well, of course, but—"

"Then you have to abide by my decisions." It was like a door slamming in her face.

She felt herself bristle like a cat who has seen a foe. She crossed her arms. "You do not have leave to order me about, Nicholas Redford." She rapped her parasol on the ceiling. "Stop the coach!"

The horses whinnied and the wheels slowed.

Nick swung his head out the window, shouting, "Don't you lose that royal servant, Jon! Get moving!"

"Heyah!" Jon Driver called to the horses.

The carriage lurched forward, throwing Lillian back into the seat.

"You cannot order my servants about!" she cried.

"You told them to accept my commands. When you were of a more rational mind, that is. Now, at least, you will be safe. If Windsor isn't secure, then I don't know where is. And I cannot do my job there while worrying about you haring off straight into danger."

The nerve! Her anger rose like a righteous inferno. "Who the blazes do you think you are?"

"I'm the man in charge of ensuring your safety."

"If I wanted a bodyguard I would have hired one!"

"You got a double service for one price. I save your beloved Beaumont and watch your back. I'd say you made off pretty well in the deal and should be happy for the service."

"Don't tell me what I should be feeling! You have no idea what I want, what I need—"

"Oh, I have an idea." His arms were around her in an instant, pulling her across the small space and into his lap. Firm lips pressed against hers, silencing her cries.

She tried to struggle but knew that it was simply for show. She wanted his lips, his taste, the feel of him pressing against her. Being around him all morning was like being surrounded by the aroma of melted chocolate but not being able to taste the candy.

His tongue conquered her mouth, sweeping across her teeth in broad, demanding strokes. She shivered, never having experienced anything like it. His tongue met hers, sending thrills rocketing to her toes. Wrapping his arms tightly around her, he kneaded her bottom as if he had been dying to do it all day. He groaned inside her mouth. She could not catch her breath from the intoxicating assault on her senses.

In his kisses, he demanded her obedience, and she rose to fight him. Defiantly, she kissed him back. Boldly she lathed his mouth, tasting a hint of eggs and bacon. Taking his quick lesson and turning it against him, she pressed her hips into his manhood, feeling her effect on him, how much he wanted her.

Passion was both their weapons, sweeping over her with a force that left her winded.

Nick pulled away, his breath coming in pants, his heart pounding so hard that it drummed in his ears. Carefully, he set Lillian down on the seat beside him and then shifted across to the opposite cushion. He would have gone to sit up top if it wouldn't have forced them to stop the coach.

Moreover, it would have shown his weakness, and he was never one to admit an Achilles' heel for a woman.

She watched him with satisfaction glinting in her azure eyes. Her lips were red and swollen, and her breast rose and fell with each shallow breath. Her peaches-and-cream cheeks had two high spots of color, and she looked so delectable that he wanted to yank her back onto his lap and finish the job he'd started. But he had made a promise to himself, one he was going to try to keep despite this slip.

They rode along, the silence only broken by the jangle of the wheels and the clatter of horse hooves.

"Not a way to win an argument," she finally remarked, wiping a gloved finger across the corner of her lip.

"I wasn't trying to win. I just wanted . . ." What the hell had he wanted except to be inside of her? To taste her, hold her . . . But she was an innocent. He would be a selfish bastard to take advantage of her. And she would hate him for it, in the end. Her words haunted him, *Fanny's idea, my execution.* Looking back, she viewed their first coupling as a death sentence. In a way it was, for she was ruined. And he was the one who had stolen her innocence.

He was not about to do her another injustice simply to feed his lust.

"We need to call a truce," he finally declared.

"I didn't know we were at war." She stuck her bottom lip out, reminding him of a lush cherry.

"Look, Lillian, we're about to arrive at Windsor, and I can't have you distracting me." As if she could help it.

"I'm not the one who started"—she licked her lips—"that."

"I know." Removing his hat, he ran his hand through his hair. "It was a mistake. My mistake. And I will not repeat it again."

"Kissing me was not your mistake, trying to control me was. I am not yours to be ordered about."

"No." He let out a long breath. "You are not. But I do need your help."

She crossed her arms, looking out the window. "I will not be manipulated into doing your bidding."

"You're right. I suppose I was tense about the summons. I had not expected it. And certainly not now when I need to be working on Beaumont's defense." He worried the rim of his hat with his fingers.

She sat up, alarmed. "What do you expect will happen?"

"I cannot ignore the summons."

"Of course not."

"So I can only hope to resolve whatever the matter is at Windsor as quickly as possible, then return to London and finish the job for you."

Anxiety furrowed her brow.

"Don't worry, Lillian, I will not desert Beaumont."

"But what if you have no choice?" Her voice had risen.

"I won't let that happen. If things turn south, then I can always try to get a postponement of the trial."

"Dagwood won't give it."

"He might, if the circumstances were compelling. We just have to wait and see what's to greet us at Windsor. Then try to deal with it as expeditiously as possible."

She swallowed. "What can I do to help?"

That she was able to see past her anger so quickly and focus on what needed to be done amazed him. Lillian was a remarkably intuitive lady, and her practicality would have impressed even Dunn.

"You can help me traverse the political waters of Windsor more quickly . . . ," he offered.

"You are assuming that I won't be tossed out on my cheeky bottom."

"If there is a true emergency, then that's unlikely to happen."

"You don't know royalty."

"Exactly. Which is why I could really use your help."

"I don't think that I'm going to do you one bit of good."

"But you will accompany me?"

"I don't see that we have an alternative. Dillon is counting on us."

He thanked his lucky stars that she was so pragmatic.

They rode along in silence, the sway of the carriage bringing Nick a sense of calm he would never have dreamed of when going to Windsor on a job. Perhaps it was having Lillian along with him. He might be headed into trouble, but he had a capable ally on his side. Now if he could only keep his hands off her. She could not help how she looked, how she moved, how she drew him like a bear to sweet berries. But he refused to be tempted. A promise made was a promise kept.

"I have always wanted to see Windsor," she commented, staring out the window at the countryside flashing by. "I have only seen renderings."

Leave it to Lillian to try to put a sunny face on a tense situation.

"Perhaps you will meet Queen Charlotte," he offered.

"Heaven forbid! I am not dressed for court. This is hardly acceptable attire—"

"Don't worry, Lillian. All will be well. I promise."

Her eyes flashed, and she settled back in the seat. "Don't make promises you cannot keep, Nick."

He swallowed.

They rode the rest of the way in silence, and from opposite sides of the coach.

Lillian could not help herself; as the carriage rolled down the long drive, she almost hung out the window for a better view of the magnificent gray stone castle. With its formidable walls sitting up high on a hill above the Thames, it rightly took her breath away. It was an imposing patchwork of both rounded and square towers, narrow windows and tall walls. But the forbidding quality of the buildings was softened by the green lawns rolling alongside the carriage, the thick emerald forests flashing by and the hundreds of flowers in all shades of red, orange, gold and purple spattered on the grounds. Despite the nervous butterflies swarming in her middle, she could not help but appreciate the amazing mixture of man's progress amid nature's plenty.

Spotting the King's colors flying in the cloudless sky, Lillian felt a rush of pride for her homeland. In the opposite seat, Nick seemed confident but preoccupied, obviously realizing the enormity of his task. Lillian had had no idea that he was on retainer to the queen. The prospect was daunting and filled with enormous opportunity. If Nick was successful, his enquiry agency would receive a great sponsor. But if he failed . . . well, she did not wish to consider the consequences. Whatever the outcome, it had to come quickly, for Dillon's sake.

The carriage lurched to a halt, the door swung open and a stool was set.

Nick jumped out and offered his hand.

Stepping out, she gripped it tightly, anxiety making her mouth dry as dust.

A servant of middle years with wispy gray hair and a lanky frame rushed forward to greet them. "Thank the heavens you're finally here! But who is this?"

"Lady Janus will be assisting me," Nick replied, trying to instill some steel into his voice. For all of his seeming confidence in the carriage, he was nervous as hell for dragging her along with him. But he was not about to abandon his obligations, even for the queen of England.

"Well, this way, this way." The servant rushed agitatedly before them, twittering like a nervous bird might. "Come, come."

They followed the man at a brisk pace, and Nick was glad for the opportunity to loosen his legs from the long ride. He felt as if every muscle was stretched taut. Lillian looked up at him and smiled, but it was a tight, tense motion. A small crease marred her lovely brow, and her lush lips were pinched. He knew that she was apprehensive about their reception, and so was he.

They were led down a long hallway capped by high, ornately carved ceilings. The hall smelled of wax and wool, and slightly fresh, as if recently aired. Ornate gilded frames held portraits of elaborately attired men in battles, hunting on horseback and formal portraits. Nick did not dare dawdle, as the servant was charging down the hall at a breakneck pace, though he didn't walk too briskly either, fearing he'd trip on the thick, red-and-gold tasseled carpets and fall flat on his arse.

The servant opened a door and ushered them into a dark, wood-paneled study. In the center of the room was a large brown desk, surrounded by round-backed walnut chairs. The odor of wax, ink and parchment permeated the room. It seemed both a work chamber and meeting space.

"Mr. Redford. Lady Janus," the servant called, then after one last twitter, spun on his heel and left the room.

Lillian looked at Nick, her brow raised in question. The room was empty. Then a paneled door opened, and a stout, gray-haired man in a fine purple woolen coat with ivory ruffles jutting out of the sleeves stepped into the chamber. "Redford!" he bellowed.

Nick stepped forward, nodding. "At your service, sir."

"It's about time." He had wide eyes, a flat nose and loose jowls, reminding Lillian of a bulldog. Raising his hand to his nose, the man sniffed a pinch of snuff. Whipping a large square white cloth from his pocket, he blew a ferocious sneeze into the bandanna. Sniffling, he asked, "And who is this lovely lady?"

Lillian curtseyed.

"May I introduce Baroness Janus," Nick announced.

He bowed stiffly. "Daniel Hogan, Secretary and Comptroller, my lady."

"Your messenger indicated a great emergency, sir. How can I be of service?"

The man sighed. "Dreadful business. Dreadful business indeed." He sniffed. "Lancelot's gone missing."

"Lancelot?"

"The queen's favorite."

"The queen's favorite what?"

"Pug."

Nick felt his brows rise to his hairline. "You call a missing dog an emergency?"

"How terrible," Lillian interjected, shooting him a scolding glance. "Her Majesty treasures her pug dogs as if they were her own family."

Hogan scowled. "She is beside herself with worry."

Nick wanted to shout at the absurdity of being dragged away from a murder investigation for a runaway dog, but instead he bit out, "How long has he been missing?"

"Just over five hours."

"I assume a search is underway."

"All of the footmen and grooms have already begun looking for him."

"Where was the . . . Lancelot last seen?"

"Near the path in the garden, by the river."

Nick suddenly realized that this could truly be an urgent situation. "And that path leads to where?"

"The village."

"Which has been searched."

"Yes."

"Is there any chance that the dog was stolen?"

"Kidnapped, you mean?"

"Yes."

"That is my fear. Which is why I sent for you."

"The queen—"

"—agreed that it was the best course. Anything to find Lancelot, you see—"

"Mr. Hogan!" a steely voice shrieked from the hallway.

Hogan stiffened, and Lillian peeked up at Nick, trepidation in her blue gaze.

"Mr. Redford has arrived, ma'am!" Hogan bellowed, swiping a hand across his brow.

"Thank the heavens!"

Queen Charlotte of England glided into the room with a gaggle of servants on her trail.

Chapter 19

❧❧❧

Queen Charlotte was just as Nick remembered: short, tea-skinned, with fine, brown hair heavily streaked with gray piled high on her head, and small, darkly piercing eyes. She carried herself with a refined, delicate air, belying a tenacious intensity.

Lillian dropped to the floor in a curtsey; her head bent low to the ground.

Nick bowed deeply.

"Mr. Redford," the queen cried. "My darling Lancelot has gone missing!"

"I am at your service, Your Majesty."

"You must find him."

"I will find Lancelot." He felt the pledge burn through him and realized that he meant every word.

"Excellent." Spying Lillian, the queen's beady eyes narrowed. "Who is this?"

Nick waved his hand, trying for courtliness.

"May I present Baroness Janus. She heard the terrible news and hoped to assist in the search."

The queen huffed.

Nick endeavored to explain, "Lady Janus and I were both visiting the Marquis of Beaumont at Newgate Prison when—"

"Why?" the queen interjected. "The man is a criminal."

"No court has proven him so. He awaits trial."

"Are you committed to Beaumont?" Her tone was harsh and her eyes shrewd. "I must know this instant."

"The only thing that Mr. Redford is committed to," Lillian answered from her position low on the floor, "is to finding your precious pug."

The queen's eyes were calculating. "What business is this of yours?"

"When your servant arrived with news of your situation," Nick answered quickly, suppressing a slight flash of anger that the queen was targeting Lillian so, "I was without a means of transportation, ma'am. Lady Janus graciously offered her coach so that I might arrive here promptly. I am ready and eager to help."

"You wish to help too, Lady Janus?" The queen's tone carried a hint of challenge.

"As the rest of my family has always been, I am humbly at your service, ma'am," Lillian stated. "It would be my privilege to assist in any way that I can during this terrible tragedy."

The air fairly crackled with tension as the queen studied the top of Lillian's head. Nick held his breath, and it felt like everyone in the room did as well.

Finally, Her Majesty stepped closer. "Aren't you Baron Janus's granddaughter?"

"Yes, ma'am."

She harrumphed again. "Sinclair was a good man."

"Yes, ma'am."

"And what makes you such an authority on this situation that you *presume* that you can be of assistance, Lady Janus?" Her Majesty intoned, scowling down at Lillian.

Nick feared that he had really mucked things up this time.

"I am not an authority of any kind, Your Majesty." Someone in the room hissed, but Lillian fearlessly pressed on, "Yet my pets are most beloved to me. When one of my dear charges is in need, helpless, unable to fend for himself, then I will do anything in my power to see him well. It breaks my heart to hear of your Lancelot in such peril."

The queen's eyes widened at the word *peril*, and Nick could see her attitude toward Lillian soften. "Sinclair was a good man," she murmured.

"Yes, ma'am."

"Gone how long now?"

"Just over two years, ma'am."

After a long moment, the queen sniffed. "Very well, you may stay. But do not get underfoot."

Lillian slowly rose with her head still bowed, not meeting anyone's eyes. "Thank you, Your Majesty."

The queen turned to Nick with a swoosh of her ivory lace skirts. "Find my Lancelot, Redford. Find him at once!" She turned, sending the servants scurrying out of her path.

Before she could leave, Nick rushed on, "Ma'am, I

will need maps of the grounds for an organized search. I must speak to the servants in charge of the dogs, and specifically those on hand at the time of the loss. Do you have any paintings of Lancelot that I can view?"

Hushed silence filled the chamber. He had dared to speak to the queen without being addressed first, but he had been unwilling to miss this opportunity.

The queen's head rotated slowly, her dark eyes fixing on him with ruthless scrutiny. Raising a thin, arched brow, she declared, "Finally someone with a brain in his head!" She peered past Nick's shoulder. "Mr. Hogan, show Mr. Redford my portrait with Lancelot and Daisy. Then get him whomever and whatever he requires."

"Yes, ma'am," Hogan bellowed.

Eyeing Nick shrewdly, the queen nodded. "Bring Lancelot back to me, Mr. Redford, and you will be well rewarded." Turning, she swept from the room, her entourage following quickly at her skirts.

Nick let out the breath he had been holding, and he almost swayed with relief. "Whew."

Hogan frowned at him, but Lillian sent him a smile of encouragement and stepped near.

"Where do you wish to start, Mr. Redford?" Hogan asked.

"First find the servants who were in charge at the time Lancelot was lost. Then all of the servants who care for the dogs. In the meantime, please procure a map of the grounds for me."

"Anything else?" Hogan sent Lillian a look that indicated that he was willing to humor Nick, for the moment.

"I would like to view that painting with the dog in it."

"Certainly, sir. I will have a word with the steward about the maps, and then I will bring you to the Master of the Hounds, Mr. Glen." Nodding to Lillian with a mischievous smile, he left the room.

Lillian let out a soft exhalation of air.

"So we were not tossed out on our cheeky bottoms," he attempted to jest.

"Poor Lancelot. Over five hours. What if he is cold, hungry? Thirsty?"

"The weather is mild, he can forage for food and there's plenty of standing water around to keep him hydrated. I'm more concerned about dangers of the two-legged variety."

"You think that he was actually kidnapped?" she exclaimed, obviously aghast.

"It's the clearest reason why he's been gone for so long without anyone seeing him."

"I cannot fathom anyone stooping so low."

"That's because you are not an immoral person."

"Many of the ton would disagree," she muttered, obviously trying to make light.

"I made that mistake once, too, but now I know better. You're not immoral, just tenacious. A quality that I admire in others almost as much as I do in myself."

Slowly, her lush lips lifted at the corners, and he was glad to see her smile. She was at her most beautiful when she smiled.

Hogan stepped back into the room. "If this is an instance of kidnapping, Mr. Redford, how do you propose to ferret out the traitors?"

Nick turned to the comptroller. "I take for granted that everyone is guilty until they prove me otherwise."

Hogan scowled, nodding. "Then we begin. If you will follow me?"

Silently, they moved out into the hallway and began their search.

"So you are saying that those two men kidnapped Lancelot, Mr. Glen?" Nick demanded, leaning over the rust-haired servant.

"I didn't say that, Mr. Redford. All I said was that they were hanging about and I thought it was odd, Mr. Redford, sir." Poor Mr. Glen seemed a pitiful specimen compared to the virile investigator. He was weedy, with flapping jowls, pasty skin and hunched shoulders. His brown eyes darted around the room as if seeking rescue from Nick's inquiry.

"What was odd about it?"

"Just that it's not a well-used path."

"So what reason would they have to be there, Mr. Glen?"

"Don't know, sir, which is why I thought it was odd." His pasty cheeks shook with agitation.

Lillian watched from her chair in the corner and had to admit that she was impressed with Nick's questioning skills. He managed to explore every angle for information, going back again and again to the areas where he was dissatisfied with the answers. Thus far, Mr. Glen was providing little enough to satisfy. His assistant, Wilson, seemed more eager to please but also had little helpful knowledge.

Nick turned again to the smaller servant, a youth of about seventeen with a freckled face and brownish hair. "Did you see these men, Wilson?"

"No, sir," the lad replied. "I was on the other side of the big bushes. But Mr. Glen told me about them right away. Said it made him wonder what they were about."

"Do you take the dogs to this vicinity often?"

Wilson nodded. "Yes, sir. Most days. The dogs like to run in the tall bushes."

Since Nick had given her free reign, Lillian interposed, "That must require quite a bit of brushing."

"Indeed, my lady," Wilson replied. "We have a nasty time getting the knots out. It feels like it takes forever, but Her Majesty don't like any knots in her dogs' coats, so we take special care."

"And Lancelot has taken off in these bushes before, you say?" Nick asked.

"Quite a few times, sir," Glen answered.

"Then why do you return there?"

Wilson shrugged. "The dogs like it there. And we always find them. It might take a bit a time, but we did . . ." The poor man swallowed, and a lock of carroty hair dropped onto his forehead. He swiped it away with a white gloved hand and grimaced. ". . . before today, that is."

"Did you always hold this post in the household, Mr. Glen?" Nick asked.

Glen straightened. "I had been a Gentleman Usher of Privy Chamber, but Her Majesty removed me to my current post."

Lillian would have supposed that this was a promotion of sorts; she knew that she certainly would have preferred handling the dogs.

"Tell me what you recall about the faces of the men on the cart, Mr. Glen."

"I barely saw them."

"Think hard."

The man scrunched up his thin face and stuck his tongue into the corner of his mouth. "Well, perhaps the first man had brown hair."

"Brown hair? That's it?" Nick retorted.

"Maybe they both did?"

"Are you asking me or telling me?" Nick turned away from the man, seemingly in disgust, and looked at Lillian. She shrugged, unable to aid him. The pitiable servants seemed distraught over losing Lancelot and likewise terrified of the consequences that would befall them. And well they should be. The queen's distress trickled down to every member of the household save for one, and that was His Majesty, King George. According to Hogan, the king resided on the opposite side of the residence from the queen and was being kept well away from the hubbub. No one wanted to further disturb the already unsettled king.

Nick spun on his heel, unleashing yet another question on poor Mr. Glen. "You saw two strange men but did not report it. You lost Lancelot on your watch—"

Wilson puffed up, defensive. "He told me about it, sir, and we were to report it as soon as we returned."

"But Lancelot had been gone by then."

The lad bowed his head and a lock of brown hair fell over his eyes. "Yes, sir."

Hogan charged into the room. "Mr. Redford! The most terrible turn of events!" he bellowed, waving a white piece of foolscap in the air.

Nick strode over to him. "What is it?"

"They demand two thousand guineas for the safe return of the dog! If not, they will kill him!" Cries of shock and disbelief rang in the air.

"Let me see that." Nick grabbed the note and scanned it quickly.

Lillian stood, alarm shooting through her.

"Who delivered this?"

"A lad," Hogan replied.

"Where is he?"

"Gone. Handed it to one of the gardeners and told him to deliver it to the queen, then ran off."

The muscle in Nick's jaw worked, and Lillian just knew that he would have given a lot to have questioned that boy. Still, he maintained his composure. "Perhaps the gardener can describe the lad to the local vicar and we will see if he can recognize the boy."

"Very well, sir." Hogan swiped a gloved hand across his sweaty brow, visibly distressed. "I suppose Her Majesty must be told."

"How do you believe she will react?" Nick asked.

Hogan's face contorted. "Not very well, I'm afraid."

Nick paced the room, his broad shoulders stiff with tension. The servants hovering on the outskirts of the chamber twittered with outrage.

Lillian rose and met Nick in the center of the room. "This is dreadful," she whispered.

He nodded. "Still, word is out about the missing Lancelot . . . I must consider the possibility that someone sent the note knowing that Lancelot was missing so they might profit from this terrible situation."

"And that they do not have him?"

He scratched his chin. "Although it is doubtful, we cannot afford to make any assumptions in this matter."

Hogan hastened over, mopping his sweat-filmed head with a handkerchief. "I had best go inform Her Majesty."

Nick shook his head. "It's my case. I will inform Her Majesty of this dreadful development."

Lillian blinked. Nick had just offered to place himself in the eye of the storm.

Hogan straightened. Staring at Nick a thoughtful moment, he said, "Dunn always said you had a backbone of steel."

So that was how Nick got the post with the queen.

Nick shifted his shoulders, as if uncomfortable with the compliment. "I take responsibility when it's due, and credit just as well." Turning back to Mr. Glen, he asked, "One more question, Mr. Glen. Who knew that Lancelot was the queen's favorite?"

The man blinked and sputtered, "Well, everyone, I suppose."

Nick harrumphed.

Wilson stepped forward. "But this means that it ain't our fault."

"Who said that it was your fault?" Nick turned.

"Well, I was worried, sir. That people would think that we had something to do with it, since we was the ones caring for Lancelot when it all happened." The lad's freckled cheeks tinged pink. "And now you know we had nothing to do with it since we were here and couldn't have sent the letter demanding the money. And everyone can see that we don't have Lancelot." He turned to Mr. Glen, grinning happily. "We're cleared. It weren't our fault, and now everyone knows it. Those men took Lancelot!"

Glen's shoulders sagged. "Why you're right, my boy. This proves it! We're in the clear." The man's willowy frame drooped as he whispered, "Thank the heavens. But poor Lancy . . ." He looked around the room, as if realizing that others had heard him. He shrugged sheepishly. "I always call him Lancy. The poor love is in the hands of thieves. Maybe murderers! Lancy!" The man slumped to the floor in a puddle of tears. Several servants rushed over to give aid.

The servants at the edges of the room grumbled with growing agitation. The words *kidnapped* and *stolen* and *two thousand guineas* shot through the angst-ridden air.

"I need everyone to remain on the grounds," Nick announced, eyeing the assembly. "Danger lurks. I do not want anyone to leave the grounds unless they have my permission."

The noise in the room thickened into a chorus of distress.

Nick sent a curt nod to Lillian and strode with Hogan out the door.

Lillian whispered a parting prayer of good luck as she watched his broad back recede.

Feeling impotent, Lillian turned, seeing where she might be useful.

Mr. Glen was sitting up, and someone had brought him a glass of water. He tried lifting the glass to his lips but grimaced with pain.

Lillian stepped near. "Are you all right, Mr. Glen?"

"Kidnappers stealing poor Lancy! The blackguards! What will happen now?"

"I don't know, Mr. Glen. I suppose that Mr. Redford will help figure it out."

"Will they pay? Will we ever see Lancy again?"

"Two thousand guineas?" Wilson scoffed, then shrugged sheepishly. "I mean, it's a lot of blunt for a dog."

"This is Lancelot we're talking about." Glen shook his head. "Her Majesty's favorite. Oh, if only I'd have been closer. If only I'd have taken better care. . . ."

"You did what you could, Mr. Glen." Wilson nodded sagely. He turned to Lillian. "Mr. Glen ran himself ragged looking for Lancelot. Cut himself up but good in the bushes, bloodied his best uniform. But he would not give up. No, ma'am."

"You serve your queen well, Mr. Glen."

"We all try to do our jobs, my lady," he muttered, his pallid cheeks flushing pink.

Seeing that the man was recovered, Lillian faced the lad. "Wilson, would you be so kind as to take me to see your charges?"

Wilson looked to Glen, who nodded.

The lad beamed. "Certainly, my lady. They've been locked up since this morning and would be glad for the company."

So would Lillian, for she suspected that it would be many hours before she would be making her way back home. She just hoped that it would be with good tidings.

Chapter 20

A breeze drifted in through the open bedchamber windows, carrying with it the faint scent of honeysuckle. Staring out at the moonless night, Lillian sighed and leaned back in the gilded beech chair. She knew that she would not be able to sleep this night, no matter how comfortable the chambers that Hogan had procured for her. She was in one of the many stately bedrooms in Windsor Castle, and she could not quite believe that she was residing under the same roof as royalty, if only for one night.

King George of England was somewhere in this great building, sight unseen but very present. Had he finally learned about this abominable affair? If he'd been told, what had he understood? Rumors abounded about his madness. Lillian could not imagine how his family dealt with the grief of watching him drift into lunacy.

She stared out the window and bemoaned the black sky, nary even a star appearing on this moonless night. Poor Lancelot was out there somewhere, and so were his hopeful rescuers. She leaned forward and, yes, she could still see the golden torches bobbing up and down as people continued the search. Thus far, the hunt seemed only to have confirmed that Lancelot was indeed gone, his whereabouts unknown.

"The depraved blackguards," she muttered, wondering at humankind's capacity for evil. Recently, she had encountered a scheming murderer, and now fiends who kidnapped beloved pets. Was the entire world turning into another Sodom?

The queen must be beside herself with worry being the target of such malicious sport.

" 'Uneasy lies the head that wears a crown,' " she quoted her favorite bard. Could even Shakespeare have invented such devilry?

She worried for the poor staff, who would suffer for their failings in this travesty. Likewise, she agonized over Nick's future and that of his burgeoning agency of enquiry. She was beginning to comprehend what this enterprise meant to him. He lived for the puzzle and for the chase. He lived for justice and seeing evil punished. He had found his raison d'être and it fit him to a tee. But unless he came up with some answers for the queen, and soon, his business would be routed by a death blow from which it might not recover.

And all the while Dillon was in prison for a crime he did not commit, and the clock ticked toward his doom. The only thing keeping her chin up was her confidence in Nick. If anyone could see through this madness, it would be he.

Someone tapped gently on her door.

Pulling the borrowed wrapper closer around her, she stood and tiptoed to the rosewood-paneled entry. "Yes?"

"It's Nick, open up."

She bit her lip, apprehensive about allowing him into her bedroom, at Windsor Castle, of all places. But she was desperate for information.

"Oh, botheration," she muttered, turning the brass key in the lock.

Nick swiftly slipped into the room.

Lillian took one glance down the empty hallway, sent off a prayer that this wasn't pure folly and closed the door with a firm thud.

He looked wretchedly tired. His clothes were disheveled, dark fuzz grazed his jaw and his cocoa eyes were red rimmed and shadowed. His hat was in his hand, and his tousled black hair looked as if he had been raking his fingers through it all day. He probably had.

"What news?" she begged.

Mutely, he shook his head.

Her spirits sank even further. "Why are you not out there?" she asked, gesturing to the open window.

"What's the point?" he asked bitterly, tossing his hat onto a chair. "Colonel Thompson is here."

"Who?

"From Horseguards. Claims this is a matter for the army."

"A kidnapped pet requires an army?" she cried, aghast.

"It does when it's the queen's dog." His tone was sardonic.

"It's a damnable power shuffle."

He crossed his arms and fell back against the

wall, sulking. "I know, and there's not a bloody thing I can do about it."

"Don't say that."

His face was partially shadowed in the glow of the single candle by her bedside, but his features were a mask of defeat. "But it's true. There's naught I can do."

"You can catch the dastards who kidnapped Lancelot and send Thompson back to Horseguards with his tail between his legs."

Their eyes met and he smiled, just barely.

She suddenly realized her inadvertent pun on canines. "You know what I meant," she added, feeling absurd.

"They're going to pay the ransom."

Her hands clenched. "Is there nothing we can do?"

Pushing away from the wall, he swept past her and stood before the tall open windows. "Did you not hear me? I'm off. Dismissed. If it weren't for Hogan worrying about rousing you in the middle of the night, they would have me gone by now."

"We can look for more clues, follow the money. The kidnappers must come to retrieve it—"

"It's to be placed in a basket and sent downstream," he interrupted. "Thompson plans to follow it and catch the buggers then."

"But you can go as well . . ." she offered hopefully.

"You seem to think that I have a choice in the matter." Running his hand through his mussed hair, he sighed. "It's for the best, anyway. We have just over a week until Beaumont's trial. If I can't help here, I might as well go back to London and do some good there."

Lillian felt torn by her loyalties. She believed that Nick could help the queen. And the future of his enquiry business might be in jeopardy. But Dillon needed him too; Dagwood and Lord Langham were pressing hard for prosecution.

She chewed her lip. "Do you think the queen could get us a postponement on Dillon's trial?"

"You were the one who seemed intent on her not knowing that I was working for Beaumont."

"I know," she sighed. "Nobility do not like sharing. The queen would not have been happy if she'd felt that your allegiance and efforts were divided."

"And now?"

She pressed her hands to her eyes. "I do not believe that we have a choice. Dillon needs you. But so does our queen. I know that you can catch these kidnappers."

"I appreciate your faith in me, Lillian. But a dog, royal or no, does not equate to a man's life."

"Do you think Thompson will capture them?"

"The stream forks in many places. It'll be impossible to watch every access to the water. These men are probably locals and know every nook and cranny of that river."

"I hate to see those fiends win," she grumbled, fisting her hands.

His face softened. "Watch out, Lillian. You might just grow a righteous streak."

"I cannot stomach all the villainy. It makes me wonder about mankind's future."

"Dunn always said not to let a few bad apples turn you against cider."

She wrapped her arms around herself, knowing he was right but feeling gloomy nonetheless. "We've been dealing with a murderer, and now this. How can you be so optimistic?"

He walked over to the window and stared out at

the black night. The wind drifted in, gently lifting a coil of dark hair off his forehead. "I've felt the pain man can inflict," he said, his tone bleak. "Yet I've experienced great kindness as well. It's a mixed batch, but not all bad."

"How . . . how have you experienced pain?" she asked haltingly. She was curious about his past, so different from her own. For all of her troubles with Kane, Lillian had always had a home, loving grandparents, food on the table. She could not imagine the world that Nick grew up in.

"Dunn was not always the headmaster of Andersen Hall."

Funereal silence filled the chamber. She waited for more, afraid to press, yet afraid not to ask. "Can you tell me?"

He shrugged, staring off into the dark night. "Festus had been a sergeant major in the army. He believed that the same principles that applied to infantrymen would work just as well with small children."

She swallowed. "You mean discipline?"

"Discipline, duties, marching. Lord, how we marched. Some days, morning, noon and night. In the rain, in the snow. Heaven help us if we faltered, if we . . . cried."

"Why would he insist on such harsh training? You were children, for heaven's sake."

"If we were occupied, then we could not get into mischief. Festus liked order." Nick's jaw clenched. "Children by nature are not exactly an orderly lot."

"Didn't anyone know of this foul treatment?"

"We were orphans," he scoffed. "Most people were just thankful that we weren't picking their pockets or stealing their produce. Luckily for me, I was in the nursery for most of his tenure. Others were not as fortunate."

Chills raised the hairs on her skin. "What happened?"

"Timothy Dobbins was not one for taking orders. He pushed Festus as far as he could, in every way that he could manage. At the end of his rope, Festus decided to teach Timmy a lesson. Flogging and thirteen-year-old boys don't mix."

"Oh, my God."

"Timmy died, and the trustees of the orphanage finally stepped in."

"They retained Dunn?"

"The trustees made a couple more mistakes before finally bringing Dunn on board. It took us some time to realize how different things were going to be for us."

"And matters improved?"

"Worlds better. But it was too late for many. Too late for Timmy Dobbins."

A quiver rippled through her, and she marveled that he'd managed to come out as whole as he was.

His body was stiff with tension, his face haggard with anguish. He seemed so bleak, so alone. Her heart went out to him.

She walked over and slipped her hand into his. He did not look her way or say anything, but his fingers curled around hers, cupping her hand in warmth.

"I am so sorry," she whispered.

"There's no point in being sorry. Just in facing forward, moving on and making things better. That's why I cannot let Dunn's legacy die. We cannot let Andersen Hall close."

"Is that a possibility?"

"So they tell me. . . . Perhaps I am not meant to run an enquiry agency, Lillian? Perhaps this is a sign."

"I have never seen someone so perfectly suited to their profession."

"But what if I am meant to do more worthwhile, nobler things?"

"Saving an innocent man from the hangman's noose is not noble? Punishing Lady Langham's killer is not righteous? Helping protect the queen from villainy is not worthwhile?" Resting her cheek on his arm, she added, "I do not think that Dunn would have you give up so easily."

He sighed. "He would have liked you."

"But would he have agreed with me?"

He seemed to consider it a long moment. "Yes, I believe he would. Dunn always said to follow your heart, but be certain your skills were the ones needed to do it."

"Wise man."

The breeze drifted in, carrying with it the scent of honeysuckle. The gentle sounds of the night filled the chamber and brought a modicum of peace.

She did not know how long they stood there, side by side, giving comfort with a touch. His nearness brought the titillating warmth that he stirred inside her, but it was tinged with tenderness. He was in pain, and she felt his grief as if it were her own. For the moment, the connection between them was less about passion than compassion.

Slowly he released her hand and ran his hand through his hair. "I should not have come to your bedroom, I just . . ."

"I'm glad you came," she soothed. "I wanted to know what was happening."

"I wish I had better news."

"You must be exhausted. Have you had any dinner?"

He shook his head.

She gently propelled him over to the small table and urged him into a chair. Pushing the tray toward him, she poured a goblet of wine.

"That's your dinner," he argued halfheartedly.

"They gave me enough for an army—but I will not share it with the overambitious Colonel Thompson, only you."

"I feel honored," he rejoined with teasing sincerity. She was glad to see the tightness in his face lighten a bit.

"Try the veal, it is delicious," she added, handing him the goblet of wine.

She sat on the chair across from him and watched as he dug into the food. His movements as he ate were labored, but they soon quickened. He finished one plate and then another, his face growing more animated with each serving. The hunch slowly disappeared from his shoulders, and his features lost some of their tautness.

Sipping from his glass, he sighed. "Thank you, Lillian. I did not know how hungry I was. Tell me something good," he asked, inclining in the chair. "How have you occupied yourself this afternoon?"

"Wilson took me to visit the dogs."

"Not Mr. Glen?"

"Mr. Glen was in a sorry state. He injured himself while looking for Lancelot, and he was understandably upset."

Nick tilted his head. "What kind of injury?"

"He hurt his hands in the bushes searching for the dog. Bloodied his uniform badly."

"Really," he remarked, leaning forward. His dark gaze glittered with interest. "Did you see the wound?"

"No, he wore gloves."

His eyes narrowed, and he appeared thoughtful.

"What is so remarkable about Mr. Glen's injury?" she asked. Images of a small bloodied dog flashed in her mind. "Do you think that Lancelot was hurt in the same manner and that the kidnappers are simply trying to take advantage? That they do not have Lancelot at all?"

"We have combed the area thoroughly and would have found Lancelot even if he could not come to us. There was no blood found. Which makes me believe that Lancelot was taken."

"And is alive?"

"Yes."

She breathed a sigh of relief.

After a moment, he stood, his energies apparently restored. "I must go."

"Where are you off to?"

"I want to check on a thing or two."

"About Lancelot?" she asked hopefully.

"Yes, Lillian, about Lancelot."

She jumped up. "I knew that you wouldn't give up!"

"I will endeavor to satisfy your confidence in me." His tone was teasing.

"All you needed was a moment's rest and some fortification."

"Sincerely, I don't know what I ever did to deserve such faith, but I will not let you down."

"You mean the queen."

"Her too."

She beamed, feeling an unexpected rush of pride. "What changed your mind?"

"You reminded me that one person *can* make a difference."

Stepping around the table, he gripped her shoulders, pulled her close and set his smooth lips to hers. She was so shocked that she just stood still as his soft mouth pressed firmly against hers. Slowly her lids lowered and she drifted into the kiss, feeling like a willow swaying in a warm breeze.

He tasted of wine and veal, and the faint scent of almond enveloped her. He was solid as an oak, and she needed that support, for her knees had turned to jelly and she knew that if he released her, she would fall. But she knew without doubt that he would not let her tumble. So she melted into him, loving his mouth with a tenderness that bespoke her burgeoning feelings for this remarkable man.

Lifting his head, he murmured, "I promised myself that I wouldn't do that."

"Do what?" she whispered, her eyes hooded, her mouth lush with his kiss. This woman moved him, he realized. She was different from any other woman he had known. With those sparkling azure eyes and the melodic voice that chimed in his soul. She was like a cloud of cream and lace in her night rail, causing a man to imagine the curves being hugged by that silkily thin fabric. He yearned to rake his hands through her strawberry blond hair, disrupting her coiffure of curls and making her sigh with pleasure. But he had sworn to protect her, not exploit her.

"Give in to temptation," he murmured as he

pulled away, keeping his hands cupped on those silky shoulders.

"Where's the harm?"

"I swore to keep my hands off you, Lillian. It's not right that I take advantage."

"What if I want you to?" Her voice was husky, and he could see the desire pooling in her blue gaze.

It took every ounce of his self-control to stop him from taking her right then and there. In Windsor, no less. "Now you might want to, but how will you come to feel after?" Pressing a kiss to her forehead, he murmured, "You might come to regret it, and that I could not endure."

Leaning into his broad chest, she sighed. "I wish you were a bit less honorable, Nicholas Redford. But I suppose it's like asking a leopard to change his spots."

"If only I could be the man that you see me to be."

Pushing him away, she chided, "Oh, go off and find Lancelot. Catch the wretched bastards, Nick, and give Colonel Thompson cause to regret ever coming to Windsor. Show him what you are made of."

His face softened. "Thank you, Lillian."

"For what?"

"For sending me back out there." Releasing her, he turned and quietly left the room.

Chapter 21

$\sim\!\!\!\infty\!\!\!\sim$

As the first rays of dawn filtered through the bedroom window, Lillian decided that she could wait no longer; she would venture out of her room and find out what was happening. She was anxious about what Nick was "checking on" and certain that if Lancelot was to be found, Nick was the man to do it. She splashed cold water on her face and performed her ministrations, apprehension making her movements quick but jerky. *Dear Lord*, she prayed, *let this turn out well*.

As she walked down the plush, red-and-gold carpeted corridor, she was not surprised to see many servants bustling about and to hear the quiet hum of a waking household. A sense of urgency filled the air, and Lillian felt it thrumming through her, propelling her toward Hogan's office.

She knocked lightly on the door.

"Come," he called, not looking up from the papers scattered on his desktop. He dipped his quill, blotted it and scribbled. Lillian slipped into the large chamber and waited a few feet before his great brown desk.

Hogan's hunter green coat was clean and pressed, and his shirt ruffles were perfectly folded. But his gray hair was mussed over his ears, and dark shadows banked his eyes. The creases flanking his lips seemed more delineated than the day before, as if they were now set in a permanent frown.

Dropping his quill, he looked up, surprised. He stood. "Good morning, Lady Janus. I trust your accommodations were acceptable?"

"Wonderful, sir. I just could not dally in my rooms knowing that Lancelot and his captors are still out there. Pray tell me, is there any news?"

He inhaled a deep breath, his broad shoulders rising and then dropping. "We will pay the ransom today, my lady. And we hope that then Lancelot will be returned to Her Majesty."

"You doubt that they will keep their word?"

"Once they have the money, they have no incentive to return the dog. I fear that they will grab their booty and take off to evade capture."

"Won't Colonel Thompson be able to catch them when they come to retrieve the money?"

His steely eyes narrowed, and she realized that she had just slipped about speaking with Nick during the night. She held her breath, wondering how he would deal with this indiscretion.

After a tense moment, he seemed to let it pass. "I do not believe that Thompson appreciates the difficulty in tracking anyone over such a spread of water."

"Then let Mr. Redford have a go at it, sir."

"You and Mr. Redford will be leaving this morning. His services are no longer required."

"But Lancelot has not been found. Why send off one of your best men?"

"I did Dunn a favor by giving Nick this job. You couldn't say no to the man once he had gotten his teeth sunk into an idea. But I never really thought that it would come to anything."

"But it was not charity. It was to the queen's benefit as well. And here you have the perfect opportunity to utilize Redford's talents."

He raised his hand, declaring, "Enough, Lady Janus. My decision is made."

Her spirits and her shoulders drooped. "Then we have failed."

"We all have."

"Hogan, I need your help!" Nick announced, charging into the room. He moved with alacrity, the exhaustion seemingly gone from his person. His clothing was still wrinkled and his hair was a bedraggled mess, but his cocoa-brown eyes flashed and his handsome features were fixed with determination. Lillian's heart thrilled; Nick was on the hunt and he was magnificent.

He bowed curtly to Lillian. "Good morning, my lady."

She nodded, her heart doing the special dance that it reserved especially for him.

Hogan scowled. "You have been dismissed, Mr. Redford. There is no more opportunity to change my mind. I have a small portion for you, but otherwise—"

"I don't care about the bloody fee, Hogan. I think I have a way to get Lancelot back."

Hogan's bushy brows knotted. "This is not some sort of weak attempt at saving your skin?"

"Do you want him back or not?" Nick stood stock-still, waiting. Lillian held her breath. She knew that tone; Nick thought he had the answer.

Hogan's face hardened, as if on the cusp of a negative decision.

"Mr. Hogan, please." Lillian stepped forward. "Please give him a chance. There's a reason Dunn recommended Mr. Redford especially for the job. Redford often sees what we fail to. Trust him."

"I have little time to waste on wild-goose chases—"

"Just a few minutes, sir," Nick pleaded. "I will show you."

"How?"

"Just follow me and bring along two burly servants. I will prove it to you."

Hogan held up one hand, fingers wide. "Five minutes, Redford. Not one second more."

"Good," she murmured under her breath, relieved. Now if only Nick could deliver on his word.

Nick turned to her. "I cannot allow you to join us, my lady."

"But why not?"

"Rogues still roam freely."

"But—"

"Trust me." He shook his head, insisting, "Wait for us here."

"Your five minutes are fading, Mr. Redford," Hogan interrupted.

"No, Lillian." With a final look of warning, Nick spun on his heel and headed out the door.

Hogan waved a hand. "My office is at your disposal, my lady." Then he, too, raced out the door.

* * *

Lillian stepped through the threshold, careful not to be seen. She understood that she should follow Nick's instructions, but somehow her feet managed to enter the hallway of their own accord. Part of her recognized that she bristled at being ordered about. But truly, she couldn't help it; her very fiber would not allow her to sit by idly while Nick's and Lancelot's futures hung in the balance.

Servants parted before Nick and stared after him in his wake. The air fairly crackled with urgency, and Lillian realized that her heart was beating rapidly with apprehension. She had no idea what Nick was up to and prayed that it was not folly. She had faith in him, yes, but this was the queen's favorite dog that had been abducted.

A servant scurried past and she spun around, pretending to be casually examining a tapestry. Turning, she peered out the long corridor as Nick, Hogan and two burly servants marched down the passage like a small army preparing for battle. She scuttled down the long hallway after them, her shoes silent on the thick carpets. If Nick turned around, she wondered if she would drop to the ground, a pillar of salt, Nick's wrath come down from the heavens to smite her. She stifled a mental giggle at the thought. Egad, she was as skittish as a fox.

Nick led them down the hall to the servants' staircase. Lillian tried telling herself that she had come far enough and would cease this fool's quest. But soon she found herself at the top of the stairs and eyeing the open doors of the room that Nick and Hogan had just entered.

Could she dare?

The large room had pale-colored walls and a

sundry of mismatched but expensive furniture placed throughout. It was the servants' salon, Lillian realized, with finer furnishings than were to be found in some of Society's London homes. She slipped inside, hoping to be unobtrusive near the wall by the door.

Two housemaids huddled in a far corner, but upon seeing Nick and his party, they immediately rose and drifted out. Mr. Glen's carrot-topped head could be seen cresting an armchair facing the hearth. Wilson stood before him, cap in his hand, his brown hair mussed and hanging in his eyes.

"I say . . ." Wilson sputtered.

Glen spun around in his seat and then stood. "I pray to the Lord you have news of our Lancelot?" Mr. Glen asked anxiously.

"Take off your gloves, Mr. Glen," Nick demanded.

"What?" he cried, his pale cheeks quacking with agitation.

"I wish to see your injuries."

"I don't understand," Glen cried, his eyes directed at Hogan.

"I insist you take off your gloves, Mr. Glen," Nick urged.

"Why?"

"Because I wish to see the injuries you claim to have gotten while searching the bushes for Lancelot."

"I must protest, sir," Glen implored Hogan. "I am hurt—"

"Do as he says, Mr. Glen," Hogan replied stonily.

Glen bristled. "You will take this . . . character's word—"

Nick stepped forward, menace in his every movement. "If you don't take off your gloves, then I will take them off for you."

"All right. All right. But I will not forget this indignity."

Wilson's eyes flew from Nick to Glen, to Hogan and back to Glen, uncertainty in his brown gaze.

With painstaking care, Glen slowly stripped off his gloves, exposing white bandages with bloodstains peeking through. Holding up his hands, he challenged, "Are you satisfied?"

"Take off the bindings," Nick ordered.

"Now see here," Glen sputtered.

"Off, or I'll rip them off."

Lillian was appalled at Nick's rough treatment of Glen. Could the poor servant truly be behind this terrible crime? She could hardly credit it; he seemed to cherish his charges, especially Lancelot.

Glen swallowed. Eyeing the men, he untied the knots on the bindings and slowly unwound the cloth. Long, bloody slashes fanned his hands, some deeper and redder than others.

Wilson's eyes widened, and his freckled face blanched.

"How did you get those injuries, Mr. Glen?" Nick demanded.

Glen's cheeks reddened, but he did not answer.

Nick pressed on, "I went out to where Lancelot was taken, and the only bushes there are rhododendrons, hardly the kind of bush to cut with such ferocity." Nick stepped closer. "I ask you again, Mr. Glen, how you got those injuries?"

Mr. Glen's willowy frame shuddered. "This proves nothing."

Wilson was shaking his head, his gaze disbelieving.

"What is it, Wilson?" Hogan asked.

Wilson's voice was hoarse. "Them's dog bites."

Hogan's face hardened. "Where is Lancelot, Glen?"

Glen shook his head back and forth. "This proves nothing."

"I asked at the village pub, and it did not take long to find out that you've got gambling debts, Mr. Glen. Much more than you can make working for Her Majesty for at least seven years. So for you, a quick fix might just be the ticket, eh?" Nick stepped around the armchair and grabbed Glen's arm, twisting it hard behind his back. "Where is Lancelot?"

"If you don't let me go, the queen'll never see her demmed dog again!" Glen screeched.

Lillian's mouth dropped open.

Nick jerked his arm higher. "Who has Lancelot?"

Glen's face contorted into a pained grimace, but he gritted his teeth. "Hurt me and the dog dies. You'll have to let me go."

Hogan clenched his hands. "You dastard. You'll hang for this!"

"You're going to let me go or the queen will never see her Lancelot." His eyes glittered with satisfaction. "The queen will not take the chance of losing Lancelot. She'll let me go."

"The queen has nothing to do with this," Nick growled. He swept his boot under Glen's legs, knocking the man flat on his back. Nick jerked his head, motioning for the two servants to assist. "Hold him down."

Lillian moved along the wall, unable to help herself. She *had* to witness this.

Nick grasped Glen's left hand while the two men held down the scrawny servant.

"You must let me go!" Glen shrieked. "The queen—"

"Shut up," Nick ordered, reaching down into his boot and pulling out a long, menacing dagger.

Lillian gasped.

Glen's eyes widened with terror.

"You're going to tell me where Lancelot is and who your accomplices are." Nick sliced the knife through the man's uniform cuff, exposing Glen's pasty white wrist.

Glen screamed, "But you can't!"

"I'm no gentleman. I follow any bloody code that pleases me. For the moment, I'm liking the Bedouin way of doing things: A thief loses his hand."

Nick slowly slid the knife into the crease at Glen's wrist. Bright red blood seeped out of the gash.

Glen screamed and his body jerked. The servants grunted, locking him down.

Lillian cringed, sickened, but she could not tear her eyes away.

"Hold still, Glen," Nick bit out. "The more you move, the more it will hurt."

"I'll tell you! I'll tell you!" Glen screamed, his eyes imploring Hogan. "Just get this madman away from me!"

Nick pressed the knife on the wound. "Where and who!"

"My sister's barn! Next to the mill! My sister and brother-in-law took the dog!" His body wracked with sobs. "Please stop!"

Nick gestured to Wilson. "Do you know his sister's barn?"

Wilson nodded, his freckled face flushed with anger.

Nick dropped the arm. "Take this worm to Hogan's office. No water. No food. No contact with anyone."

The men's faces were grim as they nodded.

Hogan pulled out a white handkerchief and blotted his sweaty brow. "Do exactly as Mr. Redford says."

Nick leaned over Glen, slowly wiping the bloodied knife on the quivering servant's uniform. "I'll be back, Glen. If you sent me on a fool's errand, I'll take out your tongue."

Glen's eyes rolled back in his head.

Nick turned, and Lillian tried to melt into the draperies. "Since you don't have the good graces to stay out of trouble, Lillian, you might as well come along where I can keep an eye on you."

Pursing her lips, she nodded and stepped forward, trying not to look as guilty as she felt.

"I didn't want you to witness that," he whispered sharply, offering his arm.

"I'm a big girl, Nick," she murmured.

"Not as big as you often think."

Even though it was well deserved, she was hurt by his rancor. "Nothing untoward happened."

"But it could have. I swear you'll have me gray with fright before the week's end."

"You're not afraid of anything," she countered.

"You have no earthly idea."

Chapter 22

❦

The neglected barn smelled dank with the scents of manure and old hay. Dust sprayed the air with the stomp of the servants' footsteps as Nick led the search. Servants rummaged through hay and pails and broken tools, crying out, "Lancelot! Lancelot!"

Silence greeted their calls.

The sunlight streaked into the barn through the loft's window above, casting the building into areas of illumination and shadow. The dust drifted up into the light like a grimy cloud.

Hogan stood with Lillian in the threshold, the morning's sun on their backs casting long silhouettes onto the earthen floor.

"I don't see him anywhere!" Wilson shrieked with anguish, gripping his cap in his hands.

Hogan patted his handkerchief across his clammy face. "Was the knave lying?"

Nick stopped, looked around and then dropped onto his knees, staring at a small hole.

Lillian would have stepped forward, but Hogan blocked her with an outstretched arm. "You might not want to see this, my lady."

"I need a shovel!" Nick commanded. "Now!"

Two servants raced out the door as Nick clawed at the dirt with his fingers. Wilson fell beside him, burrowing his hands into the area.

Fear welled up within her. Dear Lord, they had buried poor Lancelot? But how could he survive?

Lillian pressed her fist to her mouth, holding her breath.

The men arrived with shovels and Nick threw off his coat, grabbed one and rammed the shovel down, digging. Another servant dug just a foot away.

Lillian began to pray.

Nick's movements took on a precise quality as he carefully worked around a circular object. After a moment, he reached down and gently yanked it out. It was a long-necked ceramic water pitcher, the bottom broken out.

"What is that?" Hogan whispered to her.

Hope rose in her chest. "I'm not certain, but it could be a channel for air to get through." Her heart pounded, and she felt like her skin was splintering from anxiety.

Nick tossed it aside, lifted the shovel and started digging again. No one uttered a word; the only sounds were the spades hitting the earth and the huffs of the men as they worked. After many tense moments, a small thud boomed through the barn like quiet thunder. Everyone froze.

"Stop digging," Nick ordered. "We don't want it to break."

Using his fingers, he excavated around a square about the size of a small traveling chest. Lillian stepped closer for a better look, and Hogan drifted forward beside her.

A dirt-covered wooden box came into view.

Nick leaned over, sticking his eye into the hole. "Damn! I can't see a thing." He sat up. "Help me get this out. And be careful."

Gently, they lifted the box out of the ground and set it down. It was square, with a small hole in the top left corner. Nick peered inside the hole. Slowly, he reached his hand inside the opening, his shirt-sleeve bunching on the outside of the box. Everyone held their breath.

Relief washed over his features. "He's alive."

Wilson cried, "Hurrah!" The other servants cheered.

Tears burned the back of Lillian's eyes.

Pulling his arm out, Nick ripped at the wooden top. Half of it came off, nails spiking. Inside, a small, blond, long-haired dog lay curled in the corner, looking filthy and pitifully dejected. Two small cups sat empty beside him. The stench of dog feces filled the air.

"He'll need water," Wilson said as he reached for the dog, then froze. "May I, sir?"

Nick nodded. "Absolutely."

Nick looked up, and his eyes met Lillian's. The triumph filling his cocoa brown gaze made her heart swell, and she found herself blinking back tears.

"Dusty in here," Hogan murmured, wiping his handkerchief in the corner of his eye.

Nick turned to Wilson. "Give Lancelot a bath, Wilson, and then take him to the queen."

"I must interject, Mr. Redford." Hogan stepped forward.

Nick looked up.

"*You* shall be the one to take Lancelot to the queen."

Lillian thought her heart might burst through her chest, it was so filled with joy.

"But first, Mr. Redford, a quick bath and a change of clothes for you." Hogan smiled wide, his eyes glinting. "I shall have Colonel Thompson take Mr. Glen into custody and chase down his nasty relations. And I will ensure that Horseguards receives a full accounting of today's events."

Hours later, Nick enjoyed the ride back to London much more than the tense journey out of the city. He did not dwell on Lillian's heart-stopping kiss in the carriage. Today, the air smelled of spring and wildflowers, and for a moment Nick wondered at the pleasure of living in the country. But he pushed the thought aside. He would never leave London, it was in his blood.

"You were magnificent!" Lillian enthused for the third time in an hour. Her azure eyes sparkled like the ocean on a clear day, and her cream-colored cheeks were flushed a lovely shade of cherry. She looked particularly beautiful without all of those unnecessary face paints.

He could not help the grin from lifting his lips. "I had a little help."

She waved her hand in dismissal. "Did you hear what the queen said about you? She said that you were 'one of the most trustworthy men of the empire!' That you should be knighted for this!"

"She did seem pleased."

"Pleased? She was elated! Thrilled! Impressed beyond reckoning! And she well should have been! You were magnificent! Admit it!"

"We did a good job today."

"Ha!" she scoffed.

"The queen thanked you as well, Lillian." He might have given up if it had not been for her unshakable confidence in him. He did not know what he had ever done to deserve her faith, but he would be eternally grateful for it.

Looking back, he recognized his mistake. He had been too focused on the hunt, not seeing the full picture. Only with Lillian's insistence had he paused, and only with her information had he recognized his target. It was not accidental that she had been with him at Windsor; he considered it divine intervention. Moreover, his triumph seemed sweeter for having her to share it with.

Through the window the sun glistened on her hair, shining it reddish gold. Her blue eyes sparkling, her lush lips lifted and she smiled at him. He felt pulled into a sensual web of intimacy. What he would have given to be able to kiss those luscious lips once more. He had not meant to kiss her again last night, but it had been like fuel to his fire, giving him that final rush of confidence he'd needed to succeed.

Her lovely brow furrowed. "I'm just angry with myself for not asking the queen about postponing Dillon's trial. I had such stars in my eyes that when I finally realized it, I had lost my opportunity."

He pushed away all thoughts of honeyed kisses, reminded again of his charge. Lillian was in his care, needing his protection. He was not about to take advantage of that position. "Hogan will help, if we need it. But I'm hoping that we don't require the additional time."

"I think you're right about Sir Hogan. He would help if he could. He's a kind person and very grateful to you."

"Well, he certainly has taken a liking to you. I was frankly amazed that he followed your suggestion about promoting Wilson."

"Wilson is the perfect man for the job. Besides, Hogan will ensure that Wilson is properly supervised until he's ready to handle his duties on his own. I suspect those dogs might be kept under lock and key from now on. Under heavy guard. And," she added dryly, "I wouldn't be surprised if Colonel Thompson gets the posting after his aggressive lobbying to come to Windsor."

"It is a matter for the army, and all," he commented, his tone mockingly serious.

"What do you think, 'Lancelot's Lackeys' or 'Royal DogGuards?' "

They both laughed. To Nick, it was a relief and a joy to be able to have made it through this thorny tangle and to be laughing about it. He sent a prayer of thanks to Dunn for the opportunity, and another to the heavens for sending Lillian his way.

She inhaled and exhaled deeply. "What a glorious day! The felons are in custody, Lancelot is well, if a bit shaken, and you, sir, are in line for a knighthood. If we could only exculpate Dillon today, then all would be well in the world."

Nick coughed into his fist, discomfited. "I would not mention the matter of the knighthood to anyone, Lillian. The queen was a bit overwrought, and I would not take anything that she said today to heart."

"I'm certain Colonel Thompson took what she said to heart. I didn't know a man's ears could turn so crimson."

"For all of his political maneuverings, the man was only following what he thought was the best course of action."

"You are too charitable by far. But you do sound very noble." She shook her parasol with two hands, declaring, "Oh, I cannot wait to tell Fanny the whole of it! And Dillon will be so diverted."

"I hope that you don't mind, but I would like to check in at my office. See if any investigative digging has yielded harvest." He motioned to the window. "Do I have your leave to change our route?"

"Of course." She licked her cherry lips. "I'm curious. Do you . . . is your office near where you reside?"

"Around the corner. I live in a boardinghouse on Pryor Street. The landlady, Mrs. Bears, watches out for us boarders as if we were her kin." He rubbed his chin. "She's probably ripping her hair out with worry that I have not been by for a while."

"We can stop there if you wish."

"Thank you. I'm sure that she will be glad for the visit, but please don't accept if she offers you her spice cake. It's like eating a brick."

"I will try to remember that." Lillian grinned, and he almost felt like it was a smile especially for him.

After giving Jon Driver the directions, Nick adjusted his coat and stated slowly, "I think that we need to talk about your refusal to follow instructions. Did I touch a nerve, perhaps?"

"Yes," she sighed. "I suppose you did. Kane was a dictator of the first degree. I do not exactly have fine feelings for anyone who tries to order me about."

"Understandable. From now on I will endeavor not to command you, and instead, sway you with logic. You seem agreeably responsive to that tactic."

"Manipulation isn't nearly as effective if you give the other person your strategy," she teased.

"Look at the sunset." Nick pointed out the window.

The mellowing sun clung to the London rooftops in a golden orange haze.

"I love this city," he remarked. "Its collection of people of every shape, size and class. Its haphazard lanes where one can purchase just about anything imaginable. And even the pungent Thames running throughout." London had a pulse of its own, and Nick almost felt like his pulse cantered in echoing response to it.

Lillian tilted her head. "I have never thought of it that way."

"Why are we slowing down? This lane is usually empty this time of day." Nick stuck his head out the window.

Lillian leaned forward. "Where is everyone going? They all seem to be headed in the opposite direction."

The faces of the men and women appeared grimier than usual, and the air seemed sootier somehow. Nick's heart began to beat a bit faster as he recognized the burned scent in the air.

She wrinkled her nose. "What's that smell?"

"Fire."

"This much smoke from hearths?"

"House fire." Every Londoner's biggest dread.

"Oh, no."

They turned a corner, and suddenly two long black plumes—portents of doom—could be seen winding heavenward. Nick's stomach sank as he tried to brace himself for the worst.

Her eyes shifted to him questioningly. "Isn't that—?"

"My boardinghouse."

The soot drifted in the air, and Lillian coughed from the ash.

"Cover your mouth with a handkerchief," he advised, pulling his own from his coat. "Jon! There's a stable down the next alley. We can walk from there."

Nick felt the calamity like a yank on his soul, reminding him once again that nothing he cherished would last. It never did.

Chapter 23

⌒◯◯⌒

Lillian clung to Nick's arm, riveted by his darkening mood and the tragedy unfolding before them. They walked side by side in silence, heading toward the center of the ash—his boardinghouse. His body was as stiff as iron, seemingly braced for what they might find.

From the steady but slow stream of activity in the streets and the smoldering scent hanging in the air, it seemed that the fire had been put out a while before.

As they neared the hub of movement, Lillian felt the muscles in Nick's arm tighten and flex. A crowd huddled in clusters around the site. Overturned buckets and blankets were strewn about the street. The former house on Pryor Street was a hulking figure of charred mounds and scrap. It no longer resembled a building but more of a gaping mouth with broken, burned teeth.

281

A tall, portly fellow with a tuft of brown hair ringing his receding hairline looked up. Upon seeing Nick, he disengaged from his group and walked over. His face and clothing were covered in black soot; his gait showed him to be exhausted. Despite the dirt, he seemed to have kind, brown eyes and loose lips that hung down in a fatigued frown.

He held out his hand, and Nick grasped it firmly. "Nick. You're a sight for sore eyes."

"This is my dear friend Dr. Michael Winner. Baroness Janus."

Lillian nodded.

"What happened?" Nick asked grimly.

Dr. Winner tried to speak, but only a hoarse cough came out. "Pardon me," he muttered, turning his face away and spitting. Shaking his head, he faced them once again. "I apologize, my lady. Fire's foul on the lungs."

She gestured that this was immaterial.

"Arson," the man muttered. "Cruel business. The bugger tied up Mrs. Bears, stole the key to your rooms and then lit the fire there."

"Is she—?"

"The bastard came back and sliced the rope at her feet, then ran. She was able to jump through the window." He shook his head. "She's a tough old bird."

"He wanted her to get away," Nick muttered. "To tell the tale?"

Winner glowered. "He told her to give you a message."

Lillian's mouth went dry. "Was . . . was the man dressed in black with his face covered?"

Winner's hands fisted. "And how did you know that, my lady?"

"Because that's the bugger who attacked Lady Janus the other night," Nick ground out, his face a mask of contained violence.

"You're sure?"

"I'm going to hunt that bastard down and kill him," Nick avowed.

"Do you know who he is?" Winner coughed, his gaze shrewd.

"I'm getting a good idea of who's responsible. It's the same fiend who is behind Beaumont's troubles."

"It's all connected," Lillian whispered. *And it's all my fault.* Everything came back to that fateful event, when her mother had been forced to marry Kane, a miserable parasite of a human being who made her life a living hell. Because she'd had no choice. Because of Lillian. Because a man had seduced her mother and hadn't bothered to take responsibility. Shame whipped through her so powerfully that she felt her knees buckle.

Nick turned to her with alarm, supporting her. "Are you all right?"

"This is all my fault," she whispered.

"No," Nick retorted. "It's bloody Kane's."

"Who's Kane?" Winner asked.

Nick pulled her close. "Lean on me."

She allowed him to support her, feeling sick.

Winner gently pressed his hand to the back of her neck. "It's the ash, my lady. It overwhelms the senses."

She closed her eyes and focused on Nick. He was like an oak, she told herself, fighting the queasiness. Solid, substantial and enduring.

Slowly the queasiness dissipated.

The doctor removed his hand. "Better?"

She nodded and opened her eyes. The feeling had passed; still, she did not leave the protective circle of Nick's arms.

"Now tell me, who the blazes is Kane?"

"We believe that he set up Beaumont for Lady Langham's murder," Nick answered, his voice rumbling through her. "He's trying to scare me off the case."

"So that's where you've been?" Winner asked. "Working on Beaumont's matter?"

Nick shook his head. "Long story." At Winner's raised brow, he added, "For another time. Where's Mrs. Bears?"

Dr. Winner pointed to a group sitting on blankets down the street. "But you should know, Nick, not everyone got out in time. The old boarder, Mr. Jenks, did not make it."

Nick's body stiffened to rock.

"Lillian?" His voice was gruff. "Will you please go with Dr. Winner? He can take you home."

"I don't want to leave you—"

"Please?" He squeezed her arms.

"Of course," she replied, disappointed. She wanted to comfort him the way he comforted her. But he needed to see to his friends. She understood that.

Nick slowly disengaged from her. "See she gets home safely, sir."

Winner nodded.

"Nick," Lillian called before he could travel two steps.

He turned but would not meet her eyes. He reminded her of a volcano, just barely contained, on the brink of eruption. Yet beneath the fury, she sensed his pain.

Slipping her hand into her pocket, she extracted her key. She pressed it into his hand. "Whatever you need."

He nodded, turned, and walked away.

"Do you have a carriage?" Winner asked.

Mutely, she nodded, watching Nick.

Reaching the cluster of women, he squatted down beside a wizened crone cloaked in blankets. Her face was black with soot, her form bent with age. Nick took her hands in his and spoke quietly to her, their heads bowed low. A loud sob erupted, and she rocked to and fro. He waited as she bawled, still clenching her hands in his.

"Mrs. Bears is a strong woman," Dr. Winner remarked. "But this boardinghouse was her life."

"Can it be rebuilt?"

"With what money?"

She swallowed, thinking, *Eleven months. Only eleven months and I will have more money than I will ever need.*

Abruptly, it was as if a window opened in her mind. She had always thought of her inheritance as her ticket to freedom. Of no longer living under the Sword of Damocles that was everyone else's rules. To travel the world, be a free spirit. No more pretending to be Dillon's light-o'-love.

Suddenly her view seemed astoundingly short-sighted. The money that she wanted to spend on herself could be better used. The world was filled with needy people. Young boys like Nick had been—homeless, without resources . . . *I could be that resource.* The prospects sent her mind reeling.

"Are you feeling unwell again?" Winner asked. "Your face is as pale as parchment."

"I would go home now, if you will." There was so much to think about.

He extended his arm, and she accepted it.

Taking one last look at Nick as he consoled the weeping Mrs. Bears, she asked herself, What would the noble Nicholas Redford do with the money if he had it? But Nick did not have her money. She, hopefully, would. In eleven months' time. Where would Nick be in eleven months? Would they still be in contact? More than mere friends? Somehow she could not imagine him out of her life, but she had no idea how he might fit. But she wanted him there, no matter how it might be. . . .

A jumble of emotions cascaded though her. The tragedy, her guilt, the capsizing of her well-laid plans . . . *Nick.* It was all too much. The only thing she knew for certain was that she wanted to be with Nick. And the thought terrified her to her bones.

Lillian's eyes drooped and her chin sank to her chest as she waited in the big armchair by the hearth in the drawing room. She had left the wide doors to the salon opened, giving her a side view of the front door to her home. The fire was toasty warm, and the chair a bit too comfortable, causing her eyelids to close with annoying frequency.

She had lain awake in her bed, pretending not to be listening for the tread of boot steps on the stairs. At half past two, still Nick had not come. Her anxiety had been like a fever, one she had not been able to quell with anything other than activity. So she'd given up pretending, and she'd headed to his rooms.

Lillian was determined to give him whatever he needed, before he could even consider asking for it.

It was the least she could do for him. So she had changed the sheets in the guest room three times, to find the appropriately cozy but masculine color.

But the thought of him lying between the sheets had brought such heat to her skin that she'd opened the windows to air herself and the room. Thereupon, she had become too cool, reminding her that Nick would need clothing. So she had lain out four different dressing gowns of Dillon's for him to choose his preference, along with four sets of matching slippers.

But that had gotten her thinking about his long, manly toes. And thighs brushed with a delicate cover of dark fuzz on moon-pale skin. Consequently she had had to take herself off to the kitchen for a glass of water. Which had brought to mind the fact that Nick might need some sustenance. He was always up for a meal.

So Lillian had meticulously arranged gamepie, cheese and fruits on a tray. After carrying the feast up to his rooms, she'd placed it on a table. Then she'd assembled soaps, towels, combs and even shaving accoutrements, in case he wished for them, even in the middle of the night.

Thereupon, she'd decided that knowing him as the undemanding man that he was, all he might want was a snifter of brandy. So she'd poured it and waited in the front drawing room, alongside the foyer, ready to greet him whenever he came.

The cavernous chair had almost swallowed her up, and she had not been able to resist the urge to curl up in its corner.

"It isn't too terrible for me to rest my eyes," she'd murmured to herself. "I'll be certain to hear him as soon as he uses the key."

Sure enough, a small click roused her from her repose. Abruptly, she sat up, her body alert but her brain muddled. For a moment, she wondered where she was. At a sound to her left, she turned.

He stood in the threshold to the drawing room, broad, dark and motionless, watching her. His face was lost in the shadow cast by the candles in the foyer. Her single candle flickered low, and the fire had waned to mellow cinders.

She stood, holding the back of the chair for support, for her knees had turned to jelly. "I'm so sorry, Nick," the words tumbled out. "If I hadn't involved you—"

Two strides and he was upon her, grabbing her by the shoulders and drawing her close. His lips pressed against hers with an undeniable hunger, and he opened his mouth to her with need.

Lightning shot through her as his tongue laved her mouth, enticing, demanding, fulfilling. Heat coursed through her, igniting the embers of the passionate longing she had held for just this man. She inched closer, crushing her soft breasts against his muscular chest. His arms snaked around her waist, hugging her close, lifting her onto her toes.

She was captivated, intoxicated by his desire for her. She felt it in every inch of his muscular form as it pressed, warm, hard and hungry, against her.

His hand reached behind her head and lifted the braid from her neck. Loosening the strands, he raked his fingers through her curls, sending shivers racing over her skin.

He lifted her hair and suckled on her neck. Moving up, his tongue traced the crevices of her ear.

"Lillian," he breathed, as if it were the only word in the universe.

Her head swam and she melted.

Reaching behind her, he gently but possessively clutched her buttocks and lifted her up. Without thought, her legs spread. His hard shaft pressed into that amazing crevice between her thighs, and she groaned with the joy of it.

Carrying her to the couch, he turned and dropped backwards, drawing her to lie on top of him.

Pressing her hands against his chest, she stilled, suddenly uneasy.

"What is it?" His voice was a harsh whisper.

"I don't know what to do . . ."

He pressed his palms against her cheeks and drew her mouth back down. "You were born knowing. . . ." His throaty voice rumbled through her, telling her that his need was as powerful as her own.

"So hot, so soft . . . beautiful," he groaned, splaying butterfly kisses along her neck.

All fears succumbed to his honeyed kisses.

He fumbled with the ribbons tying her wrapper and whipped off her rail. She yanked at his neck cloth and pushed off his coat. Baring his brawny chest, she pulled his mouth up to hers and sighed as the soft flesh of her breasts brushed against the smooth surface of his muscled torso. As she lay across him, the crisp hair coating his belly teased her abdomen with titillating pleasure. His belly was flat and hard where hers softly pressed into it. Her heart raced even more, and her breath quickened to a gasping pant.

His shoulders were surprisingly soft to the touch as she held on and slithered down his form. Remembering how good it felt, she pressed an open kiss to his nipple and sucked on the nub. It hardened, pebbling against her tongue. He groaned, shifting restlessly beneath her.

Closing her eyes, she circled the nub with her tongue. Unexpected thrills surged through her. Grazing her fingers across his belly, she marveled at the joy of touching him. Silken skin over hard muscle and bone. Sweet heat pooled between her thighs.

She spread her legs, wrapping them around him. The rough wool of his breeches pressed into the inner lips of her private core. Her body flamed. He raised his leg, pushing into her heat, lifting her to a place where all thoughts fled. Grasping her waist, he rode her on him, driving her mad with wanting.

"Wait." Lifting her up, he set her on the couch and stood, ripping off his boots, breeches and smalls and tossing them to the floor.

He sat down beside her and pulled her onto his lap. She spread her legs around his waist. It felt like the most natural thing in the world to do.

He leaned back, setting her across his manhood. The muscles in her feminine core leaped with desire. His hips bucked, driving his hard manhood across the silky crevice between her thighs. Her body quivered and she groaned with the joy of it. The tip of his manhood slid across the hard nub of her core with a torturous rub. Instinctively, her back arched, her hips flexed and she slid down his shaft. Even without entering her, his rod made her shudder with pleasure.

With a tantalizing grip on her buttocks, he slowly undulated his hips, plowing his manhood up and down in her wetness, kneading that electrifying hard nub. A harsh cry tore from her throat. Everything faded in contrast to that amazing desire thrumming from between her legs, lancing up her flesh and making her want *more*. She needed him inside her. But his manhood slid once more across that outer nub.

"Dear God," she moaned. "You're killing me."

"Not yet," he murmured.

Her pelvis rocked, moving to his primal rhythm, grinding him into her wetness. Propelling him into that most excited spot. Again and again. Urging his hard shaft to take, to give, to drive, to satisfy . . .

The muscles inside her innermost core squeezed and jumped, throbbing, pulsating. Heat surged. Rippling waves of lightning shocked through her veins. A harsh scream erupted from her throat. Awareness fled; there was only the blind rush of sensation, pulsing through her.

Slowly her senses were reborn. Her heart pounded so hard that it hurt. Her breath came in harsh gasps. Her innermost core still throbbed with the remembrance of ecstasy. She struggled to regain air, to regain sanity.

Their bodies were pressed together, slick with sweat. She swallowed hard, listening to his stampeding heartbeat. He was panting, his skin almost burned to the touch. She could not ignore his engorged shaft as it pushed, thick and wanting, into her inner thigh.

A terrified thrill shot through her; she needed to touch him, *there*. Garnering her courage, she reached down between her legs and grasped his manhood. It pulsed in her hand, stiff and throbbing with acute heat.

"God forgive me, I want you, Lillian." It was a guttural cry.

He flipped her over onto her back and pressed his sturdy frame into her body, making her feel sheltered and possessed at once. He claimed her mouth, his kisses intent, needy. His hands glided down her body, exploring, claiming, arousing her until every crevice thrummed with wanting, yet again. She was lost, wallowing in the ecstasy of his touch.

His fingers opened the hot flesh of her womanhood, fingering the inner lips with a searing stroke, edging upward to that incredible peak of pleasure. His pace quickened. She writhed, sobbed, and rocked with excruciating rapture.

"Nick," she cried. "Please . . ."

His manhood touched her core and he groaned. "So wet . . ."

She wrapped her arms around those brawny shoulders, hugging him with a ferocity that astonished her. But it felt so good. So very *right*.

He plunged inside her so wholly that the breath rushed from her throat. He filled her, warming her to her soul and meeting her aching need.

His movements were tantalizingly slow. Sliding in and out with excruciating strokes, he drew her back toward that vortex of pleasure. The pressure built inside her once again, propelling her forward, driving her, pushing her until she could stand it no longer. She cried out. Her muscles spasmed and heat filled her core. He pumped into her, spilling his seed. Warming her completely.

Chapter 24

Lillian did not know how long she lay underneath Nick's leaden form. She was blanketed in his heat, listening to his haggard breathing harmonize with her own. Time seemed to have stopped. Her world was this room, his muscular arms around her, the heady scent of passion and the darkness keeping them safe.

He slipped out of her and pulled her into the nest of his arms, wrapping his long body almost entirely around hers. She lay there, feeling his heartbeat thumping reassuringly against her back, memorizing the sensation of his smooth skin brushing hers, the bristly hairs near his manhood tickling her derriere, the scent of Nick. Man, almond and desire. She wondered if anything else would ever smell as good.

She hated to break the peace between them, but

her concern overrode her qualms. "Are you all right?" she whispered.

"Better than I was an hour ago."

She kissed his forearm. "Me too."

After a few more moments of silence, she ventured, "I was thinking, I will be coming into some funds in a few months, perhaps, if Mrs. Bears needs it . . ."

"I gave her the reward I received for finding Lancelot."

She nodded; she should have known that Nick would not let Mrs. Bears down.

"But it was kind of you to offer," he added quietly.

"Did you . . . did you lose anything of value in the fire?"

The hand cupping her elbow clenched and unclenched, and his body shifted as if he were uneasy.

"Can it be replaced?" she asked.

"No."

"I'm sorry."

"It wasn't important."

"It was to you."

He was silent a long moment. "Sentimentally, yes. It was a link to my past, but I don't know that it has any bearing on my future."

"Can you tell me?"

She felt him shrug. "It was a lady's redingote. The one they found me in as a babe."

Her heart contracted. She pictured Nick as a beautiful, dark-haired baby boy, lying alone, wrapped in a lady's outer garment. She shuddered, sensing the pain he must feel. Pulling his arms tighter around her, she held him closer still.

He squeezed her in a reassuring hug. "It was a long time ago, and I do not recall it."

Unable to fathom the anguish of abandoning a child, she asked, "Do you know anything of your family?"

"I've searched, but the farmer who found me could provide me with few clues other than the coat."

"He kept it?"

"Apparently in the hubbub of discovering an abandoned babe and bringing it to the local justice of the peace, the garment was left behind. The farmer was kind enough to keep it in case I ever came looking for my family. But I couldn't seem to scratch up much from a puce redingote with fur lining, and the residents knew little as well." He lifted her hair and pressed his lips to the base of her neck. "Perhaps I need you with me to solve the tough ones."

It was a sweet comment, but it brought the future to bear. She swallowed. "What do you think is going to happen . . . with us?"

"Hell if I know."

She smiled. "Me neither."

Content with his strong arms around her and the heat of his body warming her skin, she studied the play of shadows on the ceiling.

"Why don't you think that the redingote bears on your future?" she asked.

"I've wasted too much time trying to figure out my family connection."

Closing her eyes, she nuzzled her nose into the crook of his arm. "I feel like I cannot escape my past; that my whole life is driven by my family and the choices that they've made, for themselves and me."

"What of your natural father?"

"I got the feeling that my grandparents knew very

well who he was. But the subject was taboo." On those few occasions when she had tried asking about her father, it had been like a fortress gate slamming down with a boom that had reverberated inside her soul. *"It is of no consequence,"* Grandmother would chide. *"We will not see you suffer at the hands of that unfeeling blackguard the way your mother did."*

"Does he have any idea that you exist?" Nick asked.

"My mother would fall into these fits of crying . . . and one time . . . she confessed that she had told him in a letter and had received no response. Pathetically, she had still held a shred of hope that he might come for her. She had just set herself up to be disappointed again." After that episode, her mother had spent almost a month abed, unable to cease crying. Kane had ignored her, staying at the far end of the house, but Lillian could not escape the weeping and the fact that she could do nothing to stanch her mother's sorrow.

"Have you tried to find him?"

"The blackguard knew precisely where we were and did not lift a finger to help us. He does not deserve to know me."

"Brave words, Lillian. But I'm from Andersen Hall. You cannot fool me." He exhaled softly. "At one point or another, orphans yearn to understand who their parents are and why they abandoned them. You have not searched for him because you were afraid that he would reject you yet again."

She jerked, her eyes flying wide open. It was as if she had been looking into a mirror and he had smashed it with a hammer, shattering her reflection into a thousand shards of glass. Her heart slowed, as if searching for something in the stillness. Gradually she became aware of her anguish. It had always been there, hiding under the bravado. The pain of knowing that her father had not loved her enough to come rescue them from Kane. That he had not loved her enough to even bother to condemn her when she had so publicly chosen to be Dillon's paramour.

He hugged her close, brushing his lips across her shoulder. "It is perfectly natural to fear rebuff once you have already been forsaken."

The words slashed at her heart. She was a castoff, like a misbegotten rag. Unwanted. Ill considered. But she had been loved. Her mother had tried her best. Her grandparents. Her dear friends. She had never been truly forsaken. The pain subsided but did not disappear. She might have been better off than so many others, but that did not mean that the rejection did not hurt. Exhaling slowly, she asked, "How do you deal with it?"

"I suppose like I deal with most things. As a lad, it became a puzzle to be played with. Was my real family an old one with a weighty name like Prendregast or Edmundson? Or were they a people in trade: Glasier, Smith, Baker, or Carpenter?"

"Why names?"

"It was a start that soon became an obsession. Dunn encouraged me at first, but then decided that I needed to relax a bit. Thankfully, now I'm just shy of fixated on monikers."

She felt him shrug. "I was found on a snowy Christmastide near a low water junction where the town folk crossed the river. Hence, the Nicholas reference and 'reed ford' becoming Redford, thanks to the inventiveness of the local justice of the peace." He shifted against her. "The name suits me fine, but

I'm starting to believe what Dunn always said. That your true name, the one you make for yourself is the only one that counts."

What a wonderful philosophy, she mused. "I hope that's true—it always bothered me that Janus meant *duplicitous.* I feared that the name was apt, considering my arrangement with Dillon."

"The duplicitous connotation only came from the two opposing faces of the Roman god Janus."

"You looked it up?" She twisted around, surprised.

"I'm fixated, remember?"

"What else did you learn?"

"Janus was identified with doors, gates and new beginnings. Hence January, the first month of the ancient Roman year."

"I'm impressed."

"But that's not your true name."

She stilled, trepidation shooting through her. What did he know that she did not? "What is?"

"I have yet to figure it out." Leaning over her, he splayed butterfly kisses along her jaw. "But don't despair, the queen says that I'm 'one of the most trustworthy men of the empire,' so I shall discover it soon enough."

She sagged with relief but could not ignore the disappointment filtering through her. Nick was right; she did want to know why she'd been abandoned and who the bastard was who had done it. She wasn't so different from the other children at Andersen Hall, she realized.

"Was it like having many siblings, living at Andersen Hall?"

"Not really. We were all so very different. The

only commonality was our reason for residing there. But we all had a shared bond, I suppose." He shifted slightly, recounting, "In fact, a couple of my friends actually ended up married to each other."

"What about you? Did you ever have someone special?" The question of the innocent that he had bedded flashed through her mind.

She heard a sharp intake of breath.

"You don't have to tell me if you don't—"

He squeezed her close. "What does it matter now?"

She shrugged. "It matters to me."

He was silent a long time.

Finally, he answered, "She was at Andersen Hall with me. A few years older."

"Did you love her?"

"Yes."

"And what happened to her?" Was she still around? Did they see each other even now? Her heart began to pound as she realized how important the answer was to her.

"She's dead."

Lillian was both relieved and saddened. "How . . . How did she die?"

"She took a job as a scullery maid. It was a good house. Dunn thought it was a fine fit."

"She wasn't molested?" she cried, appalled.

"No. She just couldn't handle the work. It was too much for her." Unwinding one hand from hers, he slowly brushed her hair with his fingers, as if to soothe her and, she suspected, himself. "She was fired but was too ashamed to come back to Andersen Hall. She didn't want to face Dunn, or me. So she took to the streets. But it was like throwing her to the wolves. . . ."

"What happened to her?"

His hand caressed her hair, brushing it against her back. "I looked for her but didn't find her until she was already in the hospital. She had gotten a fever, and it burned the life right out of her."

"Did you get to say good-bye?"

"No. I was too late." Quiet shrouded the room. Still he gently soothed her hair.

"It was a long time ago. And I was a very different man then."

"How?"

She felt him shrug. "I expect I was more idealistic."

"Have . . . have there been many other women in your life?"

He leaned forward, nibbling on her ear. "You're heading into dark waters, Lillian," he teased. "Are you sure you wish to go there?"

"Just tell me, more than fifty or less."

"Definitely less. But for now there is only one that counts." Turning her shoulders, he pressed his lips to hers, sliding his tongue deep into her mouth. She welcomed him, relishing his taste and his touch. His words kindled something reminiscent of hope in her heart, but she pushed it aside, knowing that it was not meant to be. Instead, she focused on his smooth lips, the erotic play of his tongue with hers and how good he made her feel.

Slowly, he pulled back, nibbling on her lower lip. "I have answered your questions, so how about you answer one of mine?"

"All right," she replied, slightly breathless.

"Tell me why you have never married."

She traced her finger down the edge of his nose.

"I have a problem with being ordered about, remember?"

"I can't imagine a man ever subjugating you."

"Because I would not suffer it. I had enough of that from Kane to last me a lifetime." Pressing her palm to the warm column of his neck, she felt his heartbeat pounding within. "What about you? What do you see in your future?"

"You mean family?"

She nodded.

"I'm not the family kind."

Rubbish. Thinking of Mabel and Andersen Hall and Mrs. Bears, she could not help but disagree. Nick considered others with compassion beyond himself. If that was not the true definition of a family man, then she did not know what was.

"Besides," he added, raking his hand down her torso, sending delicious shivers cascading down her skin, "I'm a bear to live with."

"Oh, you're a bear all right," she teased, laying her palms on his chest. "But I like it when you growl."

"And I love it when you scream." Suddenly his fingers tickled her rib cage.

"Stop that!" she shrieked, swatting his hands away.

Ignoring her, his fingers seemed to be everywhere, tickling her to madness. She howled with laughter.

"Stop! Mercy . . . please!" she begged.

"Only if you pay the piper." He leaned his cheek toward her and patted his finger to his cheek for a kiss.

Instead she reached down and grasped his member in her hand. Smooth and warm, it swelled in her palm. "What's that you want me to do?"

"Anything the hell you want," he growled.

And by dawn he was the one begging for mercy.

Chapter 25

❦

Lillian gazed out the window of her drawing room, hardly seeing the emerald trees for her reflection staring back at her. She was in the briars, and she knew it. Fanny had been right; it was good to live every moment as if it were her last. Lillian could not deny that sleeping with Nick had been one of the most incredible experiences of her lifetime, and she would cherish the memories forever. But the busy afternoons followed by passionate, earth-shattering nights with Nick had not quenched her feelings for the dashing investigator. Instead, to her mounting distress, she was growing ever fonder of him with each passing day.

Love might be an illness that she had sworn never to catch, but it seemed to be working feverishly to corrupt her. Things could only end badly. They had no future together and they both knew it.

After that first night, she and Nick had not discussed marriage or their prospects again. It was as if each was unwilling to cross that frontier, instead enjoying the stolen moments of the past two days for what they were—breathtaking.

"Lillian," a deep voice rippled though her with a familiar quickening of her pulse.

She turned. Nick stood in the doorway, so stunning he made her heart skip a beat. He wore a forest green coat with gilt buttons, over cream-colored breeches that hugged his magnificent thighs and dipped into shiny black boots. His ivory cambric shirt had a standing collar with stiffened points high above a simply knotted linen cravat.

"From the look on your face, am I to assume that you like it?" He waved a hand down his form.

"My servants seem to have taken you into favor," she teased, smiling.

"Yes. Gillman is particularly keen on seeing me fashionably attired." Sticking a finger into the high collar and yanking on it, he added, "I'm not too comfortable in this, but it will do for today. I don't want to stand out like too much of a sore thumb when I go to Kane's club."

"Promise me you will be careful," Lillian implored as she stepped over to him.

"For the tenth time, Lillian, Kane is not about to do anything to me in his club."

"I know. But I still worry." Anxiety roiled in her middle. If anything happened to Nick. . . . She swallowed, pushing away the distressing thought. "Thank heavens Russell is going with you." Someone else to fret about, though.

"I would not have done it otherwise, but I need Mayburn to get me into Brooks's. The knave has been practically living at his club. I have no choice but to confront him there."

"Why confront him at all, Nick? I still don't understand what is to be gained from it."

"Arrogant bastards often direct us to evidence of their guilt. It's stupid, but a matter of pride. They like to gloat, trying to show their superiority. If he is as smug as you say, then it's worth a shot. And we have little time." His eyes had darkened, and his face had hardened to stone. "Besides, I want him to know he cannot hide behind his dastardly deeds. He is not immune from persecution. He's not immune from me."

Laying her palm on his dear cheek, she murmured, "You will not be of any use to me, Nick, if something happens to you."

His face softened, as he too remembered her motherly chiding when he was soaked through from their misadventure at Litchfield Park. Clasping her hands in his, he brushed his lips across her knuckles, whispering huskily, "Your concern moves me, *my lady*."

Her heart contracted with a rush of heretofore unknown feelings for this man.

"Lillian."

Russell stood in the doorway, glaring at them. He was dressed in his usual dandified splendor, from his tall black hat topping golden curls that hung unfashionably long to his shoulders, to the brass-buttoned, high-collared crimson velvet coat, to his white breeches so tight that they could have been shrunk onto his legs, down to his gleaming black Hessian boots.

Lillian pulled one of her hands from Nick's and extended it to Russell.

"Thank you for coming, Russell. Pray that I

would not have to involve you in this villainy, but I must call upon you for help."

Stepping forward stiffly, he clasped her hand. "How may I be of service?"

"We believe that Lord Cornelius Kane is behind Lady Langham's murder," Nick explained. "And that he is trying to set the blame upon your brother to get at Lillian."

The color drained from Russell's face. "Surely you must be mistaken."

"I need your help getting into Brooks's. I need to speak with him, and that seems to be the best place to find him these days."

"I'm not so sure that this is a good idea," Russell sputtered, fingering the brass buttons of his coat.

"I need you to be my champion, Russell," Lillian implored, squeezing his gloved hand. "And watch Nick's back. Kane is like a serpent, he strikes when one gets too close."

Russell swallowed. "You will be telling Kane that you suspect him?"

"Yes, and inviting him to correct any of my misunderstanding of the facts." Nick shot Lillian a knowing look. She prayed that he realized what he was doing.

Russell blinked. "That is most . . . generous of you. But wouldn't you wish to call upon the authorities?"

"This matter is *personal*," Nick replied.

"Yes," Russell breathed, his eyes filled with understanding. "Personal. Good idea, to give the man the opportunity to set the record straight."

She turned to Russell. "Please have a care for your safety. Kane is a fox who eats hounds."

His brow furrowed.

"Just be careful and follow Nick's lead."

"You must remain in the house, Lillian," Nick ordered, his face gravely serious. "No excursions, no visits to Newgate, not even a call on Fanny."

She fought the natural inclination to challenge his command. "You will come back here as soon as you've spoken to him?"

"I'm not sure where Kane's information might lead me. Let us see how things progress. Just promise that you will remain here."

"I promise. And I will take care of getting some of that Cognac to John Newman," she added. "Fanny had a few bottles more. But don't worry, I will simply send a footman to handle it."

"Thank you." Bussing her forehead, he released her hand and headed for the door. She felt bereft, uneasy. She prayed that he would come back to her soon.

"Hey now," Russell cried, affronted by Nick's intimate gesture, but Nick ignored him and was gone.

"The man takes liberties, Lillian!"

"Leave it be, Russell," she answered weakly. Her emotions were in such a roil that she had hardly any energy left to deal with Russell's inappropriate jealousy.

"I cannot sit by without speaking up."

"Your brother's freedom is Nick's foremost priority. Let us keep our eye on the target, please, and not get distracted with trivialities." Even though her feelings for Nick were turning out to be anything but trifling.

"Your dignity is not trivial. You deserve better than that . . . that *person*." Russell said the word as if it were a disease. "Even my brother is preferable to him. At least he's of noble blood."

She looked up sharply but reined in her irritation. Now was not the time to cross swords with Russell. "You were lucky enough to have been born into a wonderful family, Russell. Others were not as fortunate."

"That is my point exactly," he countered. "You and Redford are worlds apart. You come from a fine family that cares about you."

"My only family is dead."

"Not all of it. You should learn to appreciate what you have."

Had the man cracked? "You are about to go confront my supposed father because he is setting Dillon up for murder!"

Russell brushed a blond curl from his forehead. "Things are not always as they appear."

Setting her hands on her hips, she took a long, hard look at Russell as a whisper of doubt threaded through her mind. "Is there anything you wish to tell me, Russell?"

"Just that I believe you are allowing Redford to take advantage of you."

She crossed her arms. "You have not been to Newgate to visit Dillon. Why not?"

He stiffened, guilt flashing across his features. "To be frank, I don't know that I could face the prospect of seeing my brother in such a wretched place."

Relief trickled through her, but a trace of doubt lingered. "You never would do anything to hurt Dillon, would you?"

"Of course not. 'An enemy to one Mayburn is an enemy to them all,' " he intoned, reciting the Mayburn family motto.

"Good." Unwinding her arms, she patted his

hand, chiding herself for being so paranoid. "It distresses Dillon that you have not gone to visit him, but he will forgive you after all is said and done. At the end of this wretched affair, he will know your true blue colors. Know how his flesh and blood rose to the occasion and routed his enemies."

"We all do what we must."

"Come, Nick waits in the carriage," she urged, walking toward the door.

Nodding stiffly, he escorted her to the entrance of the house, where the servants had lined up, seemingly understanding that something significant was happening.

Russell bowed and kissed her hand. "Until we meet again, Lillian."

"Have a care, my dear friend."

As she stood in the doorway, Lillian watched Russell join Nick in the carriage. Nick nodded, his eyes meeting hers so piercingly that she felt her chest contract. *Have a care, my darling,* she wished, clutching her hands to her breast. What she would have given to have placed herself in danger instead of him.

As the coach pulled away from the curb, Lillian tried to stanch the pain leaking from her heart.

Russell's groin and armpits were sweating. He tried not to squirm too much as he and Redford walked up the stairs at Brooks's. By jingo, he had to pee. Stealing a peek at the dark brooding oaf beside him, he reckoned that he could hold it for a few more moments.

On the carriage ride over to the club, Russell had not been able to decide if this confrontation was a good or bad idea. On the one hand, Redford would tell Kane that someone was on to him. On the other, Kane might be furious at Russell for moving without consulting him. But wait. It had not been Russell's idea to bring Nick. He had had no choice. It was either go along or let Lillian know that something was afoot.

And she *had* been suspicious. He was quite pleased with himself for dealing with her so handily. Still, her questions had left him feeling uneasy, like he had eaten a bad egg.

So Kane could not fault him for this encounter with Redford. Could he? Russell was having difficulty keeping track of exactly what he was supposed to do today. And what Kane might do in response. Did Redford expect him to leave? Perhaps, now that they were inside, he might excuse himself and let Redford go it alone. But should he stay for Kane's sake? Would Kane expect him to do something? Like what, exactly? Oh, it was all so boggling!

All of this thinking was giving him a headache, and he wished that he had never gotten up this morning. Setting that fire at the boardinghouse had been more harrowing that he had expected. Only at the last minute had he remembered that he had tied up the old biddy. Then he had had to risk life and limb to go back and untie her. Not that she'd been thankful, mind you. She had punched him in the chest, and it still hurt in that spot. He wondered if she had made it out after he'd knocked her over. The blaze had been a nasty thing to navigate. Recalling the heat, the flames and that terrible burning in his throat and nose, he shuddered.

"Don't worry, Mayburn," Redford boasted. "I will handle Kane."

Cocky bastard.

They entered the card room with its bare walls and myriad of tables. It carried the familiar scents of beeswax, leather and stale cigar.

Kane sat with his back toward them, at one of the first tables. The newspaper was spread out before him, and a snifter of brandy rested beside it, near his hand. He was the only one in the room.

Redford waved for the footmen to leave. *Overstepping boor, ordering our servants about,* Russell grumbled to himself. Gallingly, the footmen turned heel and scurried away. One just could not count on the help these days.

They edged forward toward Kane's expansive shoulders. Russell heard a pounding and wondered what it was. Then he realized it was his heart. *You have nothing to be afraid of,* he told himself. *You are Russell Mayburn, future Duke of Greayston.* The thought made his back straighten. Still, he was thankful that he had worn his Weston morning coat today. He'd had the shoulders padded for good measure.

"Lord Kane," he declared, with just the right touch of authority.

"Don't bother me, Mayburn." Kane did not even turn.

Russell eyed that broad back, embarrassment growing in his middle with a sickening twist. That Kane should be so rude in front of lowly Redford. Well, it was too much. "My lord—"

"If I've told you once I've told you a thousand times, do not disturb me when I am reading the broadsheets!" He huffed, as if greatly put out. Russell did not have the nerve to look at Redford's face. Kane flipped the page of his newspaper, growling, "And stop hovering over my back like a blunderbuss. Go away."

"I think that that's a good idea, Mayburn." Redford stepped forward. "I'll take it from here."

Kane swiveled in his seat. "Who the bloody hell let you in?"

"Mayburn did me the honor," Redford supplied, moving around the table and smoothly sitting in the seat across from Kane.

"Oh, did he now?" Kane glared at Russell, and the youth fought the urge to turn tail and flee.

Russell puffed out his chest and opened his mouth to declare his good reasons, but Kane gave him his back. Russell closed his mouth, relieved that Redford had Kane's attention. Sweat had popped up on his nose and he scratched it, irritated.

"They usually don't allow bastards in," Kane sneered. "It's the stench, I suppose."

Russell's eyes widened.

"I thought they kept out spongers as well," Nick retorted. "Tell me, Kane, is it more difficult outrunning the creditors or the constable?"

Kane's back stiffened.

Russell felt overwhelmed by their vicious banter. "I'm . . . I'm . . . going to . . ."

But they paid him no mind, they were so focused on each other. Slowly, Russell shuffled backwards, toward the door. Perhaps after relieving himself he could go back to Lillian. Redford was out of the house. She would be happy for the company. He would tell her how he had fulfilled his promise, her champion—

"How does it feel to be swiving another man's castoffs?" Kane snickered.

Russell stopped in his tracks.

"But then again, she's a randy slut, just like her mother."

Russell's bladder grew more insistent, and he fought the sudden urge to be sick. He had been right about Redford and Lillian? Had things progressed that far? But no, that was not possible! Lillian was too pure, too . . . *Randy slut just like her mother*? He stiffened like a bowstring after a shot.

Redford looked like a storm drawing clouds, on the brink of violence.

Russell began to tremble, very upset.

"And just like her mother, she will crumble before me," Kane declared. "Beaumont couldn't protect her, and neither can you." Swiveling in his seat, he crossed his ankles. "You're nobody, unworthy of even this pithy conversation. You're too low to even lick my boots. Now get the hell out of here." Lifting the newspaper, he snapped it open before him, blocking Redford out.

Redford stood and plucked the broadsheet from Kane's hands.

"How dare you!" Kane shrieked.

Redford slowly ripped the paper in two, the tear earsplitting in the empty chamber. "I know that you killed Lady Langham."

The silence was so deafening that Russell could hear his own breathing.

"I'd like to see you prove it, by-blow," Kane finally ground out.

Redford dropped one piece of the paper, and it drifted on a wayward course to the floor. "People are waking up about your shifty investment scheme.

The shareholders are talking. Stein is talking." He tore another section with a loud rip. "The money's dried up." Shred. "It's only a matter of time before we pull the evidence together to hang you." He dropped the tatters like confetti, polluting the floorboards.

"Well, time is not a luxury you have," Kane droned. Russell could tell by his voice that he was smiling. "Beaumont swings in a handful of days. And for Dagwood to come after me then would only mean . . . Oh, no!" he cried with exaggerated drama, pressing both hands to his cheeks. "He could not have hung the wrong man!"

"Beaumont hangs over my dead body," Redford growled.

"That can and will be arranged. By the way, how are your quarters these days? A boardinghouse on Pryor Street, isn't it? It's a shame about the fire."

"Not everyone made it out alive, you murdering bugger," Redford lashed out, his face contorted with fury.

Russell's heart skipped a beat. "The old woman," he whispered.

Redford's eyes flicked to him. "What did you say?"

"Nothing," Russell muttered, stepping backwards, away from the judgment in his gaze.

"Too bad you weren't inside when it burned," Kane declared. "But, oh, I forgot, you were out, bedding your client's mistress."

Redford's hostile gaze latched onto Kane. "What did you hope to accomplish? I will not desert Beaumont no matter what you do."

"Wouldn't you like to know . . ."

The words trailed on, the hard voices grinding at each other, hammering at his brain. Russell rushed from the room, unable to stand it. He felt sick, afraid, confused by all of the words, the harsh innuendo. What was real anymore? Had Lillian betrayed him? Was she so unfaithful as to have taken up with Redford? Her paramour was in prison, and she had hardly waited two weeks before inviting another man to her bed? A lowly wage earner?

And the old woman. Had she died in the fire? Burned in that horrid, scorching heat that felt like hell licking at your heels? The scent of the ash haunted him still. Was the fire a taste of his afterlife to come?

Jealousy, anger, fear and guilt swirled inside his gut. Hanging on the banister railing, he vomited all over the stairs.

He was panting, the foul taste of returned kippers lining his mouth. Sweat blanketed his face and privates. And he could not endure the stench by his feet.

"My lord!" One of the footmen appeared at the top of the stairs.

"Clean up this mess," Russell ordered, feeling like the world was slowly ceasing to spin.

Wiping a handkerchief across his brow, he realized what he was going to have to do. It was a good thing he had been smart enough to have brought his pistol.

Straightening his coat, he headed for the door.

Chapter 26

Lillian wandered in the back garden with a plate of food for her cat, trying for a semblance of normalcy on this maddening afternoon. She was at her wit's end for all of the waiting. She was not very proficient at it, she realized. It was a good thing that she had promised Nick that she would remain at home; otherwise, she might have been tempted to get out of the house. As it was, she was ready to yank out her hair from feeling so impotent. Fear for Nick plagued her like a festering wound. She could not ignore it, but the more she picked at it, the more it stung.

Her black-and-white friend strolled over, brushing his shiny coat along her skirts.

"Hello, Jack," she sighed. "I hope that you are doing better than me today."

Standing on two legs, he meowed for the salver in

317

her hands. She set down the plate with some of Cook's sliced turkey, and he attacked it with voracious intensity. Watching him tear into the meat, she muttered, "I'm glad that someone can enjoy Cook's food today."

"Lillian," a soft male voice called from nearby.

She looked up sharply. Russell stood on the other side of the black iron gate just paces away. His brown eyes topped the gold-tipped spikes of the entry.

Rising quickly, she started. "You're back! What happened? Where is Nick?"

"Nick is still at Brooks's."

"With Kane?"

"Yes."

Sunlight flashed on something silver. From between the bars, a small pistol with a dark black barrel was pointed at her chest.

"What are you—?"

Then it crashed into her consciousness. She had not been paranoid, simply blinded by her unwillingness to believe it was true. Dillon's embroidered handkerchief left next to Lady Langham's body . . . Dillon's personal correspondence . . . Russell's aversion to visiting his brother at Newgate. He wore Canterbury violet cologne! It was he who had attacked her in Litchfield Park!

"Russell," she whispered. "What have you done?"

"It wasn't supposed to happen this way. But it's *your* fault. Everything was because of *you!*"

She turned and dashed for the house.

"Stop or I'll shoot!"

She froze, petrified. Her heart was hammering so loudly that she marveled he couldn't hear it. Would he actually shoot her? He had just tried to pin a murder on his brother, so he was probably capable of anything.

Swallowing, she whispered, "What do you want?"

"I need to know what is real. You owe me that. After what we mean to each other, you have not been honest with me."

"And pointing a gun is supposed to endear me to you," she charged, anger seeping into her voice. "Convince me to be more forthcoming." Slowly, she turned, facing the guppy that had turned into a shark.

He swallowed, and she noticed the perspiration gleaming on his brow.

"Come here and open this." He waved to the gate. A new shiny brass lock sealed the entry closed, keeping him out and her in.

Bless you, Nicholas Redford!

"Nick must have placed the lock on the gate. I do not have the key."

"I suppose he knew that you were in danger."

Was that a threat of his intentions? Her blood chilled. Her childhood friend had turned into a terrorizing stranger. Was he also a cold-blooded murderer?

"Stop this, Russell," she urged, her mouth dry as dust. "Put the gun down and we will talk."

"About what?" he sneered. "About how you have taken a lowly bastard to your bed?"

"It was your doing," she lured.

"Don't be absurd."

"He had nowhere else to go. You burned down his house."

His face blanched. Revulsion twisted inside of her as she realized that her gambit had paid off.

A righteous anger filled her, and she shouted,

"What is wrong with you? You're killing people. Targeting your own flesh and blood! What did you suppose was going to happen, Russell? Was I going to fall in a faint into your arms?"

The redness flushing his cheeks told her that her supposition was correct. Her belly flipped with repugnance.

He'd cracked. The lad had gone 'round the bend, and she was not about to blame herself for his sickness.

"I'd sooner die than ever take up with you."

"But you took up with Dillon—"

"To get away from beastly Kane!" She couldn't believe that she was standing there talking to a madman. She wondered whether he would actually shoot if she made a dash for the house. More importantly, would he actually hit her? But all of the Mayburn men were crack shots.

With his free hand, he tugged at one of his blond tresses. "I don't understand. . . ." He looked so distressed, so lost. "Please tell me why this is happening."

"Because you're mad?"

"It made perfect sense when Kane laid it out."

Kane. Her heart sank. She felt a rush of responsibility. "Kane put you up to this?" But if she died, Kane got nothing. Where was the benefit in that?

"Dillon was using you. He was taking, taking, taking, as he always did," Russell cried bitterly. "It was the same old story, but now he was hurting you. I was trying to help you."

"How was Dillon supposedly hurting me?" she asked, unable to stop herself. It was like a passerby being drawn to a carriage smashup; she was appalled, and yet fascinated.

"You deserve to be the Marchioness of Beaumont. Not sport for his pleasure."

"But I did not wish to marry him," she bit out. This was an old story; it had not changed.

"He should have made you."

"How? By holding me at pistol point?"

"The man *deserves* Newgate."

Lillian knew someone else who fit that bill. A couple of men, in fact. He might be mad, but she was crazy for staying and talking to him.

"I know that you were doing what you thought was for the best, Russell . . ." She edged backward, figuring that if she got far enough away, it would increase her chances of escape.

"I'm not ready for you to go, Lillian," he insisted, raising the fireman.

She halted. "What do you want from me, Russell?" Jack rubbed up against her leg, and she jumped. Carefully she tried to nudge him out of harm's way with her leg. Fortunately, he somehow seemed to understand and took off. She almost sagged with relief.

"I want you to recognize all that I've done for you." Russell pounded his free hand to his breast in a tight fist.

Anger blazed through her. "Attacking me in the gazebo in the park? You did that for my own good?"

"I did not mean to hurt you." The pistol wavered. "But you struggled and tried to run away. You gave me no choice. And then that blasted Redford showed up. He wasn't supposed to be there. I was just trying to tell you to make him go away."

"What other fine things have you done for me, Russell? Murder? Arson? You cannot claim these things for my benefit. I would sooner cut out my own heart as do the terrible things that you have done. You are a *wretched* human being, and if you cannot see that, then you are more witless than I could have imagined." The litany was out of her mouth before she could stop it. Belatedly she realized that she was egging him on. Who was the witless one now?

He seemed to be huffing, struggling to breathe. His cheeks paled, and the firearm quivered in his hand. Slowly, he raised the pistol and extended his arm through the bars, aiming it at her chest.

Time seemed to stand still; the birds ceased their chirping, the sun darkened and the wind died. Lillian closed her eyes, waiting for the blast. So this was the end, and astoundingly, she was not afraid. She had not exactly led a righteous life, but it had not been completely without virtue, especially at the end. Her affairs were in order, everything would go to charity. Fanny would be all right. Nick would save Dillon. Nick . . . Her heart contracted. Tears burned the back of her eyes. She was abandoning him, just like everyone else that he had ever cared for.

"Drop the gun, Mayburn!" She would know that deep, rumbling voice anywhere.

Nick! Her heart thrilled. Her eyes flew open. She felt him, like a potent presence, behind her.

He was holding a long-necked black pistol before him as he slowly stalked forward. "Get in the house, Lillian."

"Don't move!" Russell screamed. His pistol shifted to target Nick's chest.

No!

"Kane made him do it," Lillian cried, trying to end this madness without spilling blood.

"Go inside," Nick growled.

"Tell him, Russell. Tell him how Kane played you for a fool."

Russell blinked rapidly, as if dazed. "Oh, my God. Oh, my God." He swayed slightly.

"It was all Kane's idea," she cried. "In the end he knew you would take the fall."

Russell blanched. He slowly lowered the weapon.

Relief washed over her so powerfully that she felt faint.

Nick raced forward, yanking the pistol from Mayburn's grip and sticking it into his coat pocket. Keeping his own firearm leveled at the knave, he pulled a key from his coat and unlocked the door.

Mayburn fell forward onto both hands, landing on a rock. Nick had no sympathy for the stupid bugger. He'd brought it all on himself by coveting his brother's mistress.

Mayburn's blond head bobbed up and down, and a sob escaped from his throat. "He played me, he played me . . . for a fool . . ."

Hicks came running up.

"Send Gillman to the Bow Street office, Hicks," Nick ordered. "I need Kim and Kelly here, post-haste!"

"Yes, sir!" The butler turned heel and ran.

Pinching his nose and blinking wildly as if fighting back tears, Mayburn moaned, "I didn't mean for any of it. I never expected . . . never supposed . . ."

Nick turned to Lillian, trying to stem the violence that was surging through him. Still, he barked, "I told you to get back to the house, Lillian."

"I was not about to let him kill you." She stepped over and snuck under his arm, being careful not to disturb his pistol hand.

Nick squeezed her close. Now that she was all right and the danger had passed, he almost quaked with the power of his terror. Seeing Mayburn standing there with a pistol pointed at her chest had been like experiencing his worst nightmare. His mouth still tasted the tang of fear.

It had been an awful moment that had crystallized everything he felt for Lillian into one pinpoint of light. Perfect. Beautiful. His. It was as if God had created her especially for him. He adored her beyond anything that he had ever held dear, beyond everything he had ever experienced. Beyond reckoning.

"You scared the bloody hell out of me," was all he could say. There were no words to describe his feelings. The vulnerability of seeing her so close to death had shaken him to the core.

"I'm all right." Her smile was tight. "Now that you're here." She hugged him, and he wanted to hold her forever and never let her go. But he did not tell her this. Hell, he could hardly comprehend it himself.

Shaken by the intensity of his feelings, he fell back on what was easy. He turned to Mayburn. "When the police officers come, you are going to tell them everything. Everything that Kane put you up to."

"How did you know to come?" Lillian asked.

"Something Mayburn said at the club. Only the arsonist would know about Mrs. Bears. I didn't catch it right away. But something else was nagging at me." He had had his sights so set on Kane, his anger raised to such a fury, that he had almost missed it. He had almost taken too long to figure it out. When the realization had hit him, he had raced out of Brooks's like a rabbit in bow shot. If he had not acted right away . . . if he had lost Lillian . . . He swallowed hard, unable to face the prospect of a world without Lillian Kane.

"What was nagging you?"

He shook off his emotions, focusing instead on the facts. "His cologne. I recognized it as the same one that Beaumont wears. It made perfect sense. Mayburn was the insider, your turncoat."

"He told me that Lord Langham killed his wife." Wiping his eyes with his hand, Mayburn shook his head. "That the man was distraught . . . that we were doing good from bad."

"And you believed him?" Nick scoffed.

"Were you supposed to marry me?" Lillian asked. "And then sign over my entire dowry to him?"

Mayburn's features flushed red. "Yes," he whispered.

Lillian pressed her face into Nick's chest, and he squeezed her tight. He hated that she had to suffer this way. To see the filth that was a mockery of a man. He wished he could protect her from it, forever. Today, at least, was a start.

"You gave Kane your brother's handkerchief?" Nick demanded.

"Yes," he whispered.

"And the letters?"

"Yes."

"This makes no sense," Lillian muttered. "Russell was crazed enough to do these horrible things but rational enough to see them through? He must be sick."

"He is. But there was method to his madness," Nick avowed. "He is a murderer."

Facing Mayburn, she charged, "What of the Mayburn motto? What about protecting your own flesh and blood? You *knew* what you were doing was wrong."

"Yes," he whispered miserably. Tears lined his pasty cheeks. "I guess, deep down I did."

"I wonder how Kane is going to enjoy John Newman's amenities," Nick murmured.

"You think that there is enough proof?" Lillian looked up, anxiety permeating her beautiful gaze. As if Kane's demise was beyond what she could hope for. Anger surged through him at the pain the bastard had caused her. He would stop at nothing to ensure that Kane paid the piper.

Nick kissed the top of her golden hair as conviction filled him. He would protect her from Kane and anyone else, or die trying. "Kane will never get near you again," he vowed, feeling the pledge down to his soul.

Her eyes slid to Mayburn. "Hanging?"

He nodded. "Between Russell's account and what I've already gathered, Solicitor General Dagwood will have more than enough to make *both* of them swing."

Sadness filled her gaze. That she could still feel compassion for that miserable wretch of a human being did her credit. But Nick was not as forgiving.

"By tonight, Beaumont will be freed." He was glad for it. But where did this leave him and Lillian?

"Thank you, Nick. Thank you." She hugged him close. "I don't know what I would ever have done without you."

Chapter 27

∼◦◦◦∼

Lillian rolled over, reaching for him, but Nick was not there. She tried to clear the sleepy cobwebs from her mind. Sudden fear gripped her. She sat up. "Nick?"

"Oh, you're awake." He stepped out of the dressing room, wearing only an ivory linen shirt and smalls.

Pressing her hand to her heart, she willed it to slow.

"Are you all right?" he asked, worry knitting his brow.

She nodded. "I couldn't find you."

His handsome face softened, and he sat on the edge of the bed. "Well, I'm right here."

Scooting over on the mattress, she laid her cheek on his wide, muscled thigh. He grazed his hand over her hair, brushing it gently.

"Can we stay in bed today?" she implored, trying to keep her voice from sounding too desperate. "Let the world go on without us just for a few hours."

His hand lowered to her back, swirling in gentle circles. "I cannot do that, Lillian. I still have much work to do with Dagwood on the prosecutions against Kane and Mayburn. Greayston might be horrified by his younger son's actions, but he is still paying for some pretty forceful counsel for Mayburn's defense. The man is making noises, trying to blame it all on Kane."

"Greayston only sees what he wants to. If Kane is the villain, then Russell is not to blame."

"Well, the barrister he retained is fighting the prosecution tooth and nail."

"But Russell confessed."

He glowered. "There's a lawyer for you."

"What difference would it make to the prosecutions if you stayed here with me one afternoon?" she argued, trying not to sound too forlorn. "You have been working almost nonstop since Russell's arrest seven days ago. You deserve a break."

"There is still the business at Andersen Hall."

"What is so important that it cannot wait?"

His hand stilled, resting flat on her back. "The Board of Trustees meets today, and I cannot miss it."

"Will Marcus be there?"

"Unless he's a complete wastrel, he will show at the meeting."

"I do not like him," she murmured, sifting her fingers through the coarse hairs around his knee.

"You have not even met the man."

"But you do not like him."

"I did not like him as a child." She felt him shrug. "I expect that I have to see how he has managed to turn out. The lad I knew was not one to become a war hero, but Marcus has done just that."

"So you will give him the opportunity to prove himself?"

"If he manages to stay around. The Marcus Dunn I knew was quick to take off at the first sign of trouble."

Rolling over, she stared up at this man who was so dear. "Then the query is: Can leopards actually change their spots?"

He moved his hand to her neck, grasping it in a gentle hold. Her pulse pounded against his palm. "I, obviously, changed mine."

"Don't sound so desolate," she chided. "We have done nothing wrong."

"I broke my pledge."

"Do you regret it?" she asked, knowing the answer. They were too well suited for him to truly regret it.

"I can't," he murmured, leaning over and pressing his lips to hers in a delicate kiss. "But I know that I should."

Opening her mouth to him, she pushed away the flurry of worry. She had been seeing signs that Nick was not wholly content with their arrangement. She had been trying to ignore it, but her nightmares would not let her hide her head in the sand.

In her dreams she was looking for Nick, calling out to him, reaching for him, but he was not there. Where could he be? Fear washed over her like a tide of longing. Often he came, only to disappear like a ghost misting into a cloud. Once in a dream, he appeared before her as a king, adorned in blazing armor to the hilt, a ghost, just like Hamlet's dead father. Again, he faded away into the haze of the dawn at the ramparts, before ever telling her that he loved her.

Closing her eyes, she pushed away all morbid thoughts, living for the moment, living for his kiss on her lips. Raking her hands through his hair, her tongue met his, and the familiar thrills shimmered through her. She groaned. Intensifying the passionate play, she showed him with her body that she wanted to evolve the kiss from sweet to more fiery.

His tongue glided over hers and tingles raced up her naked skin, igniting the flames that had scorched her in the darkened shadows of her bedroom. Now, in the light of day, she longed for him still, yearned for him to be inside of her, a part of her, never to leave.

She pressed her hands to his manhood, feeling the stretch of thin fabric cloaking him. Stroking him, she felt him harden. Stiff, he throbbed in her hand. A satisfied sigh escaped from her mouth.

"Lillian," he murmured, his voice husky. "I can't. I have things to take care of. I don't want to be late."

"The carriage got stuck in a rut." She kneaded his shaft with eager fingers, feeling it jolt. "The road was congested." Leaning forward, she pressed an open kiss to its head, tasting a gratifying dampness beneath her lips. "I had a headache and needed—"

"You never have a headache," he groaned, running his hand through her tresses. "And I thank the heavens for it."

Setting her mouth to his shaft, she gently bit it, teasing the length of his member with delicate nibbles. It jumped under her ministrations, straining against the fine cloth.

Reaching up, she pressed him down onto the bed,

rising up before him on her knees. "I never would have thought that sleeping without nightclothes could feel so good," she breathed, running her hands down her sides.

His eyes roved over her with predatory satisfaction. He grazed her nipples with the backs of his hands, down her flank, caressing her thighs. "You're so beautiful."

A thrill of pleasure shot through her at the hunger she heard in his rumbling voice. "So are you." He was. He was the most magnificent man she had ever laid eyes on.

His hands fanned out, bracing her thighs and squeezing. "You are too much of a temptation. I cannot keep my hands off you."

"Then don't," she murmured, closing her eyes.

His fingers tickled at the fine hairs between her thighs, edging toward that warm and magical place. Spreading her inner lips with nimble fingers, he slowly stoked the fires of her passion.

She threw her head back, rocking her hips in rhythm to his strokes. "Oh, Nick," she moaned.

He grasped her hips, lifting her up and shifting her off of him. Disappointment flushed through her. "Don't stop now."

"I want to try something new," he murmured, rotating her and pressing her gently into the soft mattress.

She lay flat on her stomach, waiting for him. Excitement pooled in her belly.

He tossed his smalls to the floor, leaving on the linen shirt. He rocked over her, laying a hot, wet kiss between her shoulder blades. The tails of his shirt raked across her buttocks. She shivered. His velvety lips traveled, teasing, licking, sucking his way down to her waist. His breath trailed across her derriere, raising the fine hairs in that most private crevice.

His tongue slid across her buttock. Nervous, she pulled up onto her elbow. "Nick?" she asked, unable to hide the jumpiness from her voice.

"Trust me, Lillian. I will not do anything that you will not thoroughly enjoy."

She lay flat on her belly, waiting, tingles quivering in her middle, wondering what he was going to do. She trusted him with her life and knew that his only agenda was pleasure.

He slowly parted her legs and kissed her inner thigh. Her pelvis bucked and she groaned. Warm breath slid across her heated core, making it throb with wanting.

His hand slid beneath her, finding that hard nub that begged to be touched. Lightning flashed from that amazing juncture to every extremity and back again.

Slowly he stroked her, bringing her back to that peak of pleasure. Her body flamed. She was panting, groaning, needing him to fill her, to make her whole.

Sliding a pillow beneath her abdomen, he raised her onto her knees, lifting her buttocks into the air. He grasped her hips, spreading her thighs with his knees. His manhood pressed at her core, thick and wanting.

She felt open, like a flower waiting to be plucked. Her breath was heavy, her body shimmering with a need only he could satisfy.

Planting one last kiss on her shoulder, he reared back and plunged into her womanhood, filling her.

"Oh, God!" she cried out as her inner muscles

clutched him in welcome. He hammered so deep inside of her that she felt besieged by his body. Conquered in heated passion.

He rode her, and carried her, taking her with him on a wild rampage. The world honed into one perfect rhythm as his thrusts drew her closer and closer to that divine place that they shared. . . .

Her womanhood convulsed, her senses shattered, and she was lost. He thrust once, twice more, warmth gushing as he poured his seed inside. He fell on top of her with a shuddering groan.

She lay beneath him, blanketed by his weighty warmth. Her heartbeat slowed, her breath returned to normal and her senses awakened once more.

Panting, he slipped out, rolling onto his back beside her. His hand rested lightly on her shoulder.

Leaning over, she rubbed her nose in his raven hair, marveling at the softness. He smelled of sex and the familiar scent of almonds. She was grinning, so very content. She kissed his bold, dark brow, those piercing cocoa eyes, his aristocratic nose. Lips soft as heaven. And that angular chin with just the hint of a cleft.

"You shaved," she whispered, nibbling on his smooth jaw.

"Um hum."

"Wait." She stopped. "How do you smell of almonds?"

"Yesterday was the first Tuesday of the month."

Hope filled her. "And you had your soap sent here?"

"Only for this month. Don't worry."

Her heart sank, and the familiar fear shuddered through her. This time she did not bother to hide her distress. "You do not expect to be here in a month's time?"

"I never said that." He lifted up onto his elbow. "I just did not want to presume anything."

She shifted to the edge of the bed, sitting up, upset, confused and angry with herself for being so stupid. Sex was not a way to keep him. It was not what Nick was about. He had told her from the start that he did not believe in long-term commitment. That it was likely to fail in the end. What did she expect from him?

"What do you want from me, Lillian?" He sat beside her and grasped her limp hand.

"I don't know," she lied, lifting a shoulder. She wanted him with her, simple as that. But Nicholas Redford was not the type to be a kept man. Though he would be anything but, it might appear so to the world. His pride would come into play, and moreover, she could not bear to sully his name. He was too good a man to be tainted with London's most notorious mistress. How would it impact his business? She did not know. How long would he stay with her? She knew that he still feared abandonment. That he was set against marriage and children for that very reason.

Children. Nick's children. Small, raven-haired minxes . . . But they would be less serious, less scared. She would protect them, never let them feel the pains that their father had.

"Lillian, you're crying," Nick murmured as he traced a finger down her cheek. "What is wrong?"

"I don't know," she sniffed, turning her head to him. He wrapped his steely arms around her and hugged her close. She bawled into his chest, a huddling jumbled mess of feelings thicker than a quagmire. She was so very confused.

He rubbed her back with smooth, round strokes. "Tell me what is bothering you, Lillian. I will try to fix it."

How could he, when he was the problem?

"I'm ruining your shirt," she muttered through the haze of her distress. "I'm sorry."

"No, I am, Lillian. I know the last few weeks have been difficult and it's still hard."

She nodded mutely, not knowing what else to do. She hated being such a puddle of tears, hated the mishmash of feelings conflicting inside her.

"Things can't go on like this," Nick said.

She stiffened. *Oh dear Lord in heaven. What did he mean by that?* But she was too much of a coward to ask, letting him speak instead.

"I have to take care of some things today. There's this board meeting, but when I come home, we will talk. All right?"

Swallowing, she nodded, wiping the final tear from her eye.

"Good." His lips brushed across hers. "All right, then."

Standing, he headed back toward the dressing room.

She fell back onto the soft feathered mattress, curling up into a ball. She dragged the sheet over her. She felt chilled, alone and very afraid.

Chapter 28

"**L**illian! Lillian!" Dillon called, snapping his fingers in front of her face. "That's the third time in half an hour that we've completely lost you."

"Oh, sorry," she mumbled, burying her nose in her cup and sipping the lukewarm tea.

"It's hard to have a decent scandal-broth when one of the guests of honor is mentally absent," he chided.

"Oh, is there some gossip?" she asked, trying to feign interest.

"Only that Dagwood's political ambitions have mired for the moment. He's still smarting from trying to hang an innocent man." He clapped his hands. "I wonder if his career might not be over."

"Wishful thinking." Fanny snorted. "The public might have a short memory, but for politicians it's the length of a nose."

"You should be happy to see Dagwood so humiliated, Lillian," Dillon remarked, ostensibly surprised by her lack of reaction. "You hate the man."

She shrugged. "Yes, he is overambitious, but in the end, he was simply doing his job."

"What ails you?" Dillon cried. "If I had given you this intelligence last week, you would have been dancing a jig."

Fanny slid a fruit tart into her mouth. "She's in love."

"Redford is quite the handsome bloke," Dillon remarked. "And I do owe him my life, well, along with Lillian. Too bad he carries himself like a peasant. Otherwise, he might just manage to get along in Society."

Fury rose in Lillian so overwhelming that she screeched, "Why, you self-centered prig! You try growing up in an orphanage and—"

Dillon laughed. "You *are* in love!"

Lillian's mouth closed and she eyed her friends, sinking back in the settee, deflated. "I suppose I am."

"Why so glum?" Dillon asked. "Father has agreed to continue paying your expenses for as long as you need it, even if we are no longer an item. And he lets you reside here indefinitely, he is so grateful to you for exposing Kane's villainy."

"Dillon is right," Fanny added. "It's not such a terrible fix. Redford really is a wonderful man. And between saving the queen's dog and Beaumont's arse, his enquiry agency will be in the bull." She grinned wickedly. "Besides, it couldn't have happened to a nicer girl."

Lillian wagged her finger. "You knew this would happen! You set me up for a fall!"

"Flat as a pancake." Fanny's shoulders lifted proudly.

Dillon sighed, sipping his tea. "I suppose it was only a matter of time until you left me."

"That's the problem," she moaned. "I don't know where I'm going."

"You mean Italy is out?" Fanny flipped open her fan and waved it languidly. "Just take him with you. Love in Venice is supposed to be divine."

"I'm not going to Italy, there's a war on. Besides—" Lillian studied her teacup, embarrassed. "I've found a better use for my money."

"Like what?"

She shrugged. "I'm giving it away to charity."

"What?" Fanny screeched, flicking her fan closed with a snap. "After all of our hard work?"

"Not all of it!" Dillon cried.

"No, not all of it. I still have to live. But a whole lot of it. It's more money than I will ever need. I just wish that I could give it to Andersen Hall now and not have to wait until I turn twenty-four."

"Nick was telling me about the mess at the orphanage," Fanny added. "He worries that the trustees will vote to dissolve the foundling home if there's not enough confidence in the new headmaster."

Lillian nodded. "Nick is working with Headmaster Dunn's son, Marcus, to ensure that the orphanage remains open and functioning in the spirit that Dunn would have wanted." The plight of the orphanage and its charges had been taking up a lot of Nick's time recently. Between the prosecution against Russell and Kane and the troubles at Andersen Hall, Lillian felt that she hardly saw Nick these days. And now he wanted to *speak with her* this afternoon.

"You can pick your face up off the floor now, Lillian," Fanny chided. "Everything's going to be fine."

Dillon scooted forward on his seat. "So if you're not going to Italy, what are your plans now, darling?"

She realized that the endearment Dillon used so easily had never crossed Nick's lips, nor had he ever uttered a word about his feelings for her. Today was going to be bad.

"I don't know," she stated glumly. She feared that the only thing she knew for certain was that she was going to shrivel up into an old crone and die a lonely woman.

"Oh, stop it, Lillian. The man loves you madly."

"He has not said so. And," she swallowed, "I worry that he is going to end it."

"Why would he do a stupid thing like that?" Dillon asked. "You're probably the best thing that ever happened to him."

"Thank you, Dillon." She was not about to expose Nick's insecurities. That he avoided intimacy because he feared being abandoned. "Nick, well . . . he does not believe in marriage."

"So? Neither do you."

"But he has this blasted code of honor. Oh, I don't know. All I do know is that I fear he is not being fully honest with me. I'm afraid that today he's going to tell me that he is no longer happy with me."

Fanny grimaced. "That is not good." She and Dillon exchanged a meaningful glance.

"What?" Lillian asked.

"Well, Nick asked us to be around this afternoon. He thought you might be needing us."

Heaven help her. Wilting into the settee, she groaned.

"What if he is going to propose marriage?" Fanny asked, watching her carefully.

"I doubt that," she muttered.

"And if he did? What would be your answer?"

"No, of course," Dillon supplied. "Lillian's sworn against the marital state for as long as I've known her. And let us just recognize that despite Redford's obvious charms, he is the dominant kind. Used to giving orders. Lillian would never sit for that."

"Just because he gives orders does not mean that Lillian has to take them," Fanny shot back. She turned to Lillian. "So what would your answer be?"

"I, I . . ."

"Dr. Michael Winner to see you, my lady," Hicks announced from the threshold.

"Oh, please send him in."

Lillian stood nervously. Dr. Winner was one of Nick's oldest and dearest friends. She wondered why he was calling.

"Good day, Lady Janus." He entered and bowed. He looked better than when she had last seen him, covered in soot, coughing and sad. He was tall, if a bit portly. He had a kind face that crinkled at the corners of his eyes and mouth, as if he easily slipped into a smile.

"Dr. Winner, may I introduce Lord Beaumont and Miss Figbottom." Lillian motioned to the tea service laid out before them. "Please join us."

She waited for an answer, but the man seemed struck dumb.

"Dr. Winner?"

He shook himself as if startled from a daydream.

Carefully, he removed his hat and stepped forward. "It is an honor and a pleasure to meet such a fine actress as yourself, Miss Figbottom." His pale cheeks and balding head had flushed to a high cherry, enunciating the tuft of brown hair ringing his receding hairline.

Fanny sashayed over, extending her hand. "The pleasure is mine."

"I used to go to the theater just to see your shoulders." His eyes drifted to the swell of pale curves rising up out of her bottle green gown, taking in her shoulders, as well. He blinked toffee eyes. "Did that come out as stupidly as it sounded to my own ears?"

"Not at all," Fanny cooed, obviously thrilled with the attention. "Come sit by me, Doctor."

Shooting Dillon a glare to move off, Fanny led him to the divan. "Some tea?"

He nodded, his loose lips lifting into a smile. "Miss Figbottom, I feel so very honored."

"You already said that," Dillon muttered under his breath.

Lillian waved at him to behave.

"I had asked Nick for an introduction," Winner went on, oblivious, "but I expect he's been too busy these days. . . ." His eyes shifted to Lillian, and she tried not to blush.

"He had not mentioned it," Fanny replied, obviously irritated that Nick had not spoken of the good doctor. As if Nick could have known that Fanny was on the prowl and the doctor was just her type.

Fanny poured him tea, and even Lillian had to admire her grace and form. It was like watching water spilled over glass, fluid and seamless. Fanny was an artist. And she had a captive audience.

"Thank you, Miss Figbottom." Winner accepted the china cup and sipped.

"Call me Fanny."

He just barely stopped himself from sputtering into his tea.

Lillian almost felt sorry for him. Once Fanny turned on the charm, it was easier to get out of the way of a runaway carriage.

"Nick had not told me how nice you are."

Rolling his eyes at Lillian so that Fanny could not see, Dillon helped himself to another fruit tart and sat down in the armchair. "So how do you know Redford, Doctor?"

"I've known Nick, well, since he was a drip-nosed, fist-ready lad."

"You worked at Andersen Hall a long time?" Lillian asked, almost jealous that he had known Nick for so long and she only a short time.

"I was still fresh from Edinburgh. Had barely been out of the Royal College of Physicians and newly married to my dear Eleanor." His cheeks tinged, and he turned to Fanny, explaining, "My wife."

"Oh, you are married?"

"Widowed."

Fanny practically preened. "Go on, my good man, please."

"Dunn had come calling on behalf of the orphanage. I told him that I didn't have blunt enough to be giving it away, and he somehow convinced me to donate my time and 'handiwork' instead."

"Very charitable of you." Fanny bustled her skirts sideways, exposing just a hint of ankle.

"And?" Dillon urged.

Eyeing Fanny, Winner tugged at his cravat. "Nick

had had the fever and was segregated from the other children in the dormitory. He was a mere slip of a thing, really—"

"I find that hard to believe," Dillon declared.

"He was not always the mighty Nick he is today. No." Dr. Winner sighed, looking wistful. "He's grown up, our boy." He smiled. "I can't really take the credit, but I'm proud of him just the same." He turned to Fanny. "He's the enquiry agent to the queen, you know."

Fanny nodded sagely, tracing a finger across the line of her jaw. "I had heard something of that. But I would love to know more."

"He saved her beloved pug, Lancelot." His brow furrowed, and he turned to Lillian. "But you were there, Lady Janus. You can certainly tell it better than me."

"Nick was magnificent." Lillian shook her head, still impressed with Nick's abilities. "He could see what we could not. The wretched Master of the Hounds, Mr. Glen, was a foul character of the worst sort. But I had no idea. I was completely fooled. But not Nick."

"He knew straight off that the scoundrel was behind the kidnapping?" Dillon scratched his ear. "Or is it dog-napping?"

"Nick came to it by piecing together all of the facts and seeing which did not fit. It was all very logical. . . ." Lillian's thoughts drifted off. The spark of an idea flickered like the wick on a candle. Gradually, it intensified. Nick was a creature of logic. She just had to find a way to let him know that it went beyond all logic for her to abandon him. So that she would never do so. But how to elucidate that point?

"And?" Dillon urged. "Then what happened?"

"Oh," Lillian blinked. "What did you say?"

"You were telling us about the Master of the Hounds . . . Mr. Glen . . ."

"You tell it, Dr. Winner, I feel the sudden inclination to stretch my legs a bit. I'll be in the back garden." She rose. There was too much thinking to be done for lazing over a chitchat. She needed a plan. And a good one. She headed for the door.

"Oh, I was so distracted, I forgot to ask," Winner declared, drawing her from her reverie. "Is Nick around?"

She stopped midstep. "Isn't he at the meeting of the Board of Trustees?" Then it struck her. *"With you?"*

Winner's mouth worked. "That's not until tomorrow."

Lillian felt as if a bucket of icy seawater had been dumped over her head, drenching her to the bone. And it stank.

"Oh, dear," Fanny muttered, rising.

"Lillian, you're as pale as plaster," Dillon declared. He rose. "What's wrong?"

Lillian suddenly found it a trifle hard to breathe. He had lied. Nick, her upright, noble savior, had lied. And he wanted to talk with her this afternoon. It was the end. *Her end.*

"Are you ill, Lady Janus?" Winner stood, setting down his china cup with a clatter. "Can I help?"

"Her affliction is most severe." Fanny wrapped a thick arm over Lillian's shoulders and squeezed. "And, I hate to say, untreatable."

Chapter 29

Nick waited in the opulent drawing room, pacing before the tall windows. His palms were sweaty, his mouth parched. He knew that this was a long shot, but he had to try.

His instincts were telling him that Lillian could not be swayed with words alone. And he could sooner ignore the voice in his head than suffer watching Lillian cry as she had this morning. It had made him want to find a way to make it stop—either that or hit someone. He knew that she was not happy. He could almost see her struggle as she fought with her feelings for him.

She would not be won over with expressions of affection. No, it would take a broad stroke for her to finally understand that love was not a malady to be suffered poorly, contained, or, better yet, recovered from.

Not that he was an expert on the overpowering feeling. It was so new, so compelling. It was like his world was awash in a prism of color that blinded him of everything else. At the center of light was his golden-haired beauty who made the pulse in his veins drum with intoxicating vigor. When she was around, he felt more alive than he had ever been. More aware of the significance of being a part of something greater than himself. When she was away, he longed only for the moment when he would be back with her.

His feelings were so fantastic, so foreign to his experience, that they terrified him to his bones. But he figured that if he was going to be scared out of his wits, then he might as well be with the woman that he loved. But she needed proof, something so rock solid as to make her *believe.*

So he paced in the drawing room, waiting to see if his suspicions would bear fruit. Waiting to see if he could take this incredible ardor and make it whole, with Lillian.

"Mr. Redford." The sinewy Viscount Rece stepped through the doorway. His gray hair tufted around his head, reminding Nick of a barn owl. Nick recalled a moonlit night when he and Lillian had met; they had each been escaping a crowd and had found each other.

Lord Rece scratched his head. "I suppose you're here about our failure to visit. There is no manipulation on my part, I assure you. My wife has been suffering from a cold."

Nick shook off the memory, focusing on his charge. "I know, my lord. Lillian received Lady Rece's note."

His bushy gray brows lifted. "Oh."

"I'm not here about your wife. I am here about you."

"Will this take long?" Rece frowned. "I have an appointment."

"It depends on how quickly you answer my questions. If you please. It is important." Vitally so.

"Very well." Rece waved him to a seat. "But I will not delay my business for long."

"Thank you, my lord." Nick felt his heart begin to pound as he settled into the armchair by the window. The afternoon light bathed the red carpet in golden color, reminding him of Lillian's lovely hair. "I wish to ask you about your falling out with Lillian's family."

"It's a bit late for trying to clear the air, Mr. Redford."

"Perhaps you are correct, but my instincts are telling me that it is worth exploring." Nick pulled at his coat sleeves, assuming the mantle of enquiry agent. "What was the nature of the falling-out?"

Rece studied him a long moment, then shifted sideways in his seat. He straightened his coat, looking away. "I don't know that I'm comfortable discussing this with you."

"Please, my lord."

"There is no good to come from it."

"Did you and Lady Janus's mother have an affair?"

Rece's face darkened to an angry scowl. "How dare you insinuate any such thing?" He stood, pointing to the door. "I'll have you tossed out!"

Nick rose. "Was it three-and-twenty years ago? Before she had ever met Lord Cornelius Kane?"

Rece looked as if he had gulped down a whole

fish, bones and all. "Out! Out! You impudent knave!" His extended arm was quivering.

"Did you promise to come for her, only to leave her high and dry?"

"Stop it." Rece's voice was a harsh whisper, and his eyes slid to the open door. Slowly, his arm lowered. "Stop it now."

Nick felt the truth lock into place like a dungeon gridiron. Satisfaction filtered through him. Now it was only a matter of bringing Rece around to the facts.

Nick strode to the entry and slammed the door closed with a thud. "Did you have intimate relations with Lady Janus's mother? Yes or no?"

"What is it any of your business?" Rece cried harshly, looking cornered.

"Anything that affects Lillian is my utmost concern." Nick took a deep breath. "And I believe that Lillian may be your daughter."

Rece's face drained of color. "What queer tricks do you play? If this is a callous ruse to deceive my poor wife—"

"Lillian's mother married Kane because she was forced to. The man she loved, the father of her child, never came for her as he had promised."

Rece's brows knitted together, unwound and rejoined. "This cannot . . ." He swallowed. "How do you know these things?"

"Lillian told me. She does not know that I am here today. She has no idea, but I had the suspicion. It was the eyes."

Rece raised a trembling hand to his face. "What do you mean?"

"Azure."

"Many people—"

"Not with that depth of color."

"Can this be?" he muttered, dropping clumsily into the chair. "Is it possible?"

"You are the only one who can tell me."

Rece shook his head, looking older, lost even.

"Did you have intimate relations with Lady Rece three-and-twenty years ago?" Nick asked softly.

Slowly, Rece nodded. "Yes," he whispered harshly.

"And did you promise to come for her?"

"Yes."

"What happened?"

"I received a missive. My father was ill. Near death, it said. So I sent a letter to Iris, telling her that I had to go. That I could not meet her . . ."

"Was your father ill?"

"No. But how?" he cried, rubbing his eyes.

"Kane."

Rece flinched, as if struck.

"I believe it to be true," Nick avowed. "He tried the same trick with Beaumont to get him away from Lillian. False notices of illness, even death. A ruse to try to get him out of the way."

"Don't tell me . . ." He rubbed his eyes. "He did not succumb to the subterfuge?"

"He knew that Kane was a serpent. How were you to suspect?"

Rece seemed to wilt before Nick's very eyes. "I thought . . . I thought that she could not have loved me if she couldn't wait. . . . I was so angry. Felt so betrayed . . ."

"Likely, she never received your letter. I presume you never received her posts."

Mutely he shook his head.

"I venture that the posts from Lillian's mother to you were interrupted. Bribe a servant and the world's intercourse is undone."

"I came back and she was married. . . ."

"She thought you had left her. That you had forsaken her, and your child."

His shoulders slumped. "It was my fault. My own doing . . ."

"I can see where Lillian gets her overblown sense of responsibility."

"Overblown? Nay." Guilt flashed in his eyes. "I had told Kane. We were friends, you see. I thought that he would be glad for me. I had boasted of my great love . . . Even of her sizable dowry . . ." His eyes glistened with unshed tears. "I led him to my Iris as surely as if I had handed him the wedding ring and sent him to the vicar myself."

"Kane is a viper. He has wrought destruction in his wake. Even if you had inadvertently given him the idea, it was his evildoing. The fault lies with him."

"The monster!" Rece hammered his fist onto his thigh. "I could kill him!"

"Lord of the Manor of Tyburn shall have that honor. And it cannot come too soon, in my opinion. Solicitor General Dagwood is taking special care to ensure that he has the right man this time, but he cannot ignore the evidence. Kane will hang."

"So much lost," Rece ground out, anger reviving him. "So many years of pain that I owe that bastard."

"Regret can only do so much. Now is the time to right the wrongs. You have the golden opportunity to show Lillian that she was not abandoned. That had you known . . ."

"I would have stormed into Lord Janus's household and claimed what was mine!" His voice rose with conviction. "The lady I loved and my unborn child."

"Lillian believes what her mother did. That you knew about her but did not love them enough to come for them." Rage made Nick's hands clench at the pain his beloved Lillian had suffered. "That you did not care enough to protect them from Kane."

"What have I done? My pride. My foolish pride. Oh, how I wish I could cut it from my character." He swiped his hand across his wrist. "Cleave it away and bleed it out of me."

"What is all of the yelling about?" Lady Rece cried from the doorway. "I could hear you all the way in the parlor." Her nose was red, her eyes glassy. Otherwise, she looked alert.

Nick stood, looking over at Rece for direction.

"Mr. Redford? What are you doing here? Is it Lillian? Has something happened?"

Slowly, Rece rose. "Dorothea. There is something I must tell you. . . ."

"What is it?" She blanched. "Oh, dear. Where is a vinaigrette when you need one?"

She swayed slightly, and Rece was immediately at her side. He and Nick helped her over to the couch and settled her there. Rece pulled a vinaigrette from his coat pocket. Obviously this was not uncommon.

Opening the tiny silver box, Rece held it under her nose. She blinked, the color returning to her cheeks.

"Tell me, Donald. Tell what ill has befallen my dear friend."

"Actually, Dorothea, I am pleased to be able to share with you good tidings."

"Really?" She looked doubtfully from Nick to her husband and back again.

"I"—he cleared his throat—"I mean *we* are parents."

"Wh-what?"

"It turns out that Lillian Kane is my daughter."

Lady Rece's mouth opened, then closed. Her brow furrowed.

"Really?"

"I, ah," Rece's cheeks reddened. "It was a long time ago . . ."

"So Kane is not her real father?"

"No," Nick supplied, wondering how much to say and what he should leave for her husband to handle.

"I've never liked Kane. Hmmm." She scratched her chin. "No wonder she always veered the topic away whenever I mentioned him."

"He's a scoundrel of the first order," Rece declared.

"You do have exactly the same eye color," she interrupted, staring off. "And that obstinate streak . . . hmmm. Makes a certain sort of sense."

"You think so?" Rece asked, blinking, as if taken aback. "You don't seem very shocked."

"You act as if I didn't know about Iris," she huffed, sitting up.

Rece's cheeks reddened. "You did?"

"Of course I did. You carried your pain around like scars of battle."

"I did?"

"Why else do you suppose I befriended Lillian in the first instance?"

"You knew that she was my daughter?"

"Don't be silly. Had I known that, I would have

tried to take her here to live with us. No. I simply wished to know more of the woman who had broken your heart. By chance I met Lillian at the milliner's one day. Since Iris was no longer alive, I hoped for intelligence from her daughter. But that fortuitous meeting grew into a wonderful friendship, since she is such a charming lady." Excitement filled her gaze. "Do you know what this means, Donald?"

He smiled with such affection that there was no question he loved his wife well. "What, Dorothea?"

"I have my girl!" Tears sprang in her eyes, and she threw her arms around her husband. "This is wonderful! Wonderful news! I love you, Donald! You have made me so very happy!"

Nick rose, stepping back to give them their moment together. He felt a tug of longing for such caring, for such a secure bond of affection.

"Oh, Donald," Lady Rece sighed, pulling back from his embrace. "Iris may have been your first love. I am just so very glad to be your last."

Nick cleared his throat loudly. They turned to him, as if recalling that he was there.

"Lillian does not know yet," Nick stated. "We must tell her."

Rece exhaled loudly, sitting beside his wife and clutching her hands in his. "Will you enlighten her, or shall I?"

"She is unprepared. This will come as a great shock to her." He could only imagine how he would feel being united with his natural father. "There is much emotion involved—"

"So what do you suggest we do?" Lord Rece asked. "I must confess I am a bit nervous about her reaction."

Rece was not the only one. Nick was worried about how Lillian would receive the intelligence. And how she would view his role in the affair. She claimed not to want to know her natural father. He had not believed her, but what if it was true? What if his strategy blew up in his face? Instead of her overcoming her fear of love, what if Lillian turned against him for his heavy-handed behavior? Should he have come to her first with his suspicions *before* confronting Rece? He had not wanted to cruelly raise her hopes. It was a mighty gamble he was taking, and the stakes could not have been higher.

"I can speak to her first, if you wish," Lady Rece offered. "Smooth the way, so to speak."

Nick shook his head. "No. It's my responsibility. I went behind her back to uncover the truth. I will be the one to tell her."

"You sound as if she might not be glad for the tidings," Rece said, worry marring his brow.

"She has not had it easy—"

"Devil take Kane." Rece shook his fist. His cheeks blanched. "Oh, how poorly I have treated her! My own daughter!"

Shaking his head, Nick offered, "You did not know—"

"Is that why Lillian took up with Beaumont?" Lady Rece asked. "To get away from Kane?"

"Yes."

"I suspected as much, though she never said." She patted her husband's hand. "We will make it up to her, you and I. I know that she longs to have a family. She would never admit as much, but I can tell."

"Will she . . . be angry with me, you think?" Rece questioned, apprehensively.

"To be honest, I'm not sure how she will react at first," Nick replied. "But she is a woman of great sense. She will understand who the true villain is in this piece."

"You admire her well?" Rece asked, studying him with a keen eye.

"More than you can ever know."

Rece looked fondly over at his wife. "Oh, I think I have some idea."

Chapter 30

⟡⟡⟡

"Oh, dear Lord in heaven," Lillian murmured. "I really need to lie down."

"You're already prone, darling." Fanny clucked over her like a mother hen.

"Can I get you a vinaigrette?" Winner asked from over Fanny's shoulder. His brows were knotted in a scowl.

"Or how about a brandy?" Dillon cried, pacing along the back of the sofa where she lay. "I know I could certainly use one."

"What the hell is going on here?" Nick demanded.

Winner, Fanny and Dillon melted away.

Nick stood in the doorway, stealing the final breath from her throat. He looked resplendent in a navy coat with pearl buttons, white ruffles spilling out of his cuffs and an ivory neck cloth framed by a high collar. He wore black breeches, and his black boots had been buffed to a bright gloss. The man had no right to look so magnificent when she looked like a carriage smashup.

"Lillian!" He strode to her side. "What's wrong?"

"I'm fine," she muttered, rising up on one elbow and then swinging her legs over to sit. Adjusting her skirts, she assured him with false bravado, "I was just a bit tired."

"Are you certain?" he insisted, concern marring his gorgeous face.

A mortified blush slunk up from her toes all the way to her hairline. "Absolutely."

He cleared his throat. "You are positively certain that you're feeling all right?"

"Yes," she ground out. "I am not a powder puff, you know."

"Of course you aren't."

Oh, this was bad, he was patronizing her now. She could not stand it. She dreaded the moment, yet she would have it now and be done with it. "Do you have something you want to tell me, Nick?"

"Do you two want to be alone?" Dillon asked.

Fanny swatted him on the arm, hissing.

"That is probably a good idea, Dillon," Lillian agreed.

"Are you certain?" Fanny asked.

"If one more person asks me if I am certain, I am going to scream."

Looking askance, Fanny turned to the men. "Let us give them a few moments alone."

"I'm taking the brandy," Dillon declared, grabbing the snifter and clutching it under his arm. "Unless you need it, Redford."

"I'm fine." Nick waved him away.

The door closed behind them with a resounding click of the mechanism.

"They're probably listening at the keyhole," Lillian muttered.

"Winner wouldn't let them."

"He'll let Fanny do just about anything. He's infatuated. Makes men injudicious." And silly young women too.

He swallowed, sitting beside her and grasping her hand.

Blast, his palm was clammy, another sure sign. The fear that had been simmering inside her bubbled forth and she wanted to expire on the spot. But she was not a coward and wanted to make him say the words.

"Since Dr. Winner is here, I suppose that you've already figured out that I was not at a board meeting," he began haltingly.

"The thought had crossed my mind," she murmured, rubbing her free hand up and down on her gown, trying for something to hold on to in order to bear the onslaught.

"I know that it was not right to lie, but I just could not abide by telling you where I was going."

She waited, her back so tense that she felt like she was bearing creeling stones. But she was not a Scottish bridegroom facing pre-wedding trials; she was a woman about to be cast off.

"I know I had no right, but I went to see your natural father."

His face faded in and out of focus, and for a moment, she thought that he had said that he had seen her natural father.

"Lillian? Did you hear me?"

She shook off the daze. "I'm sorry, what did you say?"

"I know your true father."

"What in heaven's name are you talking about?" To her dismay, her voice had risen to a shriek.

"Your natural father is Viscount Rece. He had no idea that you were his child."

Lillian pressed her hand to her breast, trying to stop feeling like she was splintering into a thousand fragments.

Wrapping his arm around her shoulders, he squeezed her close. "Breathe, Lillian. Take deep breaths."

She swallowed a gulpful of air, and it sounded like a shuddering wheeze.

"Rece had not discarded your mother. Kane fouled their relationship. Just like everything else, he was poison to them. He turned them against each other. Probably so that he could snare your mother's dowry. Your name is Lillian Rece. It is your true name."

Anger, fear, elation, surprise, apprehension and exasperation shot through her in a cascade of discordant emotions. "You knew that Rece was my father?" She turned to him, aghast.

"I suspected—"

"And you did not tell me?" She stood, thankful that her knees were only slightly wobbly. "How could you not tell me?"

"I wanted to confirm it first. Not give you false hope—"

"Wouldn't that be my decision?" she cried, so angry she quaked. She was furious, and she did not know where to place her anger. So she directed it at the bothersome oaf who was at the center of her tribulation.

He rose, his face having shuttered into a mask of disquiet. "You're upset—"

"You had better believe that I'm upset!"

"I'll tell him to go. That you're not ready—"

"You brought him here?" she shrieked.

"I'm sorry, Lillian, I thought that this was for the best. I guess I was mistaken." He turned and walked out the door.

She stood trembling from head to toe, feeling confused and afraid. As if she was a ship that had lost its moorings. Slowly the knowledge sank into her consciousness and locked into place. Nick had uncovered her natural father's identity. She now had a name other than Kane. And it was all due to Nick. He had done the one thing that she had been afraid to do for herself.

He had given her a gift. To him, an orphan who yearned for his true name, it was the most precious thing that he could possibly grant her. He had presented her with something completely selfless, wholly for her. The one thing that he believed could change her life for the better. The one truth that could turn all of her negative assumptions on their heads.

Her mother had not been discarded. They had not been abandoned. Lord Rece was a good and honorable man. She knew this from knowing his dear wife. He would not leave his child in the clutches of a monster like Kane. He must not have known how much her mother had loved him. He could not have known about his babe.

Love was not the poison that had destroyed her mother, Kane was. Kane's greed, arrogance and narcissism.

Love was not an illness; it was a reward, granted to those favored by its touch. A magical thing that grew between two people, a living, beautiful entity in its own right. Undeniable as the air that she breathed, the sun in the morning and the compassion of Nicholas Redford, the man she loved beyond her wildest imaginings.

He had given her the greatest gift he could think of. And she had tossed it back in his face like yesterday's trash.

"Wait!" she screamed, heading out into the hall. But he was already gone. "Nick!"

Unmindful of the servants passing by, she hastened toward the foyer. Gillman jumped aside to let her pass.

At her approach, Hicks coolly stepped forward and swept open the door, letting in the afternoon's golden rays. Through the glow, she spied a familiar figure standing on the steps outside. Tall, raven-haired, well-built, make-no-bones-about-it gorgeous; yes, that was the love of her life.

Her heart swelled and she quickened her pace. "Nick!"

She rushed out the door. In her haste, the toe of her half boots snagged on the doorsill, hurling her forward. Her arms whirled for balance and the sky spun madly, until strong arms caught her about the waist, bracing her against a solid mass of man and muscle. She clutched him and held on for dear life. "My dark knight," she breathed.

He hugged her close, and suddenly she felt like she had made it *home*.

"I'm so sorry," she cried. "I'm a cuckoo of the first class!"

He slowly set her down, holding her gently just

on the tips of her toes. "I'm the one who's sorry. It was presumptuous of me. I should not have—"

Pressing her fingers to his lips to stop his protestations, she shook her head. "You just gave me the most wonderful gift imaginable. I am so very grateful."

"Really?" he asked, his broad brow knitted with insecurity.

A line from Shakespeare's *Henry IV* suddenly popped into her head. " 'While I live, I will tell truth and shame the Devil.' " Kane was her devil and she would exorcise him from her life. There would be no lies, no questions left unanswered, and no unwarranted pride between herself and the people she loved.

Confusion clouded his beautiful, dark gaze.

"I was afraid you were going to leave me," she explained. "I thought that was what you wished to discuss with me. Your big news about my parentage simply tossed me into a bumble broth. But now I'm rational. I appreciate your gift, Nick. Beyond estimation. Your wonderful generosity of spirit—"

"You thought I was leaving you?"

She bit her lip. "I feared it."

"But you're mine." He said it with such certainty that her heart melted.

"And you are mine." She grinned, knowing it down to her soul.

Lifting her into his arms, he kissed her so soundly that her head spun. She clung to him, showing him without words how much she cared.

He pulled back, his face grave. "I needed to find your father, Lillian. So that I could ask his permission for your hand in marriage. But I do not make the same mistake twice. So I ask *you*, Lillian Rece. Will you marry me?"

Her breath caught. Deep in those cocoa brown eyes she saw his vulnerability, his apprehension at being rejected. The orphan who had been abandoned by his family feared being forsaken still. His body was taut with tension, his dear face a mask of anxiety. The darling man had no idea how much she loved him.

She tenderly brushed a lock of black hair off his forehead, wanting to take away all of his pain, all of his fear. "I love you, Nicholas Redford. Your true name is etched on my heart, and I swear, I will never leave you even if you beg me to go."

"But will you marry me?" he asked hoarsely. "Will you share my name with me?"

She exhaled a dramatic sigh. "I suppose it will take a man like you to make an honest woman out of me," she teased.

The tightness in his handsome face lessened. "You're serious?"

"I am." She beamed up at him, loving him so much that she thought her heart would burst.

"I don't want a farthing of your inheritance."

"I know, which is why I want to share it with you. It is *my choice* to be with you and *my choice* to share my life, and everything I have, with you." She tapped her finger on his broad chest. "I choose you."

His lips curved up into a grin so wide that it filled half his face.

"Hurrah! Bravo! Congratulations!"

They turned and realized that Hicks, Dillon, Gillman, Fanny and Dr. Winner stood crowded in the threshold, gawking at them.

"Congratulations!" Dillon shouted. "Well done, Redford, you've made the catch of the century!"

"I'm the maid of honor," Fanny declared. "And I

know who will be my escort." She peered at Dr. Winner through fluttering eyelashes.

"A wedding!" Lady Rece exclaimed.

Lillian turned, and her breath caught. Lord and Lady Rece sat in the coach by the curb.

"I love weddings!" Lady Rece declared, beaming.

Lord Rece stepped out of the coach, moving hesitantly, as if afraid of his welcome.

Nick slowly released her, and Lillian drifted forward, as if in a daze. Here she stood, facing the man that she had never expected to know. She was more than a little terrified, she realized. But she could handle anything with Nick beside her.

Rece's eyes roved her features, searching. Slowly, he nodded. "Lady Janus," he murmured. "I believe that I owe you the world's biggest apology."

Her arms were around him and her nose in his coat before thought came to mind. He smelled pleasingly of Jockey Club Cologne. This was her father. Her own flesh and blood. He had not left her. He wanted to know her. She had a family that wanted her.

Gradually, he wrapped his arms around her and gently patted her hair. "I am so very glad to know you, Lillian."

Tears blurred her vision as Fanny and Dillon came charging down the stairs. Hearty congratulations rang out. Exclamations of wonder. Cries of gladness. And many tears.

Gently, Nick pulled her away from the crowd of well-wishers. "You're certain you wish to marry me?" he asked huskily, a trace of awe in his voice.

She beamed up at him, love flooding through her with a certainty that this was the only man in the world for her. "I love you so much, Nick, that I don't know that I could bear not to."

Epilogue

Ten months later, Lillian celebrated her four-and-twentieth year giving birth to an azure-eyed, raven-haired, howling little boy. The child's grandparents were so overjoyed that they posted announcements in the newspapers and the proud grandfather emptied the tobacconist's shelves. It seemed that not a man in London was without a cigar that afternoon.

The couple's happiness, however, was marred by one trifling issue: They could not decide on a given name for the fledgling baron. Lillian chose Nicholas, for the man she admired most in the world. Nick, on the other hand, wanted the boy to have a name of his own, with a solid family history. He suggested Donald, for Lillian's father.

Lord Rece demurred, saying that the honor of the firstborn should go to Lillian's grandfather,

Sinclair. Dorothea whispered in Lillian's ear that Donald was hoping that the second Redford might be named after him.

Still unable to agree on a moniker, the couple asked the child's godparents. Dillon suggested his own name since he knew that he would never have children of his own. Fanny recommended William for hers and Lillian's favorite bard. Her husband, the good doctor, proposed Lancelot, for Queen Charlotte's pug.

After much discussion, the parents finally agreed on a name that was sturdy, noble and linked to the past: Sinclair Donald Redford, nickname, Dunn.

News of the baby's healthy arrival was greeted with joy in all parts of London, from drawing rooms, to taprooms, to Newgate Prison itself. Even at Newgate, Warden John Newman toasted to the happy family with his most excellent libation—Cognac, aged twenty-five years.

Coming in August from Avon Books, romance so sizzling
it will burn up the pages!

A WANTED MAN by Susan Kay Law
An Avon Romantic Treasure

Laura Hamilton has spent her life sheltered by her tycoon father's protectiveness, until she finally takes a bold step toward independence—a trip that will lead her to Sam Duncan. Sam's steely nerves have made him one of the most famous hired guns in the West, but can he react to Laura's allure fast enough to save his heart?

THE DAMSEL IN THIS DRESS by Marianne Stillings
An Avon Contemporary Romance

J. Soldier McKennitt, detective-turned-bestselling author, is just trying to find out who is panning his books in the *Port Henry Ledger*. His trail leads him not to a nasty shrew but to charming Betsy Tremaine, and suddenly romance comes down off the shelf—but first they've got to get Betsy safely out of the path of a stalker who has "true crime" in mind . . .

Also available in August, two beautifully repackaged
classic Julia Quinn love stories

MINX

When untamable Henrietta Barrett's guardian passes away, her beloved home falls into the hands of William Dunford—London's most elusive bachelor.

BRIGHTER THAN THE SUN

The dashing—if incorrigible—Earl of Billington needs a bride before his thirtieth birthday if he hopes to earn his inheritance. And the vicar's daughter, Miss Eleanor Lyndon, needs a new home.

Discover Contemporary Romances at Their Sizzling Hot Best from Avon Books

SOMEONE LIKE HIM   by Karen Kendall
0-06-000723-0/$5.99 US/$7.99 Can

A THOROUGHLY MODERN PRINCESS
0-380-82054-4/$5.99 US/$7.99 Can   by Wendy Corsi Staub

A GREEK GOD AT THE LADIES' CLUB   by Jenna McKnight
0-06-054927-0/$5.99 US/$7.99 Can

DO NOT DISTURB   by Christie Ridgway
0-06-009348-X/$5.99 US/$7.99 Can

WANTED: ONE PERFECT MAN   by Judi McCoy
0-06-056079-7/$5.99 US/$7.99 Can

FACING FEAR   by Gennita Low
0-06-052339-5/$5.99 US/$7.99 Can

HOT STUFF   by Elaine Fox
0-06-051724-7/$5.99 US/$7.99 Can

WHAT MEMORIES REMAIN   by Cait London
0-06-055588-2/$5.99 US/$7.99 Can

LOVE: UNDERCOVER   by Hailey North
0-06-058230-8/$5.99 US/$7.99 Can

IN THE MOOD   by Suzanne Macpherson
0-06-051768-9/$5.99 US/$7.99 Can

Have you ever dreamed of writing a romance?

*And have you ever wanted
to get a romance published?*

Perhaps you have always wondered how to
become an Avon romance writer?
We are now seeking the best and brightest undiscovered
voices. We invite you to send us your query letter to
avonromance@harpercollins.com

What do you need to do?

Please send no more than two pages telling us
about your book. We'd like to know its setting—is it
contemporary or historical—and a bit about the hero,
heroine, and what happens to them.

Then, if it is right for Avon we'll ask to see part of the
manuscript. Remember, it's important that you have
material to send, in case we want to see your story quickly.

Of course, there are no guarantees of publication,
but you never know unless you try!

*We know there is new talent just waiting
to be found! Don't hesitate . . . send us
your query letter today.*

*The Editors
Avon Romance*

Avon Romantic Treasures

*Unforgettable, enthralling love stories,
sparkling with passion and adventure
from Romance's bestselling authors*